Praise for

'A fascinating story that never s[...] in human nature' *Guardian*

'An unnervingly believable struggle for the future. The story of Moremi and Orpheus has classical antecedents but with a satisfying eye for the future' *Booklist*

'Tightly crafted, weaving science fiction, mythology, and more to tell a tale that feels pertinent right now' *Kirkus Reviews*

'*More Perfect* is a deeply character-driven dystopia that explores memory, connection, and controlling the narrative, with vibes sort of like V *for Vendetta* mixed with *Inception*' *Tor.com*

'The London you encounter in Temi Oh's *More Perfect* is grittily familar – making the near future she paints queasily plausible ... It weaves an intriguing tapestry of references, from the classical story of Eurydice to the neuroscience of consciousness, set against a drumbeat of dread' *New Scientist*

'With refreshing nuance and a seamlessly built world, the award-winning author of *Do You Dream of Terra-Two?* takes readers on a high-octane journey with deeply moving stakes: What does it mean to *truly* empathize with another person? If you could alter traumatic memories, would you? And lastly, what is the price of privacy?' *Oprahdaily.com*, **Best Sci-Fi books of the Summer**

'Feverishly inventive' *The Washington Post*

'A spectacular exploration of the power of technology. Upon finishing the final page I was left breathless and bereft. A feat of creativity, written with great heart, this is science fiction at its best' **Saara El-Arifi**, *Sunday Times* **bestselling author of** *The Final Strife*

Also by Temi Oh

Novels

Do You Dream of Terra Two?

Short stories

Zoya The Deserter in *Black Panther Tales of Wakanda*
Davros in *Dr Who: Origin Stories*
Almost Too Good To Be True in
Black Sci-Fi Short Stories

MORE PERFECT

TEMI OH

SIMON &
SCHUSTER

London · New York · Sydney · Toronto · New Delhi

First published in Great Britain by Simon & Schuster UK Ltd, 2023

This paperback edition published in 2024

Copyright © Temitoyen Ochugboju Douglas-Scott, 2023

The right of Temitoyen Ochugboju Douglas-Scott to be identified as
author of this work has been asserted in accordance with the
Copyright, Designs and Patents Act, 1988.

1 3 5 7 9 10 8 6 4 2

Simon & Schuster UK Ltd
1st Floor
222 Gray's Inn Road
London WC1X 8HB

Simon & Schuster: Celebrating 100 Years of Publishing in 2024

Simon & Schuster Australia, Sydney
Simon & Schuster India, New Delhi

www.simonandschuster.co.uk
www.simonandschuster.com.au
www.simonandschuster.co.in

A CIP catalogue record for this book
is available from the British Library

Paperback ISBN: 978-1-4711-7131-4
eBook ISBN: 978-1-4711-7130-7
Audio ISBN: 978-1-3985-0065-5

Epigraph from *Under Milk Wood: The Definitive Edition* by Dylan Thomas
reproduced with permission from The Dylan Thomas Trust.

This book is a work of fiction.
Names, characters, places and incidents are either a product of the author's
imagination or are used fictitiously. Any resemblance to actual people
living or dead, events or locales is entirely coincidental.

Typeset in Sabon by M Rules
Printed and Bound in the UK using 100% Renewable
Electricity at CPI Group (UK) Ltd

MIX
Paper | Supporting
responsible forestry
FSC® C171272
FSC
www.fsc.org

For Benedict, for everything.

And for Jubilee, who we longed here.

PART ONE

1

MOREMI

'Will it hurt?' Moremi asks the girl from the sixth-form who sits opposite. The girl is lit in zebra-print by the slats in the blinds, holding a hot-water bottle to her stomach, and her hazel eyes keep flitting up to the muted television screen at the far end of the waiting room.

'Only at first,' she says.

'That's what everyone says.' Moremi is nervous. She's only been waiting in the school nurse's office for a quarter of an hour, but already she's chewed her thumbnail down to the quick.

'Where does it hurt?'

This morning she'd been excited about the procedure – she is the last in her class to go through with it and has been begging her mother to sign the medical waiver for almost a year now. There is an asterisk next to her name on the school register, which indicates she is still 'Pulseless'. Even the word, she hates.

The sixth-form girl casts Moremi a sideways glance as if considering how much of the truth to tell her. 'Everywhere,' she admits finally. 'Your whole body, but only for a minute. Less than, maybe.' Moremi swallows. 'And not just your body, also . . . your mind.'

'You mean, my head?'

'No, it's deeper than that.' The girl frowns in recollection. 'It's a weird sensation. As if something is there that shouldn't be. That feeling you get when someone is looking over your shoulder, only this is deeper, the machine eavesdropping on your thoughts, your memories.' She touches her forehead with the palm of her hand. 'It's as if you're not alone in here anymore.'

'But that fades away after a while, right? That feeling?'

'Not really,' the girl says, fiddling with a loose thread on the edge of her school skirt.

Moremi rubs the miniature ballet slippers that dangle from a keychain on her school bag. For luck, like a rabbit's foot. She's done it so often, before an audition or a dentist appointment, that the satin at the toe-box has frayed now. She'd only been thinking of the moments after, how good it would feel once it was done; she'd forgotten about this, the scalpel, the pain.

The bulk of the device is the size of a five-pence coin, placed under the temporal bone. The sixth-former must have had hers implanted a while ago because the skin around it has completely healed over. Moremi can't help but stare, even though she knows it's rude. Around its central processing unit is a cluster of accessories – the pin-headed RAM, HPU, sensors and transmitters as well as optional drives – that make a 'constellation' of LEDs and metallic notches in the skin behind her ear. The girl wears her hair, as a lot of people do, to one side in order to make the lights of her constellation visible. Pinks right now, indicating that she is in mild discomfort, steady beat of her heart, the brightest light, throbbing like a distant drum. Moremi's friend, Zen, had been the first to get one a few years ago and Moremi remembers leaning close to her head to marvel at it, an unnatural fusion of organic and mechanic that she used to find almost viscerally repellent.

'How old are you?'

'Thirteen,' Moremi says.

'Isn't that a bit old?' the girl asks, regarding Moremi with a familiar suspicion; some people consider parents who refuse to give their children a Pulse the same as parents who turn down vaccinations. 'Have you watched the video?'

On the screen above them, it's running on mute with subtitles. An informative broadcast about the implantation procedure. Moremi catches words like 'direct neural interface' as they flick across the monitor. 'I've seen it a few times,' she says. In doctors' and dentists' waiting rooms, on television. Something about it, today, makes her a little queasy. Maybe it's the spongy pink schematic of the human brain. The nanoscopic fingers of the Pulse are called arrays. They measure less than one thousandth of the width of a human hair. Once the Pulse is implanted under the bone, millions of arrays extend, penetrating the thick membrane of connective tissue that surrounds the brain. The arrays spider through grey matter, routing around for cranial nerves: the optic and auditory neurons, the hippocampus – where memories are stored – and the amygdala to interface with.

'So . . . it's like brain surgery?' Moremi says.

The girl snorts derisively. 'Don't be dramatic. My dentist does, like, ten of these a day. It's like getting your ears pierced.'

They've learned a lot about the brain this year in biology. Moremi has discovered that it contains around 86 billion neurons. That the external world can be fractured into lines of analogue or binary code for it to interpret. The colour of the sky right now is a specific wavelength of light that sends a pattern of impulses into the back of her brain. A kiss on the cheek sets off fireworks of its own in her facial nerve. Strange to consider how rich her inner life appears to her – including at this moment, the smell of the waiting room, the glitter of dust in the air, the sound and sight of schoolchildren playing on the Astroturf out the window – even though it is simply the result of some chemical code disseminated through grey and white matter. Just as hard to believe that the whole of the internet, every picture and video, email and game, is written in the binary language of machines: 'on' and 'off' switches, 1s and 0s. It's these similarities which make it possible for the machine to interface with her brain.

The Pulse is programmed to transform neural signals into lines of computer code and vice versa. The whole process has been called 'neural digitisation' and it allows the Pulse to turn the brain into another node on the internet. This means that once the procedure is over, Moremi's head will be part of the internet in the same way a phone or a tablet computer is. The thought of it is astonishing and terrifying.

Her console makes a noise in her bag. Moremi scrabbles for it, and when she sees that it's her mother, she races into the bathroom to answer.

'How did it go?' her mother asks.

'It hasn't happened yet,' Moremi whispers. Through the window, she can see a group of girls from her class ambling to their final lesson.

'I thought it was this morning.'

'Oh! The audition.' Moremi makes herself look away, focus. 'Well, I think ... I mean, I fumbled the last part of the adagio but—' Even before she finishes she can hear her mother sigh. 'I'm sorry.'

'It's not me you have to apologise to.'

Moremi wants to say, 'Isn't it?' Her mother almost never calls her out of the blue. These past few months, preparing for the auditions for the Regency Ballet School, have been some of the happiest of her life. She's cherished the time they've spent together. Those late nights and early mornings in the kitchen, listening to her mother clap out the beat and say, 'again', 'again', 'again', with feeling. That elusive glimmer of pride in her eyes, the blessed light of her attention. It will all evaporate, Moremi knows, if she doesn't make it through the next round of auditions, and her chances don't look good.

'If you could only focus,' her mother is saying, and as she does, Moremi flips the tap, waving her hand to make the setting hotter and hotter, then forces herself to hold her fingers under the stream for as long as she can bear.

'Where are you now?' her mother asks.

'I told you last week.' Moremi grits her teeth at the pain in her fingers. When she finally snatches them away, steam curls like cigarette smoke off her nails. 'I'm doing the . . . thing today.'

Heavy silence on the end of the phone. She can already imagine the expression her mother is making, her lip curling with disgust.

'I forgot,' her mother says finally.

'I figured.'

'You know, you don't have to go through with it.'

'But that's the thing,' Moremi says, 'I want to.' She would have had the procedure years ago if it wasn't for her mother's hesitations. Her older sister Halima had done it as soon as she was old enough to sign the consent herself.

'I don't understand you and your sisters. You're already "connected" all the time. You have computers, consoles—'

'Not connected where it matters.' Moremi's gaze drifts back to the girls who are walking into class, the same dozen feet, black leather Hush Puppies, almost in step. The other girls live on a different plane of existence. They live in the Panopticon, the network of networks, connecting everyone's constellations to each other, and tethering them all to the internet. It's the Panopticon that allows them to talk without opening their mouths, or to watch each other's memories. She's heard that they all wear filters on their skin, bat wings or cat ears that she can't see. Sometimes their class teacher raises her hands like a musical conductor and everyone but Moremi says, 'Oh!'

Over the past few Pulseless years, Moremi has lost

every single one of her friends; she can't understand them anymore.

'Is that what you want?' her mother asks. 'To be like everyone else?'

Moremi says what she always says: 'Of course!'

There is a knock at the door.

'I have to go,' she tells her mother.

Moremi's resolve weakens a little, though, when she steps out of the bathroom and remembers how afraid she is of pain. If only there was a way around it, she thinks.

The nurse is calling her in now. Moremi stares at the door to her office and wonders what she will be like when she emerges. Will she emerge fundamentally altered? Or will it be different like turning thirteen was different, only an incremental change? The seconds before and then after midnight on New Year's Eve on the dawn of some millennium? Different the way people say losing your virginity is different?

'More-rem-me?' says the school nurse, an overweight Filipino woman, before frowning at Moremi's last name. She makes a familiar halting attempt, sounding out every syllable with none of the certainty of Nigerians.

'Hi,' Moremi says, and follows her in. The detergent tang of the room threatens to turn Moremi's empty stomach. Lemon and pine-flavoured floor cleaner. Sponges soaked in iodine. The curtains drawn, and the place cold as a mortuary. She was told not to eat anything for twelve hours before the procedure, and now her gut is twisting itself in knots. It's like getting your ears pierced, she tells herself, reaching her hand up to the little silver stud in her left ear and reminding herself of the day her mother took her and her two sisters to Claire's Accessories to get them done. Her older sister, Halima, had been so nervous about the procedure that when the technician touched a Sharpie pen to her lobe, she burst into horrified tears. Moremi had been braver, but she still recalls that her terror in the moment before the needle punctured her skin was so much worse than the event. She still remembers how silly she'd felt on her way home, compulsively touching the gold hoops just to remind herself it had happened. It had been such an easy thing. Such a short moment of pain, nothing compared to the rest of her life.

In the centre of the room is what looks like a dentists' chair. Several monitors have been set up to measure her vital signs, a glass console with a projection of her brain, as mapped half an hour earlier by the scanners, turning like a bloody moon.

'Okay, then,' the nurse says cheerily. 'Are you ready?'

Moremi tries to smile, but then she spots the scalpels glinting on the equipment tray, blades silver under the sun-bright surgical lights. 'Um . . .' She can't bring herself to say 'yes' yet.

'It's been a while since I've done this procedure on a pupil so old.' The nurse eyes her suspiciously. 'Are your parents . . . ?' She doesn't want to say the word 'Luddites' or, worse, 'Revelators'. She doesn't want to ask if Moremi's mother is the kind of person who burns down cell masts and carves stars into her skin as a sign of protest against the Panopticon.

'No, nothing like that.' Moremi is quick to jump to

her mother's defence, even though she has noticed that whenever the Revelators are arrested, her mother will never denounce their actions. Instead Moremi says, 'I'm scared . . . it will change me.'

'Of course it will *change* you,' the nurse says, 'but what doesn't change you?'

She tuts near Moremi's head where she guesses her date of birth is projected. 'Thirteen. It's too late, really. The way things are going, give it a generation and most people won't even remember when they first get it. Which, they say, is the best thing, really. You know, the solid-state drive inside the Pulse is capable of storing a lifetime's worth of memories.'

It is made up of a virtually indestructible quartz crystal capable of storing a zettabyte of data. That is, Moremi has seen in her study console before, one sextillion – one followed by twenty-one zeroes – bytes. A number so large it means almost nothing to her at all.

'Research suggests we only remember about a tenth of the information we are presented with. Which is pretty appalling. If I ask you what you were doing at this exact moment last year? Seven months ago? Can you tell me? Probably not. And do you know that every time you recall something, the way your mother sings, your tenth birthday, the first time you ever jumped on a trampoline, you change the memory just a little. It's not like replaying a DVD – oh, I know you don't remember DVDs – you change a memory every time you recall it. Most of them slip right out of your head. Whole days, whole years, it feels like. More when you get older. Before we had the

Pulse, there used to be this disease of forgetting, a real epidemic. It happened in the elderly. I'm a nurse, I still see what happens to old people who don't get the procedure.' She shakes her head sorrowfully. 'A home I worked in a few years ago. This lady of eighty-five tossed all her family pictures in the trash. She kept shouting at me, "Who are these people? I don't want these pictures!" It was heart-breaking to watch. You see it less and less, and in your generation, we won't see it at all. For that reason alone, if it ever comes time to vote over "total adoption", I know I'll vote to give the Pulse to everyone. Let's not forget anything. Not a thing.'

As Moremi sits down, the nurse adjusts the height of the chair then takes her wrist and says, 'Okay now, you'll feel a sharp scratch.' Barely a moment, and the needle breaks her skin, cool liquid pours into her veins. Quickly, a numbness sets in and her muscles unspool.

'This is a unique cocktail, devised by the Panopticon to aid this procedure. It's called nox.' The nurse straps a mask to Moremi's face, and her jaw flops open as she breathes. 'You might notice the taste' – like bitumen and burnt sugar in the back of her mouth – 'especially cali-brated for your height and weight, this concoction will keep you asleep for the duration of the procedure.'

As Moremi's mind peels away from the inside of her skull, the nurse's voice takes on a tinny discordant ring.

'The machine will wake you to a cue we recorded.' The cue is a song that comes through a speaker with a childish soprano trill.

Frère Jacques, Frère Jacques

Dormez-vous? Dormez-vous?
'... the cue will help you sleep as well ...'
Sonnez les matines! Sonnez les matines!
'... Sleep paralysis sets in when ...'
Ding dang dong.
She feels as if she could shrug her bones right off. Her mind is flung into a graveyard orbit, spinning out, out of her body, of school, of the sprawling city.
'... here comes the machine.'
'Is this the part that hurts?' she wants to ask, but can't. It is. Her mind is shunted back into a body full of pain. She screams, an animal howl of agony, every joint locking, every nerve on fire. They say it lasts a few seconds, but there is no time in this agony.
'No!' she shouts. But the machine is inside her now. Although she knows it's impossible, she thinks she can feel its microscopic needles puncturing her skull. Spidering into her grey matter.
'Make it stop,' she cries. This was a bad idea. A mistake. Too late, now, to change her mind. 'Make it stop!' When she opens her eyes she can see nothing but the blinding surgical light, all faces eclipsed. Nothing but white-hot, searing rods of pain thundering through her bones. *How much longer,* she wonders, *before it turns on?*
They say it feels like falling. That falling asleep Pulseless for the final time really feels like tumbling off a cliff. And it does. She slips right out of her skin, elevator-drop plunge in her gut, like falling in a dream. Her life will never be the same. Her mind will never be the same.

*

What does it feel like to wake up in the Panopticon? It's like waking up for the first time ever. It's like waking up with a third eye. The nurse is beaming at her. 'What can you see?' she asks. It looks as if Moremi is staring at her from behind the lens of a digital camera. Her vision is dotted with points of light that resolve into letters, numbers. Cross-hairs appear around the nurse's doughy features, as the retinal interface searches the Panopticon for a match. The nurse's profile appears in a nimbus of translucent light floating around her. Moremi learns that her name is *Julliana Sanchez, DOB: 3/04/2001, Occupation: Paediatric Nurse, Pimlico School, Children: 6.*

'You have six children?'

Julliana rolls her eyes. 'That's the part that everyone asks about. Did it tell you, too, that I speak five languages?'

'Spanish, Portuguese, English, Malay and French, but only to a B1 proficiency.'

'Senegalese ex-husband.' She waves dismissively.

Moremi can't help but try to reach out to touch the words, the way it's hard to stop yourself from grabbing at bubbles. People call them 'holograms', but they are really 'phosphenes', hallucinatory points of light produced when the microarrays send electrical signals to her optic nerves, physiologically similar to the explosion of stars she sometimes witnesses when she rubs her eyes.

When she turns left, a projection on the window pane tells her there is a 90 per cent chance of drizzle between 4.26pm and 5.40pm, tells her that it's T-shirt weather until then, expertly feeding information about her core body temperature against the weather predictions for that day.

An architecture app spies the newly built maths block of the school and the profile of the architects is summoned up; Moremi waves a hand to dismiss it. After a while, the Panopticon will learn her preferences and only feed her information relevant to her profile and interests. It will point out her friends in a café. It will tell her if a celebrity she likes frequents the same coffee shop; it will define words she's always wondered about. Answer questions before she's thought to ask them.

When Moremi closes her eyes, the nurse activates the GrapeVine, the main memory-sharing app that she used to access on her console. Moremi already has a profile, and so her familiar dashboard floods the darkness behind her eyelids with light. Video tutorials, ironically spliced cartoon clips, Michael Jackson lighting up the sidewalk with his toes. Commercials. People liked to upload their own memories recorded off their quartz, which always look like poorly edited videos captured on a handheld camera. As Moremi's Pulse configures to the local TV channels she sees space cowboys, beach getaways, a map of Manchester's sewer system, discount sofas, gardening shows, sit-coms, a laugh-track running and running ...

Group chats run audibly in the background, which gives the room the ambient sound of an overcrowded diner, different people talking, people she hasn't spoken to in months, the school eco-society, her old ballet class, the girls on her apartment block who promised that they'd get together to make a newspaper but now do nothing but send each other ironic memes. All of their voices are in her ears, and Moremi feels as if her head is a radio, and someone is twisting the dials up and down. The nurse demonstrates the hand and eye motions that control the volume in her cochlear nerve.

She does a few more checks and then sends Moremi on her way, warns her to take it easy, give herself time to get used to it. 'If you like, you can watch a couple of the tutorials on the Vine. But most people like to experiment. Think of this like a relationship, you need to get used to the way things are from now on.'

The school day is already over and when Moremi heads out into the street, it is gorgeously transformed, awash with hallucinogenic light. The sky spells 'Hello, Moremi' in soft ivory contrails. She strides past the brutalist red brick of the World's End Estate, and onto the far end of the King's Road.

Lots of the fun of the Panopticon is in the filters, which she can change with a swipe of her hand. It's quite intuitive; Moremi is used to manipulating images and displays in the same way on her console. There are hundreds of millions of filters, arranged like apps with the most popular for her demographic first. There is the default one called InfoWorld, which fills her vision with relevant information. If she looks at a bus it tells her where it's heading and what time the next one will arrive, street names float up in Comic Sans bubbles, there is an endless ticker-tape scroll of news headlines on the edge of the pavement. Moremi summons up the profiles of strangers, their names and ages. The Panopticon has a function that lets them know she is new to the network and lots of people smile and greet her.

Moremi heads into the local Polski Sklep and with the flick of a hand all the newspaper headlines are legible to her. *'Czy mogę ci pomóc?'* asks the woman behind the till after ten minutes of watching Moremi hold newspapers up to the light. 'Can I help you?' An automated voice reads in her cochlear nerve. The woman's profile tells Moremi that her name is *Zuzanna Wysocki, 26,* and Moremi is so thrilled they can understand each other that she just grins widely.

'No,' she says, 'Zuzanna.' She can go anywhere now, with this device in her head. Talk to anyone and, as she steps back outside, she imagines conversing with a tuk-tuk driver in Bangkok, or a begging monk on the streets of Ginza.

It's fun just watching the adverts playing in the shop windows. A translucent family lounging in striped pyjamas in the Sofa Workshop. Models dressed up for Ladies Day at Ascot in the window of Jane Taylor, invisible horses churning up the grass before their feet. There is a filter that turns the world sepia-toned so she can imagine she lives in an old photograph. There is a filter that the Year 7s love which gives everyone elf ears and manga eyes. Moremi has heard rumours of some X-rated filters that her child-locked Pulse won't give her access to.

There is a girl walking her PanoptoPet, a pink creature with rabbit ears. Someone has built a Minecraft Taj Mahal in the middle of a garden square, and Moremi peers through the gates to admire the pixelated detail on the ivory blocks. At the bus stop, a girl casts a Patronus, a spectacular leopard the size of a bus that bounds down the street and then turns to smoke. Everyone who sees applauds. Moremi does, too. This new world is magic. Reality can be remade with the turn of a hand.

There is a couple outside Chelsea Old Church who've just got married. Moremi lingers for a while, taking in the satin of her dress. *Annie Ross, DOB: 2/04/2023*, and *Peter Emmerson, DOB: 3/10/2015*, their profiles say. They make her think of her parents, for some reason. There is only one picture of her mother and father on their wedding day, and Moremi has stared at it so often, the edges have faded a little. She would have given anything to have been there, to see them that happy – never so happy again.

It's saved forever for this couple, though. Moremi imagines that this wedding is over and, very soon, the couple will leave behind the laughter, the music and the quick clicking of heels outside the courthouse. The grinning faces of their guests will vanish like smoke. Their few witnesses, who have lined up to say goodbye, along the cracked pavement, tossing dried petals. Annie and Peter run between them, she clutching her satin train, he flinching from their balled fists. Two people have lit sparklers even though it is daylight. Moremi imagines that the sweetest impressions of this moment will be saved in five dimensions of digital code, etched by lasers into the pound-sized quartz crystals in the sides of their heads. With a flick of her hand, Annie might be able to replay the instant again, or to share it with anyone. Only a generation ago, moments like these were made of nothing but memory, saved on nothing but neurones; carbon, salt and lipid membranes delicate as soap bubbles. So, maybe love doesn't last forever. This exact moment can last until the end of time on a virtually indestructible disc; their young faces on the courthouse steps, naively optimistic, splashed with hysterical light.

During the same year that men first landed on the moon, two computers 560 kilometres away from each other made first contact. Moremi has seen a couple of black-and-white pictures of it, the birthday of the internet. She's seen the computer scientists in flared trousers at the University of California and the Stanford Research Institute. They had meant to transmit the command 'login' but the transmission sputtered out, spelling only the two letters 'L' and 'O'; 'Lo,' people liked to say, 'lo and behold.'

The Panopticon was born in 2025, five years before Moremi was. She has seen the videos, photos, memes and spoofs of it, too. A crowd of scientists stand behind a pane of glass that overlooks a spartan exam room. Among them are the three founders, known as the Magi: Professor Jitsuko Itō, a Nobel-prize winning neuroscientist; Bertram Fairmont, a billionaire philanthropist; and Hayden Adeyemi, a young hacker. In the videos, Itō sits with her eyes closed in the middle of a room, cross-legged and barefoot like a monk. There is a large machine on her head and her eyes are closed as she wills her mind to speak to their computer outside.

In the video, Hayden is standing before it, teeth clenched in anxiety. 'Say something,' he commands, over the intercom, the way that Alexander Graham Bell may have demanded when he picked up a telephone for the first time. A bated-breath silence as they watch the empty screen waiting to see Professor Itō's words.

'Lo and behold,' she had said, in a nod to the way that history always repeats itself, and all the scientists gasp. The first time a brain speaks to a computer. In the recording, Bertram can be heard shouting for joy the way that Archimedes might have shouted, 'Eureka!' *I have found it*.

Hayden Adeyemi bursts into tears. And Moremi always wondered if they were tears of relief. Because life affords few moments like that. Few momentous thunderclaps of triumph. In between, and for years before, only failure and striving, exhaustion and self-doubt.

With all that came after, the recording has taken on the sheen of inevitable history.

In a TED talk a couple of years ago, Hayden asked the audience, 'How many of you have ever felt lonely?' Of course, every hand went up. He explained that the current incarnation of the Panopticon is only the beginning of his design. He promised that a time would come when the Pulse would not only store your own memories – incorruptibly and eternally – but soon it would be possible to inhabit the memories of others: loved ones and friends.

'It will bring us together,' he explained. Solve a fundamental human problem. The problem of other minds. 'At the moment we are essentially alone. Consider sorrow. Pain. Consider love. The only experience we have of any of these phenomena comes from inside ourselves. You are the only person in the world who has ever been in pain. You only know what the sky looks like from behind your own eyes, and you experience the entire world, from your cradle to your grave, locked inside a cage of your own bones. What if you could be freed? What if you could understand what it really feels like to live behind your lover's eyes? What if you could traverse their dreams as you would an island? You might never argue again. You might never say, with forlorn disappointment, "You don't understand me at all."'

What is the sky like from behind her mother's eyes? Moremi asks herself as she crosses Battersea Bridge and into the park. Does her heart break with wonder too, sometimes? It's almost spring and a brisk wind whips up from the Thames as Moremi walks. Her Panopticon lets her know that she's receiving a call. The lovely thing about a call on the Panopticon is that you hear your own name, in the caller's voice, and it rings like a bell in a deep part of you. Remi: she could listen all day to the sound of her own name in her mother's mouth. *Remi.* Such a strange sensation, someone's voice inside her head. She fights the urge to turn around, or to touch the back of her skull.

Mum? She thinks the reply, imagining her mother on the other end, leaning into the speaker of her old console.

'It went well?' she asks, her voice full of tension. 'No side effects. No headaches?'

'It was fine,' Moremi says. 'Better than fine. I feel . . .' How can she explain it to the uninitiated?

'. . . like you'll never be alone again?'

There is a sourness in her mother's voice but Moremi only says, 'Exactly!'

'I'll see you after work, okay?' her mother says.

21

'I love you,' Moremi says, but her mother has disconnected before she hears.

Moremi takes a left, strides past the sub-tropical garden and into the woods. Last week, her younger sister, Zeeba, had told her that trees are social creatures. Apparently they 'talk' to each other through an underground network of roots. It turns out that even trees have their dramas. A dying tree divests itself of resources for the benefit of the community; a mother tree pushes nutrients to her sun-deprived sapling. A plant under attack from pests sends a warning to its neighbours. Some scientists are suggesting that the entire forest could be considered a super-organism.

There is a filter called Wood Wide Web that allows her to see it. Moremi stands in a wooded glade and turns it on with a hand gesture. It lights up the soil, revealing a root system that looks like molten lava, pulsing with life. Moremi drops to her knees in surprise at its beauty, buries her fingers in the loam. It's so wonderful it's almost terrifying. Under her knees are patches of moss as thick as a bear's pelt, and she pushes her face in the dirt, tears in her eyes. She hadn't realised how much pain she had been in until it was gone. Her loneliness. She imagines herself as a spindly oak, integrated, only now, into the network.

Moremi knows that Hayden believes there is a future where everyone has a Pulse; he called it 'The Singularity'; had said, 'We'll be complete, like lovers – everybody. We're calling it the Singularity. Science will take us there. Science will usher in the time of everlasting joy.'

There are people all around her. In her head, Moremi

can feel their presence. Hear the susurrus of their voices. She will never be alone.

Hayden says that the Singularity is almost upon them. 'It's almost here,' Moremi says to the network in her head. A promise that brings goosebumps to her skin. 'Our mind will be an open eye, the eye of God.'

2

ORPHEUS

His father had warned him that, one day, they would have to leave everything behind, and Orpheus is fourteen when that day finally arrives. In the tiny hours of a winter morning, his father, Warsame, appears on the threshold in a camouflage jacket and hiking boots. Sleep-dazzled, for a second Orpheus thinks that it's a dream. But they have practised this drill a hundred times, and so it is not long before Orpheus slips into autopilot, climbing out of bed, and shuffling into his clothes without turning on the main lights.

He knows the way around the back, to sneak out of the house, making no sound at all. He knows where to find the 'bug-out' bags that his father keeps by the back door with enough supplies to last them seventy-two hours on the run: first-aid kit, water-purification tablets, fire-starting tools, maps and batteries and knives. Sometimes his father jokingly refers to them as GOOD bags: Get Out Of Dodge.

They do it without a word. Orpheus' hands are shaking too much to lace up his boots and so, balancing the LED torch in his mouth, his father does them quickly for him. Zips up his jacket, indicates the back door.

It's midwinter and, outside their house, a gust of sea-breeze hits Orpheus like a bucket of water. Adrenaline floods his veins. They live on a tidal island, in a house his father built. It is barely visible from the mainland and, when the tide is high, they have to take a boat across. It's only a rickety wooden thing that his father hammered together, but it makes almost no sound at all. Orpheus ducks into it, hugging his knees as his father begins to row. They are almost a mile away from their house when he dares to look back, and his gut buckles with regret.

On the other side of the house, Orpheus thinks he can already see it, a speedboat slicing the water, throwing up ribbons of sea-foam. Armed officers from the Panopticon stand at the stern, ready to tear the house down looking for them. Orpheus almost has to rub his eyes at the sight of them. Men and women in masks, with helmets and suits. His father has invoked the notion of them so many times to get Orpheus to behave. He's not allowed to leave the island on his own, not allowed to talk to any strangers, if he sees a drone flying past he must duck and run. His father has told him that the Panopticon is the puppet-master playing the whole world. His father has given up everything to run from them, to build a life for his son off the grid. 'It was only a matter of time,' he says now, his breath a plume of white air in the darkness. Every hour, for the past fourteen years, his father has been on the lookout for them.

'Will we ever go back?' Orpheus whispers. His father doesn't reply so Orpheus knows the answer.

According to his father, the police who work for the Panopticon have a machine that reads minds. Orpheus has been warned that once they are discovered, the officers will connect it to his brain and search his memories for information. As insurance against that day, his father has told Orpheus very little about his own life before he came to the island.

Although Orpheus has begged to hear more, all he has been able to piece together is that his parents committed a serious crime before he was born. 'Something necessary,' is the most that his father has ever said about it. They became fugitives, neo-Luddites on the run from the Panopticon. Because they were on the run, Orpheus was born analogue – 'born free', his father likes to emphasise. All Orpheus knows is that he was born on a beach, and he has imagined the moment so many times that it is as if he can remember it himself. Believes that he can remember the unfused bones in his skull grinding together. Holy agony as he emerged brow-bruised and half-blind. A baptism of clamour and light. Rush of freezing air into the hollow spaces in his body. How could he do anything but scream? Everything had been abrasive and alien, his nerves were like un-insulated wires. A fierce briny mist gusted up from the surf and invaded his mouth, his throat, his belly. A first breath. When he had exhaled a sound like thunder rolled from his lips. Everyone had been crying. He didn't know the word mother or father, but they loomed over

him like giants, like shouting, joyful gods, their chests a
storey high. Perhaps the first thing he saw was the sky.
Gun-metal grey, tossing clouds violently around. That
would have been the first time he ever saw light – noon-
time cloud-obscured sun a sublime thing. Perhaps his
entire life is just a vain striving for those initial ecstatic
seconds. They registered his birth with no authority, told
no doctors or family. As far as the world knows, Orpheus
does not exist.

Orpheus' mother died when he was a newborn, of
eclampsia. A word that, Orpheus discovered, means 'light
burst', and he imagines death taking her with that same
quickness. That is the problem with living off the grid,
living analogue; they had been at least an hour away from
the nearest hospital and by the time her seizures started
it was too late.

Orpheus knows so little about her that, to him, it is as
if she never existed. He might as well have hatched out of
an egg. After her death, his father, Warsame, built a home
on a tidal islet in south-west England, an hour's boat-ride
from Penzance. Far from any town or village, nothing but
dirt road and forests on one side, granite coves and the
English Channel on the other.

Warsame is the patron saint of solitude, teaching the
doctrine of self-sufficiency to a congregation of one. They
grow all their own food and vegetables on the acres of
land around their home. Orpheus or his father collect
water every morning from the well, bathe in the evening
in a solar-powered bathhouse that heats rainwater. Their
home is a Faraday cage, designed to block electromagnetic

signals from coming in or out. Their only news comes once a month, in the papers his father manages to smuggle from the mainland. Otherwise, they pass most of their days reading and fishing and farming. Warsame says that he is teaching his son to be a 'philosopher king'. He teaches him dead computer languages, how to tell the time by the direction of the stars, they play chess every single day, read Karl Marx, Nietzsche, the *Confessions* of St Augustine and Plato's *The Republic* on real books made of real paper. His father reminds him regularly that they are fugitives, tells him that something bad is going to happen soon, in London. One evening as they talk by lamplight he says, 'It's bad already. You don't know what it's like for children out there these days. They're probably tagging them at birth with that Thing now.' He points to his temple and shudders.

'It's only going to get worse after the flood.'

'The flood?' Orpheus asks, and his father's eyes flash with warning. That look he gets when he won't say any more.

'I'm just trying to protect you.'

He tells Orpheus that the life he has taken care to build for them here is as delicate as a soap bubble. 'If anyone or anything ever sees you – any of the Summer People, the patrol drones or the coastguards – the Panopticon will come to find us and they will kill me.'

Four months ago, Orpheus had tried to run away, just for a couple of hours. His father had taken the boat out in the morning, on his monthly excursion to the one store on the mainland that he can trust. There is an old man there who he can barter with. His father exchanges garden-grown herbs for tin cans, the alphabet spaghetti and cherry-flavoured Pepsi that Orpheus likes, aspirin, copper wire. That morning, when Orpheus awoke, he knew that his father would not be back for hours. And the thought occurred to him with crystalline clarity: if he ran, now, along the beach at low tide, he could make it up to Hunter's Tryst to see the Summer People, and if he timed it right he could return before Warsame.

Orpheus is forbidden from leaving the island without his father. But he knows that the Summer People flock in for the weekends during the warmer months. They are like aliens to him. Their cars drive themselves, they ride up and down the cliffs on surfboards called Zephyrs which – his father had explained to him – float on currents of ionised air. They have implants in their heads that allow them to speak without moving their lips. 'Not magic, just science,' Warsame had insisted. But it's almost the same thing, to Orpheus. For almost a year, he's longed to examine them himself. To see how close he can get.

The morning of his attempted escape, Orpheus buckled his shoes, headed out of the house and sprinted across the beach. He had forty minutes to get to Hunter's Tryst – the highest point of the cove where he can get the best view across the bay – and turn back before the tide rose again to sever his home from the mainland, leaving him stranded. He'd never done anything except exactly what he'd been told, but that morning a wild recklessness had overtaken him as he realised that this was his chance.

29

The run felt good, terrifying and exhilarating all at once. Across the sticky sand and wet cobbles, up to the outcropping of granite rocks piled high like a cairn, the Hunter's Tryst. He'd heard that at the top of it, on a clear day, you could see all the way to the Scilly Isles. His feet struggled to find purchase between the algae-slicked stones; as he climbed, he tried to imagine that they had been tossed there, right at the beginning of time, dented and pounded by the waves to make these divots the perfect shape for Orpheus' cupped hands, for the soles of Orpheus' scuffed boots. And when he made it to the precipice, winded but triumphant, he couldn't help but let his gaze whirl around. For a moment he was sun-blind, his vision bleached electric-blue. The tinnitus roar in his ears resolved into the sound of the sea and when his vision returned he felt as if he could see the flattened crust of the entire earth. It had been a beautiful sight, near the southernmost point of England, the depthless blue vault of the sky faded into the silver heat haze that evaporated off the surface of the sea. Gulls circled then descended, their claws razoring the water. To his left, on the opposite side of the bay, miles and miles away, were the Summer People.

He had spent years imagining them, reading about them in books, reading stories about them in the newspaper, baffling dispatches from their lives. That day, his heart beat wildly at the sight of them. He stood and watched for a long time, imagining their lives. Perhaps they do everything in groups; take their boats out onto the long surf in laughing teams, bat sherbet-coloured beach balls at each other, trek up to the coves to make love out on the empty beaches, an ivory tangle of sun-blushed limbs on gingham picnic blankets. Just contemplating them, in their happy gangs, made Orpheus feel a pain for it. He didn't know yet that the word for the ache, the one he had gritted his teeth against for most of his life, was 'lonely'. Sometimes he would go whole years without speaking to anyone but his father.

He noticed, then, a glimmer in the sky. Was it a seagull? A plane? It moved like a wasp, heading straight for him. Orpheus realised too late that it was a drone.

'No!' he gasped, covering his face. Had it spotted him? If it scanned his face no profile would come up, and it would report him automatically to the authorities. In his panic, Orpheus scrabbled around at his feet for a rock, and pitched it at the thing's spinning blades. They whined as it struck them. Another throw, aimed at the camera lens, but it missed and then panic overtook him. Covering his face, he decided, too late, to try to flee.

By the time he got back down to the beach it seemed to have flown off. The tide was rolling in. By then, the stretch of sand between himself and his home was covered in a transparent film of water and with each lap the waves came in further, rushed into the dunes and dinted gullies, covering everything.

His feet sank into the sand as he made his mad dash from one end of the beach to the other. The further he ran, the harder it was. The sand began to change under his feet, turn to liquid, suck at the heels of his shoes. He tried to counteract the effect by imagining himself as fleet-footed Hermes, winged shoes, his soles barely touching the ground.

The water was still coming in. It was at his thighs when he realised that he was going to have to swim for it. Kicking off his shoes, Orpheus paddled home as freezing water lashed at his face.

His father met him on the edge of the island, incandescent with rage. He grabbed his son by the arm, pushed him into the house, unbuckled his belt and beat him. Each strike of the leather against his back tore a scream from Orpheus, caused him to arch his spine, to howl and try to crawl away. Warsame held his son's right arm steady, beating him with the energy of a woodcutter, each hit like a tongue of fire. *I hate you!* Orpheus thought, tears in his eyes.

Hours later, he lay in the half-darkness of his bedroom, a T-shirt draped over the window in place of a curtain, white jets of setting sunlight spearing through, listing, in his mind, all the ways he could try again to run ... though he had no idea where he could go. By nightfall, Orpheus examined himself in the bathroom mirror and discovered that long welts had risen up all along his spine and shoulder blades, radiating out like wings. When he returned to his bedroom, his father was sitting on his bed, by the lamp. He had tears in his eyes. Told Orpheus that he was sorry. That he only wanted to keep him safe.

Orpheus doesn't look anything like the man. Warsame is a giant, six-foot-five, barrel-chested, with a dark beard and matted afro, skin like varnished oak. Orpheus is lighter-skinned, green-eyed and wiry. More like his mother? He often wonders, although his father has no holograms or photographs of her.

'You don't hate me,' his father said then, so that Orpheus didn't have to.

A father is a first love. A fierce kind of love. Three years ago, Warsame fell off the roof while fixing a solar panel. Orpheus had seen the bit of tiling under his feet give way, seen it in slow motion, his leg swinging wildly, his entire body flailing and then crashing to the ground. It had been like watching the ground gape open like a pair of jaws during an earthquake. Orpheus had been struck dumb with horror. The man is his entire world.

How to say it? Orpheus thought carefully that night. 'Only sometimes . . .'

'. . . sometimes you feel as if the world I've built is too small for you,' Warsame said. 'Something in you is longing for more.' Orpheus agreed by staring down at the fraying edge of his duvet cover. 'And it will be satisfied, Orpheus. Soon. We just need to keep safe as long as we can. At least until after the flood.'

'The flood?' Orpheus asked, but his father's expression came down like a shutter, and Orpheus knew that he was scolding himself inwardly for saying too much.

Orpheus was silent for a while too, distracted by the memory of the spinning blades of the drone he had seen earlier that day. But then he tried to shake it away, the distant concern. The camera lens that had definitely spied him.

Warsame claims that there is a price on his head. People hunting for him who will be glad if he's killed.

The threat, of course, fills Orpheus with horror. Reminds him again of that day his father had fallen off the roof. It had been the first time it occurred to him that this man could die.

Orpheus had asked him then, and asked again that night, 'What happens if you die?'

What happens to me? he was really asking. His father had laughed both times and said, 'I've been working on a way around it. Death. A way to defeat it.'

After twenty minutes of furious, silent rowing, his father brings them to the other side of Angharad Cove. During drills, this is normally where it ends, with his father taking out his stopwatch and checking to see how fast they evacuated. But this time, Orpheus knows, from the maps his father has drawn, that they will have to climb up the rocks and head into the forest. Behind an abandoned ranger's cabin his father has parked a car they can use to ride out to Silo 6 – an old farm, home to a colony of neo-Luddites – where they will be safe.

Their pursuers are closing in on them, the sound of drones score the air, a high-pitched whine that brings Orpheus' mind dizzyingly back to the other morning. 'Who are they?' he asks his father. There is a speedboat whipping up foam behind them, its blinding headlights rendering the passengers as shadows.

'Bounty hunters, hired by the Panopticon,' his father says, and then, 'Come on. We can outrun them.'

His father moors the boat near the rocky outcropping of the cove, on the other side of Hunter's Tryst. This side of the cove looks like a cliff face, about five metres high. Orpheus feels the boat rock under his boot as he climbs off, setting his thick rubber heel on a barnacled rock. His father hurries after him, kicks the boat away, and then silently indicates the crest above them. They will have to scale this to get into the forest without being seen. Even as they stand there, Orpheus can hear the blades of drones slicing the air behind them. His heart is racing, his fingers already numb, but his feet find purchase in a crevice half a metre high, and he begins his climb.

It's below freezing, a freak winter chill in the air, colder than Orpheus is used to. Under his parka, he wears an old woollen jumper he has almost outgrown, and cotton pyjamas. His socks are so threadbare that, as he climbs, cold creeps up his ankles and wrists.

His father, scaling the rock beside him, is almost super-human. They have practised climbing before, trees and a few knobbly cliff faces. But never like this, in the dead of night, midwinter. Orpheus reaches up above him, and his fingers find purchase in another crevice; he pulls himself up, stretching out his left knee, but then the stone below his heel loosens from its divot and gravity snatches him. Orpheus screams, suddenly, horrified. His feet have lost purchase and he clings on with nothing but his trembling fingers. His momentum causes half of his body to bash against the rock, winding him, and he kicks in panic as his fingers begin to slip.

'Son!' his father cries out at almost the same moment as Orpheus flounders, as if they are attached to each other. He is about two metres above, almost at the top of the cove. He looks down in relief to see that his son has not fallen. Shouts, 'Hold on!'

Orpheus' gaze whirls around as he scrabbles to find footing, but the cliff-face feels deadly smooth. He is going to fall. At a few metres above the sea-level, perhaps he'll survive. But when he looks down at the rocks below, terror grips him. Night-black ocean lashes the granite outcropping, tossing rocks against each other with a sound like a car crash. He shakes away a vision of his skull spilled on the sharp edge of them, bones rubbed raw by the waves.

'I've got you,' his father tells him, though he has to raise his voice now, over the sound of the approaching speed-boat. With one shaking hand, he unlatches a rope attached to his belt; it unspools like a tongue and he swings it towards his son. Everything in Orpheus strains not to fall as it swings forward and then back.

'You need to catch it,' his father urges. But Orpheus is too terrified to let go of the rock. What if he lets go and misses, falls to his death? Tries to grab it but tumbles into the freezing water?

'Catch it!' his father shouts, more urgent now. The rope swings away, slows, slumps back. Orpheus tells himself that this time he will catch it. The rope gets closer. He'll let go of the rock, and grab it. 'Catch it! Son, come on!' It's gone again.

'I can't do it!' His heart is in his throat and tears spring from his eyes. 'I can't let go.'

'We don't have time,' his father tells him. Orpheus can hear it too, the sound of a drone sweeping the darkened shore, looking for two people running along the beach. In a minute or two, it will cast its light on them.

'Just go without me,' Orpheus replies. The thought of being caught is suddenly less terrifying than the thought of letting go. Letting go and falling into the black water.

'Orpheus,' his father says fiercely, 'I will never leave without you. Do you hear me? I will never leave you. Tonight, you have wings. When you see the rope coming, imagine it. This is the beach on which you were born. There is nothing to fear.'

Orpheus tries to imagine it. Tells himself that he is actually Icarus, taking a first fateful leap into the air. He'll let go of the rock and he'll be surprised that gravity's forgotten him. He'll be surprised that he doesn't fall. 'Okay,' he says.

'Okay!' his father shouts back. 'Three, two . . .'

An explosion of light and the air erupts into sound. Orpheus lets go of the rock and his palms burn on the fibres of the rope.

Fugitives detected! A mechanical siren explodes from the speaker at the base of the drone. Orpheus is holding on for dear life and his father's terrified face is illuminated in blue, white and red. Orpheus finds a space for his foot in one of the rocks, pushes himself up, up, imagining he has wings, that he is a creature of the air. He won't die here.

The shutter of an automated camera going off like lightning bolts. The people who are chasing his father won't be far behind. Orpheus can already hear them coming in their speedboats.

Orpheus scrabbles up the cliff-face, his blood pure adrenaline. His father makes it first and then is quick to lean down, taking his son's hand in his. 'It's okay,' he says again, his voice steady. 'Out in the forest, we have a chance to lose them.'

Two drones are circling like helicopters, beating the cold air above them. When Orpheus gets unsteadily to his feet at the top of the cliff, he sees three speedboats in the water. Two men, mooring theirs by the rock below, steady at their heels.

'Run!' his father tells him, and they flee into the forest.

Orpheus struggles not to trip in the thick under-growth; frosted leaves crunch like eggshells under his boots. Brambles and nettles whip his ankles. This part of the run, though, he has trained for. He has been, since aged seven, running relays with his father across Angharad Beach.

'They went that way!' someone shouts as Orpheus and his father turn a sharp corner past a frozen pond. His ears are filled with the roar of drones. They swoop like Valkyries down through the leafless canopy, sending shuttering daggers of light across the forest floor. Howling sirens, propellers tearing through the boughs. The noise of their pursuit is an assault on all his senses.

'Freeze!'

Orpheus allows himself a fleeting glance over his shoulder and sees four people in dark armour, holding hunting rifles. They sweep through the forest on Zephyrs. Orpheus is mesmerised for a moment by the sight of them, the way they look. Flying. Actually flying. These people from the city, they are something more than human. It's almost sickening to watch the way they move.

His father is a few paces ahead, shouting, 'Hurry!' But where are they going to go? Orpheus is not convinced anymore that they can outrun their pursuers. He feels like a fox dashing through the undergrowth, a half-visible hunting party at his heels. They are several metres away, although closing the distance every second.

A bullet makes a sound like a mosquito in the air, a suffocated squeal and then a branch near Orpheus' arm splinters, erupting in a tiny blizzard of frost. Another gunshot and this one would have hit Orpheus if he had not ducked just at the right second. These men really want to kill us.

A rat-tat-tat-tat of gunfire through the branches, and Orpheus takes cover behind an old elm, his heart pounding, sick with terror. They are almost at the cabin where his father parked his car. An old rusted thing that runs on diesel, it would stick out in the city but is good enough, his father has assured him, to get them where they need to go. It's less than half a mile away, Orpheus knows. If he and his father can make it there without getting shot, they might have a chance.

If he leaps between this tree and the next one, he can take cover. His father is a few paces ahead, and as Orpheus dashes through the wood he feels as if the forest has turned against him. He has to hold his hands up to protect his face from the gnarled branches of trees, bullets zip past, exploding above his head. Tears blur his vision and sear his throat, but he keeps running, fighting the waves of black dread that threaten to seize his muscles. A quarter of a mile. His father is slaloming through trees, leaping over the undergrowth, missing bullets, careful to keep out of the spiralling spotlight pouring down from the drones.

We might make it, Orpheus thinks. But just as he does, the heavy heel of his boot is gripped by a thick root that bulges from the soil. He loses his balance all at once, flies forward into the dirt, biting down on his tongue so hard his mouth fills with blood.

'Orpheus!' his father shouts, although his voice is half drowned by the sound of sirens, and the blood beating in Orpheus' ears. He hits the ground so hard his lungs turned into a vacuum. And, by the time Orpheus looks up, he knows he's going to die. A man in a dark suit appears overhead, and Orpheus is facing down the barrel of his gun.

'No!' his father shouts.

Gunfire. The smell of burning. Orpheus doesn't feel it at first. Looks down at his left hand and sees that the bullet has cut a hole clean through it, flesh, bone, tendon. It's like a trick of his vision, although, before he knows it, the forest floor is slick with his blood.

A second shot.

His father hurls a rock at the man balanced on his Zephyr, knocking the machine so it rocks like a kite, causing him to reel, and miss. Crash of shot branches, birds leap into the lightening sky.

I'm going to die, Orpheus thinks.

His father throws another rock at the Zephyr, angled just the right way to hit its corona wire. There is a squeal of threatened mechanics and the man loses his balance, toppling onto the forest floor with a crash and a howl of pain.

It gives his father enough time to run over and scoop his son up in his arms, the way he used to do. 'It will be okay, son,' he tells Orpheus. 'We have medical supplies in the van. There is a doctor at Silo Six.'

The pain is already beginning for him, though. Orpheus grits his teeth and tries not to scream. He feels as if his arm is on fire, as if it's been skewered by a red-hot poker. Everything he touches is slippery with his pulsing blood.

Orpheus can see the cabin a few metres away. Relief, they are almost there. Almost safe.

'I need you to trust me,' his father tells him. Blackness for a moment, a ringing in his ears. When Orpheus opens his eyes, his father has tucked him into the leather back seat of the car. He is rummaging around for a piece of cloth to fashion into a tourniquet, which he ties around Orpheus' arm. In the rear-view mirror on his right-hand side, Orpheus can see almost a dozen people climbing off their Zephyrs, surrounding the car.

His father says, 'I don't think I can outrun them.' His breathing is ragged, eyes wild with fear. 'So I'm going to go back ... it's me they want. Not you. You need to stay here, and keep quiet.'

'No,' Orpheus gasps. 'They'll kill you.'

'I know,' his father says evenly. 'I want you to close your eyes when they do it. I want you to close your eyes and understand that I've found a way ... I think I've found a way to defeat death.'

'What?'

'Yes.' His father smiles then. 'You're going to live. You'll live long enough to wonder. So I promise you now, that you will find me where you lost me.' When he leans down to kiss his son, Orpheus realises that he's crying. 'I love you, Orpheus. You will be the fulfilment of all our dreams. We have a plan for your life. A design. This day is part of that.'

'Dad . . .'

Before he can stop him, his father is gone. It's all he can do to haul himself up on his one good arm. His blood has turned to tar between his fingers, black and cold.

Through the car windscreen he sees his father outside, silhouetted by searchlights.

'It took you fourteen years to find me,' his father shouts at the glass eyes of one of the drones. 'With all your technology.' Orpheus can only see his father's silhouette. A dozen officers approach him, their heavy boots snapping branches in the underbrush. They grab his arms and apprehend him. Drag him forward. Orpheus sees his father start in surprise; he's caught sight of something outside Orpheus' field of vision.

'You came yourself.'

'You know what they say,' a man replies, 'about getting a job done properly. We've destroyed everything, you know, every part of Milk Wood.'

'That you've found.'

'There's only one thing left.'

'Me,' his father says.

'Yes, and you might have divined already that your plan ends this way. Here, tonight.'

'That's not what I've seen.'

A click of a rifle, another voice. Someone says, 'If we kill him now, it's over.'

'You can't stop the future,' the man says.

Before he fires, Orpheus hears his father say: 'It's already here.'

3

Moremi

Moremi is a member of the post-flood generation, now. One of the millions whose lives were torn apart when a terrorist organisation hijacked an unmanned British drone and used it to drop four bombs on the Thames Barrier, the steel dams that protected the floodplain of Greater London from high tides and storm surges moving up from the North Sea.

It happened nine months after her Pulse was implanted and Moremi spent the weeks after watching it from behind thousands of eyes. Now, she's seen enough quartz recordings to patch together a vision of the flood's entire motion. 'Twenty-eighth of January, 2045,' she'll tell the directory, 4pm, high spring tide, London reeling in the wake of freak blizzards, the snow melting off the Cotswold hills and surging back into the bursting banks of the Thames. The worst day for it.

If she plays back the recording, she can find her own memory of the afternoon before the hit. She'd been heading out of a ballet class, a hot coal of joy in her chest. She'd just discovered that she'd been accepted into the prestigious Regency Ballet School. That had been half an hour before the explosion. Moremi had bid goodbye to her form tutor, grabbed her gym-bag and rucksack, and slid down the banister the way that she had been warned several times not to. School had only just finished, and all the pupils were dispersing. There had been a long line of people waiting outside the music hall for detention to start; inside, the choir were finishing up practice, and their buoyant melody resonated down the corridor. Moremi had wanted to shout her good news out to the stragglers in the playground: 'I'm going to ballet school!' She wanted them to know that all her years of blistered practice had paid off. From her first wobbly arabesque on the worn shag-carpet in her living room, Moremi had danced every day of her life for over a decade. She knew that it would take many more years before she came close to skimming the perfection of the professional dancers in a company, but she was willing and excited. She had worked hard, asked the universe a question and it had answered 'Yes'.

Moremi waited in the playground for her younger sister Zeeba, impatient, scanning the faces of the smaller students for one she recognised. 'Zeeba?' Moremi called halfheartedly, breath misted on the brisk January air.

If her sister had had a Pulse, Moremi would have been able to track her location, but Zeeba had refused the implant for the third year in a row.

'Remi!' came a sing-song voice, unnervingly close by. Moremi looked up to find that her sister had climbed the old oak tree in the corner of the playground. It was her first year in the secondary school, and she looked too small for her blue blazer and the heavy turtle-shell of her rucksack. Zeeba was hiding just above the sightline, a couple of metres perhaps, holding on to a bough like Tarzan and grinning, her school skirt bunched between her legs in a way that exposed her bleached cotton briefs, one arm swinging wildly.

'Get down from there!' Moremi shouted, her joy disappearing almost at once. 'You could break your neck.'

'I won't though,' she said, already twisting around and angling herself to climb down.

'You'll get another detention.'

'You just hope I will.' Zeeba leaped between boughs, her scuffed shoes finding purchase on the branches.

Zeeba was twelve and a source of constant irritation. Even that high sing-song cadence of her voice, Moremi found grating.

'I heard you have one tomorrow.'

'From who?'

'On the GrapeVine,' Moremi said. 'What did you get this one for?'

Zeeba looked embarrassed.

'Fighting?' Moremi guessed, correctly. 'Again? Zee? Mum's going to kill you.'

'You would have done the same if you'd been there. Bobby K called our family Luddites.' She lowered her voice at the last word as if it was obscene.

'Because you don't have a Pulse yet?'

'Yet? I'm never going to get one,' Zeeba said.

'Don't say that.' Moremi rolled her eyes. 'You'll change

your mind when you're older. And, if what they say is true, it might be impossible not to have one in the future. Like, living without a phone, or the internet or ...' She strains to think of something more essential. 'Electricity.'

'Some people do,' Zeeba said, kicking her bag against her leg as they headed towards the school gates.

'Yes, but ...' Moremi rolled her eyes again. 'That's crazy.' It has been nine months since hers was implanted and she shudders to consider how she ever lived without it. Sometimes she dreams in analogue, dreams not splashed with holograms or metadata, and then she wakes like an expat who's grown to despise her mother tongue.

'Maybe me and Mum think all of you are crazy,' Zeeba said.

Her words aggravated Moremi; she gritted her teeth, tightened the strap of her rucksack over her shoulder and said, 'We'll be late to meet Mum if we don't hurry.' Once a month, the three of them went to the Odeon in central London, with the discount tokens that her mother collected, and watched a movie. Moremi loved to sit in the dark with her head on her mother's shoulder, and this time it was her turn to pick the film.

As Moremi and her sister walked through the streets of Pimlico and up towards Westminster station where they were to meet their mother, Moremi had been filled with an unfamiliar love for the city and everyone in it.

London hadn't always felt like home. Although her mother's parents had lived in Peckham for over fifty years before they died, they had always called Lagos 'back home'. They sent most of their savings to distant relatives there, still cooked jollof rice and boiled spicy stews with bony meats, sliced Scotch bonnets like tomatoes and turned their noses up at chips or pasta. While growing up Moremi's mother liked to tell her not to forget where she 'came from'. As if Moremi could remember anywhere but London. After her father left, their mother had maxed out two credit cards on a sudden caprice, buying flights for them to go to Lagos. Going 'home' aged nine, Moremi understood a bit of what her grandparents meant. It had been the first time she'd looked up at the billboards on the dusty road from the airport and seen that every face looked like her own. 'There are black people on the *money*,' Halima had said, her voice light with wonder. Five hundred naira, a scuffed yellow note with Dr Nnamdi Azikiwe's – first president of the Federal Republic of Nigeria – round familiar face on it. She held it close, it was too precious to spend.

Moremi remembered that they'd met a lone Canadian woman by the buffet table after a four-hour church service, who had told them, 'You know, I was the only white person in the hall,' and Moremi realised for the first time in her life that she hadn't been counting.

And yet, she also remembered the damp feel of the air when she returned to London. The sky, stony-grey and threatening rain. That smell of dew and petrol, of brushed steel and wet concrete, that was the smell of her childhood. The sight of a red bus sweeping through traffic outside Earl's Court station, the voice that declared 'Mind the gap' on the underground. Dowdy Jehovah's Witnesses in long skirts and loafers giving out leaflets by the Sainsbury's with a sign that asked, 'Is this all there is?'

'You bet,' shouted a commuter in a Burberry trench coat, ducking from the downpour. It felt like returning to the window to find nothing but your own face staring back at you. When she thought 'back home', it meant back here.

Moremi loves the city with the sad fervour of the neglected and lovelorn. It regards her not at all. Her family can barely afford to live here.

Moremi considered it as they headed from their school in the heart of Pimlico, past the tenement flats on Page Street with their chessboard facades, rectangles of buff-grey brick and rendered panels, children playing out in the concrete square. She and her sister needed only to turn a corner and they would emerge on another quiet street lined with stately 19th-century homes. It was something that Moremi could never reconcile about London; on one road, there might be five to a bedroom in a condemned flat with no central heating while, just around the corner, would be the listed townhouse of a billionaire banker, an ambassador or a baroness. White porticoed terraces worth millions, dead-eyed bay windows reflecting private gardens, homeless men sleeping on benches in front of them. Or else gathered just two streets away, in mud-streaked sleeping bags under the Victorian arches of the railway track, rattling used McDonald's cups in hopes of change. On the one hand, envy scissors through Moremi at the sight of such wealth, and on the other she burns at the unfairness. Although she's been told that she is lucky, in an abstract global way, last month she piled all of her pillows and blankets in the bathtub, in order to make herself a private place to sleep.

As Moremi and Zeeba emerged on Milbank,

overlooking the Thames, her mother messaged to say that she was running late. There had been a delay on her tube and she was likely to arrive at Westminster station after they did. 'Stay there and wait for me,' it said. It had been all Moremi could do not to burst out right then with her good news and spoil the surprise.

'If she's going to be late,' Zeeba said, dragging her heels with a bored whine edging up in her voice, 'why can't she meet us at the cinema? I hate standing outside the tube station, especially at this time of day.'

'I don't know. If you had a Pulse, or even a phone, you could ask her yourself,' Moremi said.

The first and second bombs exploded almost half a city away from where she and her sister had been standing. In her memory, they had just crossed the road. They had been heading by a hotdog stand with wind-chimes hanging from its shuttered window. In the second after the hit, they made a ghostly tinkle, as if a sudden hard breeze had picked up. It drew Moremi's attention to the street behind her. Moremi remembered that she felt the third and fourth barrier strikes like the sub-sonic disruption before an earthquake. Tectonic plates buckling under the earth's lithosphere. But perhaps that's only her own mind embellishing the moment. The traffic went quiet. Everyone received a TERROR ALERT on the Panopticon. But there had been a few terror alerts that winter and, though everyone in the city had been poised for disaster, it was difficult to shake that 'it can't happen here' disbelief.

Almost two thousand years ago, the Romans had built Londinium on the north bank of the Thames, on ground that sloped upwards. But as the city expanded into its floodplain, the river had been carved into narrow bends. Without the Thames Barrier, at high tide and with the pressure of the recent snow runoff, the river was unleashed to reclaim its old dimensions. It did so with such force that, for a few minutes, it appeared to reverse direction. The dark waters swung out into the sea only to bound back in a huge swell, bursting embankments, surging up streets, between the pickets in gates, over tarmac and asphalt. In some places it came up several metres high, like a black mountain.

Moremi and her sister had been standing on the pavement just outside Victoria Tower Gardens when people began to run. Cars skidded to a halt, one bus juddered up onto the kerb, and Moremi had to duck in order to avoid its yellow mirror clipping her head. A cascade of terror alerts scattered across Moremi's vision. Although Zeeba could not see them, she could tell that something was wrong. They were just around the corner from Westminster Bridge, which was the second worst place to be as it was on lower land, near a bend in the river where the force of the water was like a truck turning a sharp corner. If they'd been standing outside Westminster station at that moment, they would have seen the wave coming, lashing foam at the London Eye. (The people in the lower capsules all drowned, those at the top bearing horrified witness.) They would have seen throngs of tourists drop their cameras and flee as water thundered up Victoria Embankment with the speed of a bullet train, unearthing trees and lifting cars from the tarmac. From some vantage points the wave looked about two storeys high, made of foam and rubble, debris and bodies tossed up like life rafts, aluminium bonnets of cars, the glass panes of bus shelters.

Before they saw it, they heard it. A sound Moremi herself would never forget, rising over the screams of the commuters. A terrible roar, like the churning metal in the jaws of a rubbish truck, bent steel, snapped wood, gargled howls of the drowning. It had been like a lucid dream, the ancient river doubling back to devour the city.

Commuters scrambled from their cars and spilled onto pavements. Buses opened their doors suddenly to let their passengers flee in the opposite direction from the river. Everyone began to run, abandoning briefcases or shopping bags, scooping their children from buggies and car seats. But where to run? Where was safe? Was another bomb going to explode, and if so, was it better to take cover? Or was it better to flee from the river, try to get inland, up to higher ground?

Moremi simply froze, squinting up to the darkening sky at the storm-cloud of smoke and ash in dizzy disbelief. Then she had turned to see the water coming in a black wave over the side of the embankment, maybe a hundred metres away from them. It had only been when Zeeba screamed, 'Run!' that Moremi's limbs had unglued. They had about five seconds before the wave reached them, and Moremi remembers it in a blur. Remembers the sight of the water crashing through the park like a scene from a disaster movie.

Zeeba and Moremi pelted in the opposite direction, up Great Peter Street, which had been lined with large bare-knuckled trees and red-brick terraces. As they ran, metal manhole covers unbuckled from the road, lifted upwards by rising water. Mud oozed between cracks. All around, the less able-bodied had been shouting for help. A school-boy with crutches. A pregnant waitress in an apron. A Romanian beggar. Moremi had glanced over to them, but then shouted, 'I can't . . .', her own face a mask of terror.

They made it some distance before they realised that they couldn't outrun the tsunami. Zeeba shouted, 'Up there,' and scrambled up a wall next to a block of flats. Moremi watched as her sister's feet found purchase in the knobbled bark of an overhanging plane tree. By then, the water had been up to her shins, and it was pulling at her with a furious force. Screams, all around her, as people were felled like bowling pins.

'Hurry!' Moremi could barely hear her sister over the tumult.

Moremi grappled for the top of the wall and jumped, letting the water slide under her feet. Her heart had been pounding so fast that by the time she found balance on the wall her vision blackened. She was wet all over. With one hand she gripped the branch of a tree, but the water was grabbing at her thighs, pulling her in the opposite direction. Bark splintered into her fingers; it took all her might not to let go. The wave was two metres high by then; it wasn't a river, it was a leviathan, intent on swal-lowing the city.

Moremi began to let go.

The wave had already gulped down railway and power stations, centuries-old landmarks, turned streets to rubble. Moremi could feel herself surrendering to it. It was vanity to hope that her own flesh might prevail where steel and iron could not.

From many accounts, in the couple of minutes after the initial blast, the power went out across the city and the Panopticon was temporarily disabled. Distant alarms resonated through the empty halls of buildings and apartment blocks across London and then went quiet.

Moremi must have passed out, and so her quartz had stopped recording. When she opened her eyes, she was lying on the floor of a room she had never seen before. A school hall or gymnasium.

For a moment she almost concluded that she'd dreamed the whole thing.

With shuddering sobs, Zeeba explained that she had hauled Moremi out of the water, using the strap of her rucksack like the scruff of her neck. 'I thought you were dead,' she kept interrupting her tale to shout. It had been the police officers on Zephyrs who had come to save them forty minutes later. The officers had helped to transport the girls, along with any other survivors they could find, to a nearby church.

As Zeeba spoke, though, Moremi was distracted by the fact that her Pulse seemed to be offline. Only a couple of holograms still flickered about her vision; there were tabs around the church displaying notices or an option to read the hymns displayed on the board. But the ticker-tape news feed normally scrolling to the right of her field of vision had been filled with ugly error notices. The voices of her group chats had faded to silence.

The silence, more than anything, had filled her with a

strange kind of dread. That phantom-limb pain familiar from the old days. Once, she'd reached into her pocket to discover that her phone had been stolen. With a stab of terror she'd realised that she'd lost something as integral to her as a sense.

Over three hundred people were gathered in the hall. Gym mats and blankets were laid out across the aisles, in chapels and between pews. From the window it was possible to see the sunken city. It wasn't just the water, it looked as if the streets had been digested.

'What about Mum?' Moremi asked, her voice scratched.

'I don't know,' Zeeba said, more tears spilling from her eyes.

'She would have been in an underground station,' Moremi reasoned. 'So she's probably safe.'

Their older sister Halima had left the city a few days earlier for the Hilary term at St Hilda's, so she, at least, was miles away from the devastation. Her mother, too, Moremi imagined, was probably safe somewhere. Perhaps on the floor of another church, or a school gymnasium.

Moremi reached reflexively for the holographic menu, selecting the option that would allow her to make a call, but – of course – it was not working. Not the map, either, which was normally populated with reassuring bubbles with the names of everyone she knew. *Will Mum be okay?* Moremi thought into a search-box, *Will we?* Neither returned anything.

Zeeba suggested that they head out and look for their mother, which seemed like a vain effort to Moremi even before the officers stationed at the door explained that it was safest for them to stay put. When Zeeba protested, they insisted that no minors would be allowed to leave without a parent or guardian.

While waiting in the church, Moremi and her sister were briefly insulated from the anarchy on the streets outside. Moremi would only see it on the news later; a mother running up roads carrying the drowned body of her five-year-old son, screaming. Fires ignited in trash-cans. A group of truanting teenagers smashing the windows of high-street shops and – the security system disabled, police at breaking point – stealing as much as they could carry. Emergency services had struggled to meet demand. The army had been dispatched onto the roads.

Two girls in her year-group had been discovered wandering the streets. They were delivered to the church by a police officer, where they relayed to Moremi in excited tones how they had escaped from the wave by scrabbling atop a bus shelter. Someone else had saved himself by grabbing a displaced road sign and clinging on to it like a raft. They told wild, miraculous tales of escape that made Moremi herself feel blessed and giddy in spite of her worry. She felt improbably fortunate – though she'd only later discover, when she learned the death toll, quite how fortunate – and something about the elation of surviving turned the rest of the day into a surreal holiday. Like a snow day. She imagined telling the story again and again – that night at dinner, next week at school, over a decade of Christmases – of how the wave came and her sister saved her. Moremi had resolved, in her mind, never to be cruel or short-tempered with Zeeba again.

As the sun set outside, the church's vicar went around lighting candles. The cold began to set in; Moremi and Zeeba played Go Fish with an incomplete pack of cards Zeeba had found under a pew. They were fed packets of crisps and Snickers bars by apologetic volunteers. Moremi had a ballet class scheduled for tomorrow morning.

As night fell, she took the initiative and began practising for next week's recital on her own. Moremi was supposed to play the duck in a ballet of *Peter and the Wolf.* So, she used the back of the chair as a barre and practised her solo with closed eyes. In her mind, she recalled the bird-like chirp of the oboe during the duck's theme. In the ballet, the duck is swallowed whole by the wolf. At the end of their first rehearsal their ballet teacher, Annette, had told them, 'If you listen very carefully, you'll hear the duck quacking inside the wolf's belly, because the wolf, in his hurry, swallowed her alive.' She had been looking forward to performing, but she didn't know then, even as she danced, that icy water had crashed through the windows of Annette's basement ballet studio, drowning her and seven other women in minutes.

Every hour without her Pulse made Moremi feel even more disorientated and sick. As if she was trying to navigate life without one of her senses. She could tell the people around her were getting restless as well. It was maddening to know so little about what was going on.

As midnight came and went, dread began to creep up her back. By then, about a dozen people from her school had been recovered – caught up in the flood on the way home – and they brought with them more harrowing news of the disaster. Hannah Wellbank – the blonde girl in the form group opposite, best in the school at netball, who still wore the tarnished steel 'best friend' necklace she was gifted in Year Seven – had stayed home from school that day because of a stomach bug, and Sandra Sanchez had heard from her neighbour that everyone in Hannah's block of flats had drowned. Meera Patel – with the waist-length black hair, put up a year because she was so good at maths – was found dead on her way back from an orthodontist appointment. Ira Medina's father, a tube driver, was killed, along with hundreds of others, in London Bridge station.

Every now and then, someone left the room in hysterical tears. A scream might echo down the corridor. The vicar led everyone in a chorus of 'Abide With Me', pointed to the crucifix on the wall, reminded them, 'For He must reign until He has put all His enemies under His feet. The last enemy to be defeated is death.' Words Moremi would turn ponderously over in her mind for years to come. Then another song; a tearful rendition of 'Nearer My God To Thee', sung the way it might have been before the *Titanic* sank.

At around 1am, Moremi went to sit in one of the side chapels, lit by the offertory candles and a dim chandelier. Mary holding Jesus. Her old friend Zen was there. They used to sit next to each other in maths class before Zen got a Pulse and they stopped talking. Zen was shivering in her rumpled school uniform, her feet up on the bench, hugging her knees, silent tears rolling down her face.

'I miss it,' she said when Moremi approached. And

Moremi knew that the girl was talking about the Panopticon.

'Me too,' she whispered. 'I feel sick without it.'

'Worse,' Zen said. Her teeth had been chattering and Moremi could not tell if it was from the cold or terror. 'You didn't have it as long as I did. I already feel this pain for it. Grief, kind of. And a grief for everything else too. Everything that will be different now.'

'Do you think it will be?' Moremi asked.

'There's talk of school being cancelled for the rest of the term.'

'That doesn't sound possible,' Moremi replied. 'What about exams?'

'They'll probably be cancelled too,' she said. 'They're setting up checkpoints throughout the city, the army were deployed, there's a curfew.'

'That sounds crazy.' Moremi's head was spinning.

'This whole thing is crazy,' Zen said, looking into the distance. 'I keep thinking about last week, yesterday, this morning. This morning! Myself at the bus stop not knowing that everything was about to change. I just wish my Pulse would come back online,' she said again, rubbing the dim lights of her constellation.

'You children.' A rueful laugh from the bench two rows behind made them both start. An old lady was sitting there, only the whites of her eyes clearly visible in the gloom. 'You easily bruised peaches. A mere thought can floor you.'

'This is a big deal!' Zen said, turning to her. 'They're saying this bombing, it was an act of war.'

'Everything we know could be gone,' Moremi said, half to herself, dizzy with disbelief.

'Oh,' said the old lady, 'you don't know yet? You haven't lived long enough to learn that everything you rely on can disappear like this.' The sound of her fingers snapping echoed like a gunshot. 'Everything you hold dear. You kids. You've been lucky all your life. That's all. Not safe, just damned lucky. One day your prime minister is assassinated. One day there's a coup and none of your laws exist anymore. There's a flood, there's a famine. A dictator. A pandemic. Just because it hasn't happened to you doesn't mean that it can't happen. Doesn't mean that this isn't the human condition to fight for and then lose and lose again what you fought for.'

'This isn't just about us,' Moremi said, suddenly frantic, 'it's about everyone. I saw London vanish. The Houses of Parliament.'

Zen said, '"The centre cannot hold",' and the woman replied:

'So we find a new centre.'

The rest of the night was spent on the floor, on a vinyl gym mat. The air smelled of incense and dust, and though at around 3am the vicar blew the candles out – nothing but the old moon through the stained-glass window – Moremi could tell that nobody was asleep. Zeeba, who had curved the little bones of her back into her sister's chest, was crying quietly. The whole day had curdled into a nightmare.

The next morning, their older sister Halima came to

pick them up. Some of the water had receded and it had been possible for her, she explained, to take a circuitous route from the train station past the hastily erected checkpoints and to the 'safe houses' dotted around town where children were being held. Her cheeks looked hollowed out, her face harrowed. She said that she had spent all day and night looking for them. Their mother still hadn't turned up at any of the checkpoints or rescue centres. 'She will though,' Halima promised as the three of them left the church, struggling to keep their fragile hope intact.

One time, Moremi had left the house during a blizzard and had been shocked by the sight of the world made new and dreamlike by white drifts of snow. That morning, instead of childlike wonder, her body was clenched with horror. By then, the waters had receded, but the city had crumpled in their wake. The slip roads had turned to rivers, as the contents of houses sailed into gutters. Sanitary towels bloated by water, wads of newspapers, punctured deodorant cans, cracked picture frames, globs of faeces. Halima lifted Zeeba onto her back and told her to close her eyes.

Moremi kept waking up in the middle of the night and forgetting. Thinking she could hear her mother's footsteps in the bathroom, the wood floor somewhere creaking under her soles. And then she'd remember and fight to breathe. Some of the magical thinking from her childhood resurfaced; one magpie meant their mother was gone forever, two and she was coming back tomorrow; a crack in a kitchen tile could undo them all.

Two days after the flood, Moremi woke at 4am as the

Panopticon came back online. Wonderful data, chatter, discord and news. How had she survived without it? Moremi gripped her bedsheets, fists wet with sweat, surprised that she could find herself so relieved when, technically, almost none of her problems had been solved.

The feeling didn't last for long, though. It was only a couple of minutes before she opened the tabs and read the numbers. Thirty-five power stations and almost a thousand electrical substations were affected. Trillions of pounds of damage: 400 schools, 16 hospitals, 3.3 million homes – most especially the basement homes of poor residents and people who lived in poorer areas. There were Vine recordings of authorities carrying water-damaged paintings from the shattered entrance of the Tate Modern. Millions of pounds of damage to priceless pieces of art.

Moremi couldn't comprehend any of the numbers. There was only one she cared about. To help with the recovery mission, people posted their quartz recordings of the flood on a public directory that Moremi became obsessed with watching. She saw the flood from behind hundreds of eyes, but never the two that mattered the most.

Moremi stayed up most nights, searching the memories of survivors for the face of her mother. Sometimes Moremi thought she saw her, her profile or her wax-print headscarf, but it was almost never clear. 'Have you seen this woman?' She'd send messages out like flares across the Panopticon; they would vanish, of course, because everyone in London could count on two hands the number of people they knew who had died or were still missing. The map of the city had been scarred and repatterned by tragedy.

Moremi asked the Panopticon how to stop a bad thing from happening. Apparently there are lots of ways: hide your thumbs when you pass cemeteries to protect your parents from death, the 'parent finger'. Moremi took this to heart and tucked them in even when she passed those spray-painted murals on street corners, the memorials pinned to the gates of every school, taped to lampposts, the ones with words like 'loving grandad and brother', next to wilted garlands of carnations spelling the word 'NAN'. Unlit candles, rain-soaked teddy bears, overexposed Polaroids.

Moremi would go out at night sometimes, tears in her eyes, just looking. It was then she would feel as if she could sense it, ghosts in the air. And that smell, sewage and damp, sulphur and flesh. Death. She'd try to scrub it off herself as soon as she returned, wash it out of her hair. Burn incense, open all the windows; maybe she could banish it from her home forever.

In the weeks after the flood there had been riots, people in masks looting empty flats, malls, boutiques. A wild take-what's-ours spirit. An end-of-days breakdown of every kind of law. Bodies like piles of meat, eyes and mouths filled with mud, nameless, or shovelled into mass graves, unidentified. Everything felt too horrible to be true.

The prime minister reminded them that Londoners had made it through a great fire, through the plague, through the Blitz, 'and we will make it through this'. His own sister and her family numbered among the thousands still missing.

Every morning she woke and Halima made them breakfast; Moremi would stare at the blue flame and tell herself that this was not forever. If she could still picture her mother frying the eggs, brushing Zeeba's hair, then she might still return.

Halima had interrupted her studies at university to come back to London and take care of her younger sisters. To make some money she took a job with a Clean-Up Crew, the fleet of thousands who were paid less than minimum wage to shovel the streets. They used an implement that looked something like a metal detector to latch on to the signals emitted from a nearby Pulse, which helped them to locate bodies under cars or rubble. In the early days, a few of them were still alive: two drivers trapped in their taxis; a child curled like an Inca princess in the orchestra pit at the Royal Festival Hall.

The majority of the missing were poor, people without a lot of family, widowed, elderly. It was impossible to know what had happened to them all. Perhaps they were carried back out to sea with the tide, bones smoothed like coral on the rocks. 'We would have found her by now, you know,' Halima would say sometimes, 'if she'd had a Pulse.'

Moremi's mother's body was finally discovered during an excavation of a flooded underground station. What was the last thing that her mother had seen? It's likely that she had been waiting on the platform of the tube station, checking her watch, thinking about her daughters who she knew were waiting for her. Maybe it happened in an instant. A swill of mud between the tracks, a distant roar like a train approaching and then, all of a sudden, it rumbled through the tunnel, drowning everyone on the platform. Moremi can't help but imagine it, sometimes she'll dream about it, and wake up covered in sweat, clutching at her throat.

But she's spent so long training herself into magical thinking that Moremi begins to tell herself that her mother's death is a problem that can be solved. She says it, this evening, to Halima, who only stares at her blankly.

'Death is analogue. It's just a collection of processes: organ failure, respiratory arrest, unravelling of atomic bonds ... it's probably possible to turn it back, untoll the bell.'

'She's just in shock,' Zeeba says, and adds something else about the stages of grief, denial. But a couple of hours later, Moremi searches the Panopticon for stories that prove her point and she finds one: there is a doctor at the St Erth teaching hospital who brought a boy back from the dead.

He was a cardiologist who occasionally oversaw surgeries that required putting the patients into deep hypothermic circulatory arrest, a surgical technique that involves cooling the body and stopping the heart and brain function in order to repair large arteries in a still heart. A week before the flood, a boy with a gunshot wound, no Pulse and no records was admitted to A&E after the coastguard found his body washed up on the beach.

In the story that Moremi reads, when they found him, his body temperature had been 13.7°C. He was brought into an operating theatre where a team of doctors worked for hours to save his life. They connected him to a heart and lung machine machine and rewarmed his blood before pumping it back into his body. Eight hours after they started, a heartbeat was recorded, and his temperature had increased.

It can happen, Moremi tells herself; technology can save us. It will.

He'd regained consciousness on the day after the flood, in a video captured by the quartz of one of the nurses. 'What's your name?' she'd asked him. And in the air, with a finger, he spelled out the name 'ORPHEUS'.

His story goes viral. And, when she watches it, Moremi understands why.

She, too, becomes fixated with the video of Orpheus waking up. Watches it forwards and then backwards. His eyes close and then open, he draws breath, the blood runs back up his nose and she can't help but wish that all of time could move in that direction. That the flood waters could draw themselves back in like a held breath, the city reassembles, everyone's eyes unclose. Bricks and stones, shrapnel and glass, the hulls of speeding boats defy entropy. Inhale. Hearts start. Bombs fly back up into the sky, drones scatter like pigeons, smoke and cinders fall like rain. Her mother kisses her 'hello' on the threshold of their flat. Moremi walks backwards into her home, drops her keys in the bowl by the door, says, 'I'll see you later,' but never leaves.

4

ORPHEUS

They will never stop asking what Orpheus had seen when his heart stopped.

His entire life? Fourteen years marooned like Miranda on that island with his father. Had he begun to see the light? Had he glimpsed the face of God?

It is almost impossible to piece together everything that happened. Orpheus supposes, now, that the men who killed his father had thrown both of their bodies off the edge of the cliff. Which might have been how he was discovered the next morning, washed up on the beach at dawn, blue with hypothermia, his heart a stopped clock.

He'd been flown by air ambulance to the St Erth teaching hospital. According to the reports, it had taken them around eight hours to reheat his blood and get his heart started again. He didn't open his eyes and regain consciousness until a full week later. Had drifted for days in the hinterland of the half-dead, dreaming wild dreams.

When he'd opened his eyes, the first thing he'd seen was a nurse, haloed by mid-afternoon light. They told him he'd slept for almost eight days. Only, he couldn't shake the sense that he'd been asleep for a century. In her eyes he could see the distorted reflection of his own bruised face. He had been shaking. One of her quartz recordings is now a viral Vine. A five-second memory of Orpheus looking around as if he'd lost something. Telling the nurse that he saw something that filled him with awe.

'What?' she had asked.

'Where?' he asked back, increasingly frantic, tears in his eyes, terrified, clutching at his throat and mouthing, 'Where did I go? Where did I go?' as if anyone, the doctors, the nurses, the bemused medical students, could tell him.

In the weeks that passed, the hospital psychiatrist, the news reporters and the other teenagers on the paediatric ward would ask him the same question. 'Where did you go?'

Where did you go when you died? They asked him the way the Trojans might have asked Aeneas when he returned from the underworld. Enkidu told Gilgamesh, 'If I tell you the order of the nether world, sit down and weep!' What did Martha and Mary ask Lazarus after Jesus called his name and he returned, eyes unclosed, from the grave?

Orpheus remembers the week after they found him only in snatches. Waking up to the sight of doctors and nurses, the relentless glare of hospital lights, the din of monitors, the smell of antiseptic and latex.

When they had found him, he was a Pulseless minor with no parents and no biometric data recorded on any system, a face that no camera recognised. Anonymous, they call it, which, of course, is a crime. Orpheus wakes to discover the nurses, the doctors and social workers have already agreed on their own narrative of his life. They tell him that the way his father brought him up – totally isolated from the outside world – was a form of abuse. They treat him like a survivor, the sole escapee from an extremist religious sect.

When he is stable, they transport him to the city, which has better facilities. London is totally alien to him. Eleven million people – the idea of them makes his gut recoil. He imagines them like a time-lapse video of E. coli cells multiplying. Orpheus can count on one hand the number of people he's spoken to in his entire life. He is Rip Van Winkle woken three hundred years too late to a digital-age nightmare. Flood-ravaged city, half-run by machines.

During the weeks that he's in hospital, three police officers are stationed outside the door of his room at all hours of the day and night. All nurses and doctors entering and exiting are vetted and when Orpheus is finally deemed well enough by the lead consultant, they enter to question him.

They look like people Orpheus has been taught to dread. Protection Officers for the Panopticon. They wear a navy uniform, armoured vests with visors, elbow pads and guns. A Union Jack on one lapel, the logo of the Panopticon – an eye with the globe in its iris – on the other. The men who killed his father, he thinks, clutching the papery cotton of the bedsheet in sweaty hands.

It's a small room, and while two of them are stationed at the far end of his bed, the third positions himself by Orpheus' side. So close, that Orpheus can see the gun in its holster. He has buzz-cut ginger hair and in the skin on the side of his head are the little divots and lights, flecks of metal and raised tracks of skin. *Is that it?* Orpheus wonders to himself. The machine that his father talked about: the Pulse. The sight of it makes his stomach twist and he looks away.

A red light begins to flash in the corner of the officer's head. 'Never mind this,' he says, noticing Orpheus staring. 'It will just transmit this interview.'

'Interview?' Orpheus' voice is still a rasp, even though it's been almost two weeks since they took him off the ventilator.

'Yes,' says the first man. 'Can you tell us your full name to the camera for our records, please?'

'Where is the camera?' Orpheus asked, still confused.

'Just look into my eyes.'

'Orpheus,' he says, squinting into the man's blue irises.

'Can you give us your surname?'

'I ...' His father had always called him Orpheus of Angharad. But when he explains this, the officers exchange wary looks.

'What was your father's last name?' the first officer asks.

'Warsame ...' Orpheus bites his lip. 'He never told me.'

A silence again that fills Orpheus with dread. It looks as if he's lying, being uncooperative or rude. But he is not sure these people will believe him when he explains how much of his life his father kept from him. He can only sketchily fill in some of the details, and only from the small nuggets of information that his father let slip, mentioned in passing before he stopped himself. He knows that his father was born in Somalia. He came to London and met Callie, Orpheus' mother, at university.

He turns the question around and asks, 'Who are you?'

'We are protection officers,' says the man closest to him. 'You can refer to me as PO1, and my colleagues as PO2' – motioning to the silent man at the foot of the bed – 'and PO3.' He nodded at the short-haired woman nearest the door.

'Protection ...' Orpheus says the word slowly. 'Protection from what?'

PO1 smiles. 'I don't know how much you understand about the current political situation, Orpheus. But almost two months ago, London was the target of a devastating terrorist attack. Over a million people died. A new government came to power promising to keep the country safe. Our corporation, Protect, is owned by the Panopticon. We won the government contract to oversee the policing and counter-terrorism operations in Greater London and – hopefully, soon – the rest of the UK.'

'So, you're like police officers?' Orpheus asks.

'Imagine if police officers could see everything,' PO1 says.

'You couldn't see my father,' Orpheus says, the words tumbling out. And he regrets them a moment later.

'The man who you claim is your father has been known to us for a while. Though you know him as Warsame,

71

we have identified him as Mustafa Matan. A known terrorist who escaped from custody fifteen years ago.' The words make Orpheus dizzy but then his mind shunts against them.

'That's a lie. Or, I don't know, a mistake,' Orpheus says.

'We've identified his body. Though he burned off his fingerprints, and altered his dental records, his DNA matches the samples we have of Mustafa Matan.'

'Terrorist . . .' The word tastes like ash in his mouth. He doesn't believe it, he won't.

'Unfortunately, it's true. And now we need your help, Orpheus. We believe that he is part of a wider system of organisation – possibly associated with the Thames Barrier Bombers – of neo-Luddites, anarchists and eco-terrorists who organise themselves in groups known as silos. We think that when we intercepted him he was on his way to a place known as Silo Six.'

PO3 steps forward and says, 'You could help us to stop them. To stop a similar attack from happening again.'

'I'm not helping you do anything,' Orpheus says, gritting his teeth. 'You people killed my dad.' He finds the rage inside him and holds on to it. 'You killed my dad!' he shouts again, hoping that everyone in the hospital will hear.

PO1 lunges forward and slams Orpheus hard in the chest, knocking him onto the gurney, turning his lungs into a vacuum for a moment, IV bags and tubes swinging like bells. Orpheus gasps, hit so hard that stars flitter across his vision. One of his monitors is knocked off and a shrill alarm starts ringing.

'If we hadn't killed your father then, we'd have killed him today. He'd be on Tower Green with all the other terrorists, getting the punishment he deserves. And if I had my way, his kid would be too. Do you know how many of our kids, whole schools of children, died eight weeks ago? This isn't a game. People's lives are at stake. The last attack crippled the city and we have intelligence that your father was part of planning another.'

It's only now that it occurs to Orpheus how much danger he might be in. At the mercy of these men who killed his father. *Can they kill me, too?* he wonders. He doesn't know anything about the laws of this country.

'I don't know anything,' Orpheus rasps.

'Imagine if police officers could see everything,' PO1 says again, pressing his index finger against Orpheus' temple. 'Could see right into your hippocampus. Could see your memories.' The thought is disgusting, Orpheus thinks. Exactly what his father warned him about.

'That's the great thing about the Panopticon. In the past, we might have sat here for twenty, thirty hours, trying to wring out of you what information we need to continue our investigation. But now we can do it digitally.'

'What does that mean?' Orpheus asks, but as he does the door swings open and three doctors appear by the door. The shrill sound of the alarm filters back into Orpheus' consciousness.

'What are you doing?' asks Dr Bailey, one of the consultants who's been treating Orpheus. Nurses descend upon him, checking monitors and IV lines, machines.

PO1 lets go of Orpheus and steps back to allow them access, turns to the doctor defiantly.

'Questioning a hostile witness.'

'You mean a vulnerable witness. A child.'

'This child may be hiding information that is vital to our investigation.'

'I believe that you asked the hospital to fast-track your request to tag him?'

'He's a ward of the Kingdom now, and a minor. By law, he must have a Pulse.'

'He's still very fragile.'

'Tag?' Orpheus asks, sitting up again in bed. He stares at Dr Bailey in horror. They are talking about the Pulse. That repulsive machine. The thought of one inside him fills him with horror. 'I don't want it!' he shouts. *I'd rather die*. The thought comes to him suddenly but he realises that it's true. His father taught him, 'Nothing is yours except the square inches of matter inside your skull.' Already, trapped here, they have his body, but he can't let them have his mind. His memories. 'I'd rather die,' he says aloud.

'Now you've upset him,' Dr Bailey says. 'Look, he's my patient, can you please—'

'For now,' PO1 acquiesces. He heads towards the door with the two other officers then says, 'He's already been scheduled for interrogation and then re-education. It's our duty at Protect to ensure that all anonymous minors are tagged and re-educated as quickly as possible.'

'Re-educated?' The word gives Orpheus goosebumps.

'He's scheduled to undergo the procedure tomorrow.'

*

That night, Orpheus decides to run. He waits for forty-five minutes past midnight. The changing of the guard, the thirty seconds when the men will not be staring straight through the glass window of his hospital room, and then he leaps out of bed, barefoot, naked under his papery hospital gown, no plan in mind except that he must run.

From what the doctors explained to him after the protection officers left, Orpheus understands that tomorrow they will insert a Pulse into his skull. The police will not only use it to scan all of his memories but they will be able to track him wherever he goes. He will be a ward of the Kingdom until adulthood, so an alarm will ring, alerting the authorities whenever he is not where he is supposed to be, at school, in his dormitory. If he doesn't manage to escape now, he won't be able to leave the city until his eighteenth birthday. Four years. The thought is too horrible.

The window is sealed. Orpheus struggles with it for a while. On the other side of the glass he can see the fire escape. He thinks he could climb out and make it to the street, but there is no way to do it quietly.

He spies a ceramic vase of artificial flowers on the console table at the far end of the room. Orpheus lifts it like a basketball and pitches it at the window so hard he thinks he feels the ground shudder. It's an old building, and there is a crash of glass so explosive that it trips an alarm, which sends the guards hurtling into the room. The roar of traffic and the rain outside surges in.

He knows there's no time to think. Orpheus clambers through the break, glass slicing his shins as he goes. He climbs over the thick stone ledge and sees the city, nine storeys below. Night-time, the streets lit like rivulets of mercury. If he falls now, he'll surely die. But in his brief walks around the room, he has seen the external fire escape, three metres to his right. As Orpheus clings to the ledge, flashes of that terrifying climb with his father come back to him and his heart flutters. He reminds himself that he's done this before. Years of labour in his father's care means that in spite of his injuries he is still strong.

Orpheus grapples the ledge and manoeuvres himself to the right as fast as he can. A protection officer leans his head out the window and shouts, 'He's headed for the fire escape!' Orpheus hears the thunder of boots as his own feet find purchase on the ninth-floor landing of the wet fire escape. It doesn't feel very safe. When he leans over the edge the street telescopes below him.

'Stop him!' someone bellows, struggling with the locked door.

A few people on the pavement below look up.

'Don't jump!' someone shouts, half in jest.

Orpheus braces himself, clutches the rusted banister and rushes down the stairs. The staircase trembles with every step. Although he feels like a tightrope walker – his bare feet searching for purchase on the uneven ground – it's nothing compared to the terror he experienced a moment before, hanging off the window ledge.

The staircase shudders as two officers clamber down. They are two storeys above him, only a few metres away, but Orpheus is at an advantage; fleet-footed and small, he practically floats down to the wet pavement, landing near a row of tall bins that reek of rubbish. A quick glance over his shoulder and he sees that the officers are gaining on him. Orpheus kicks over two of the bins with his bare feet, watching as bags split and fly all across the bottom of the staircase, hoping it will slow them down.

Sirens cut through the traffic.

'Stop him!' a couple of people shout, but Orpheus slaloms through the pedestrians and turns down an almost deserted lane, his lungs on fire. There is no way that anyone can miss him, a barefoot boy pelting down the street, naked except for a white hospital gown. Rain spatters in his eyes, icy splinters of it coming in heavy cataracts down from the iron-coloured sky. His only hope is that he might find a place to hide long enough for the protection officers to lose him. And then after that? Can't they see every corner of this city using the Panopticon? All he wants to do is go home. Take a train down to Penzance, then a boat maybe, but how will he possibly get that far without being caught?

Never mind, he thinks, taking another left and dashing across a kerb. He will come up with a plan once he's lost the protection officers, whose shouts he can still hear about fifty metres behind him.

Orpheus leaps across another road. He doesn't see or hear it, the car. Experiences it only as an explosion of headlights. He freezes in terror and watches as it swerves right off the tarmac. 'Jesus Christ!' someone shouts through the open window. He needs to run, but the ground lists under him, and his head spins, flushed with adrenaline and terror.

Orpheus scrabbles back to his feet, fighting the stars floating at the edge of his vision, and runs down an unlit alley between two tall buildings, out into a leafy square, Georgian terraces facing a private garden with six-foot fences all around. Orpheus scrabbles over one of them, jumps down, and his bare feet sink into the wet loam on the other side. Then he crouches for what feels like a long time in the hedgerow, listening as the sounds of sirens fade away.

A tear rolls from his eye as it occurs to him how futile and reckless this flight is. Of course he will be discovered. Where can he go? He can't board a train out of this city without the authorities catching him. And even if he could ... he considers the way that his home had looked that last night, lit by searchlights. He considers his father, the way he had looked on the threshold that afternoon Orpheus had sneaked out to see the Summer People, and a horrible realisation occurs to him, something he'd tried to make himself forget. The drone he had seen that day. The drone that must have taken a photograph of him and reported his location – unregistered minor – to the authorities. And the line of consequences that led him here.

My fault. A thought like a thunderclap in his head.

Fugitives detected, a flash of light. Orpheus looks up with grim recognition and sees a drone. As he leaps to his feet, almost slipping in the mud, Orpheus hears sirens coming back up the road. He dashes into the garden, heading for the nearest gate, but as the streetlight glimmers on, he sees a troop of protection officers closing in on both sides. He freezes in terror, and the next thing he knows they've descended upon him, hands everywhere. Someone grips his skull like a bowling ball and grinds his cheek into the gravel path. His hospital gown is riding up but Orpheus is too panicked to care. 'Restrain him,' shouts a voice.

He puts up some fight, kicks and shouts. There is a boot on his ribcage. The snap of a zip-tie on his wrist and around his ankles. A needle-sharp scratch, cold pour of liquid into his veins.

'What are you doing to me?' he shouts, arching his spine and grinding his jaw, doing everything he can to resist. *Stay and fight,* he thinks. But his body is already ceding this battle, his vision going white.

'You can't have them,' he slurs, as his eyes roll back in his head. 'You can't have my memories.'

The scanner sees your whole life backwards. Sees Orpheus waking up in the hospital, the dappled streetlights flicking across the linoleum.

His father dies again, a bullet slides out of his skull and he gasps for the last time. They run through the woods. Orpheus lives it all again, the metal bite of panic, the winter air ripping his lungs raw.

It takes him back through his childhood with his father on their island and Orpheus sees it in beautiful relief for the lovely rare thing that time was.

They'd lived like monks, the two of them. In lonely harmony. There is a story that Warsame liked to tell about a Benedictine prioress, who asked the novitiates, 'Why do we pray?' In the story there had been a roll call of pious answers (the answers were different every time his father told the story) – 'Because we love the Lord'; 'Because we want to show him our devotion' – and, to each one, the prioress would answer, 'Yes, but that is not why we pray.' Finally, to the puzzled nuns, she said, 'We pray because the bell tolls.'

For the two of them, 'the bell' was as much the waning tides of their own enthusiasm as it was the turning of the earth, the changes of seasons and the work they had to do on the island. Waking up with the sunrise, sowing seeds in the spring when the ground was warm. Harvesting broccoli, using cloches to protect the squashes from frosts. Turning animals out onto the grass. Late summer and the back-breaking work of harvest, long days, the smell of wheat, the two of them picking top fruits from large trees, wild berries, peas and beans.

Winter had been Orpheus' favourite season, when the hard work of the summer paid off. Days were shorter, so his father would spend more of the winter teaching him lessons. A season of science, some weeks of history, languages every day; Arabic and French as well as coding and cuneiform.

One of Orpheus' happiest memories is the day he finally beat his father at chess. He says 'checkmate', and his father bangs his chest and roars. Orpheus flinches, expecting punishment, but his father lifts him above his head and says, 'This boy!' He holds him high like a trophy. 'This great boy!'

Orpheus laughs. His father turns to an imaginary crowd. 'This boy is a genius,' his father says. In Orpheus' imagination his mother is there too, smiling as his father shouts, 'This boy is the greatest thing we ever made.'

Although the quality of pre-Pulse memories are inferior, the machine manages to tease out things Orpheus thought he had forgotten. The feeling of his own weight on his feet for the first time. The smell of the lining of his Moses basket. The sweetness of powdered milk. The blood matted in his mother's hair, her amber eyelashes sticky with pearls of tears.

Being born on a beach in both of their arms.

Waking up to the Panopticon is like waking up in the tempest of a storm. Orpheus is screaming when he opens his eyes, reaching out reflexively to grab the icons, the lights and holograms resolving in his field of vision. A blizzard of data, the roar of voices, people he doesn't know talking about things he's never heard of. 'How do I make it stop?' he asks the doctor, who replies, 'It never will.'

Hard to hear him over the screaming, Orpheus bangs his head against the bars of his gurney and shouts, 'Cut it out!' He'd do it himself if he could, with a scalpel or a shard of glass.

The nurse is a young man in his twenties. He reaches over and presses his cool hands over Orpheus' clammy eyes. Icons are still flitting around in the dark, but a second or two later they fade.

'You know that Socrates feared what writing would do to society?' the man says. '"It will introduce forgetfulness into the souls of those who learn it."' And now all our memories are saved on a disk. There were Victorians who trembled at the monstrous speed of the steam train.

Maybe there were cave-dwellers who shunned fire and what it could do.

'Natural,' he says. 'It's natural to be frightened of the future. To shudder at the light. I remember when I discovered I needed laser surgery, aged seven. How I cried all the way to the optician's office. Cried when I fell asleep, and when I woke up ...' He takes in an awed breath. 'Had it always been this way? The flattened baby hairs on the side of my sister's face? The variegated specks on those leaves? Had the world been more exquisite than I had ever discerned?

'The rest of my life began that day. The part of my life when I could see. And so it will be for you, Orpheus, today.' He removes his hands and steps back.

5

ORPHEUS

Ten months now, since the flood. November. The leaves are flaying off the trees, the sky is getting dark at four. Constant driving rain. Orpheus has settled into a depression from which he will never properly recover.

After his Pulse was implanted, he had remained in the hospital for two more weeks until a social worker arrived and drove him in a van to Children's Division 11, a home like a prison for three hundred or so orphans in Stoke Newington. It's a part of London that was not hit by the flood and so has undergone rapid expansion – neo-gothic skyscrapers are shooting up, glass and steel towers like cypress trees, tall enough so the inhabitants will never drown. The purple flags of the Legacy Party hang from every official building and, since the attack, every train station or post office has at least one or two protection officers stationed outside.

Orpheus reminds himself every day that he is a prisoner,

biding his time in this city until his eighteenth birthday when he can leave. Nothing that his father taught him has equipped him for the life that he must lead off the island. He can fish, has spent the past decade growing all of his own food, but he has never set foot in a supermarket. The teachers are not sure how to teach him. He can recognise every constellation, has taught himself how to write in cuneiform, but he has never seen a computer screen. He still stares at holograms, still prickles all over with dread at the monstrous roar of the underground trains.

Most of the children in his division were orphaned by the flood, although a few of them are climate refugees from far-flung places, separated from their families at the border. Orpheus tries his best not to talk to any of them. They are like another species to him, children and teenagers raised by the Panopticon. Orpheus can't even imagine what it is like to be them. Wonders if all of their memories are scattered with holograms, their entire child-hood encrypted in quartz. Hackers and cyber-shamans. Some of them know how to disable the school's security locks with the click of a finger. Others can make their minds run algorithms to predict the weather. Think in five dimensions. Dream in code.

Growing up in the division, his life is governed by routine. He shares a dormitory with four other boys. An alarm rings every morning at six-thirty, which gives them ten minutes to climb out of bed, fold hospital cor-ners into their sheets and then jump into the shower. Breakfast is served in an over-lit canteen, a rotation of processed food – nothing like his own eggs collected just that morning from their coop – that Orpheus is expected to finish before getting into the bus which takes them to school. It's at school where Orpheus feels the most like a prisoner. Growing up, his lessons with his father were governed as much by his own interests as his dad's. They might begin the day learning about computer programming and end it reading about Ada Lovelace, and then the poetry of Byron. Learning had been an adventure, totally exhilarating, and he would always come away from lessons in awe of his father, at how much the man knew, and how many questions he could answer. Now most of his lessons are spent watching the clock, keeping quiet and wishing himself out of this body, out of this city.

Some features in the Panopticon are beginning to win him over, though. Orpheus has only to think of the question before it provides the answer. Although his access is restricted through an age filter, he feels like a mariner seeking the edge of the world. He wakes every morning hungry for answers, music he's never heard, films he's never seen, people he doesn't recognise.

Even his dreams are different here. He dreams of things that have never happened to him. Sitting in a crowded living room watching a screen. The tang of cider in the air, the sun peeping through slats in the blinds. A dog barking out on the lawn. A father he never had, a white man in a football shirt, watching with bated breath as England score the winning goal in the 2034 World Cup.

He dreams of road trips out to the countryside, lying with his friends down in the wheatfields, laughing. The smell of baked grass, the sting of hay fever in his eyes.

His dreams are spliced with memories that aren't his, but they stick like a thorn in his mind even when he wakes. When he was six his father took him to see an execution. It's one of his earliest memories. The convicts stood on a platform and, with the few coins his father had given him, he had bought an orange to eat. In his most salient memory of the day, he is watching the old orange-seller cut the rind off in one continuous motion; a clementine curl of flesh that flopped like a fish into her basket. He ate it while the prisoners shouted, bit into it like an apple, still smiling, and then the explosion of bitter citrus happened at the same moment as the gunshot.

'Are there executions in England?' he asks that evening at dinner, sitting in front of his melamine canteen tray, his eyes fixed on the squares in the ceiling as a thousand answers heed his call.

Orpheus discovers that after the flood Stella Stratton campaigned for the Thames Barrier bombers to be executed. Once she was elected on a landslide victory, a heated public debate began over the merits of reinstating the death penalty even for extreme cases. In the end, the party's home secretary had settled on a strange compromise known as the Sleep, where a tiny device, called a Nerf, is implanted into a bundle of neurons in the hypothalamus that control wakefulness. The implant puts the prisoner into a strange REM sleep that ensures they'll never wake.

'Do you think they dream?' Orpheus asks his room-mate Sherif. Sherif is a loner who used to cry himself to sleep at night. With his bronze skin, jet locks and darkly lashed eyes, people have often mistaken the two of them for brothers. They are sitting opposite each other at the canteen table now. There is a rule that children are not allowed to leave until they've eaten everything on their tray, but Sherif has allowed his pasta to go cold and is, instead, leaning over a notepad sketching furiously, his fingers blackened with charcoal.

He looks up at Orpheus' question though and says, '... *alsujana'i*?'

'Sorry.' Orpheus sets his Babel app to *English:UK*.

'The prisoners?' Sherif's voice plays in Orpheus' ear like a badly dubbed movie, and with the same stiff monotony as the voice that says 'Mind the gap' on the underground station.

'I've heard that they do,' Sherif says, and then looks back down at the page he is drawing. Orpheus watches in silent awe for a little while as a skyline emerges from his wild lines.

'I do not have any pictures,' he says, 'of home.' Orpheus has not heard much about Sherif's life, only that he was forced to flee his home and that his mother and brother died on the journey.

'I never took any pictures of my father,' Orpheus says. 'And now, it's terrible, I can feel it evaporating. You know the way memory works. The details are gone already, but I can't even remember now which ones.'

'They say that smell is the last to go,' Sherif says, still gripping the worn bit of charcoal between his fingers. 'Not anymore.'

'Yeah,' Orpheus says, observing the flickering lights of

Sherif's new constellation – he likes to wear his hair to one side to cover it.

'This sounds crazy,' Orpheus says, 'but I think I'm having some dreams that aren't my dreams.'

Sherif eyes him suspiciously and Orpheus continues, 'I keep having dreams that are as vivid as memories. Of people and things and places that I've never seen before. I know this probably sounds—'

'No,' Sherif says, glancing now across the room. Looking around for the social workers or officers, perhaps.

'Last night I dreamed I saw an execution.'

'You too?' Sherif's eyes widen.

'Yes, and then I looked it up on the Panopticon and found that executions actually happen in this country. My father seemed to have the idea that the death penalty was outlawed in the UK in the 1950s or 60s.'

'This is not the same thing,' Sherif says.

'I know. They put people to sleep, but that's why I was just wondering if—'

'I've heard that they do dream,' Sherif says as he had before. 'That they all have the same dream. I've heard that in their dreams, the prisoners are trapped inside a maze with not a single other soul. And because it's a dream, they live for thousands of years. Alone, haunted by figures from their own nightmares.'

Orpheus feels that night's dinner roll in his stomach.

'It's part of the punishment. The dream is designed by the government, and broadcast into their sleeping brains.'

'Designed?' Orpheus asks, incredulous. 'That's possible?'

'Of course! The technology is already here, inside all

of us. They simply write a program that's a bit like a memory, play it into the cranial nerves – are you okay?'

The blood has drained from Orpheus' face, he thinks he feels the room spinning. He recalls all the dreams that he's been having. Memories that aren't his. A rose-tinted childhood that he never had. People he's never met, places he's never been. Orpheus looks down to find that he's gripping the vinyl lip of his dinner tray so hard his knuckles are turning white.

'I think . . . I think they're doing that to me.' Sherif gives him a look of detached sympathy.

'Welcome to our world,' he says.

Orpheus gets up from his seat without saying another word. He feels, right then, that if he opens his mouth he might scream. He heads across the crowded canteen, and when he gets out to the basketball court he begins to run. The rain is pouring and he is still in his school shirt, dizzy with horror, shaking.

He gets as far as the chain-link fence at the end of the court, and drops to his knees, crying. Orpheus feels as if a fissure has opened in time and space. He can remember so vividly a dream-father, a football-loving, rule-abiding, homely man. A man who cried during the Olympics and took Orpheus out to the neighbouring common and taught his son how to ride a bike. Orpheus feels as if his own father, his refusenik, genius, rebel, polymath father, is fading away.

When they had let him out of the hospital, the social worker had given him a bag of the personal effects they had found with him the day he was admitted to A&E.

Even then, only a month after his father had died, they'd seemed like such curious things. Relics from another life, already. A good dream.

You can only see your childhood the moment that it's over. The boots that his father had mended for him with an old rubber tyre with sand from Angharad still encrusted in their treads. Orpheus had run his index finger over them and promised himself, then, as he did now, 'It happened.' After a brief inspection of his other possessions, he discovered his father's broken pocket-watch in one of his own shredded trousers and wondered how it had got there. Examined his distorted eye in the dented chrome lid. The social worker said, 'The broken-hearted look different from the rest of us.'

In the car, on the way to the children's division for the first time, Orpheus had played with the watch nervously, flipping the spring-hinge open and closed. He had been thinking, *If something funny happens, who will I tell now?*

The next morning, on the bus on the way to school, Orpheus asks the Panopticon, 'Who do my dreams belong to?'

The government calls it the Good People Project, piloted by the Panopticon, and adopted recently by the Legacy Party. Since the rise of computer-brain interfaces, a department of the government has been set up to investigate sleep. They describe the project as 'Good dreams for vulnerable people'. When Orpheus sleeps, a signal is transmitted across the Panopticon to his Pulse the same way as a software update. His quartz then executes a set of instructions that cause a certain pattern of electrical activity in his brain. This all happens while he sleeps and so he experiences it as hallucination or a 'dream'.

It turns out that a 'good' dream is one that meets the standards set by the Ministry of Sleep and Dreams. Government-sanctioned, patriotic dreams, happy dreams, hollow visions of a rose-tinted kingdom.

According to the Ministry of Sleep and Dreams, the Good People Project is being trialled in a number of prisons, detention centres and children's divisions across the country and has been judged, so far, to be an overwhelming success. During the Panopticon's controlled trials, prisoners who had undergone dream therapy for at least six months were half as likely to reoffend. Many of them went on to seek gainful employment, apologised to their victims. They became model citizens, compassionate fathers or hard-working women. His form tutor explains to Orpheus that children who have lost their parents and undergo this course of therapy are less likely to be depressed or anxious, have fewer instances of suicidal ideation, form more secure attachments.

'But nobody asked me,' Orpheus says, clenching his teeth in frustration. 'No one even told me. I thought, for weeks, that these were *my* dreams.'

'They are yours, now,' she says.

In his head, Warsame is laughing at his son's naivety, at his hope that the Panopticon might set him free. 'Nothing is yours,' he imagines his father saying, 'not even the wrinkled pounds of flesh between your ears.'

That afternoon, in the playground, Orpheus sits, as he always does, on the benches facing the boys' makeshift cricket pitch. Orpheus watches the boys in their uniforms, loosening their ties, shouting at each other, their voices thick with laugher. Do their dream-fathers look the same as his?

That evening, he finds Sherif again, and sees that he's watching something on the glass console at the far end of the division's TV room. The news playing on mute, with subtitles. An attractive fair-haired family emerges from a car and wave at the press. A man in his late fifties is wearing a white polo-neck. He has thick blond hair, slicked back from his high translucent forehead, neon-green eyes and a toothy smile.

'People say they look that way because of in-breeding,' Sherif says, lifting a forkful of curry noodles into his mouth.

'Who?' Orpheus asks.

'That man is Bertram Fairmont,' he says. 'The man who helped to create the Panopticon. Him, Hayden Adeyemi – this Nigerian whiz kid – and a neuroscientist. I can't remember her name. She has long hair. Kind of old. The Fairmont family were a big oil family. They were rich for generations. And now Bertram is the richest man in the world.' Orpheus has heard the three founders of the Panopticon referred to as the Magi.

Sitting beside Sherif now, Orpheus reaches his hand, as he's used to doing, into the pocket of his trousers. He pulls out his father's watch and flicks it open. It's heavier than one might expect, with a glass face that reveals the delicate skeleton inside. They can see into his mind in the same way.

'You know what I think freedom is?' Orpheus says, clenching his jaw and snapping the watch shut. 'Dreaming your own dreams.'

Sherif puts his fork down and examines his friend for a moment. Orpheus wonders if he can see it too, the blistering core of rage in him. Disgust at his situation.

'Shall I tell you a rumour?' Sherif doesn't wait for a reply. 'There is a warehouse in east London where people gather, people who know how to build their own dreams.'

'Yeah?'

'I've heard all about it from a girl here. They call it God's Own Junkyard.'

It's an easy thing to make your Pulse 'go dark' for a short while, a hand motion that mutes all notifications and messages for a couple of minutes. Once he learned how, Orpheus would try to do it as much as possible, but then the timer would count to zero and the light and noise would rush back once more. The software in his constellation only allows him to go dark a couple of times in a day. Someone in his design and technology class had taught him how to make a 'muzzle', a home-made device a bit like a helmet that stops electromagnetic signals from penetrating, taking his Pulse completely offline for a short while, and deactivating the GPS system. It allows Orpheus to stay dark long enough to trick the attendance drone by the main gate and sneak out of school at lunchtime.

He hops on the back of a bus, stashes his uniform

behind a trashcan, and heads to the location he was given by a girl in his division. Sherif had introduced them, and she'd explained that she knew all about God's Own Junkyard. In the UK, like in most countries, people who want to design dreams must register with the Ministry of Sleep in order to practise. And the content of every dream is processed through a censoring software to check it complies with regulations. People who do not submit to this process – college students who code pornographic dreams on their laptops, teens who build dreams of parkour and train-surfing – are called dream-thieves. They are subject to the same punishments as people who sell class B drugs, and about as easy to get a hold of.

God's Own Junkyard is a warehouse in east London where the dream-thieves gather. But, she'd warned him before he left, the place attracted some unsavoury characters. Orpheus wants to go anyway. He wants to learn how to make his own dreams; it seems like the only way to take back some control of his mind.

Orpheus is lost in London without the Panopticon. He wanders for half an hour, up quiet residential streets around Walthamstow until, almost by accident, he finds the place. A rundown warehouse guarded by a child of eleven or twelve who sits on a battered office chair, reading a book. The kid holds out her hand, without looking up from the pages.

'Is this the place?' Orpheus asks, trying to peer over her shoulder. She smiles to herself as if at a private joke, then holds out a hand and rubs her fingers together in that old symbol for money.

'How much?' Orpheus asks. Although, he has nothing he can give her.

'You give it to me and I'll decide.'

'I don't have any money.'

'I don't want money,' she says, 'I want a memory.'

'Of what?' he asks, and the girl shrugs.

'Something fun.'

Orpheus is hesitant to take off his muzzle to connect with her but her eyes float up to the roof of the building and when his gaze follows hers, he spots a signal-blocker. He's safe from being tracked while he's here.

Orpheus chooses Guy Fawkes Night, when the children in his division were allowed to watch the fireworks. It had been the first time Orpheus had ever seen them, pyrotechnic glitter against the cloud-darkened sky. Electric lime diadems tearing seams in the darkness, tight clusters of stars spraying outwards in cloudy contrails. His blood fizzy with stolen Prosecco. Orpheus takes his helmet off and makes the motion to transfer a copy of the file to the attendant, but the girl shakes her head, performs a hand gesture Orpheus has never seen before, and the file vanishes completely from his quartz. As if it never happened.

'That'll do.' The girl slides away and lets Orpheus through the door behind her.

Although unassuming on the outside, inside the place is lit like the Las Vegas Strip. It's an Aladdin's cave of salvaged neon signs, clearly stolen – some of them have bits of plaster stuck to the edges – or repurposed from red-light districts. Stickmen and women bent double in sexual positions, 'Peepshow', says one, 'girls, girls, girls'.

The iconic one from *Top of the Pops*. 'Stage door', a sign that looks like it's been stolen from the back of a theatre, 'APPLAUSE' in potassium-blue bulbs, a dressing-room mirror, a shattered chandelier, the door of an old phone box. Gaudy red lips and a poster from outside a Tokyo love hotel reading, '休憩 ¥3,000'. Sun-faded Jesus with a neon halo, and a light-up heart in his chest, stigmata illuminated at his bare feet, which rest on gold-leafed clouds. Someone's put a discarded can of Mountain Dew on his upturned hand. Orpheus rubs his eyes as his retinas are bleached with light. The place itself is like a dream, salvaged memories, fragments of fantasies, dim glimpses of distant places.

Entering is like arriving late to a party where he knows no one. He wonders through the hectically illuminated procession of rooms, and catches glimpses, through half-open doors, of dreamers. Almost everyone is asleep, in bathtubs and blow-up pools. Cracked tiles and discarded needles.

The girl in his children's division had explained to him that while the Panopticon can transmit short clips to a sleeping brain – fleeting 'memories' that last only a couple of minutes – to transport one's consciousness into the dreamworld for hours, to enjoy a fully lucid dream, is a far more involved process which requires a lot more technology, sensory deprivation in tanks or baths, advanced computing power, and certain drugs.

The air is damp on the lower landing, and as Orpheus descends, goosebumps rise on the back of his neck. Some of the rooms are storage cupboards, filled with machinery, bundles of wires and routers. Others are stacked with racks of flashing servers, water-cooled radiators for the high-performance processing that Dreamtime – the illegal app that allows users to create, buy, sell and experience their own lucid dreams – requires. Orpheus is not sure what he had been imagining when he pictured the place; something like a capsule hotel or a hospital ward with long pristine ranks of beds. He had not imagined this foul smell, the stink of damp, the ripe scent of human bodies, the ferric tang of blood.

There must be over a hundred people in these different rooms, half-drowned in tubs. The sight of their puckered and bloated skin makes him think of London in the wake of the flood. The bodies retrieved from under cars and in basements. Here, they writhe and groan in restless drug-induced REM. People of all ages, their Pulses flickering.

Two young people sleep like Hansel and Gretel, sharing the same dream. There is an old man, his dreaming eyes blind half-moons. In the thin illumination Orpheus can see that the veins in the backs of his hands and arms have collapsed. There is an IV bag taped to his inner thigh, the insertion site darkly bruised. That must be it, Orpheus thinks, at the sight of it. Nox, the highly regulated lucid-dreaming drug that allows the sleeper to escape into the dreamworld for hours.

What are they dreaming of? Orpheus wonders. Dreaming that the flood never happened, that the people they love never died? Dreams of adventure, or flight. Though even Orpheus knows that most dreams are not so innocent. There are rumours of a man who came to the Junkyard in order to buy dreams where he brutally tortured and killed his manager every night. Of course, most of the dreams bought and sold involve sex. People make love to each other wearing fantastical bodies or wake as sultans on the other side surrounded by a harem.

'Buying or selling?' asks a man in a mask.

Orpheus says, 'I heard there was someone here who could teach me how to build dreams.'

The man nods, and leads him into another room where a girl he introduces as Nanu is sat cross-legged on the floor, playing a game of chess against herself.

'Orpheus,' she says, without turning around, reaching out to touch a knight but then recoiling her hand as if it burned her. She is a skinny young woman with an afro and a silver bomber jacket. Orpheus knows that she graduated from his children's division only last year. He's heard that she was abandoned as a baby, sent from one children's division to another. She taught herself how to code, and hacked into the division's security systems several times, broke out, disappeared for months on end only to be found by the Panopticon and brought back to the division or to detention centres. She's been in and out of jail for theft, hacking and selling unlicensed dreams.

'There are some different theories,' Nanu begins, moving a pawn to D4. 'From what I've heard there is a whole lot that scientists still don't know about sleep. But some ancient civilisations used to believe that when we dreamed our soul travelled to another world. Ancient Egyptians believed that dreams, like oracles, conveyed messages from the gods. And now, of course, we think that our own brain is the dream-maker. Maybe it's like playing chess against ourselves. We instantiate the fear, the question, the fantasy, and then we react to it.'

Nanu turns then. She looks older than eighteen. Possibly because of the hollows under her eyes, but possibly because her afro curls are scattered with silver hairs. Orpheus' palms are sweaty as he steps further into the room. It's half the size of the dormitory he shares with Sherif. There's a bunkbed on the far wall. The bottom bunk is littered with the familiar detritus of a teenager, rumpled clothes, twisted Coke cans and crisp packets. Interspersed with more strange things, motherboards and darkened monitors, sealed Tupperware boxes filled with fuses and cables, batteries.

'What do you want?' she asks Orpheus.

Orpheus wants none of the past year to have happened. He wants to go back to the island where he was born, for his father to be alive. Sometimes he thinks about the day he ran away, ran up to Hunter's Tryst to see the Summer People. I want to go back, he thinks. The drone that had seen him; 'my fault', the notion that jolts him from any sleep. I want to go back and do something different.

But he says, 'I want to learn how to code dreams.'

Nanu smiles. She tells Orpheus, 'Information wants to be free. Wants to set us free. Right now the government code the dreams and we dream them. But I'm about turning that all on its head.'

'How?' Orpheus asks.

'I teach anyone who asks me. Anyone who really wants to learn how to do it. Some people have a knack, like with any other art. Painting pictures, composing librettos, picking locks. And others.' She turns up a palm and shrugs.

'I want to,' Orpheus says, 'I want to learn.' There is a vain hope in the back of his mind; *if I can control the dreams, I can control everything.*

'It's not safe,' Nanu explains to him. 'It's like living on the edge of a black hole.' She makes an 'O' of her finger and thumb. 'Most people, the ones out there, linger on the outer edges, the place of dreams and fantasies. But further in is like a maze. Time slows, your nightmares seek you out. I've seen people trapped for years on the other side. But you . . .' Nanu leans in and stares into Orpheus' eyes. 'You've seen it before, haven't you? The tempest of the dream. Saw it and came back.'

'Once,' Orpheus says, shifting uncomfortably. He knows immediately what she's referring to, the thing that he saw when his heart stopped.

'Maybe that's why you want to go back,' Nanu says. 'It'll never stop calling you.'

That night, Nanu helps Orpheus download a pirated version of the app called Dreamtime, which allows them to use the Panopticon to build wild hallucinations that are experienced like lucid dreams.

Building dreams, though, requires learning an entirely new programming language, the Dreamtime Modelling Language (DML), to build 'virtual world' files that they can run on the app. It begins slowly for Orpheus, with Nanu showing him the word for 'blue', which the compiler in his Pulse converts into a string of binary code, then a selection of neural commands directed at his optic nerve. The word for 'sky', for 'ocean'. She teaches him the command 'let there be light', which Orpheus copies meticulously into a file.

'Set it to "preview",' she tells him, 'and then close your eyes.' When he does, he sees the dark static of the application's command-and-control interface. Strings of code appear in response to his instruction and a second after he closes his eyes Dreamtime stimulates his optic nerve, creating an explosion of sunlight that triggers a memory retrieval function on his quartz: the sun rising across the bay. The image lasts for just a second, but when Orpheus opens his eyes, even Nanu can see that he is in love.

'It'll take a lot more, if you want to do anything more complicated than that,' she tells him, though he almost doesn't hear her. They say that alcoholics can always remember their first drink. Once he returns home, Orpheus doesn't sleep at all the rest of that night, lies almost paralysed in his dormitory, thinking about how soon he can get back to learn more.

The next time he returns, Sherif wants to come too. Soon they're going almost every day, talking to Nanu or any of the other coders, begging to learn anything the others are willing to teach. After a couple of months, Orpheus discovers that he is grateful for some of his father's pedagogy. Unlike Sherif, he is a quick learner, fearless and experimental; he becomes fluent in the programming language of dreams faster than anyone Nanu knows.

At God's Own Junkyard he encounters the whole underground of dreamers, nerdy kids who like to code.

They take days off school just to gather in the basement of the children's division, where they fill old laundry trolleys with water and share Dreamtime files.

They all dream of home. Dream of adventure. Of everything they've ever lost.

On the other side, Nanu is a creature with a thousand eyes. She lives with her four brothers in an abandoned museum, in a dream city made of fake landmarks; the half-scale replica of the Eiffel Tower on the Las Vegas Strip, the Statue of Liberty in Tokyo Bay, Christ the Redeemer's majestic arms outstretched across the blue skin of the River Tagus in Portugal.

Sherif likes to fly among the skylines he draws. And Orpheus builds his own island. Builds it on a planet where the sun rarely sets. And in every dream, he awakes in his bedroom to the sound of his father out tending the herbs in the garden, or reading Dylan Thomas in his favourite chair.

It's a good year. For others, coding dreams is hard mental work, as exhausting as chess or calculus. For Orpheus, though, it is play. It is an easy thing, to make castles out of clay, to cut plates of sunlight into stained-glass windows, an easy thing to halt the whole earth in its orbit, and draw the moon right out of the sky. He can say a word and make rivers run backwards, he can coax the trees and rocks into dance. He is a sorcerer on the other side. A necromancer in the hallucinatory world in the bowels of the Panopticon.

Nanu says she believes that he is good at it because some part of him still belongs on the other side, still longs for it. And maybe it's true.

Orpheus loves dreaming so much that meat-space takes on a lack-lustre sheen. Sometimes, he stays under so long he wakes to find that in the real world, days have passed, and he can no longer feel his legs. His grades begin to slide, and soon he is failing all his classes. But Orpheus doesn't care; he believes that his body is a tool, good for nothing but to take him back. To the island he built on the light side of a moon, a quiet beach with a scale replica of his childhood home. He often recreates the day that he ran away. The beach he dashed across, the drone that spotted him. If he'd done something different he'd probably still be there.

His father had named the island 'Angharad' and told Orpheus that it means, 'The most loved'. Orpheus does, only now, with a broken-hearted fervour.

He could spend forever lounging on the sand, painting Aurora Australis in rippling parabolas of pink and lime-green. Long afternoons under drone-less skies lit by nothing but Saturn's steely rings.

6

MOREMI

It's been just over five years since the flood and Moremi can never shake the feeling that her entire world might be devoured in an instant. Even now, whenever she is stressed or frightened her mind will conjure it: the wave. She'll imagine the ground rumbling under her soles or potholes oozing black slime, the shadow advancing.

She'd thought that the constant glad roar of noise from the Panopticon would save her. She'd thought that dance could save her. She'd thought that her life would be different by now.

Moremi is stuck in a job that she hates, shift work with a pollinating company that requires spending her days hunched, nettle-stung and sunburned in brambles with a paintbrush. She's paid almost nothing to do the work that insects used to do for free.

This evening she's been invited to audition for a role with a new ballet company. All week, she's been nursing the tentative hope that it could be a way out for her, a way back into the life she had dreamed of after she graduated from dance school. But, on her way to the studio, Moremi received a message that Zeeba has had an accident and has been taken to the hospital. As soon as she heard it, she changed direction, leaned forward on her Zephyr and coaxed it towards the speed limit.

Ducking and weaving through the mid-afternoon traffic, terrible images flash through her mind: Zeeba knocked off her board and onto the road, dead or dying, some terrible diagnosis. It's late afternoon and the sun scythes dramatically between the tall buildings. Tree blossoms sweep like confetti across the pavement and dissolve in gutters. Early spring, and the winter feels like a war she's barely survived. She struggles the most during the colder months with her mood, gets inexplicably weepy and exhausted. Gets hopeless enough to believe that the sun will never return and yet, implausibly, improbably, here it is, on her back.

Moremi is too unhappy, though, to enjoy the beauty of the day. On her way to the hospital, she banks left and her board turns up a quieter road near Vauxhall Pleasure Gardens. As she does, memories rush back to her. Only three weeks ago she had lived here with Lionel, her ex-boyfriend, who had locked her out suddenly and piled all her things in bin-bags out in the hall. He'd been a dancer for the Royal Ballet. She'd fallen in love with him the first time she glimpsed him in an advert for *The Magic Flute*, turning lithe arabesques up the curved wall of Marylebone Station.

After they broke up, Moremi had returned to live in Halima's flat, to the bunkbed she shares with Zeeba. Moremi is still reeling from the heartbreak. She feels like an open wound; whole street corners and shops and restaurants are on fire with his name and the time they'd spent together. She should have gone a different way, but she chose this route – past his flat – just to hurt herself.

St Thomas' Hospital is right in the centre of the city. Moremi baulks at the entrance to the A&E department. Hospitals fill her with dread. It's the smell of them, the bots riding up and down, polishing the linoleum, the gaunt people leaning over IVs, or being wheeled out into the courtyard to enjoy the sun. The humanness of it all.

This is the hospital she woke up in after Lionel left her; Moremi had tried to make herself forget.

'You're here.' Halima's voice over the Panopticon is a blessed distraction from the memory. 'I can see you on my finder. A&E's the other entrance.' Halima shares her location and the way lights up for Moremi, who follows a line of green chevrons that appear on the floor. As she walks, Halima explains that Zeeba was knocked off her Zephyr by some protection officers.

'Is she okay?' Moremi asks.

'Bruised and upset. She lost two teeth and they think she might have some concussion.'

Moremi finds the two of them sitting in the hall a couple of minutes later. Zeeba's shirt is spattered with blood. 'You look worse than me,' Zeeba lisps.

'Oh, yeah? How do I look?' Moremi's been working since sunrise in a field. 'Like I'm dog-tired and hate my life?' She had been planning to go home before the audition to shower and change out of her fluorescent overalls, but she won't have the time to now.

'You hate your job, that's not the same thing.' Halima is sat on the edge of the gurney, readjusting the band of her maternity jeans over her belly. Five and a half years now since they lost their mother and Halima's maternal tone still sometimes grates on Moremi.

'And she's been heartbroken,' Halima reminds Zeeba, 'so we should treat her delicately, like someone who's broken a bone.'

'You should,' Moremi says, ignoring the sarcasm in Halima's tone. What happened with Lionel has happened before; Moremi always hurtles headfirst into love with dizzying velocity. Two years ago, a closeted drama student whose long strands of copper hair she could not bear to rinse out of the sink for two weeks after he'd disappeared. Before that, a heavy-browed politics student. Holden Fraser, her first love, whose name she'd carved into her forearm in a bid to beg him to stay. 'Lionel was different,' Moremi adds.

I found the quartz recordings,' Halima says, changing the subject, 'for the incident.' She shares the file with Moremi.

'Aren't any of you going to ask *me* what happened?' Zeeba says, holding the icepack back up to her bruised face. But Moremi is already watching it. In the recording, Zeeba looks like Hermes, riding above the streets of London on a Zephyr. Protector of heralds, misfits and thieves, wearing her new uniform: winged helmet and satchel, fluorescent lanyard and dark sunglasses. This spring she's been trying to raise money for art school by working for a start-up called Zip, which leaves solar-powered Zephyrs all over the city for commuters to pick up and discard once they arrive at their destination. The company employs a fleet of temp staff to locate, charge and service the devices. Though Moremi has always regarded rented hoverboards as somewhat of a nuisance, she is glad that her sister has found a job.

In the recording, a drone appears to broadcast a message for her to stop, but Zeeba is listening to music and can't hear. 'The next thing I knew I was flying out of the sky,' she says.

'I think they fired a rubber bullet,' Halima says.

'And my face goes crunch' – she smashes a fist into a palm – 'on the pavement.'

In the video the police descend on her and ask for ID. All police quartz footage is on public record, so Moremi can watch the rest of the encounter from behind one of their eyes. They push her sister against the hood of a parked car, hold up a scanning device to her head and start when they realise that she has no Pulse.

'Can you provide an alternative form of ID?' the female officer asks. Zeeba spits a bloody gob of saliva onto the hot pavement.

'I haven't done anything.' A slight lisp rounds her words as her mouth begins to swell.

'Yet,' says one of the officers.

'We have information that there is going to be an incident at Balfour Place.'

It's a lovely street, lined with listed red-brick houses, just off Mayfair. Impossible to imagine any crime taking place there.

'You know why they stopped me,' Zeeba says. Halima sighs and looks away. 'I read that protection officers are four times more likely to stop black people. And a black girl carrying some Zephyrs, they probably thought I stole them.'

'I doubt that, you were in uniform. And you were flying in a no-fly zone,' Halima says.

'They'd only just put up the sign,' Zeeba protests.

'You would have seen it if you had a Pulse,' Moremi says.

'Of course, that's what this is about.' Zeeba scowls at both of her sisters. With her front teeth missing, Moremi has a sudden tender flash of memory. Zeeba aged nine hoping for the tooth fairy.

'I don't know why you didn't show them your ID when they asked you,' Moremi says.

'I guess I'm the only one who cares about privacy.'

'It's the law,' Halima says, 'and if you have nothing to hide—'

'You know,' Moremi says, 'privacy is actually a pretty analogue idea. What happened on the street back there and this, the three of us standing here, at this point in time, is part of history. This conversation is part of history and no one owns history.'

'Can this argument not be part of history?' Halima sighs, and then says to Zeeba, 'I don't know how long you think you're going to keep this up.' After their mother died, Halima had begged her sister to get the implant but Zeeba had refused. At first by promising she would in a year or two, and then being conveniently sick on the days that the school nurse was performing the procedure. Now, she point-blank refuses. 'How do you think you'll get a job without a Pulse? And once the TA bill is passed—'

'If!' Zeeba says. It's the argument they all keep having. Maybe everyone is having. There's a referendum coming up in the summer; the country will decide whether or not to follow the example of Denmark and Norway and require every citizen over eighteen to get a Pulse. The choice seems straightforward to Moremi when she considers that ninety-five per cent of people under fifty already have one. Moremi wants Total Adoption to win. She's heard that countries with the highest adoption rate have historically low levels of almost all crimes: domestic abuse is virtually non-existent, children can walk to school on their own, vulnerable people stride down unlit alleys without fear. When everything is seen, everyone strives to be the better version of themselves. Moremi has heard that scientific research thrives in these places, because universities are able to carry out the kind of longitudinal studies that were never possible in the past and the discoveries have been tremendous. 'Ready for the better world?' the Vote YES slogans read. Years ago, Moremi might have said 'not yet', but everything changed for her after her mother died.

In the months after it had happened, Moremi had come to develop a strange sickness at the sight of flesh. It was the mounds of it she'd seen, piled in graves, or covered on stretchers. Everything about the human body seemed to be about to tip over into rancidness and rot. It was a losing game, she'd thought miserably, to be born at all when she knew now where they were all heading.

But some things may come to her aid. Medicine, science, art. Moremi's love of ballet is part of it; over torturous years the ballet dancer turns her body into an instrument, a portal to the sublime, to the world of symmetry and flight, immortal things. She might only touch it for a moment, but one day, she fervently believes, her Pulse can transport her consciousness there forever.

It turns out that the officers who stopped Zeeba were contracted to the Metropolitan Police's Pre-crime Department. Officers use a software that analyses data from everyone's Pulse to predict where a crime will happen next.

'Okay!' Zeeba shouts on the video. 'Arrest me for something I haven't done.' Except, as she does, there is a squeal of tyres at the end of the road. A car comes speeding in the wrong direction and crashes into a bollard. A woman runs out of the passenger seat screaming, and the police, as well as the ambulance, are on hand to help.

'Those were my favourite teeth,' Zeeba says quietly, now.

'I'm sorry,' Halima says. 'Once the dentist is done, though, you'll be your beautiful self again.' Moremi knows Halima is thinking about the money she doesn't have to pay for any of this treatment.

'I bet you're wishing this had happened at a more convenient time for you,' Zeeba says.

'Like when?'

'Like when you take up that job working for Evil Corp.'

'Wait, what?' Moremi looks between her two sisters.

'She means the Panopticon,' Halima translates.

'I know what she means.' Moremi brushes Zeeba's dramatics away. 'They offered you the job?' Halima smiles and for the first time that day her face seems to light up. Moremi hugs her sister. 'This is great news!' she says. 'I know how hard you worked for it.'

'Tell her your lame-ass job title,' Zeeba says.

'"Technical Evangelist",' Halima says with a grin. 'It's in the sales and marketing team.'

'I can't believe I'm related to you,' Zeeba says. 'I can't believe I'm going to have to eat food paid for by the Panopticon.'

'You'll be eating it with teeth paid for by the Panopticon,' Halima says. 'I'm sure it must be a real bruise to your Luddite street-cred. You know,' she says to Moremi, 'half the kids in whatever gang she's joined don't have a Pulse? Her generation—'

Zeeba tosses the icepack across the room and it whacks the opposite wall with a hard crunch. 'The Panopticon did this to me!' she yells, pointing at the bloody crater in her mouth. People in the hall look around in surprise. Halima looks around in alarm – she hates attracting attention.

'Do you know what kind of people they are?'

'Keep your voice down,' Halima hisses.

'Didn't you hear that stuff on the news, about the expanding rollout of the Good People Project? The thing that they were doing, projecting happy memories into the minds of people orphaned by the flood, or young offenders ... I mean, doesn't that sound kind of sick to you?'

Moremi had been moved to hear the testimonies of the people whose lives had been changed for the better by the project. Adults who went on to live more peaceful, fulfilling lives than they had hoped they could. 'Lots of people are grateful to that programme,' she says. It's hard to argue with Zeeba when she's like this.

'I bet you'd have been happy if they gave you dreams where Lionel stayed with you, or our mother didn't die.' Zeeba says it like an insult, although this doesn't sound unappealing to Moremi. 'Or one where we had a different mother who made us all banana pancakes in the morning and never complained about the dancing career she never had. You can't change the past, Moremi.'

'We can change anything we want,' Moremi says. 'It's in our hands. It will be.'

Zeeba stares at Moremi in horror, tears in her eyes. 'It's true what they say about you people, you've all been lobotomised.'

Hurt, Moremi looks away from her. In the window behind them is the parking lot, ambulances coming and going and all the weekday drama of the hospital. People in wheelchairs, or paper gowns, carrying flowers or balloons, strapped to gurneys.

'It's been good things, so far,' Moremi says. 'I'm happy I got the Pulse. Most people are. Less lonely, connected to everything. I have these quartz memories of Mum in the months before and I would have got the Pulse sooner just to have more. It's not even practical, it's emotional. I'm close to it, it's part of me.'

She feels as if she can't say the other thing. That sometimes she feels that the Panopticon is the scaffolding that holds her whole heartbroken self together. Where would she be without it? How would she have survived when Lionel left her, or when her mother died?

'It's emotional for me too,' Zeeba says, squinting her eyes against a flash of sun through the slatted blinds. 'It's not about privacy or letter-writing or whatever Luddite stuff. It's about trust. I don't trust them, Moremi. The Panopticon, this government. We saw with our own eyes that they don't care about us. After the flood. You saw what it was like. For us. That week we were evicted.' Halima shudders at the memory – it's still painful for her. 'After Mum died. How poor we were, with just you looking after us.'

'I tried my best,' Halima says. She'd been nineteen, just a child herself. Dropped out of university to take care of them.

'I always think about how rich Hayden and Bertram Fairmont are. You know, Bertram's the richest man in the world? Whatever I make riding Zephyrs around the city, they make in a millisecond. And they say that we live in one of the richest countries, but why the hell don't I feel rich? Why was I hungry? Why did I have to stick my school shoes together with superglue because I was too scared to beg Halima for money I knew she didn't have?'

Moremi wishes Zeeba would stop talking. She hates

to remember that time, those years when they were dirt-poor and wretched with grief. She's deleted most of those memories off her quartz because the only way to bear that pain is to try and forget it.

'What does any of that have to do with you getting a Pulse?' Moremi asks.

'Everything. The questions the future is asking us are not technological. They won't be solved with engineering. They will be solved by good government. Singularity? I just want equality. I just want to feel like my body belongs to me. I just want to stop worrying that I will get raped walking home alone at night, I'd just like to live as long as my white friends and not worry that death or disease or childbirth or a rogue protection drone is way more likely to kill me.'

'Zeeba, obviously we want all of those things too.'

'I just think that unless we address those issues first, technology will only entrench inequality deeper in our society.'

'Zee,' Halima says, 'Remi, both of you please stop this. We believe different things, okay, we don't have to act like we hate each other. And she has an audition today.'

As Halima says it, Moremi's heart lurches. If she doesn't leave soon and is late for the audition, it could be months before she is offered another chance. 'And Zeeba has to finish her shift.'

'She doesn't get time off for being injured?' Moremi asks.

Halima shakes her head. 'She wanted to ask if she could borrow your Zephyr.'

'Please,' Zeeba says, cowed now, looking away. 'Mine

broke when I fell and I can't afford to get fired from another job.'

'Hey,' Halima says, as her attention is caught by something on the side of Zeeba's face. 'What is that?'

Her younger sister's back straightens instantly and she flinches.

'Is that blood?'

'No.'

'Did they—?'

'No!'

But Halima moves quickly, leans forwards and pulls back her sister's long braids. On the side of her head, where a constellation should be, she's carved an asterisk into her skin. It looks painful and fresh, possibly infected. Keloid bumps and crystalline scabs. Zeeba pulls away, tears in her eyes now. Halima looks as if she's going to be sick.

'No wonder they stopped you,' Moremi says under her breath. It's a sign of defiance. A sign Moremi has begun to see carved into trees and graffitied on the underside of bridges. A group of neo-Luddites the government are beginning to call terrorists. 'Are you one of them?' Moremi can't even bring herself to say it for fear they will be heard. 'Those people who shoot drones out of the sky and beat up engineers?'

'The people fighting back?' Zeeba's eyes are wet but defiant. She nods almost imperceptibly and the word rings like a bell in Moremi's ears: *Revelator*.

In the end, Moremi had grudgingly agreed to lend Zeeba her Zephyr, a decision she regrets immediately once she steps out of the hospital and asks the Panopticon the best route to the audition. It indicates that the tube will be the fastest way and Moremi finds herself held up in the shadowed rabbit warren of Lambeth North station, where there has been a death, a suicide probably, somewhere underground, and the next five trains are cancelled. All along the platform, the delayed commuters buzz with silent rage. Moremi is sandwiched between walls of suited bodies and it is difficult not to picture the faceless Londoner who leaped onto the dark tracks. The thought of it makes her sick. Five years after the flood, and she still avoids the London Underground whenever she can.

But it can't be avoided today. Overhead, there is a notice from Transport For London informing everyone that there are severe delays on the Bakerloo and Piccadilly lines and the thought of the wave comes to her unbidden. It could come through the tunnel like a tube train, smelling of sewage, and sweep them all up. The hundred or so sweaty commuters standing on the platform. Moremi turns the music up on her Pulse to silence the thought.

Whenever she glances at the time, the hands of the holographic clock in the corner of her vision look as if they have skipped a few minutes. She'll be late, she thinks, catastrophically, and pictures growing old in the fields pollinating plants.

The train finally approaches just as she is about to give up. She can tell it's coming because of the way the hot metal tracks hiss and groan. The wave. She shuts her eyes against imagining it, tries to focus on the song she's listening to, but when she closes her eyes she can see it. 'No.'

In the corner of her vision, the pink icon that indicates her Pulse is flashing erratically. 'Not again.' She breathes in deeply the smell of the underground. Dust and other bodies. Not enough air. If the platform fills with water, she imagines her fist pounding the curved ceiling of the tube station, tons of concrete between her and freedom.

'No . . .' But her cry is drowned this time by the roar of the train, steel and aluminium dragon, bellowing and surging through the dank tunnels under London. A sound like a car crash as it stops and disgorges a hundred people. Her heart is pounding now. 'Please mind the gap,' the overhead voice tells them, and she can't do it.

Moremi turns, pushes back against the tide of people heading towards the exit, unable to breathe in the stale air of the station. She takes the steps two at a time until she emerges into the roaring traffic near Lambeth North station.

Moremi checks the time – she's set her Pulse display to look like a clock, which hovers ominously above her now. The audition begins at 2.30pm and, already, the minute hand reads that it's almost two. The Panopticon indicates that it will take an hour to walk, but perhaps she can run? It recalculates based on her typical running speed and tells her that she will still be late.

'Show me which buses are going there?' she asks, and a few buses heading past light up in green. Moremi jumps on the nearest one, her heart pounding.

She disembarks near Monument station with only fifteen minutes to get to a venue that is twenty-five minutes away. Moremi glances around, panicked, and then decides to run. Clutching her bag, she makes a mad dash across the road, even though the pedestrian light is still red. A bus driver blares his horn and swerves. Workers glance at her in alarm. 'Sorry!' she shouts to no one, and keeps running. Out onto London Bridge where the sun's clear light is unobstructed by skyscrapers and reflects off the river at an angle which makes it glimmer black and silver. She runs through the packed train station on the other side of the bridge, dodging commuters, and almost upturning a magazine stand. Twenty-five past. She imagines a lithe row of dancers already lined up by the stage door.

Two minutes, the home stretch. If she keeps running, she'll make it. Taking a short cut she knows through King's College Guy's Campus, her heels echo off the Portland stone alcove as she rushes under the colonnade. Either side of her are prim courtyards bursting with tulips. She slows for a moment, conjuring the directions up on her Pulse again. A translucent green arrow appears just above her sight line, directing her past the bike shed, down a one-way road, past two sets of council flats to a church. Then a ping in her ears tells her that she's reached her destination.

'Almost late,' says the woman at reception. She makes a motion, presumably crossing Moremi's name off a list.

'Isn't that the same as on time?' she gasps, rubbing her sweaty palms on her overalls.

The woman gives her a withering look and points her up the side stairs that will lead to the attic space of the church. Moremi has been in this dance studio once before, for a previous audition. She didn't get the part.

She exhales deeply as she enters the main hall of the

studio. At this time of day the sun is pouring with almost violent intensity through the high-arching mullioned windows on either side of the room. Chandeliers hang low, strung with cobwebs, scattering rainbow prisms like shards of glass across the floor where millions of *pas des bourrées* have long kicked the lacquer away, so that only the far edges of the room and the square of floor around the piano are still shiny.

Her name has not yet been called, and one of the assistants tells her that there is time for her to go to the bathroom. Moremi heads there quickly to change. Examines herself in the mirror. She's spent a year and a half working in fields and it shows in the muscles she's developed in her arms, the calluses on the palms of her hands and the chickenpox pimples of mosquito bites smattering her forearms and shins. No bees to pollinate the trees, but still plenty of mosquitos keen on her flesh. Nothing she can do about it. Nothing she can do, either, about the scars on her arms and thighs. She is always careful to pull the sleeves of her long-sleeved leotard down to hide them. Hunger and anxiety hacksaw her gut. She is down to her last pair of pointe shoes. She examines the frayed satin at the toebox, her heart sinking. She'd bought four at the start of the month, and outside of a school or a dance company, spending £50 on a pair of almost disposable shoes is as painful as pulling teeth. If she does not put too much weight on them, she thinks they can last the whole audition. 'Fingers crossed,' she whispers. And then laces them on.

Glancing at herself one last time in the mirror, she tries

to imagine what Rafael Gabor – the choreographer – will think when he sees her. She imagines him admiring her perfectly executed steps, and the hundreds of thousands of steps that came before. The blistered years of practice. The pain of trudging through every day when she had danced the skin off the soles of her feet. All the other company directors have turned her away, but perhaps they have turned her towards this moment when Gabor welcomes her into the world of the ballet.

Moremi emerges from the dim bathroom, emboldened by the dream. The light in the airy studio stings her eyes.

They have been allocated into numbered groups and when hers is called up, a dozen of them head into the centre of the studio. The pianist stretches his hands at his stool, seizes the keys and performs a playful jingle that everyone laughs at when they recognise it from a viral commercial.

In this room sit the people who will decide their fate. The company's director, set up by the large window, young assistants in tow, shouting orders at the dancers who have already taken their places by the barre.

'Moremi? Right?' a woman asks, as Moremi leans over to tuck her canvas holdall under a bench. 'Yes?' she says. The assistant pins the number 27 on the front of her leotard and she heads to the back of the room.

'As you may have heard,' says the gaunt, bespectacled director of the company, 'we are looking for four new dancers to join our company for this season.' A susurrus of whispers start in the corners of the room. Hopeful girls give each other meaningful looks. 'Rafael Gabor has come to the UK, and will be joining our company as choreographer for this season.' A ripple of excitement at the name. 'His session will be quite intense, very fast, so before he starts, we would like to have a good chance to watch you warming up. Then, we will be working with you on a variation for the corps, from the ballet *Giselle*.'

The dancers have shed their clothes and, before her, Moremi can see long lines of legs, reflected infinitely in the mirrors on either side. Flesh-toned leotards, neon leg-warmers, scruffy ribbons pinned at ankles. The stager, Anastysia, is a hip-looking woman in her early forties with thick tortoiseshell glasses and leopard-spotted leggings. She steps forward, motions to the pianist and the class begins.

Class is a dancer's daily bread, the rhythms of it as natural to Moremi as breathing. 'Okay, girls,' says Anastysia, 'two, demi, one grande, port des bras, rise . . . first, second, fourth, fifth . . .' As the music begins, Moremi shakes away her nerves and a familiar calm descends. Dance is like a meditation for her. This is where the ballet happens. In this quotidian discipline. People imagine that it is at night on stage, in a tutu, beneath blazing lamps, during exhilarating bounds, that a dancer is made. But really it is in these faithful steps.

After they are warmed up, Anastysia stops to give a few girls some words of correction. Moremi breathes deeply, glad to discover that, as always happens when she begins dancing, her nerves have fizzled away.

All the dancers freeze at the sound of heels striking the stone stairs on the outside. When she closes her eyes she can feel the sweat erupting in the palms of her hands. She opens her eyes and Rafael Gabor is standing on the threshold. It is as if he has emerged from her dream. He looks exactly the way he did six years ago, when she saw him perform at the Royal Opera House. When Moremi recalls it, a lightning bolt of desire rattles her bones. He played Romeo, and she will never forget the way that he looked taking his bow at the end. He'd been dressed in a blue silk tunic, a muscle-bound creature light as air. He looks similar now, although rays of afternoon sun illuminate the greys that pepper his iconic head of curls. There are wrinkles around his eyes too. But he still looks like a dancer. He arrives in a polo shirt and chinos, but she can see, in the rigid line of his shoulders and calves, that none of his muscle has gone to fat.

'Let's get right to it,' he says, clapping his hands, and the dancers all straighten into military lines of first position.

Moremi is somewhere near the back, staring down at the frayed edge of her pointe shoe. She thought she could push one more dance out of it but now she is not sure. Her mouth is dry; she wants this so badly.

They are dancing the scene from *Giselle* where the Willis – the ghosts of jilted women – awake in a haunted glade. Just before they try to compel Albrecht – Giselle's former lover – to dance to his death.

Moremi couldn't believe her luck when she'd been sent the audition details, because she already knew the dance by heart. Giselle had been one of the roles her mother had performed, and Moremi loved watching recordings of the performance. As the music begins, she conjures that stage again in her mind. Blue light, dry ice in a low ebb over the lacquered floor, symbolising a haunted glade in the Bavarian forest.

Every one of the Willis has been heartbroken or betrayed, maidens abandoned on their wedding days. Now, they are a sisterhood of avenging ghosts, led by their merciless queen Myrtha, exacting revenge on any man they encounter, forcing their victims to dance until they die. What a gorgeous fate, Moremi always thinks.

She is always grateful to be part of it: the corps, the 'body' of the ballet. A snowflake, a swan, a flower. During the dance, she transcends her body entirely, hers two of the fifty feet that leave the ground at the exact same time. Another heart pounding as if the dance is a spirit that has possessed them all, and they will exorcise it together.

'No . . .' Rafael gestures to the pianist. 'No, no . . .' And the notes skitter away like marbles. The dance comes to an ungainly halt and everyone looks around in confusion. 'I can't feel it,' he says to them. 'You are heartbroken. Have you ever been heartbroken?'

The music starts again and they dance, from the top.

But even as Moremi dances she can feel the burn in her chest. Even his name is a thorn. 'How do you make someone love you?' she'd whispered to the Panopticon three weeks ago when Lionel changed the locks and threw her out of his flat.

If she'd dared to look, she would have seen their relationship hurtling towards the end. When she'd told him that she loved him he'd said, 'No, you don't! You need me.

That's a different thing. You're a monster of need.' That word, 'monster', even this afternoon, is a knife-twist in her solar plexus.

Moremi channels the heartbreak into the dance now. Vaults and hurdles through the haunted glade, borne aloft by the music. All the while, Rafael Gabor walks around them. He pauses when he reaches Moremi. This is the worst part of the dance. The part that she always fumbles in practice. Moremi clears her mind as she executes a series of tricky pirouettes, a clean turning jump and then a heroic *grande jété*. For a fraction of a second, she actually flies. Gabor, the stager and the company director all turn to her in surprise as she whirls through the rest of the variation.

There is a thrill that she feels in the marrow of her bones when she knows that she is dancing well. Better than the other dancers, fleet-footed and precise, with feeling. 'Beautiful,' she thinks she sees Gabor mouth, and the company director smiles.

The clatter of the piano dies at the end of the variation. All the dancers hold their positions in fifth, arms in an elegant bow above their heads.

'Number twenty-seven,' Gabor says, staring straight at her now. Moremi's heart is pounding, sweat dripping down her back. 'Can I see that again? Just from you.' He pauses for a moment, the choreographer whispers something in his ear and he nods as if the thought had only just occurred to him too. 'We prefer to see our dancers "go dark",' he says to her. 'Just for a few minutes. When we're on stage, you know, the constellation lights and, maybe

I'm old-fashioned, but I just want us all to be here.' The dancers all look uncertain. Look as if they've been asked to surrender their valuables or sign a form without reading it. Moremi's first and they're all staring at her. 'That won't be a problem, will it?'

In some nightmares she's faced with choices like this. Should she tell him that she's a special case? Should she tell him that she has to be vigilant about the sadness, that she needs the chatter and the ticker-tape scroll of headlines and updates, the commentary and the music? That without it, she doesn't know what thoughts may come?

'Oh, um, sure,' she says, and she knows he must be able to see the wild flickering of her heart in the lights of her constellation. An unnatural hand motion she's only executed a few times, for exams or certain medical appointments. When the holograms fade it's as if the room is black and white. She blinks fiercely, trying to focus. But the atmosphere is different now, the air deadly thin. And there is a whine like a tea-kettle in the back of her head. Has that always been there? Is that the silence?

'Whenever you're ready,' the choreographer says. Moremi works hard to compose herself, to focus on the dance. There is a panic in her chest, the kind she feels when she realises her keys are missing. That's how everyone feels, she tells herself.

But when Moremi glances at him she thinks she can see mud in his eyes.

'Y-yes,' she stammers, rubs her own eyes again. 'Of course.' But it's happening to the other dancers as well, the choreographer, the stager, the assistants. The pianist coughs surreptitiously into a handkerchief and she sees the black water that spatters out.

Something is wrong. 'No,' she whispers under her breath. 'Not this. Not now.'

'Ready when you are,' Gabor repeats, but his lips are blue and the ground under her feet is beginning to shudder and groan the way that it does before a tube train approaches. It could happen any second. Death is coming, she thinks, for all of them.

'Sure, um . . .' She tries to shake the dread away but she can't help the hammering in her heart, the sudden fast pace of her breathing. The dancer's bodies are bloating with rot. Moremi knows, now, what happens to a body when it spends three weeks underwater, corneas like jelly, worms making a nest in its guts.

Not again. Not now.

Moremi manoeuvres herself into first position but all the air has been sucked out of the room. She wants to be sick. She wants to run. The piano music starts again but all she can hear now is the roar of the wave. Make it stop. She slams her hands over her ears.

'Are you . . . ?' someone asks.

'Yes,' she manages to say. 'I just need to take five.' And then, ashamed, terrified, before someone can ask, 'What is wrong?' Moremi turns on her heels and flees, past the dancers who part in stunned waves. Shame thunders over her as she rushes down the curved stairwell. What a fool she's made of herself.

By the time she reaches the street, she realises that she has forgotten her bag and all her things. But there is no way that she can go back. Moremi races outside in pointe shoes, sick with herself. Running, tears prickling at the corners of her eyes that she fights hard to blink back.

A few hours later, Moremi is wandering the streets, walking barefoot, ballet shoes slung over her shoulder. The asphalt pavement is hot as coals under her heels. The sun casts off the last of its light and she inhales the gasoline breath of the city. She might as well be naked in her black leotard and footless tights, but she does not want to go back to the studio for the clothes she left behind.

She finds herself sitting near Battersea Bridge, hoping, distantly, that he will call. But instead, it gets dark. A few people pass and ask her if she needs help, a woman thinks she's homeless and offers her money. Moremi just tells them that she is tired. And it's true. She really is exhausted. She rests her head on the metal slats of a bench and looks up at the cool indifferent light of the moon and it's as if Lionel left her a million years ago. He's never coming back, she thinks, she will never recover.

She thought that she would never recover after her mother died. Halima had come home one night with the news and Zeeba had screamed as if she'd been shot. 'What are we going to do now?' Moremi had asked, the grief hardened like a bone in the back of her mouth. *What are we going to do with the rest of our lives?* When Halima had poured herself a glass of water, her hand had been shaking so much that it shattered on the floor in an explosion that made them all cry and keep crying.

The three of them slept together, that night, in their mother's bed. Just hoping to inhale the smell of her before it evaporated for good. Moremi woke up clutched with pain at 3am, covered in goosebumps. That night was her first dream of drowning. When she awoke, what she wanted more than anything in the world was a mother.

In the kitchen, she stepped on a shard of broken glass. The one Halima had dropped earlier. In the dark, she fumbled around for the light switch and by the time she found it smeared pools of her own blood made crimson lily-pads in the shape of her heel. It looked like a lovely thing, in the moonlight, fire opal and sunstone scattered between the tiles ...

'Oh God, you must be in so much pain,' Halima had said months later, her eyes wide with horror, when Moremi had come out of the shower wrapped in a towel, her forearms uncovered. The look of repulsion in Halima's eyes made Moremi suddenly see that what she had been doing for the past few months was something shameful. 'You must be in so much pain, to do that to yourself.' She felt as if she'd been caught masturbating.

'Why does it help?' A question she'd asked the Panopticon again and again. Was it the endorphins, an explosion of neuropeptides in her central nervous system that left her feeling giddy and comfortably numb? Some people said it was about making internal pain external. Something to do with grief, suicidality. Moremi still can't understand it. Can't understand why it never feels exactly like pain, her skin opening up like an eyelid, the sight of her own pink flesh. It feels like walking on hot coals or eating fire. She has a habit of pressing hard, for a week or two after, on the fiercely swollen scab. Marvelling at the trick her body can play. It can mend everything, all it needs is time.

Moremi is different now. She will be different now. That whole thing is in her past. And when Lionel had asked her delicately about it the first night they slept together – tenderly running a thumb over the keloid stripes on her forearms and shins – she had told him, 'I think everything will be fine from now on.'

Maybe he had wanted to believe her. But sometimes she caught him looking at the name of the last boy carved into her arm.

After they met, she had flushed three months' worth of citalopram down the toilet. Threw away everything in his house that was sharp. She wouldn't need any of those things anymore.

In the dull glow of the streetlamps, the world has taken on a kind of menace. Everyone she loves will leave her and the wave wants to be fed. Moremi hurls her ballet shoes at the river, watches them with satisfaction as they lance through thin air.

Her feet take her back to her old house. It's a ghost-town now, the council houses where she grew up. Black-eyed buildings with smashed-in windows. Neon scream of graffiti across walls and doors. It's in a part of town called the Slough, the dead zone by the river that hasn't yet been swallowed up by luxury housing developments.

The police mostly steer clear of it, few drones fly overhead. In the shadowed doorways of condemned buildings sit children gaunt with hunger. As Moremi heads past they call out to her asking for money, for food, but they quiet down when they see that she has nothing on her, no bag, no pockets.

As she heads around the block of estates where she used to live, the smell overpowers her. Rubbish rotting on the sides of cracked pavements, bags cannibalised by foxes, green slime of composting food, banana peels, babies' nappies.

Although the estate was never beautiful, it makes her heart sink to see the place now. To see so much poverty in one place. People living in tents, beggars on every street corner. The one shopkeeper still in business has employed a bouncer outside the door to deter shoplifters, and even so, Moremi sees schoolchildren rifling through the bins at the back for food to take home with them.

When she reaches her block of flats, she finds that the door is wide open. A water main has burst and there is a pool of putrid-smelling stagnant water filling the landing. Leaping over it, a tuft of flies buzz up around her face. She takes the stairs two at a time and comes across a man, half-asleep in a pool of vomit, on the next landing. The sight is enough to make her want to turn back but she's got this far.

As she walks up the steps memories flood back. This is the block of flats that she grew up in. She remembers that the stairwell between the fourth and third floor always smelled faintly of curry. She thinks she remembers leaning over the banister to hear her father shout, 'We've brought you a sister', Zeeba swinging in a car seat. Running down those stairs when she was seven to see snow for the first time, a mere dusting on the cars in the front courtyard. She remembers taking a ball of it in her fist, hoping to keep it until later, opening up her hands at the threshold of her house and bursting into tears to find that it had vanished. Her mother had said, 'Oh, sweetheart, that's another one of the good things that doesn't last.'

Her whole childhood.

Moremi's heart swells as she makes it up to the fifth floor, where the door is open. Inside the unlit hall her feet take her to her mother's old bedroom. There is no bed anymore. Signs of squatters: sleeping bags, cardboard boxes, tin foil and blackened spoons. If she closes her eyes, though, she can go back. Moremi's legs give in, and she lets herself drop onto the worn carpet, which smells of cigarette smoke and damp.

She presses her face into the rough pile and closes her eyes.

When she dies, Moremi hopes that she'll wake up in bed with her mother. It's a love story, between a girl and her mother. The first. Moremi slept in bed with her until she was seven. And even later, when the family went on a trip, Zeeba and Halima with their dad, to the funfair and Moremi had been too sick with chickenpox to leave the house. She'd climbed from her own bunkbed and curled up into her mother's sweaty body.

She liked the musty smell that gathered in her mother's folds of skin, yesterday's perfume, vanilla beans and patchouli. She marvelled at the way her mother could just be silent and stare into the distance as if her head was a good place to be. Watching the rain roll down her skylight, trailing drops, streetlamp-lit, a race against friction and gravity, surface tension and time. Moremi had slept with her head on her mother's chest, flush with fever, and her mother had said, 'You big girl, still sleeping in bed with your mother.' Only she'd said it as if she was relieved.

Moremi had wondered and continued to wonder every time she woke up in bed with men, if she would spend her entire life pursuing that feeling. The feeling of being safe. Of being at the kind centre of the known world. Would she circle the whole earth just to get back home?

Moremi has always hoped that when she dies her mind will mercifully catapult her back there. To rain and fever dreams, forever, and her mother's quiet breath.

Moremi is jolted awake by a woman screaming. She smashes a beer bottle on the windowsill, and Moremi gasps, rubbing her eyes. The sun has set outside the window of her parents' old bedroom and there are three figures on the threshold.

'Who the fuck are you?' the woman slurs, waving the bottle top like a bayonet, making unsteady lunges for Moremi.

'I'm sorry!' she shouts, getting to her feet. It all comes

back to her. And she sees how she looks, a stranger in a leotard sleeping on their carpet. 'I used to live here.'

'Well, you don't live here anymore, love.' A man pitches a bottle at her and she ducks, shaking in terror as it explodes on the wall behind her.

'I know,' she says, and, as they enter the room, she realises that she's cornered. Three burly men and a woman. Moremi begins to realise that she could be in danger. Nobody knows that she's here. Anything could happen to her.

'I'm sorry,' she says again; she watches for a gap between the two men, and dives right past them, her heart in her throat. Then she is in the corridor, running as they lunge after her. The woman in the lead, picking up bottles and tossing them at Moremi. One catches her shoulder with an explosion of pain that propels her forwards, out the open door, and she has to slow herself down to turn and not go flying straight over the banister. Down two flights of stairs, but the sound of the three pursuers is like a hurricane echoing up the unlit stairwell. Moremi runs, broken glass crunching under the heels of her bare feet.

'Here, piggy!' shouts the woman. She lobs a tin can at Moremi's head and this time she doesn't miss. The strike makes Moremi's vision blacken, her foot slides out from under her and she goes flying. She experiences the moment almost in slow motion. Hits every step as she falls, faster and faster until her head cracks hard against the cement and the world vanishes.

7

ORPHEUS

At some point in the dream he is always running, and this time it's through the back streets of Old Cairo. He's a boy again, eleven, his friends are shouting his name, 'Sherif!' He has their ball, tucked under his arm as he runs. He knows this place well, and it's fun to lead his friends in this game of chase, past traffic-choked roads, the narrow cobbled lanes between apartments, past tombs and schools, sandstone mosques, shuttered warehouses and fountains.

Sherif turns left past a bazaar selling incense burners that gleam like brass baubles in the midday sun. He almost knocks over a Ramadan lantern seller who is balanced precariously on a wicker chair, smoking a pipe. Nearly tripping over a woman, who shouts at him, he turns a corner again and finds himself in the exact same street. Like an Escher drawing, an optical illusion. The road is a serpent that's swallowed its tail. At the sight of it, Sherif experiences a familiar roll of vertigo. He stops running and reaches reflexively into his pocket. When he doesn't feel the weight of his father's watch he thinks, 'Is it true?'

A second look back at the street answers the question. The market before him has transformed into a bazaar of memories, merchants selling trinkets from his childhood. An old wooden horse, painted yellow, a book of children's stories.

When he takes another left, Sherif discovers that the streets branch off in kaleidoscopic lanes. This is what he came looking for, the mouth of the beast: the labyrinth.

If the dream is a solar system, the dreamer wakes at the outer edges. This is the landscape of memory, of wish-fulfilment, where an hour in the dream will cost the sleeper eight hours in meat-space. The dreamer must keep asking himself, 'Is it true?' so as not to forget. And, even so, he will be drawn like a comet into the burning centre of the dream. The labyrinth. At first, it may feel as if he's running through hedgerows – sometimes it's the streets of Tokyo or Marrakech curving into themselves, sometimes the pottery-lined corridors of the British Museum – but if he ever manages to climb up to gain a good vantage of the world down below, the dreamer will always notice that the streets – or alleys, or well-trod clearings in a forest – are arranged in baffling geometric shapes, loops and fractals as complex and intricate as the whorls and arches on the tips of his fingers.

Whenever Sherif has mustered the courage to explore deeper, further in, he's noticed that the dream changes, becomes darker, time slows. Further in the maze, the brain hides its nightmares. Everything that the dreamer is ashamed of, or repulsed by. The nature of time changes too, it slows. The closer to the centre the dreamer gets, the longer they spend there; they can spend years, decades, lost in the dark. Sherif has heard of people who have lost their way in the labyrinth, spent centuries in Dreamtime navigating narrow halls, only to wake up a few hours later in meat-space, addled and traumatised, out of time.

'Sherif!' Another shout, choked with laughter. 'Sherif, where did you go?' It's his friend Fares. Fares who he loves, who grew up next door to him. *'Khalas!'* He reaches out to grab the ball.

Sherif gestures to surrender it but just at the moment their hands make contact the sky rips open. There is an ear-splitting blast, and then a sudden blistering wind picks up and sweeps everything – the bead-curtains in the darkened alcove of a teashop, the patterned shawls decorating the stall tables – away.

In the blink of an eye the street is transformed, and Sherif looks around bewildered, like a shipwrecked sailor, at the street now blanketed with ash. Blood on the sandstone. The sky, black as sin. Air saturated with the acrid smell of gasoline, or melted rubber and roasting flesh. A whine like a tea-kettle in his ear. His skull a fractured seashell. As Sherif drops to the ground, his hand touches something. A ball? A bird shot out of the air? He looks down and sees that his fingers are buried in a nest of human hair. Recoiling, he attempts to push the thing away only to discover that it is as heavy as a bowling ball, and when it rolls he sees the surprised look on Fares' face, mouth half-open as if he's about to say something.

'Orpheus!' A real voice, real alarm. A spasm of pain tugs him violently from his drugged sleep, and Sherif awakes gasping in a tub of tepid water. He flings his arm out involuntarily and sends a lamp swinging. He's back in his flat in east London, locked in the bathroom, his heart galloping in his ribs.

He sees his face reflected in the water-stained shower door; his lips look dark purple, brown skin, night-black eyes and long lashes. 'Orpheus?' He says the name with some uncertainty, as if it's an equation he can't solve. His name is Orpheus.

'What have you taken? Your friend is here. I mean, he says he's your friend.' It's the landlady, Mrs Dulwich, who's staring at him in horror, the blood drained from her face. 'You didn't answer when we knocked.'

'Is he breathing?' A man's voice from the hall. The room tells the rest of the story, he can see that someone has knocked the door off its hinges. 'People die doing this,' Mrs Dulwich says.

Even as his sleep-dulled eyes begin to focus, Sherif thinks that he can smell burning. He looks down at his hands, half expecting them to be covered in blood. But no. Even now, though, the streets of Old Cairo razed to rubble are superimposed on this half-lit space.

'It's not real,' he says. He is not Sherif, he is Orpheus.

An image from the dream is still frozen on one of the Oneiroencephalograph (OEG) monitors. A fuzzy projection of the child's dismembered head in a puddle of blood. All the things that can happen to a human body. Since that day, Sherif has not been able to eat meat. Orpheus is about to reach up to switch the console off when he feels a hot rush of lava up his gullet. Mrs Dulwich reaches for a bin too late and Orpheus vomits across the rim of the tub, and the linoleum floor. He feels instantly better, well enough to try to haul himself out of the bath, fingers sticky with bile and water.

'Should I call the ambulance?' she asks. 'Or what is it, the fire brigade? Don't they have to carry those injections for drug addicts?'

'Not those kind of drugs,' Orpheus says, and as he pulls electrodes off his chest he feels suddenly exposed. 'I'm fine.' Although, it's a pretty revolting sight, and he knows it. The vomit-slicked tub, the flickering OEG machine. He can already see Mrs Dulwich appraising the room, her eyes narrowing. 'Can I have some privacy please? Now you know I'm not dead?'

'This time,' she says, her concern curdled quickly into contempt, as she turns back into the hall.

The bathroom looks like the cockpit of an aeroplane. It is filled with machinery that he's built, stolen or borrowed. You don't need much equipment to enter another person's dream – just a constellation that runs Dreamtime and a bathtub – but over the past couple of years Orpheus has come to rely on a number of gadgets. His favourite is the OEG, which collects recordings from the Pulse of a sleeping person and translates them into images. Using this technology, it's possible to 'watch' a dream. It can also transmit back to his Pulse when he is sleeping, superimposing someone else's dream onto his own sleeping consciousness. The other devices are ones you might find in any clinician's office – a heart-rate monitor, a pulse oximeter, a console that connects to the arrays in his Pulse and displays a 3D reconstruction of his entire connectome. On the screen, his neurones fluoresce like a coral reef.

Orpheus is standing before the bathroom mirror as his Pulse comes back online. 'Oh, shit,' he says to himself at the sight of the time. He overslept. Eighteen meat-space hours, no wonder he is prickling all over with pins and needles, fingers wrinkled and peeled from the water, dizzy with low blood sugar. And if he doesn't hurry, he'll be late for work.

'Whose dream is that?'

Orpheus thinks that he's imagining things when he sees the face of the man in the hall reflected in the mirror.

'Yours,' Orpheus says, hardly daring to turn around. 'Sherif?'

'Brother!' Then the two of them embrace fondly. As they do, Orpheus can feel his friend's Pulse in his head. Growing up together in the children's division, they'd dream-share often. And now, some old circuits in Orpheus' mind are tuning into his like an analogue radio hitching onto a pirate station. Orpheus gives into it and receives a flash of Sherif's memories like an electric shock. The last time they saw each other, Sherif had been in hospital. Orpheus can see it now, paint peeling like ash on the bars of the window, night sweats and diarrhoea, withdrawing from Nox on a beaten-up mattress. Sherif pushes him away.

I'm sorry that happened to you, Orpheus says in his head.

140

'I'm better now,' Sherif says out loud. He looks it. His white hair is the only giveaway that he used to be a Nox addict, but he's put on some weight, and the dark circles under his eyes have faded. Though, he still has scars on the side of his face. Still walks with a limp.

'Where did you go?' Orpheus asks. It's been two years since they saw each other. Orpheus had returned to the hospital to discover that Sherif had checked himself out and vanished.

'I hear that people were saying I died,' Sherif says. 'I could have.'

'I knew it wasn't true though,' Orpheus says. 'If you'd died I would have . . .' *Felt it,* he says in his head, touching his chest.

Orpheus has hung a towel as a black-out curtain across the sash window, but grabs it now to dry himself off. Morning light pours into the room and he has to fight the urge to reflexively shrink from it.

'What are you doing with my dream?' Sherif asks, pointing to the image on the OEG screen.

Orpheus heads back into his bedroom, looks for a Sharpie, and begins drawing as quickly as he can, his gaze turned inward to the fading memory. 'Drawing a map.' Orpheus does it as quickly as he can on a clipboard in the corner of the room. As soon as he wakes the details begin to fade, but Orpheus knows how to quiet his mind in order to allow them to float back into his consciousness. The streets of the city, the way they curved into each other, the route that he ran.

'I've been using this one for years, to draw a map of the

labyrinth. It's a good one, the way the streets are built. I can climb up the walls and commit to memory everything I see.' He's embarrassed now, though, he feels as if he's been caught holding another person's underwear. Even though Sherif shared this dream with him years ago, it's hard to explain why he kept it, why he revisits it.

'I've made a discovery,' Orpheus says, stepping back from the drawing. Sherif raises his eyebrow. 'I've realised that the layout of the labyrinth is actually the same in every dream. It's a theory I've heard before, but—'

'Don't they say it's like a black hole?' Sherif says. 'People die getting lost in there. Or end up like I was.'

'I'm being careful, only exploring a little at a time and if I manage to make a map ...' But Sherif is casting a wary eye across the bedroom. There are incriminating clues everywhere. Glass vials of Nox, flushed-out syringes scattered across his desk, wadded-up tissues sticky with blood. It's possible to run short flashes of dreams or memories on a constellation – like the kind that the Panopticon broadcast as part of the Good People Project – but to stay in the dream and stay lucid for hours at a time, Orpheus has discovered that the most efficient way is using Nox. Before he'd tried Nox, staying in Dreamtime for longer than a couple of minutes had required a certain focus. He and Sherif had been together one night in God's Own Junkyard when someone first offered them the drug. Orpheus still remembers it with a vivid lightning flash of pleasure. It had been like hot-wiring his consciousness into the Panopticon. The freest he'd ever been, his mind totally untethered from his body, set loose to flit like light across the surface of a brook. He could do anything. Be anyone. The dreamworld is wild, ungodly, running on planes of perverse logic, and Orpheus felt as if he belonged there.

'Do they know you're doing this?' Sherif asks, and Orpheus almost flinches from the sudden prickle of hostility coming off his friend. 'I've heard that you've been working for the Panopticon.'

'Of course they don't. And I didn't really have a choice about working for them,' Orpheus says. He'd sacrificed most of his adolescence on the altar of Dreamtime. Both he and Sherif had graduated from school with no qualifications and almost no prospects. They had lived together for about a year after they'd aged out of the children's division. They'd shared rooms in run-down flats on the outskirts of London. Sherif had tried to make his living as an artist and Orpheus had decided to pursue the one thing he was good at: building and selling dreams.

At first it had been grimy work that Orpheus disliked. Clients paid for dreams of sex, violence or adventure. Though, in his unhappy experience, mainly sex. But Orpheus had managed to make a name for himself by creating visions that were intriguing and completely new. People began to seek him out, bid high prices for his dreams. He'd been proud of himself, because it's delicate work, making a world, akin to a locksmith or a jeweller, or an artist. Glass temples on mist-shrouded mountains. Copper Zeppelins. A merry-go-round made of memories. A more perfect world.

He'd been caught eventually, inevitably, and thrown

in jail for a couple of weeks. During that time, they'd scanned his memories – though by then he'd discovered how to wipe his quartz files – for incriminating information. They'd been looking for him for years by that point. Knew him only by his codename: Lazarus.

He might have stayed in jail for a couple of years if it hadn't been for Sai Kaur, director of the Panopticon's School of Sleep and Dreams. He'd been fascinated by Orpheus' work and for the knack he had of bypassing the Panopticon's security systems. They'd agreed to cut his jail time if he came to work for them.

'I'd have chosen jail,' Sherif says now.

'It's good work, though,' Orpheus says. 'I'm proud of what I'm doing right now. Designing dreams for people who have suffered trauma. Trying to find ways to make them better.'

Orpheus has spent so long in other people's bad memories that he feels as if he has been all around the world. He has lost a leg to frostbite, climbing Mount Everest in 1997, he was stabbed once behind a bodega in Riverside, he fell asleep on Christmas Eve only to find his own baby daughter had died in the bed right next to him. It's his job to fix people using their dreams. He codes happier alternatives on his computer; writes the heartbreak that didn't happen, or the son who only moved away. He writes the father who lived three weeks longer to walk his daughter down the aisle, the teacher who said, 'I'm proud of you'. It's emotional work, long, exhausting hours. Orpheus spends so much time in a bathtub with his eyes closed reliving dreams or else programming new ones that he's grown thin and weak, vitamin deficient. It's worth it, though, because he loves Dreamtime.

'I could . . .' He doesn't want to say that it was his grief and guilt about what had happened to Sherif that had drawn him to this work. Sherif shakes his head.

'I don't need your help. Or anything from the Panopticon.'

Orpheus needs to leave for work soon, but he is shaky with low blood sugar. Heading into the kitchen, he grabs a litre of cherry Pepsi from the fridge and drinks in long desperate drags.

'You look like a twitcher,' Sherif says, eyeing his friend from the hall. Orpheus can see it too, the reflection of himself in the window. His gaunt body, and greying hair. Twitchy and pin-pupilled.

'You would know,' Orpheus says, and then immediately regrets it. Sherif had become addicted to Nox when they were seventeen. Orpheus remembers the worst of it. The way that Sherif spent most of his day comatose in their tub and would wake at all hours like an astronaut coming into Earth's gravity. Starvation-thin, totally unable to tell the dream apart from meat-space. It had been Orpheus who had tried to talk him down from the roof of their shared flat that night he wanted to jump, convinced he was wearing a set of wings he'd sewn for himself. Orpheus hadn't managed to, and even now he's haunted by the sight of his friend's body, twisted on the roadside, blood pooling under his head.

I'm not like him, Orpheus tells himself with a shudder.

'Why have you come here today? To judge my life. After

all these years?' Orpheus asks, tossing his empty Pepsi bottle into a pile in the corner of the room. 'Where did you go? Where have you been?'

'All over,' Sherif says. 'Back to myself.' Sherif shudders at the memory. 'It's not the same for everyone, some people can tolerate it better; you, clearly. But you saw what it was like for me at the end? All those other dreams in my head, reality split in two and the dreamworld seeping into everything. Some nights I couldn't remember my own name.' Sherif leans in and sweeps the straggling hair from the side of his face; Orpheus gasps at the sight of the skin there. It's puckered and scarred, parts of his constellation scratched and dented.

Orpheus swears, 'My God, Sherif, what did you do to yourself?'

'Tried to gouge it out with a screwdriver.'

Orpheus' stomach twists with nausea.

'You can kill yourself that way! You know what happens to people who try to take out their own Pulse?'

'They die, or ... fall into comas. Get locked into their bodies.'

Orpheus shudders again, burdened with guilt that he had not been more help to his friend when he needed him. 'I'm sorry,' Orpheus tells him.

'It's okay.' Sherif smiles beatifically. 'Because I was saved.'

'What are you talking about?' Orpheus asks. 'Who "saved" you?'

'The Revelators. They took me in, drove me to Silo Ten. Nursed me through the worst of it, the Nox withdrawals, the psychosis. It was long and slow, I had to piece my identity back together. But they gave me hope and a purpose.'

'And what is that?'

'To save you.' Sherif looks urgent now, serious, a stranger to Orpheus, who lets their minds touch again and receives flashes of what it had been like with the Revelators: sweet memories of family, older people telling stories, learning to make things from clay, the boy he'd taught to swim, watching someone get baptised in a river and everyone on the muddy bank cheering. Nothing like what Orpheus imagines when he hears the word Revelator.

You don't have to live this way, Sherif says in their minds.

'Maybe I like living this way,' Orpheus says.

'You call this living?' Sherif says. 'This life you spend asleep?' He reaches over to shake Orpheus' shoulders. 'Wake up, come back to the upper world.'

Orpheus pushes his friend away, a hot coal of indignant rage in his chest.

'You think I want this? This insipid world? This wretched life. It's not enough for me, Sherif, I want more. I need there to be more.'

'There is,' Sherif says, 'and we're fighting for it.'

'You and the Revelators?' Orpheus asks.

'Yes, the Magi are planning something. There is an update they're going to roll out at the end of the summer, if the country votes 'yes' on Total Adoption. Something that will change everything, everyone.'

'So you came back to stop it?'

'To try to,' Sherif says. Now Orpheus feels sorry for him. *Poor you,* he thinks at him, *you still believe you can change the world.* Change anything at all. The past five years have taught Orpheus better.

'It won't be me,' Sherif says. 'It'll be you.'

Orpheus has heard enough, and he's late for work. 'See you later,' he shouts, and hurries down the hall. 'Or maybe in another two years.'

'There's a design!' Sherif shouts after him. 'Aspects cannot be chosen or escaped. This day, you, here, and your particular make-up. You're part of it, Orpheus . . .' But he's already slammed the door when his friend shouts, 'You will be!'

8

MOREMI

'What do you think it feels like?' Moremi asks. 'To wake up for the first time. Conscious?' There is a flash of pain through her still-bruised ribs as she presses her cheek against the taut drum of her sister's belly. Halima smells of sweat, and organic deodorant, white musk and baking soda. They're in a taxi, heading to Halima's new office on the Panopticon's Quantum Hill campus.

'They say he – or she – already is.' Halima's voice takes on the dreamy quality it always does when she talks about her baby. 'At twenty weeks, the baby can already see light and hear sounds and dream, apparently.'

'Do you think it feels like waking up? Like, do you think it happens all at once? Or is it like the sun rising, slowly?' Moremi imagines a blind creature becoming first aware of its toes and then, gradually, the muted thunder of voices. Glimmers of light.

It's been two weeks since they found her at the bottom

of the stairs in their old apartment block after her failed audition. Her Pulse had released a distress signal and she woke up, half a day later, in a hospital, in a body full of pain, her sisters floating over her like nervous ghosts. The concussion had been the worst of it. The doctors had advised her to 'take it easy' for a couple of weeks; they'd asked if she'd been taking her antidepressants. Some of her old tendencies have crept back. She's having trouble again getting out of bed, brushing her teeth, getting to work on time, eating much. She suspects Halima has organised this trip in order to keep an eye on her.

Halima looks up as the car rides up to the North Bank entrance of the campus. 'We're almost here.' She pulls her shirt back over her bump, and it's a shame to watch it disappear. Moremi wants to press her cheek against it again, to run her index finger down the *linea nigra*, dark river that circles the whole longitude of the earth. She wants to ask what it feels like, never being alone? She wants to know how it happened. When Moremi asks who the father of her child is, Halima says that Zeus appeared to her in a shower of gold coins and made her pregnant. That's easier to believe than the alternative. Up until now, Moremi would have sworn that her sister was a virgin, too cerebral for the fleshly drama of sex or childbirth. Even now, Moremi suspects that if Halima could reproduce by mitosis, she would have.

'I always program in the wrong entrance.' Halima motions for the GPS system on the car and redirects it, changing their ETA by a couple of minutes.

The Panopticon's east London campus was built on an artificial island during the post-flood construction boom.

In aerial photos it looks like an atom, with looping canals connecting the different departments, which are called 'schools'. Halima works with the sales and marketing team in the 'School of Progress'.

Although she's seen it many times in videos and photographs, the sight of the Panopticon's main building that day takes her breath away. A New Baroque palace built of glass and steel. Dark stone pilasters and bright windows glistening with phosphene light. Solar-panelled architraves and columns twisted like a double helix.

'I still can't believe that you work here,' Moremi tells her sister, her voice a mix of pride and jealousy.

'Me neither,' Halima laughs. 'I'm just glad it means I have a chance to help you.'

'You know,' Moremi says as she's said before, 'I didn't throw myself down the stairs on purpose?'

'Right . . .' Halima looks unconvinced. 'It's just . . . what were you even doing there? In our old house? Wearing a leotard?'

'I've told you—'

'That you walked out of your audition.'

'Right,' Moremi says.

'Walked out?'

Moremi flinches. She doesn't want to explain what else happened. To tell her sister that, even now, she's haunted by visions of the wave. But there is some understanding in Halima's eyes. They flicker down to Moremi's arms, the tiger-stripe scars there. When Moremi reflexively covers them with her hands, her sister says, 'I want you to be happy. Well.'

Halima has told Moremi that a friend of hers is working on a way to cure depression forever. A promise which seems far too good to be true, but Moremi knows it will be better to meet with this person than to argue with her sister for the next few months.

'I get scared sometimes,' Halima says more quietly. 'Sometimes I think about Mum's sister.'

Moremi, too, is haunted by the spectre of their aunt. Everyone suspected she suffered from some kind of personality disorder, although it was never formally diagnosed. She'd had a way of whirling into their lives on one storm of chaos or another, making fantastical promises and then vanishing a couple of weeks later. Her every relationship had been characterised by disaster. By the age of thirty, she had been hospitalised several times following different attempts on her own life. Moremi, aged eight, had found her in a bath marbled red with her own blood. After that, their mother had cut her out of their lives. And after the flood, she disappeared altogether.

'I'm not like her ...' Moremi says, a scratch in her throat.

'Of course not!' Halima is quick to agree and then she tries to change the subject. 'You know something? I was having lunch the other day with an old colleague from RELIEF. Initially, we were discussing what in our personality had drawn us to working for a charity, and the conversation was sort of a black hole. I ended up telling her the whole thing. About how our dad walked out when I was sixteen and I had to look after my two younger sisters while my mum worked two, sometimes three jobs.

How I still managed to do well enough in my A levels to get accepted into Oxford, but then the flood came, and my mum died. I had to drop out and look after my siblings. I took the first job I could get and ended up at RELIEF. I told her about cleaning the streets, how it was kind of cathartic, making everything new again. Restoring order. The kind of order I never had as a child.'

'You've never told me that.'

'Haven't I?' Halima asks absent-mindedly. 'Not in so many words, probably. Anyway. So our bill comes and I reach over to figure out how we can split it but then this woman grabs it from me and says, fervently, "No!"' Halima mimes her heroic gesture. '"I'll get it. You had a bad childhood …"' She bursts out laughing before she's even delivered the punchline. 'You had a bad childhood, so here, you deserve some free risotto.'

'You should try that at Tiffany's, see how far it gets you,' Moremi says.

'Good idea …' The car decelerates and makes the little jingle that means it's arrived. The two sisters climb out and walk up the promenade, past the Panopticon's elaborately landscaped gardens with its futuristic fountains and light-sensitive pavilions. It's late morning and there is already a hectic energy about the place. People racing electric sailboats up artificial canals, in spite of the day's heat, people flying along on branded Zephyrs, racing to conferences or to the glass refectory where some celebrity chef is trialling an artificial beef he claims will solve world hunger. According to Halima, a Nobel Prize winner is expected to give a lecture in the main atrium in a couple of hours. Members of the public are already queuing up to watch. To Moremi's left, employees from the School of Money are gathered under a stone pavilion, conjuring stock-market projections from thin air.

The employees look like initiates of some cult. At least half of them have shaved their hair off. Halima explains that it gives a more vivid reading on the OEG machine. But, as a group of coders from the School of Sleep float silently past in their white lyocell pyjamas – Pulses flickering with wordless chatter – Moremi concludes that it must be more of a fashion statement. They are novitiates, preparing to make their vows and enter a new order of science, progress and sleep.

'Oh, hello!' Halima turns then, so quickly it makes Moremi jump. They both turn to find that Halima's friend has arrived. Moremi recognises her before the crosshairs in her eyes retrieve her profile. She's small and bald, wearing those same white pyjamas with specks of coffee stains around her collar.

'Zen says that you two went to school together.' That hokey 'old friends' icon flashes between them. It says nothing about how the two of them had stopped speaking during those lonely months when Moremi was the only Pulseless pupil in her class. Or that Moremi had been gripped by a pain, then, as keen as any heartbreak.

Does Zen remember? The last time they saw each other was in the church after the flood. Moremi had heard later that Zen's entire family – living in a small basement flat – had been killed. She'd been taken to live in a children's division and they hadn't seen each other again.

'It's been so long,' Zen says, striding forward to embrace Moremi. 'It always does seem so long ago, doesn't it? The time Before.'

'As if we dreamed it,' Moremi says.

'But maybe that's how everyone feels about their child-hood.' Zen turns then and says, 'You look beautiful,' to Halima, whose just re-done her hair, in celebration of her new job, with waist-length box-braids, a subtle colour – 33, her favourite – which glimmers auburn in the late-morning sun. In her bold-print kaftan and their mother's old amber necklace, Moremi thinks, she's made such a good life for herself; why can't I get better and do the same?

'Senior dreamscaper at the School of Sleep,' Moremi reads aloud from Zen's profile.

'Yeah,' Zen says, with a modest nod of her head, 'the "senior" is relatively new.' And Moremi tries to shake away her self-consciousness that her own profile reads 'pollinator' and bears the logo of no dance company.

'It must be a great job.'

'Oh,' Zen says, 'it feels strange even calling it a "job".' Then she looks between the two sisters and beams. 'They like to pair newbies up with people who have been work-ing here for a little while. When I saw Halima's name on the new intake list I volunteered to partner with her this week. It's such a big company and this campus is so large, that you'd be surprised how many old friends or friends of friends or sisters of friends I've got to reconnect with since they started work here.'

Moremi likes that Zen still refers to her as a 'friend'.

155

'Halima says you're working on some ground-breaking cure for depression.'

'That's right,' Zen says, 'though, everything we're doing here is ground-breaking.'

They all begin walking together, towards the school, where there is a granite plaque which reads: 'We are such stuff as dreams are made of and our little life is rounded with a sleep.' Moremi stops for a moment to press her fingers into the cool stone.

Halima has to head back to work, but Zen has managed to carve out some free time to talk to Moremi. As the two of them enter the School of Sleep's expansive glass atrium, the sound takes on the distorted echo of a cathedral. A jazz machine is currently playing, automated saxophones, trumpets and vibraphones, moving as if they are being played by ghosts. 'I've never seen one of those in real life before,' Moremi says.

It's a modernist palace, with marble columns and soaring trees. There is a statue of the three founders in the atrium of Quantum Hall. Hayden Adeyemi, the Panopticon's inventor, stands in the centre, between Professor Jitsuko Itō and Bertram Fairmont, cast in bronze, his heavily shadowed eyes mica black, head like the edge of an onyx stone. It's slightly larger than life. Of the three founders, Moremi has always been the most fascinated by Hayden. He's the most mythical figure, the focus of all the bio-pics and documentaries. They say that if the internet could dream of a man it would have dreamed of him. But perhaps it's the other way around. He came from nothing, he's said, a council flat in south

London. Early tragedy. A younger brother who was stabbed outside his family home. Hayden returned to find his body on the way back from school. He never recovered, he would tell the world later. He devoted his life to this work, to building the Panopticon, and the machine that, he hoped, would one day bring about the next stage of human advancement. End strife, separation, death. People are saying he's almost there.

'Have you met him?' Moremi asks Zen. 'Or any of them?'

'Once,' Zen says, 'Hayden, at the symposium.'

'What was he like?' Moremi asks.

'I can believe everything they say about him,' Zen says. *Everything?* Moremi wonders. She wants to know if it's true that he's aged like Dorian Gray. That he looks the way that he did a decade ago on the cover of *TIME* in advance of the Panopticon's IPO. Like a teenager. His face placid and unlined. They say that he sleeps sitting upright and fasts intermittently, a practice that fills him with uncanny energy. Perhaps he can feast like a willow does on sunlight and thin air.

Together, they take the elevator up to the thirtieth floor, turn down a corridor into a room that looks a little like a wing of the Natural History Museum. It's small and wood-panelled, with the oniony smell of formaldehyde. Zen explains that it's a good place to talk, as these rooms are normally empty.

It feels as if there is a lot to talk about. After Zen had been released into the care of a children's division she'd felt as if her life fell apart. Moremi has to grit her teeth as she listens to Zen's accounts of the depression she suffered.

How unmoored and lonely she had been, the attempts she'd made on her life.

'After my mum died,' she confides in Zen, 'I kept dreaming about the flood, I used to get these . . . flashbacks?'

'Me too,' Zen says in a whisper. 'That's really common, I've found in the work that I've been doing here with post-flood victims. They seem to relive it all the time in their dreams. I do, as well. Or, I used to.'

'Used to?' Moremi says.

Zen nods and the marble crescent of her hairless head reflects like a moon against a display of papery wasps' nests. 'They turned it all around for me,' she says.

'The Panopticon?'

'Orpheus,' Zen replies, then asks, 'Have you heard of the Good People Project?'

'The programme where the government beams good memories into people's minds?' Moremi remembers the argument she had with Zeeba in the hospital corridor.

'Yeah. Growing up in the children's division, I've seen the effect it has on people, its positives and its shortcomings. The biggest one is that the memories they give you aren't specific. It was Orpheus really who invented this method, he was doing it for years in some underground lab in east London before he got arrested. He uses the machine to find your worst memories and saddest moments, and then codes something better, happier. Does it in such a way that you wake changed.' She does look changed. She seems calm and happy, she's living this life with a kind of stability and purpose that Moremi longs for. 'From everything that your sister tells me about your condition, I think you might be a perfect candidate for our therapy.'

Moremi's eyes float to the glass wall on her left. From her vantage point she can see the main atrium far below. A bright hive of activity.

'It's very experimental at the moment,' Zen admits. 'We're still monitoring the effects a couple of years out from the treatment, but there are a few case studies where patients with post-traumatic stress disorder benefit from it. Wounded veterans, sexual assault victims—'

'But I'm not—' Moremi begins.

'I know,' Zen says, 'but we have been running a study for about a year focusing on early childhood trauma.'

'Trauma,' Moremi mumbles.

'Anything can be a trauma. There are big and small traumas. Losing your mother in the flood is a devastating one.'

Making a stylus motion with her fingers, Zen draws a holographic line in the air. 'So here's your childhood,' she says, indicating the line, then she draws a red cross through it. 'And here is "the accident".'

'The accident?'

'The unfortunate incident that resulted in damage or injury. For some people it's a divorce, for others a childhood disease, and others, not getting into the elite university of their choice. For a lot of people like us, in the post-flood generation, it happened the day the Thames Barrier was breached.' The line takes a nose dive, a 40-degree diversion into the polished wooden floor. 'And this is your life post-accident. Falling into negative thought patterns, reliving the trauma. It feels as if your life has stalled, as if your growth was stunted on the day of the accident.'

'It does,' she agrees.

Her father had described each one of them as an accident before he walked out on them. For four years she'd searched for his features in the face of every Black man she saw on her street, with his walk, or his mint-green mackintosh, or holding the yellow grab-handles on a Routemaster bus. It was Halima who'd eventually managed to track him down, and she'd discovered that he'd been living only a few miles away in Walthamstow with a new family, a woman much like their mother who was pregnant with twins. He'd made promises to meet them, to send money, to take on some of the bills, to fix that window that refused to shut, letting in the bitter winter air. Every promise he made was just as soon broken. His first three daughters were a mistake he'd made and he didn't want anything to do with them.

Moremi is still cut to the bone by her father's desertion. She carries her grief for both of her parents like a deformity, limps through Christmas and birthdays with the ache. She feels like an unfinished work. Her parents knitted her bones and then abandoned her, turned her out on the hard-edged world like an open sore, begging for dregs of love wherever she can hope to find it.

'Since that day you've channelled all your energy into trying to defend yourself from abandonment, from more sudden and devastating loss. You're doing emotional first-aid on wounds that haven't properly healed.'

'Yes,' Moremi agrees.

'And in the past, what could we offer you? The blunt instrument of medication? Years of talking with another flawed human, hoping to fix the problem at the same level of understanding that created it in the first place? Electroshock therapy, insulin therapy, leeches, prayer, a draining of excess black bile.' With an amused hand she bats all that away. All of history, all the dashed hopes of men. 'Now we have neuroscience. We've entered a new age. The space age of neuroscience. Did you know that the computer in your head' – she indicates her own Pulse – 'is a thousand times more powerful than any of the computers that sent Igor Bovarin to Mars?' Yes, Moremi has heard this before. 'As Einstein said, "We can't solve the problem at the same level of thinking that created the problem." The hard problem of consciousness. The problem of the human condition. And now we have answers, solutions.'

Moremi nods. She wants to believe. She wants to believe that there is an answer for her. And she wants it to be easy.

'So, in the last few years, neuroscience has come on in leaps and bounds. We're now able to create models of your brain that are accurate on the synapse level. So we're interested in your hippocampus.' She makes a motion with her hand, inflates a holographic brain like a balloon between her fingers. It looks strange and translucent. She waggles a finger and illuminates the hippocampus in cobalt-blue. 'There it is. Under the cerebral cortex. It means "sea-horse".' Two symmetrical structures twisted like bangles in the centre of the brain. 'This is the part of the brain that plays an important role in the formation of new memories. Imagine that the line I drew is your life so far.' It's fading in the air like the light-shadow of a camera flash. 'Your impression of your life so far is made up of all the memories saved in your hippocampus and backed up on your Pulse's quartz. Imagine if we could change those memories?'

She points to the X in the middle of the line she'd drawn.

'What if the flood never happened?' she asks. 'What if you never lost your parents? What if no one ever left you?'

In her mind Moremi is thinking of all the people who ever left, not only her father but every other man she's ever loved. Holden, Tayo, Lionel, the latest. Lionel who had called her 'a monster of need'.

'Yes,' Zen says, raising a hand, drawing a blue line with the flick of a finger up into the ceiling, 90 degrees from the downward-pointing one. 'So there's a knock on your door and you open it. And on the other side of the threshold is the Moremi who was never hurt. The Moremi who was never abandoned. The Moremi who never thought of harming herself. Who moves through life with a self-assured strength, and no fear at all. She is happy. Loved. And, more importantly, she knows that she is worthy of love.'

There is a catch in her throat when she hears Zen say this. Moremi's eyes prickle with hopeless longing. Zen is describing a dream. The dream.

'All the memories stored in your hippocampus are backed up on your quartz. This treatment involves using an algorithm to find the most traumatic memories, then they are played back to you with the most painful parts altered. You'll live your most painful moments again, like a lucid dream, only this time, we'll change the upsetting details to make them happy.'

'But they won't be true,' Moremi says. 'I might have a dream where my mother didn't die, but then I'd wake up. A good dream won't change reality.'

'No, if only!' Zen says. 'No, what happened to you, happened. But haven't you ever woken up from a good dream? A dream where something you hoped for came true. Didn't you move through the world for a few hours after waking with a foreign kind of ease?'

Moremi nods.

'That's what this treatment does. The lucid part of you will know that the accident did happen. That the traumas and the consequences of them are real and inescapable. But some other part of you will be hopeful, reconciled, able to let the pain and the anger and the fear go.' She points to the line, the one that shoots up. 'That will be your life.'

'How long will it take?' Moremi asks.

'Two treatment sessions. Re-living the accident is the worst part. That happens first. And then the good memories are layered on top, in another treatment session thirty-six hours later. So far, studies shows that patients mostly achieve good outcomes. Miraculous, even. At the School of Sleep we've seen people unable to hold down a steady job take up a place at Goldman Sachs and marry their on-again off-again fiancée. We've seen good parents made out of this. Happy sons and daughters. I've seen lifelong grudges relinquished.'

'It sounds great, but,' Moremi says, squinting her eyes at the sunlight flitting through one of the double doors, 'it's the word "experimental" that bothers me. Is it safe?'

Zen smiles. 'All treatments have a few side effects. There is the side effect of the anaesthetic Nox, which can lead to drowsiness and memory loss for twenty-four to forty-eight hours after the treatment. Then there is the fact that, for a minuscule minority of patients, the treatment can become "habit-forming".'

'What does that mean?' Moremi asks.

'Sometimes we find that a few patients request the treatment several times because they want another chance to experience the dreamworld. But most people find themselves happily cured and able to pursue their ambitions.'

'And you,' Moremi says. 'It worked for you?'

'Perfectly,' Zen says, and now she takes Moremi's hand. Says it like a promise, 'I can barely remember my old self. Orpheus is a genius, an artist, you'll be in the best hands.'

There is a part of her that has always believed that if she'd only had a good childhood then she would be well. Not running out of auditions, or throwing herself head-first into volatile relationships, no living this unsteady life, doing nothing that she wants.

Moremi releases Zen's hand and lets her gaze wander back out, far below them; outside the school she can see protestors with placards gathering like storm clouds.

Moremi feels energised in a way she hasn't for years, on fire with something new: hope. She wants to wake changed. She wants to leave her pain behind and perhaps this is the answer. Moremi had believed that the Panopticon would deliver her from loneliness or despair, but she's grown to suspect that on the other side of its neon promises are the same insecurities and psychic pain she's been trying to numb all along. What comfort was the Panopticon those nights when she'd lie awake and asked, 'Can grief kill you?' into the quiet dark?

'Okay,' she says. 'I want to do it. I want to be well.'

Zen smiles. She grabs Moremi's hand as if she's just said 'yes' to a marriage proposal. 'We can do it, Moremi. We can fix you.'

9

ORPHEUS

London is in the grip of a heatwave. Oily exhaust fumes float on gusts of humid air. The old city was not built for this heat. The steel rails of train tracks buckle under the sun. Services are cancelled or delayed. Holographic signs appear outside the stations reminding passengers to bring water. Everyone is sweat-stained and furious. Impossible to ignore, in this weather, that there is an electricity in the air. Orpheus has read that in hot weather every kind of crime is more likely. People honk car horns for longer, swear more on social media. Everyone is poised for a fight. Which always amuses him. Makes him remember that he is only a body, another termite in the mound of this city.

After leaving Sherif in his apartment, Orpheus takes the tube into the Panopticon's east London campus. On the way through the turnstiles he spots the labyrinth. There is one inside every station, a permanent artwork installed decades ago to mark the anniversary of the London

Underground. They are made of the same vitreous enamel as the tube's roundel logo. Classical looping labyrinths with dark interlocking rings, Chartres labyrinths with scalloped edges, geometric Roman labyrinths. Every time he walks past, he likes to touch them the way that people touch wood. There is one on the platform before his train arrives and sometimes he has long enough to trace his finger right to the centre before it's time to embark. Easy to solve the maze when you can see all of it.

As the tube doors close, Orpheus' nerves prickle. The dream comes back to him for a moment, on a tide of dread. He's eleven and the air is black with smoke. 'Not mine,' he promises himself under his breath. 'Not real.' He leans his head against the cool glass of the window, closes his eyes and imagines his skin filling with sand, toes, heels, calves, thighs, centring his mind again in his body. 'Not mine,' he says again to himself, as he always does when this happens, 'not real.'

When he disembarks at Quantum Hill station, the Panopticon's campus comes gorgeously into view. Orpheus is used to this walk, to the sound of the gravel under his heels, but he is startled to discover that the square outside the School of Sleep is thronged with protesters. Students in tie-dye painter's smocks are holding placards. Old men with dreadlocks are spray-painting bedsheets with the words 'VOTE NO'. A group of people sitting on the stone steps outside the canteen have set up a drum circle and are starting up a chant. Someone else is handing out hand-knitted red liberty caps.

'What's going on?' Orpheus says to one of the women

handing out flyers. The atmosphere on the green is one of febrile unrest. The campus security guards are stringing yellow tape between bollards, barking, 'Keep back.' It looks as if a fight might break out.

'I honestly can't wait until the referendum is over. If only so our lives can get back to normal,' says a pregnant woman who Orpheus spots, fanning herself with a 'Vote No' leaflet.

'Give us back our privacy,' someone shouts, and the crowd applauds. 'Give us back our dreams.' A chant starts up, and they all repeat it to the rhythm of a samba drum. Orpheus can feel the ground under his feet tremble. Almost impossible to fight the urge to shout with them.

'Vote No on July twenty-ninth,' says a blonde girl standing behind a stall covered in sign-up sheets, petitions and home-made newsletters. Orpheus takes one that says, 'Who will win the war for your mind?' The logo of the Panopticon is on the cover, an open eye with the world in its iris. He's about to ask the blonde girl a question, but a hush begins to roll across the gathered crowd. The chant fades almost as soon as it began, along with the drum. Attention turns to the memorial arch where a middle-aged woman with waist-length white braids is standing on top of a table. There is something wrong with her face. Orpheus feels as if his eyes can't focus on it, her features are coming up slightly blurred as if they've been erased by a heavy-handed censor. He turns and notices a couple of other people in the crowd are squinting as well.

'There's something wrong with my Pulse,' says the pregnant woman to the woman next to her. Her profile reads that her name is Halima and it has a little icon above her occupation that indicates she's a new employee at the Panopticon.

'Mine too,' he says, and, looking through the crowd, he notices the same issue with a couple of other people's faces. The ReCog program in his retina flashes an error message when it catches their features in its crosshairs. It's a sickly feeling.

'They're Hiding,' says one of the security guards standing by a colonnade. It's an urban legend that some people paint their faces with asymmetrical patterns of UV paint that interfere with the ReCog software and hide their faces from scanners.

'They should make that kind of thing illegal,' says Halima.

'Probably will,' says the woman next to her. Her sister, he guesses, without needing to glance at her profile. The two of them make eye contact for a moment before the woman at the front shouts, 'Welcome!' Her voice resonates across the green. 'Are you ready for this fight?' The crowd cheers their assent. 'Are you ready to fight against tyranny?' Another roar. 'For your humanity?' She points a long finger at the towering structure behind her, the watchtower, which casts its brutal shadow across them all. 'Behind those doors, there are people sleeping. And we're here to wake them up. Am I right?' Pause for more applause and she waits for their silence again. 'They've been calling us Luddites and technophobes. Fools, frightened of technology, but we're the only ones who can see clearly. We are soothsayers, we are the Revelators.

'In the nineteenth century, at the dawn of the machine age, a few dissidents saw the turning arc of history and glimpsed our destruction. They were British weavers and textile workers who objected to the introduction of mechanised looms and knitting frames. Highly trained artisans who saw the skills they had spent a lifetime honing crushed in the shadow of a textile mill. When they took up their hammers and torches to smash and burn stocking frames and threshing machines they were not backwards cave-dwellers terrified of progress. Perhaps they glimpsed it, this techno-nightmare we've charged head-first into. Perhaps they saw centuries of low-wage labour, exploitation and environmental degradation. Perhaps they saw children forced to work long hours in factories, the migration of people from farms into plague-ridden cities, climate change. The Luddites were fighting against the replacement of humans by machines. The same thing that we are fighting for this very day. "We will die fighting, or live free." Because that's what is at stake here, at this coming election. Any hope we'll ever have to "live free".'

'Vote No!' people shout in the crowd, raising their fists in the air.

'Live free. Vote no!'

The woman waits for the shouts to die down a little before she continues, 'The Panopticon is gazing into the heads of our children, our loved ones, our politicians and counsellors. It sees almost everything, it can predict to a 99 per cent accuracy the outcome of the next election. People are being arrested and interrogated on the basis of crimes they are "statistically likely" to commit – "future crimes". We have sleepwalked into a world of complete surveillance and total psychological control. The Panopticon poses an existential threat to what's left of our way of life.

'Men are becoming "mechanical in head and heart as well as hand".' She pauses and, as she does, Orpheus catches a glimpse of his own reflection in the glass wall of the refectory. He sees the way that Nox has turned his hair prematurely grey, his own sallow skin, the light of his Pulse flickering quickly under it.

'But we are machines,' says the woman next to him. Moremi, his Pulse tells him. She's tall for a woman, the same height as him, with hair cut short but growing out in fluffy uneven patches that make her look like a newly hatched chick. She has large, sad eyes and a striking bone structure that is on the borderline between beautiful and freakish. Jaw, cheekbones, lips, so dark they are almost blue. Orpheus is filled with a tenderness for her courage, speaking out against this crowd.

A few of the protesters glance in their direction. 'No one says it's unnatural when a bird builds a nest,' Moremi says to the people around her. 'No one is offended by the architecture of a termite mound or a hive. But a house? An apartment block? A power station? Fire was a new technology once, you know. And even then, some of us must have run in terror of its light and heat and some of you, a burned few, would have said then that the risk wasn't worth the brilliance.'

More people have turned to her now, and Halima looks uncomfortable with the attention.

'My sister was born two months early,' Moremi says. 'Machines saved her life.'

'Mine too,' Orpheus shouts, and he's thinking of the doctors who warmed his blood and snatched him from the cool maw of death.

'How many lives do drone strikes save?' the blonde woman behind the stall shouts.

'Or bio-terrorism!' says another.

Orpheus feels an elbow in his ribs. A small man with thick glasses is looking up at him and asking, 'Where have I seen you before?'

'Isn't he the Luddite kid?'

'Yeah!' A notification flickers in the corner of his eye that lets him know someone is checking his profile. The eyes of two students flash with recognition: 'The one who came back from the dead.'

'East London's Lazarus.'

'And now you work here?' the Pulseless man asks incredulously. 'How do you sleep at night?'

The crowd around him all begin to take notice, whisper his name. 'Orpheus?'

Moremi is ignoring their chatter, though; she leaps with surprising grace up onto the rickety stall, her ballet flats making dusty footprints on the laminated newsletters.

'Science!' she shouts at the gathering crowd. 'It's not something outside of us. It's part of us. A great endeavour. As beautiful as painting or music or poetry. You talk about what it means to be human. To invent, to innovate, and build is what it means to be human. But it also means suffering and dying. Children dropping like flies from cholera because there is no clean water. Women bleeding to death in childbirth. Alzheimer's – which doctors at *that* building have cured.' She points at the watchtower. 'Cancer. Pandemics. Dirty water. Those pose an existential threat to our existence. Sickness and suffering and a swift death, those are inherent to our condition. But science, machines, computers, have come to our aid. Will come.'

All around people are turning their heads. Orpheus can feel the blood rising in his cheeks, worried for her. He'd be terrified with so many eyes on him, but Moremi seems undaunted. He could listen to her all day, her words stir something in him. Pride? She seems to articulate, beautifully, something that's been floating on the edge of his consciousness. He wishes his father could hear her speak. Or Sherif. Wishes he'd been as eloquent this morning – not that it would have changed anything.

Her gaze flickers in a way that indicates she is searching for something on the Panopticon. After a short pause she says, 'Ali Maow Maalin was a hospital cook and health worker who in 1977 was the last person to be infected with smallpox, and do you know why? Because scientists and doctors chased smallpox like a fugitive across the globe until the last living person was vaccinated. In a spectacular effort, they eradicated a disease from the face of the earth.'

Almost before she's finished, someone shouts, 'Vaccines? She's talking to us about vaccines.' There are boos and jeers, angry shouts.

'Indeed,' says the woman in front of the memorial arch. 'Why doesn't she talk to us about climate change? About thalidomide and lead poisoning? Why doesn't she talk to us about MRSA and drug-resilient pandemics. Plastics sucked down by babies through their mother's milk, the death of all the bees.'

'Talk to us about the dead coral reefs,' says another, 'and oil spills.'

'Consumerism! Capitalism!'

'Obscene levels of social inequality.'

Orpheus is hemmed in by them, unable to breathe. Moremi's eyes flash with terror as someone grabs at her feet; another spits at Halima. The hecklers around the two of them are furious and he is shocked to see it. These people would halt the turning of the Earth, if they could, for fear of the dark.

'Get down from there!' Halima shouts, but Moremi looks too afraid to. People are throwing things at her, scrunched-up pieces of paper, an apple core.

The woman at the front of the crowd is shouting again, buoyed up by their discontent. 'Who decides what world we want? Hayden Adeyemi? Bertram Fairmont? Mark Zuckerberg? Jeff Bezos? Or the people? Us!'

'Vote no!' they shout, the chant rolling like thunder across them. 'Live free! Vote NO!'

Orpheus sees an opening among them, and dashes towards the stall. He reaches out a hand to help Moremi and she grabs it. 'This way,' he says, shielding her from the crowd. He knows a way into the building, a side entrance; one security guard helps Halima while another pushes some of the hecklers back. Orpheus can feel the sweatiness of her palms, see her Pulse flickering wildly above her ear. For half a minute they are running, and then the sensors on the door read the ID on Orpheus' Pulse; they swing open and let them in.

'Don't worry,' Halima says, leaning against the door. 'All the polls predict that Vote Yes will win. And then this will be over. Even during the moon landing there were protests.'

As the sounds of the fray vanishes, Orpheus realises that he and Moremi are still holding hands. 'Thank you,' she says, letting go, staring at his profile. 'Orpheus.' His name is like silver on her tongue. But then she says, '*That* Orpheus?' And eyes the gunshot scar in his hand. He brings it reflexively to his chest as one might an injured bird. 'The one who came back from the dead.'

'Only medically,' Orpheus replies. 'Technically. A couple of people have been known to come back, from hypothermia and drowning.'

'I bet for the rest of your life, everyone will ask, "What was it like? What did you see?"' she says.

'But not you?' he asks. 'Because you're not like everyone else?' She only smiles.

10

MOREMI

That Orpheus, she thinks in wonder. The Orpheus whose sole-shaped eyes she stared into for years in that recording. He's five years older now. Beautiful, she thinks, although he is the kind of thin that can make almost any man look striking. Razor-sharp bones in his cheeks. A mixed-race boy with bronze skin, sun-darkened smattering of freckles on the narrow bridge of his nose, druggy glaze in his green eyes, curly black hair that makes her think of Jimmy Page or John Keats. They are still staring at each other when the door behind Halima flies open again and Zen leaps in.

'It's not normally like this,' she says, flustered. 'It's normally quieter in that part of the campus.' She turns to Moremi with a smile and says, 'It looks like you're getting famous.' Zen shares a blurry Vine recording of Moremi standing on the home-made stall and shouting 'Science!' at the crowd. It's already garnered hundreds of thousands of views and reactions. Moremi looks away;

she almost doesn't recognise that bold version of herself, and is unsure exactly what possessed her to try and take on the angry crowd.

'You won't remember it, though,' Zen says, 'after you have your treatment.'

'Why not?'

'Most of our patients report that a lot of the details of the preceding day become quite fuzzy.' Moremi turns to Orpheus with a stab of regret. *This too?* she thinks to Zen. Will she forget how his hand had felt in hers?

Even his pretty face, Zen says with a smile. *Which is probably a good thing, since he'll be the one designing your dream.*

Of course, Moremi thinks. It makes sense to her that 'London's Lazarus' works in the School of Sleep.

They all head together to the research and development wing of the School of Sleep. And as they do, Orpheus and Zen tell Moremi and Halima about the different projects the scientists in the department have been working on. Compared to her last visit, there is an air of festival around, because the employees are preparing for the annual symposium, the four-day conference that takes place on Quantum Hill, attracting tech CEOs and business moguls, politicians and celebrities from around the world. Moremi has seen pictures of the opening gala on gossip Vines. It's a chance for the employees at the Panopticon to unveil their newest innovations.

'The Magi are going to announce something "big" this year,' Zen says.

'Do you know about it?' Moremi asks.

'She can't say if she does,' Orpheus says.

'A lot of people are coming from around the world to learn about Orpheus' work though,' Zen says. As they walk, she discusses some of the research taking place at the School of Sleep. Orpheus explains that a group of undergraduates have been teaching paralytics to fly in their dreams. Scientists from the Centre for Depression and Affective Disorders have been encouraging the bereaved to talk to the dead. A psychiatrist is designing dreams to treat patients with agoraphobia and addiction. Zen's partner Kimiko works in the School of Radical Togetherness, where they're rescuing couples from the brink of divorce by encouraging them to pair their Pulses for periods of time and watch the world from behind each other's eyes. 'It's life-changing,' Zen assures them.

When Moremi sees a middle-aged couple walking hand in hand she wonders if they've just received a treatment. Their eyes are bright with a giggly joy, and they keep stopping to stroke each other's hair.

Zen leads them past the long galleries of sleep-pods, which look like glass capsule hotels with still bodies on gurneys, their multifarious dreams splayed on OEG monitors. According to Orpheus they are volunteers for the Zeitgeist project – people who have agreed to add their dreams to a public database. The activity of their hearts and minds is rendered in leaping spindles. Walking past the silent rows of them, Moremi can sense busyness, the way she can when looking over a city from a great height. Glimpses of things: the evanescent flames of birthday candles, the tarnished underside of a Suzu

bell hanging beneath the eaves of a Shinto shrine, ver-
million paper lanterns strung between terraced houses
over Chinatown.

Moremi must go up to one of the labs. There, a tech will
perform some routine tests on her. He'll asks some psy-
chiatric screening questions and calibrate her brainwaves
with the OEG machine.

Don't be scared, Zen says in Moremi's head. *You're in
the very best hands.*

Moremi looks at him again, then. Orpheus and his
delicate hands. He's waving to emphasise some point he's
making to Halima. It seems almost foolish, to trust this
stranger with her dreams. But then she reminds herself
of the night her appendix burst. The surgeon she'd met
whose face had floated to her as her body convulsed in
pain and who promised that when she opened her eyes
again it would be in her old pain-free body. 'I can give it
back to you,' he'd said. Science, Moremi thought then as
she did now, modern medicine; she would put her faith in
it and it would restore everything she had lost.

The dream doctors have a script. It begins with 'I'm sorry
we're meeting under these circumstances', for the patients
who are checked in for the trauma recollection therapy.

'I'm sorry, too,' Moremi says behind her gas mask.
Is it Orpheus speaking to her over the intercom? Is that
his voice?

The sleep-pod is like a sensory deprivation chamber, a
lightless fibreglass tank filled halfway with cold water. It
is so dark inside that Moremi can't tell if her eyes are open

179

or closed. Her optic nerves are making little pinpricks of hallucinatory light. They've hooked her up, via her Pulse, to a socket in the corner of the pod, to the OEG.

'This part of the treatment is the hardest,' says the voice. 'The OEG is connected to your Pulse, and it will run some software in your head looking for memories with negative effect.'

'Bad memories,' she says.

'Yes, any time that you felt sick or frightened or ashamed. That's what the machine will find. Unfortunately, that means reliving it. It's the part of the procedure called "collection". And it's not easy. It's triggering. That's why you'll have to be kept under close observation for the next couple of hours.'

'And what happens after that?'

'After that is the treatment. I'll code a better memory. Better versions of the traumatic events, and we'll feed them back to you in the recollection. Then you'll have a series of follow-ups with the psychiatrist but you'll be free to go. To live a more perfect life.'

'More perfect,' she says.

'Okay,' he says, 'we'll be putting you to sleep now. With a cue we recorded for you.' It begins to play through her Pulse.

Frère Jacques, Frère Jacques
Dormez-vous? Dormez-vous?

'It's just a dream?' she slurs, looking for reassurance as her stomach plummets. 'It's not real?'

'It is real too,' he says. 'It's just the other side.'

*

On the other side, Moremi is waiting at the school gates. Her dad is supposed to pick her up. The summer term is almost over and the air is filled with the constant din of construction, metal on metal, the sounds of buzz-saws and drills. Every time she glimpses the skyline rising up around her, a red crane has moved. It only seems to happen when she's not looking.

She is nine years old, dangling her fingers through the chain-link fence, watching the cars pull up as parents climb out. No one will miss her father when he comes, he's tall, with an afro smooth as a leopard's pelt and he's just bought a sky-blue car. Waiting for him in the playground, Moremi thinks she can see him, riding down the road, the roof down, a driving bass, mirrored aviators and a winsome grin. She imagines the girls in her class staring, the boys stopping for just a second to look up from their ball games and cards.

Standing by the fence, knocking her messenger-bag against her knees, Moremi watches the playground empty. She keeps looking back out at the road and, for a second, every car is his. Each time her heart leaps, but then another unfamiliar face emerges from the driver's seat.

Maybe he is lost, she thinks, retreating to a bench as the last of her friends disappear. Any number of things could have happened, which is what the teachers tell her too, when she is asked to wait outside the staffroom with all the other unclaimed kids. One by one they are collected, by breathless parents full of excuses. And still Moremi waits. She doesn't know it yet, but this will be her whole life.

When someone finally comes for her, it's sixteen-year-old Halima in her too-small school uniform with the skirt that she keeps tugging down self-consciously. She's tried to be industrious, to save their mother thirty pounds they don't have by supergluing her school shoes together, and the gummy crust of it is still coming loose at her heel. This is not the first or the last time Halima will be the bearer of bad news. That day she tells Moremi that their father has left their mother. 'He's never coming home,' she explains.

Moremi had been too young to see it coming. As they head back to their flat, through the estates and the boarded-up shops, Moremi starts to cry. 'You can't do that in front of Mum,' Halima says, shaking her sister by the shoulders, 'she's had enough as it is.' But Moremi can't stop. She feels as if the ground has fallen out from under her, as if their home will slide into disaster – and it will.

'Why don't you do what I do?' Halima says, as if she's about to confess a secret. 'Sometimes when he disappoints me, when he says he'll be there but doesn't turn up, I . . .' She glances away embarrassed. 'I pretend that he died.'

A startling thing to say to a child, but it comes as a relief. She imagines her father racing down the road to meet her, running red lights, but then his car turned to scrap metal on the pavement.

Moremi and her sisters eat cornflakes for dinner that night. They switch out the lights when another debt collector pounds at the door, and all the while Moremi imagines him lying there, on the side of the road, his daughters' names on his frozen lips. With this grim fantasy comes a great thing, the freedom to cast herself in a different role: not the abandoned child, but the orphaned child.

In their dreams, does everyone return to their childhood home? Moremi opens the door to their two-bedroom flat in Camberwell. Only, the house is like a hall of mirrors and behind every door is a memory.

Her mother is crying in the airing cupboard, huge ugly sobs. 'Leave me alone!' she shouts.

Downstairs, their father really has left them, abandoned his keys on the gingham oil cloth on the kitchen table.

Every bad thing that ever happened happens all at once. Behind every door is an argument, every fridge is empty, under every duvet someone is crying desolate tears. All the boys who ever left her are walking away: Lionel, Holden, Tayo, David and Dan.

The halls of the house curve back and back into each other like an Escher drawing and Moremi soon figures out that it's a maze, with herself, her own miserable self, at every dead end.

Halima shouts at her mother. Zeeba runs into the glass coffee table, breaks her two front teeth and splits the skin on her forehead. Moremi tries to find the front door, but the lights in the corridor flicker on and off.

Moremi is the one who opens the door to the bathroom and finds her mother's sister in a tub full of blood, her face swollen, lips purple, water gushing over the sides. Moremi reacts, in the dream, the way that she did that day. She flees down the hall and vomits in the kitchen sink, washes the bile down while saying to herself, 'I didn't see it, I didn't see it,' as if saying it will make it true.

She wants to get out of this place. How to make herself wake up? 'Make it stop,' she cries as the ghosts of her family swirl around her. She hears every bad thing that her mother ever said to her. One time Moremi came back late from a friend's house and her mother called her a 'mistake'. She apologised later, said that she was stressed, that it wasn't true. But it means something different when a parent calls you a name. It will stick in you like a barb. Sometimes she'll catch a glimpse of herself in the mirror, painting on lipstick, and her mother will say it again.

How to get out of this house?

Moremi stumbles down the stairs for the thousandth time to find the living room and sees the wave rising. Bulbs spark and burst, mud rushes up the walls, takes everything, the tiny etching on the doorpost where their mother marked their heights, the little affirmative Post-it notes she sticks to the fridge, all their childhood toys. The wave keeps rising, coming up her shins, her thighs. Moremi screams, turns to run, but it has snatched her, and, just as she always feared, she is going under.

Moremi clutches at her throat, paddles frantically to try to keep her head above water. But there is no escape. In less than a minute it sloshes above her head and her muscles seize. Water roils around her, and she splashes violently, her fingers seeking something to grab on to. Moremi knows that panic will only hasten the end, and so she tries to hold her breath. Something is pulling her down, and soon Moremi's body is gripped in pain as every instinct in her tells her to breathe.

Fumbling around blindly for a window, she finds the ledge and then smacks her palms hard against the glass. If she can push it open, she might be able to escape. Moremi's fingers are clumsy in her fear though. She pounds the windowpane but it's stone hard against her clenched fist.

Moremi kicks, her heart swollen in her chest, and then the urge to gasp overpowers her. Her mouth flies open and the dirty water surges into her throat. It's a horrifying feeling. Her lungs screaming for air and then the violation of water. Moremi is filled with the base fear of an animal about to die. Blind panic and then, in that frightened moment, she sees that she wants to live.

Frère Jacques, Frère Jacques
Dormez-vous?

When she wakes she still thinks that she is drowning. She opens her eyes in the sleep-pod clutched with pain, pulling electrodes off her and screaming. Nurses rush in, unseal the chamber, drag her out of the water as she sobs. This time, when she opens her mouth, cool air rushes in and she's grateful for it.

Sonnez les matines!
Ding, dang, dong. Ding, dang, dong.

Half an hour later, sitting in the recovery room, a nurse offers her a box of digestive biscuits. Moremi devours them breathlessly. *How many hours have passed?* she wonders. The sun has long set outside and the halls of the lab are quiet.

'That bad, huh?' asks one of the nurses.

Already, Moremi feels ashamed of herself. For the tears. 'My life's not been so bad,' she explains. 'I didn't . . . go to war or anything. I didn't watch my friends blown apart by landmines or beheaded by warlords.' So why is she still crying?

'It's not rational,' says the nurse, 'it's not objective. There isn't a pain scale that your brain measures life against, with war at the top and a failed audition at the bottom.' She sighs, sets the tray of biscuits down and says, 'It's funny what comes up when you do the collection. You try to get some sleep tonight, though. And when you're back tomorrow, they will make it better.'

In the more perfect world, no one ever left. Moremi's father arrives at the school gates just as he promised at the time he promised and everyone notices him when he comes. They ride home in the sky-blue car, and in the house all her family are overjoyed to see them.

It had felt unrequited, her love for her father. But, in the more perfect world, he never leaves and their family doesn't spin out into the kind of misery that left everyone heartbroken and traumatised.

In the dream she has the perfect mother. The perfect mother is a mirror. A bundle of sacrifice. When you give her a gift she never says, 'This isn't what I wanted at all.' She says, 'A gift from your blessed hands?' Her face is a lantern of unconditional love. If Moremi ever calls out in the night she comes running. She turns up early to every parents' evening and birthday party, attends every ballet class and never takes her eyes off her daughter.

In the more perfect world all the hurt, even the little slights, are undone.

Her mother is crying in the airing cupboard, huge ugly sobs, and when Moremi opens the door she tries hard to smile. 'I'm just so happy,' she says in the dream.

Their father lost his job but it means he'll spend more time with them. It means weekend mornings in their pyjamas watching Cartoon Network, it means wild family outings. Pumpkin-picking in October, trips to the Horniman Museum, the National Gallery, picnics on Parliament Hill, playing charades on a Tattersall blanket, Zeeba laughing so much that Fanta bubbles out of her nose.

In the more perfect world her mother gets to be a dancer. One morning, her mother wakes her and asks, 'Are you ready?'

'For what?' Moremi says.

'Everybody's waiting.'

'Who?'

'Everybody you've ever known.'

Moremi follows her into a hall filled with people that Moremi recognises distantly. The woman with a snake-bite piercing she often spots, waiting on the platform at Pimlico when she's running late for a morning class. The West Indian man who always delivers their mail. And then some of the other faces resolve in her memory. The paediatrician who removed Halima's tonsils and gave Moremi a lolly for doing nothing at all. They are leaning on the banister, looking up, hoping to catch a better view of Moremi as her mother leads her down the stairs.

'Sorry,' she keeps saying. It's difficult to manoeuvre down each step with so many people gathered on them. Moremi recognises her Year Eight teacher, Mrs Newbold. She'd been disapproving, and quick to punish. 'It was because I wanted the best for you,' she says. She's aged only a little, though she was old before; there are liver spots around her eyes, which are damp now. 'Please forgive me.'

'Of course,' Moremi says, with an easy laugh. Everyone is forgiven.

There is the first boy that she ever kissed, he is still thirteen, his mouth still full of braces, lips white with dry chapped skin, only he is grinning, waving, hoping that she will notice him. Moremi does, and waves. Someone tosses confetti at her and shouts, 'Remember me!' The receptionist at her dentist's office. Hard to recognise her out of context.

As Moremi reaches the landing, children from her school are gathered, with their arms open. 'I'm so glad to know you,' says the popular girl with the nose-ring. It's the first thing she's ever said to Moremi.

'You belong,' says a boy who rests his cricket bat on the console table and hugs her without taking off his glove. For a while it's a flurry of hugs. It's like crowd-surfing, as she's nudged from one pair of open arms to another and all around people are telling her that they love her, that they accept her. That she's valuable to them.

All the boys who ever left her are weeping with regret. 'You were too good for us,' Lionel says. The boy next to him, Holden, who'd later revealed he'd had sex with her to win a bet, says, 'We had to leave you for this day to come.'

It feels like her wedding day. Everyone's eyes are on her. All the friends she's ever had are gathered near the back door. They stand under a banner that reads 'YOU ARE LOVED'. All sorrow turned to song. They tell her that she will live and will go on living. Turn her blades into salt if even once she tries to cut herself.

Moremi is nudged out into the garden and for a moment she is sun-blind, her eyes wet with tears of relief. Her paternal grandparents are holding hands on the love-seat. The other grandparents are resting under the shade of the apple tree. But they all lift their glad eyes to see her emerge. 'We've been waiting for you,' says her mother's mother. Behind her is her mother, and her mother.

'Are you ready?' her sisters ask.

'For what?' she asks.

'For the future.'

In the garden, Zeeba and Halima lead a choir of all their ancestors and the tapestry of their voices rises like smoke above the picket fence, and the sun-bleached lawn, rusted tricycle, the milieu of her own workaday world where countries collide in distant wars, where everything that rises must be returned to the earth. Her forearms are covered in scars, on the underside of everything is decay and yet somehow, on this stale earth, this music exists. What a good place it must be, she realises, her eyes half-blinded by tears. What a good thing to be alive.

Trumpets glide into the bridge with a starburst of melody. Music so beautiful it sends a ripple of terror through Moremi. Her skin rises up in goosebumps and everyone within earshot laughs.

A song sounds in the distance.

Frère Jacques, Frère Jacques.

'No!' Moremi cries out in dismay. She remembers that this is only a dream. 'No!' She doesn't want to wake. She whirls around. She is the only one in the garden who can hear the cue.

Dormez-vous? Dormez-vous?

People are disappearing in a great wave, rolling up towards her from the back of the house. 'Mum!' Moremi grabs her mother's wrist and pushes through the crowd, away from the sound.

Sonnez les matines!

If she covers her ears with one hand then perhaps she won't hear it. Perhaps this moment will pass her by and she can stay here forever. Her mother turns, as the roof of the house begins to crumble and the crowd are sent fleeing.

Sonnez les matines!

She has to let go. Moremi releases her mother's hand and shields her eyes from the debris.

Ding, dang, dong.

When she opens her eyes she's looking up at the fluorescent light of the open dream capsule and she's crying again. She's back in the School of Sleep, her heart galloping in her ribs.

Nurses descend upon her, unplugging her from the machine, taking off the gas mask.

'No,' Moremi says, flinging her arm out as she tries to sit up.

Her palm still remembers the weight of her mother's hand. She feels a gut-wrench of pain at the loss. Some part of her mind battles to remember that none of it is real. That her mother really is dead. And yet some other part of her cannot accept it. Cannot accept this watered-down world when she has glimpsed heaven.

'I don't want it to be over,' she says.

'Oh, sweetheart,' says the nurse softly. 'No one ever wants it to be over.'

11

ORPHEUS

Half a day off Nox and he's already beginning to feel the tightness in his skull that will turn, in an hour or so, into a headache. In the elevator to the ground floor of the School, Orpheus stands for a while, examining his reflection in the mirrored walls with some real loathing. This is the trouble with meat-space. On this side, he's a captive.

It's been a month now, since he met Sherif, and Orpheus senses that his life is tipping into chaos. He's felt compelled to spend longer and longer in the labyrinth, he's been oversleeping, getting to work late and, during his waking hours, the dreams of his patients have been bothering him more than usual. Moremi's especially. Since peering into her mind during the recollection procedure he's been haunted by flashes of the wave that swallowed London. He'll think he sees it as a train carriage approaches and has to blink it away. Or he'll look at the eyes of his colleagues and find that rot has turned them to jelly. Perhaps that's why his work has suffered over the past few weeks and why, this evening, he had been called in to his manager's office for a probationary meeting.

'I heard you were fired.' The voice startles Orpheus from his reverie. When the elevator doors open he is face to face with Zen, who must have tracked him on the finder.

'You heard wrong,' Orpheus says.

'So what is it, then?' Zen asks. 'Sick leave?' She says it almost in a whisper and Orpheus nods, his cheeks on fire. The conversation with his manager, Sai Kaur, had begun about lateness and absences, but everyone was alert to the signs now of too much time spent dreaming and Sai had called Orpheus out on his Nox use. Orpheus has heard a rumour that Sai himself used to be an addict. He'd joined the Panopticon straight out of university and entered a graduate programme where his main task was coding video games for the School of Fun. Like dreamscapers, those employees are licensed to use Nox in small doses for their work, but dependence happens often.

'You have to jump through their hoops,' Zen says, 'tick their health and safety boxes. How long did they put you on leave for?'

'Until the symposium,' Orpheus says. 'Then they'll do a blood test to check I haven't used Nox for a month.'

They head out of the School of Sleep together, taking a different exit this time – near the canals and the cedar trees – so they can avoid the 'Vote No' protestors who congregate in the forum almost every day now. In spite of the distance, Orpheus can still hear them, the steady drum beat, the chant. Everyone is surprised that the police or campus security haven't cleared them out yet, but the rumour is that the Magi plan to address them sometime today.

'A month.' Zen lets out a low whistle. 'Sai must think you're a pretty desperate case.'

'It was that or lose my job.'

Orpheus feels humiliated. Ashamed at being caught, at letting his use get so far out of hand. He doesn't want to be an addict, but he doesn't want to stop using either.

'Maybe just for a bit?' Zen says.

'Maybe . . .' Though for as long as Orpheus remembers, his nightly routine has involved returning to his flat, eating some meagre dinner and then climbing into the bathtub to venture into the labyrinth and work on his map.

'I was so close.' He doesn't realise he's said it out loud.

Zen eyes him suspiciously. 'To what?'

'The other side.' Something about Sherif's scepticism has made Orpheus want to confide in someone else about the work he's doing. 'There is a labyrinth in every dream and I've heard a theory that there is a portal in the middle of it.'

'A portal to where?' Zen asks.

'I don't know, but I believe it.'

'Why?'

Orpheus hesitates but then says, 'Because I saw it.' The night his heart stopped, and the doctors wrenched him back from the dead. He'd been in the labyrinth then, right in the deepest part of it, about to pull open the door. Behind him, a frenzied crowd had been shouting his name. Orpheus believes that's why he feels so at home in Dreamtime, because he's been to the other side before, glimpsed the sacred blackness, and now he wakes every day sick with longing for it. He wants to know if he can touch it and come back.

Zen looks concerned now. 'Orpheus,' she says, 'this sounds kind of alarming. Pseudoscience . . .'

'You don't believe me.' His shoulders slump in disappointment.

'Of course I don't,' she says. 'You know that heavy Nox use can sometimes lead to this kind of thinking . . . obsessive, magical . . .'

'You don't understand,' Orpheus hisses. It's a mistake, he shouldn't have told her. Though he wishes that she might see him the way he sees himself: a maverick, an adventurer. A cartographer of Dreamtime. The same kind of courage as Sir Francis Drake or Captain James Cook. 'I'm close to . . . something.'

'Maybe. But is it worth losing everything to find it?' Zen asks.

'I don't have anything to lose,' he says.

In spite of the heat of the day, cool air wafts up the path by the canal. The lights of the electric boats flick across the skin of the water. The campus is already slipping into penumbral shadow. Seems like yesterday when the sky was still iron-clad, the trees naked and bright. Now the last of the apple blossoms are dissolving. The smell of horse-chestnut overtaken by the scent of cut grass and the wilder things that are permitted to flourish by the edges of the canals. Orpheus can't imagine what he'll do with his days if he's not working and he's not allowed to use

Nox. The expanse of time that yawns before him seems almost frightening.

As they get closer to the school's entrance, Orpheus notices a hush around them. A quiet sweeps over the voices, in the air and on their Pulses. Zen and Orpheus turn in the same direction to see a rare sight, Hayden Adeyemi, Bertram Fairmont and Professor Itō, walking through the grounds together. The crowds part in stunned waves around them, while they're having a silent conversation over the Panopticon. They're going to the forum to speak to the protestors, Orpheus guesses, as it's been rumoured they might. Is it Orpheus' imagination, the way that the light seems to bend around them?

They won't be around for much longer, Zen says to Orpheus.

'What?' he whispers out loud.

We heard today that Professor Itō is finally going to do it.

All three of the Magi have publicly promised for years that when the time is right they will put themselves into a cryogenic sleep. Lots of people do it, Silicon Valley billionaires, Scientologists and Formula One drivers, a hedge against death, a hope that they may be revived in the future, when the technology exists to cure them or to upload their mind onto some server.

'Is it even legal in this country?' Orpheus asks. 'Don't they have to go to Switzerland or somewhere to do it?'

'I think it's a grey area. Legally.'

'I know that Itō is kind of old, but I always thought Bertram didn't believe that he could die,' Orpheus says, thinking back to a TED talk he delivered a few years ago about 'living long enough to live forever'. He is famously germaphobic, and currently adheres to an intensive regime of intermittent fasting and stem-cell injections, all to stave off the inevitable.

'It's not like dying,' Zen says, 'it's not euthanasia. She describes it like pressing the "pause" button. On all her bodily processes. And ... there are rumours ...'

'What?'

'A cancer of some kind, a few months to live.'

Orpheus examines the professor again. The three of them are all dressed the same way, in white trousers and a shirt with a monk's collar, bare feet. According to the Panopticon the professor is almost sixty. She's probably the most likeable of the three of them, because of her high-profile philanthropic endeavours. The Jitsuko Itō Foundation has reportedly almost vanquished dementia in the global South.

Young, he thinks, to die. Although his own father had been forty-five, a number branded into his mind. And, of course, like millions before her, Professor Itō doesn't believe that death is the end.

Orpheus is startled to see, then, that she's looking right at him. Her dark eyes finding his, in the shade of the cedar trees. And then, with the synchronisation of a school of fish, all three of them turn to him. Orpheus feels the heat rise in his face; they're walking towards him now. What to do? It's hard to resist the unfamiliar urge to bow or genuflect, as he might before a priest or a bodhisattva. Like Thomas Edison or Tim Berners-Lee, their visions have already changed the course of civilisation. How do you greet people whose faces deserve to be carved into the mountains of history?

At first, Orpheus thinks that Professor Itō is reaching out a hand for him to shake, but then she touches him. Her cool palm on his cheek. Orpheus closes his eyes.

You look just like him, she marvels, her voice like a cool wind in his consciousness.

Orpheus opens his eyes then, and examines her.

You knew him? he replies in his mind.

They only smile.

12

MOREMI

For a while, she is different. As she hoped she'd be. It's as if the sun has risen in between her ears, some tectonic plates in her psyche have shifted and everything is filtered, now, through a rosy light. Her worries and insecurities dissolve. The sky is changed, the city, everyone's faces. It'll be okay, she thinks, and believes it for the first time. I will be.

'Most people don't remember the dream,' the psychiatrist tells her.

'I remember all of it,' Moremi says. The 'other side', the dreamscaper had called it. A real place, a real place where her mother is alive. After the recollection therapy, Moremi's heart is set fire with a new kind of hope. A joy that comes from being within touching distance of what she's always wanted.

'I want to go back.'

The woman smiles understandingly. 'Some people do, at first.' She repeats what all the nurses and counsellors have been saying. 'The lovely thing about this therapy is that, like a good holiday, you have something to hold on to. In just a little while, the memories of the specifics will fade – as we have programmed them to – and you'll be suffused with an all-round contentment that will carry you through.'

'But what if I don't want the memories to fade?' Moremi asks.

'It's important that they do,' says the doctor, tapping the discharge form on her console.

Seized by a sudden panic, Moremi says, 'Please ...' She's surprised to find that her heart is pounding. 'I saw my mother. My grandparents. I saw a world where they're alive. Where they're happy. I was happy ...' Don't let me go, she wants to say.

'You could be in a high-risk group,' says the doctor, like a verdict. Shaking her hand free, she makes a mark on the discharge form, then explains, 'This says that you are forbidden from any kind of recollection procedure for the next eighteen months. It's for your own good. Habit-forming happens to every one in two hundred patients, maybe. They get fixated on the dream and it distracts them from real life.' They had mentioned something like this to her when she signed the waiver.

'I just want to dream one more time. That's all,' Moremi says, feeling breathless, dizzy. 'I just want a chance to say goodbye to my mother. I didn't get to in real life.'

The doctor smiles sadly. 'That's what you say now. But another treatment will only make that worse. Recollection is just a helping hand, not a substitute. You're still going to have to face your future without her. And you're going to have to be gentle with your heart and learn to heal.'

'But . . .' Moremi doesn't hear what the doctor says, and absent-mindedly repeats, 'I didn't get to in real life.'

'That's just the thing,' she says. '*Real* life.'

After Moremi is discharged from the School of Sleep's treatment centre, Halima and Zeeba come to pick her up. They sign the discharge papers and head home together in a taxi. Her sisters keep asking her, delicately, as if they're afraid they'll startle her, how she is feeling. Moremi probes in her mind for where the thorn used to be, the way she used to probe the bloodied inside of her mouth in the weeks after her wisdom teeth were removed. Wondering, is it still there? Does it still ache?

'You look a little different,' Zeeba says. Moremi can see her eyes in the dark square of the taxi's rear-view mirror.

'Really?' she asks. Central London flies past the window. 'How?'

Zeeba only shrugs. Their eyes meet in the glass and she glances quickly away. Zeeba looks like a witch. She has painted her lips oil-black, wears a plastic choker, an ear full of piercings; she has a sceptical, mutinous look in her eye. She's saved most of the money from her part-time job to cover the school fees for her fine-art summer school, and now, whenever Moremi sees her, she has little speckles of ink or paint under her nails or across her shirt. Zeeba says, 'Does it feel the way you hoped it would?'

'I don't know yet,' Moremi says.

There are a couple of Legacy Party branded adverts flaunting across the walls of the bus shelters and tube stations. There is an image of a woman sleeping soundly, with her front door wide open. 'Total Adoption will bring Total Security,' it promises. 'Vote YES on July 29th.'

'Recollection therapy is nothing to be too nervous about,' Halima says. 'Zen thinks that they will be offering it to everyone soon enough.'

'They create the sickness, they sell the cure,' Zeeba says.

On Westminster Bridge there is a three-metre holo-gram of their prime minister, Stella Stratton. A kindly giant with her blue eyes like cushion-cut diamonds, jet hair chopped in a lopsided pixie-cut that reveals the constellation behind her ear. Apparently, in real life she is not very tall. Now, she is clenching her small fist and declaring, 'This government supports Total Adoption.' Moremi is about to remark on it, when she remembers that Zeeba can't see it. She can't see the holographic moons displaying lonely-hearts adverts, or the branded dolphins flinging their bodies out of the Thames in bright arcs of silver light; that group of women over there with cat faces and ears, Ronald McDonald on a flying saucer. Moremi feels distantly sorry for her. She can't see their mother again.

There is a certain pride that comes from wanting some-thing impossible and then getting it. Moremi finds it hard to describe to her sisters. For a while, she feels as if she can do anything, as if the universe will give her everything else that she wants, a stunning dance career, a loving family, to live forever. All she has to do is wait.

When she returns to her job as a pollinator, her mud-dusted colleagues, kneeling among the ragged patches of wildflowers, examine her from the corner of their eyes and say, 'You look a little different.' A couple of them start, the way that people do when they enter a familiar room and all the furniture has moved. Whenever she asks 'How?' they look embarrassed and shrug.

Does she look as if she's seen the curve of the Earth from space? Does she look as if she's swallowed a supernova?

Sometimes she stares at her reflection in the warped and shadowed mirrors in the Portaloos and tells herself, 'The difference is meat-space.'

For a while, she is not haunted by visions of the wave. Her heartbreak over Lionel fades into the dullest of aches and sometimes whole days go by and she doesn't think of his name at all.

But occasionally, an unfamiliar desire manages to pierce her contentment.

The difference is meat-space.

Sometimes her unconscious volleys bright flashes of the dream she'd had in the Panopticon and she wakes clutching her chest, her face wet.

'I'm scared of going back,' she explains to Zen over the Pulse. 'I don't want to be the heartbroken person I was before.'

'You'll never be,' Zen promises.

'How do you know . . .' Moremi bites her lip. 'If I could just . . . maybe if I could just go back one more time.'

'To the dream?'

'That's right. Maybe I need it just one more time to be properly healed. Healed forever.'

'Not recommended,' Zen says. 'The dream is only part of it. Now it's your job to go and live the better life.'

The better life, though, has begun to curdle somehow. Moremi begins to feel a stranger ache where the heartbreak had been. Something like lovesickness and something like homesickness. In the morning, the light through her bedroom window begins to taste of disappointment.

As the days pass, Moremi becomes convinced that she will only experience true happiness if she glimpses the dreamworld just one more time. Zen explains to her that if she has been flagged as 'high-risk' she will only be able to buy a dream illegally. So, Moremi asks a white-haired woman she works with for the details of someone who might do this for her. The woman tells Moremi that she knows a man who builds spellbinding dreams. 'You'll dream his dreams and die content.'

'That's all I want,' Moremi says.

'But I haven't talked to him in a few years. I'm trying to get straight.' The woman explains that she has quit Nox now and deleted Dreamtime off her constellation. For a while it took over her life. She re-mortgaged her house to buy dream after dream. 'I had to stop. Some people spend their entire lives chasing after them.'

But Moremi reassures herself, 'It's okay. I only need one. And then I'll be satisfied forever.'

13

ORPHEUS

Dreamtime. By the time he gets home, he's sick for it. A shutter comes down in his head and he's in the streets of Cairo, or a riad in Marrakech, a police station in Chicago. Then it lifts and he's on the London Underground. He almost misses his stop and has to race off just as the doors are closing.

The sun is still out, and as he trudges home he lists to himself the reasons he needs to quit Nox. His bosses want him to stop. His friends and colleagues, too. If he loses this job he'll likely go back to jail. And he really does care about this job.

As he takes the steps up to his apartment door, he remembers that when he lived on Angharad he could run for hours, but now walking for too long makes him breathless. If he didn't spend so much time dreaming he could build up his fitness.

The bathroom is another reason. The smell, by the time

he arrives, is vile. Vomit turned to sludge on the tiled floor, slicked down the side of the toilet, adrift in clotting floes inside the bathtub.

Orpheus cleans the room as the sun goes down, and by the end he's exhausted. Lies on his bed as sunlight scythes through his blinds, paring his muscles like a knife. His constellation notifies him that it's about to start a backup. Orpheus rolls over and looks at the backup quartz, mounted in its chassis at the far end of the bed. It's the most expensive thing he owns. The Panopticon offers one as a benefit to all its employees.

The first time he'd ever held a blank quartz had been in a biology class. He'd been taught, then, about the simple principles that underlie the technology. Teachers jokingly called them 'Superman memory crystals', a reference Orpheus has never really understood. They are made out of fused quartz, a kind of pure glass used for things like optical fibres or the windows of manned spacecrafts.

Quartz memories look a little like Morse code, a nanoscopic pattern of laser-printed dots. The laser encodes information in three spatial dimensions as well as two other dimensions – the polarisation of light and the wavelength that can pass through the quartz: 5D data storage.

Certain readable components in the hardware in his constellation may eventually fail or degrade, and all the connections between his neurons will finally weaken then die. But his quartz is a backup. Orpheus had been awed to discover that the quartz's structure is likely to remain stable for billions of years. He imagines the world in a century or seven, his thoughts playing on a loop in the darkened corner of a museum somewhere. What kind of world would it be? A thought that always strikes dread in his chest. Scorched to rubble by environmental disaster? Populated by Hayden's vision of transcended beings, post-Singularity? Or, in some of his more pessimistic imaginings, Orpheus pictures Neanderthal creatures, unable to decipher the stacks of quartz they uncover buried in the ground, using them like hammers to smash the bones of carrion.

It's so hot that it's nauseating and on the Panopticon, snippets of news reads: *Not only has 2050 brought the world's hottest ever spring, but yesterday countries from Belgium to the Netherlands to Germany have broken their all-time heat records. It has never been hotter in northern Europe. This extreme heat poses serious health risks as well as uncomfortable questions about how well Stella Stratton is preparing for these more frequent and severe heatwaves.*

When he opens his eyes, six hours have passed. It's 2am, dark outside, and his door buzzer is ringing. Orpheus rolls over, his foot tangled in a pile of his clothes, and wonders if he dreamed it. The other day, when he woke up he thought that he'd been clutching a handful of feathers. He'd been able to feel them, the sharp end of the hollow shafts buried in the softness of his palms, only he woke and opened his hands to find nothing there.

The ring comes again, and he shouts, 'Who is it?' Mrs Dulwich from downstairs complaining about a leak?

No answer.

'I'm coming.'

He heads downstairs, his body still heavy with sleep, and opens the door. It's so hot outside that he thinks he can see steam rolling off the pavement and, for a second, he's sure he's dreaming her. Moremi. The girl he met over a month ago. For a while, the thought of her stuck like a burr in his mind. He replayed the video of her facing down the crowd of shouting Revelators a couple of times and marvelled at her passion. For a few weeks, he couldn't enter an underground station without his dream-addled eyes glimpsing the wave in the forbidding darkness of a tunnel.

Her profile says: *Moremi, 20. Pollinator for Tavistock Agricultural Group.* There are bubbles that he could open up, listing education, known family, place of residence, but none of them will tell him what she is doing here.

'Um . . . hey?' He rubs his eyes, then searches hers for any sign she remembers him, although he knows she probably doesn't.

'Lazarus?' she asks.

'Who's asking?'

'I was told you could help me to . . .' She looks sheepish and says in his mind, *that I could buy a dream from you.*

I'm not selling, he says. Intrigued as he is to see her, he's in enough trouble at work at the moment and doesn't need to risk getting arrested for selling an illegal dream. But her face falls, and it's a sad thing to see.

'Look,' he says, letting some regret creep into his voice, 'I'll probably lose my job if I help you.'

'Orpheus,' she whispers as her eyes float up to his profile. He's fallen out of the habit of keeping it hidden, as he had when he worked in the Junkyard. She sees his name now, and he notices the glimmer of distant recognition in her eyes. Is she thinking about the brief moment, a few weeks ago, when their hands touched or the viral video of him waking up from the dead?

'I've done it once before,' she says, 'at the School of Sleep. I think it was the happiest I've ever been.' Orpheus can't help but shudder at these words. Should he tell her now? he wonders. Should he tell her that he's already glimpsed all the worst moments of her life? Dreamscapers at the Panopticon are advised to remain anonymous after the treatment.

'Why don't you just go back there, then? Do it the legit way?'

She hesitates, then says, 'They're worried I might get addicted to it.'

'Then they're probably right.' Orpheus reaches for the door knob to shut it but she lunges forwards to stop him. They're close then, on either side of the threshold, and he can smell the papaya in her lip balm, sweat and body spray. The longing in the dark jewels of her eyes.

'Please,' she says. And it's so hard to say 'no' that Orpheus has to make himself look away from her. 'I used to have this pain.' She tugs at the collar of her top as if it's there, inside her chest. He could touch his own chest too; he knows the landscape of his own pain so well. 'I used to think that if I could get past it, I'd have a good chance.'

'A chance at what?'

'At living a good life. Finding love. Being happy. Getting a good job.'

209

'Isn't that what they "fixed",' Orpheus asks, 'at the School of Sleep, didn't it help you?'

'Sort of,' she says, 'I don't know. My mother died, the day of the flood.' Orpheus knows this, of course. Remembers the moment Moremi heard about the death, remembers the way that Zeeba had screamed. 'I think if I could see her just one more time I could be happy.'

'That's how it starts,' Orpheus says. He doesn't want her to leave but he can't help thinking of Sherif. The way that the dreamworld took over his life for years. If he helps her he will have to use Nox one last time.

'I know this probably doesn't matter to you, but I'm a dancer. At least, I want to be, and I'm worried that if I don't get better and stay better, I'll never make it. Especially if I can't manage an audition without breaking down.'

Orpheus already knows that she's a dancer. Searching her memories during the procedure he had seen constant daily flashes of it. The mirrored dance studios and church halls, herself at five, seven, sixteen, holding the back of a kitchen chair like a barre. Peeling the calloused skin off her toes, breaking in bronze satin pointe shoes, every votive candle she ever lit in faithless desire. But her words pique his curiosity. He only knows what it feels like from inside her head; he'd love more than anything to see her dance in real life.

As Orpheus stares back at her, the motion-sensitive lights in the hall of the apartment block click off, plunging them both into darkness. He can hear her quiet breathing. The whites of her eyes flicker and she says in his mind, *Maybe there's something I can do for you?*

'Okay,' he says, as Herod might have for Salome. 'I'll help you, if you dance for me.'

She turns away from him and when she heads back into the road, he thinks – with a tug of despair – that he'll never see her again. It's 2am, as quiet as anywhere ever is at this hour in London. But then she turns and raises her hands to set a filter that he accepts. The cracked pavement becomes the black-ice surface of a stage. The streetlamps are spotlights and behind her are ghost dancers. The curtain is drawn. Orpheus watches as it rises, and an imaginary orchestra starts to play. Already captivated.

She is in the centre of the stage; she raises her arms and begins to dance.

Orpheus sits on the hot stone step in the front of his apartment block as she dances a part from a ballet of *The Bacchae*. At the climax of the dance, she tears her son limb from limb. Her holographic corps members spin around her like shadow puppets. In the dance, she is a maenad, manic initiate of the cult of Dionysus, the god of the grape-harvest and winemaking, ritual madness and religious ecstasy. Orpheus is shocked by the sight of her. On the street a moment before, in her leopard-print leggings and crop-top, plain and strange, but now she is dazzling, now she is setting the imaginary stage on fire in a virtuosic *pas de deux*. God-crazed ballerina, given over to her wildest instincts. The translucent maenads riot across a moonlit glade, pulling bones from flesh, dressed in fox-skins and bull-helmets, mouths wet with blood in mad celebration. They are like witches, wild with delight:

one breast-feeds a wolf cub, another sinks her fingernails into the mud and milk bubbles out.

Moremi is playing the role of Agave, the mother of the King of Thebes, driven mad by Dionysus when her son refuses to worship him. In the hologram Moremi is crowned with ivy vines, in a flesh-coloured dress, dancing the wild dance of the maenads. Orpheus can barely watch the climax of the ballet when the women of Thebes descend on King Pentheus. In their madness they believe that he is a lion. He dances a frantic *pas de deux* with Moremi, his eyes pleading, hoping for her to see him. It's the most tense moment. Is that a flicker of recognition in her eyes? No. She grabs his elbow, pushes her heel into his ribs and wrenches his arm from its socket. The orchestra swells, echoing the howls of his torment. Which is when the other maenads descend on him in fury, tearing at his flesh. They process into the city, his head on a thyrsus, present him to her father Cadmus and it is only then that Agave's eyes are unclouded. Only then that she sees, to her horror, what she's done. Orpheus cries with her when he watches it. And when the curtain falls at the end he feels terrified and in love.

He discovers that what she can do – casting spells with her dance – is no different from what he loves to do in Dreamtime. By the time she stops, bows, and the stage and the proscenium and the other dancers vanish, he is dumbstruck.

How can he tell her to leave now? Orpheus knows that if he lets her go, then night after night, for the next few weeks, he will wake thinking that he is Pentheus, those dancers tearing him limb from limb. He might wake up with her name in his throat, clenched with desire.

As soon as she stops, he wants her to do it all over again.

But she's in pain, he realises now, from the way that she's wincing. He runs forward and asks if she's okay, and when he approaches he realises that she has tears in her eyes. 'Did you sprain something?'

'I fell down some stairs a few weeks ago and this is the longest I've danced for a while.' She lets herself drop heavily onto the edge of the pavement and nurses a swollen ankle, darkened with old bruises. 'I've been taking it a bit easy with practice,' she says, then adds, 'Not that it matters.'

'Why doesn't it matter?'

'Because I'm starting to lose hope that I'll ever be a dancer anyway.'

After a while of assessing her injuries, she gets up, leaning heavily on the rusted banister, a few steps below him. Her face is beautiful now in the streetlamp light. 'Orpheus, you never get anything that you don't have to fight for.' Her eyes burn with determination. 'I know that you don't owe me anything. But I want to make a good way in this world. I want to be calm and creative. I want to be a famous dancer. I want to be a good sister. I feel selfish saying it, I know that not everyone gets everything they want in this life. But I want love. I want enough money to feel safe. I want to wake up every morning in a house and hear the sound of all my family, laughing. I never want to be alone. I don't want to lose anything that matters. I want to be pleasantly warm every single day. I want a mother.

213

I want mangos for breakfast every morning. I want to live forever.'

Orpheus can't help but smile, surprised, awed. It was this assertiveness that had drawn him to her in the first place. 'You know,' he admits to her, 'I can't give you a single thing that you want.'

'But maybe,' she asks, and this time he already knows that he will say 'yes', 'you can give me this one thing?'

14

MOREMI

He's a dream-thief, she reminds herself. A criminal. It only occurs to her to feel nervous when he steps back and invites her in. He lives in the attic of a townhouse split into four flats. There is a glamorous but dingy corridor, marble chequerboard tiles underfoot with one flickering bulb swinging above the landing. She follows him up the winding stairwell, three flights up to a painted black door, which is open.

'Sorry about the mess,' he mutters, kicking aside a pile of shoes to hold the door open for her to enter. Moremi is surprised that he lives in such an ordinary-looking flat.

It's a one-bedroom with an open-plan kitchen, a living room. It looks as if it was decorated in the 1990s with vividly patterned but sun-faded drapes on the windows, an airless dusty smell, the tang of food going off, a scent that is so common in the summertime. Fruit imploding in a chipped ceramic bowl, leftover takeaway on the counter furred with mould.

'It's not what I expected . . .' she admits.

'Everyone expects hackers to live in the future. Clean apartment blocks or anonymous hotel rooms. No finger-prints on anything.'

'Kind of,' she smiles.

'I don't make that kind of money anymore.'

Orpheus steps into a subway-tiled bathroom on one end of a narrow corridor and switches on the tap.

'All I can give you is one hour,' he says.

'What?' Moremi gasps. She'd been hoping for at least a day with her mother.

'One hour in Dreamtime. Outside the maze, that's about ten hours in meat-space.'

'But I've heard of people who spend centuries in Dreamtime,' Moremi says.

'An hour in our world gives you a couple of minutes on the other side. That's the same for everyone unless you get lost in the labyrinth, where time slows.

'Be careful not to. People die in the labyrinth. Or get stuck for centuries and come out addled. The layout of this dream should be the same as your last one, so you shouldn't get lost. Have you eaten in the past few hours?'

'Not much.'

'Good,' says Orpheus, plucking his socks off, his voice echoing off the walls. 'It helps to do this on an empty stomach.'

She follows him into the first bathroom. With its brightly lit displays and computer screens, the place reminds her of the nurse's office where she first had her Pulse implanted. 'We don't need any of these things really,'

Orpheus tells her, noticing her trepidation. 'All we really need is this.' He touches his head.

A moment later, he vanishes and then appears again, holding a tin bucket filled with ice. He leans across her and says, 'Watch out,' before he lets an avalanche of ice crash into the tub.

'It needs to be cold,' he explains, 'cools your core temperature. Dreamtime is probably the most taxing program that your Pulse can run. Think of old consoles, if they ever tried to run a game or something complicated they would heat up, and slow down. That's not the kind of thing you want happening to your constellation. Especially considering how close it is to your brainstem. The ice lowers the risk of Pulse failure.'

'Where will you be?'

'Over there.' He tilts his head towards the open door of the utility room, where more computers are set up around a blow-up paddling pool.

Orpheus (95.162.154.38) requests quartz access.

The message flashes before her eyes in blue, along with a couple of different bubbles specifying the level of access.

Moremi pauses, bites her lip and steps back from him. Outside the moon is high in the sky and the street is quiet. She could still leave.

'I can't do this unless you let me.'

'I know.' Moremi's mouth is dry. His face softens in sympathy. *You can trust me.*

'It's simple, look, I'll share some memories with you.'

'Okay. You mean, through Pulse-pairing?'

'For a minute, maybe.'

217

'I've never done that before,' Moremi says, though she is curious to try. He smiles. Then reaches out his hand to share access with her. After another moment of hesitation, Moremi accepts it.

The feeling of another mind is stranger than anything else. Stranger than waking up to the Panopticon for the first time. Something like déjà vu, a rushing of memories into her quartz, and something like waking up from a dream in another body. Looking around the house and thinking, 'Oh yes, there is the hall I've walked up a hundred thousand times before. That familiar wall with its asymmetrical pattern my eyes can't help but follow at 2am, jittery from too much coffee.'

How does it feel to remember being someone else? Moremi has the strange sense that she once wore his body. Those arms, her arms, stomach cramp, wisdom toothache, constant low hum of fatigue. She'd once watched the world from behind those eyes. Watched her father die.

Moremi touches her face and feels that her cheeks are wet.

'Ah.' Orpheus reaches for his temple with a wince of pain.

'What happened?' Moremi asks. As soon as they begin talking, the distance widens. She remembers that she's only ever been in one body. Moremi.

Was it her father who abandoned her in a forest she's never been to? She thinks that she was aged eleven and he told her to figure out how to make her way home using nothing but a compass and her own wits, turned her around, made sure she was lost. Left her for two days.

'Did he really do that to you?' Moremi asks. Orpheus' eyes are still squeezed shut in pain.

'He said one day I'd need to know how to make it home.' Orpheus grits his teeth and swears.

'Are you okay? Are you in pain?'

'I haven't done it for a while.' He shakes his head. 'I forgot how it feels.'

'You're used to going into other people's heads.'

'Not the other way around.' Orpheus waves a hand and breaks off the connection. As soon as his quartz stops pairing with hers she sees his shoulders visibly relax. The tension in his face vanishes and he takes a deep breath.

And then another flicker of his memories comes back to her and Moremi says, 'You've done this to me before.' She feels wrong-footed and tricked. All this time he'd been pretending that he didn't know her. That he hadn't already seen into her head. Seen the worst days of her life.

'I'm not supposed to tell you.' Orpheus winces. 'Dreamscapers in the School of Sleep are supposed to remain anonymous to their patients.' Moremi is not sure how to feel. Should she storm off in anger?

'So, it was you?' It was Orpheus who had built that beautiful dream? That bright day, the transcendent music, everyone's beaming face. From his mind.

'Okay,' she says. 'I want exactly that, again. But this time, I want to be able to say goodbye to her.'

'Okay,' he agrees, still tense.

When his eyes meet hers something flashes between them. A spark of intimacy. She's seen inside his head, which has made her feel as if she's known him for years. Somehow she knows that he is aloof and mercurial, otherworldly. A picky eater; he likes to eat his pasta with no sauce, and his bread with no butter. The taste of cherry Pepsi makes him think of being fifteen. He likes to listen to atonal jazz composed by AI. He likes the dimples behind women's knees. He is not religious but he believes in ghosts. He's unnerved by cats. He's only loved one person in the world and he's frightened he'll never love another. He prefers sex in Dreamtime to meat-space.

Orpheus shudders as if he can still feel her probing his mind. He sets about flicking on the last of the machines, doing some final checks, suddenly businesslike.

'You need to get into the bath,' he tells her. She's not embarrassed about peeling off her shirt and leggings and getting into the bath in her underwear. But he gives her privacy anyway, and steps out for a moment.

She folds her clothes carefully and places them on the shut lid of the toilet. Catches a glance of herself in the full-length mirror behind the door, in her off-white bra with its twisted underwire. Frayed briefs that bunch up around her hips.

She knows better than to ease herself slowly into the freezing water, and plunges right into the bath with a shout of pain. Ice clatters against the side of the tub, the water sears her thighs and torso, heaves up over the porcelain lip and spills across the tiles.

Orpheus asks, 'Can I come in?'

'It's so cold.' Her voice is shallow, her lungs constricted by the ice.

He apologises and looks genuinely sorry for her pain. Kneels down on the bathmat at the edge of the tub and asks if he can take one of her hands. His skin is warm and sweaty.

'They probably talked you through Nox before they gave it to you the first time, right?' She nods. 'The nurses asked you all the questions? About allergies and heart conditions and being pregnant?' When she nods again he says, 'So you should be just fine.'

He ties a rubber band on her bicep and then taps her skin, searching for a vein inside her elbow. It often takes doctors a while, but he finds it quickly. She recoils a little just before the needle breaks the skin and looks up at him, seized by terror. He tries to tell her with his eyes that she can trust him.

'I'll give you everything you want,' he promises. 'On the other side.'

15

ORPHEUS

It's getting harder and harder for Orpheus to recover after sessions like these. He wakes dehydrated, somehow exhausted, and it takes over an hour after Moremi wakes for him to feel like himself again. Even then, her thoughts creep into his.

After the dream, Orpheus warms up some food for them, knocks on her bathroom door, and finds Moremi wrapped in a towel, her eyes glazed and distant. Sorrowful. Orpheus cannot shake the twinge of guilt that he feels looking at her. She is the picture of it; what a hollow, short-lived delight dreaming can be.

'Are you hungry?' he asks, and when she nods, he offers her an aluminium takeaway box. Glass noodles with tofu, which they ravenously devour, cross-legged on the bathroom floor.

It's afternoon outside. Though everything in Orpheus' body tells him it's 3am, the sun is still shining behind his makeshift blinds. It's a Friday. People are coming home from school, or late lunch meetings. Twelve hours have passed since they first met.

Every now and then Orpheus comes to an extra-sensory awareness of her mind, an eerie déjà vu-type feeling that the present moment has happened once before, but is running simultaneously next to him, a transient mental impression of himself eating noodles, a shard of pain between his eyes. Then it vanishes and they both freeze, chopsticks halfway to their mouths, and exchange a wary glance. It feels as if Orpheus has inadvertently brushed his mind against Moremi's. And each time it does, a starburst of memories erupts in his head. After her mother died she never grew another inch. He remembers weeks of falling asleep under Halima's floral-print duvet covers, breathing in the smell of her sister, waking up every time the bed was empty, with a pounding heart. Halima would appear silhouetted in the doorway on her way back from the toilet and each time Moremi would say with a razor-edge of panic in her voice, 'I don't like waking up when you're gone.' 'I only went to the toilet.' 'Just tell me when you're going and when you're coming back.'

'I am coming back,' Halima would say, the same way a mother might say *shhhh*. 'I'm always coming back.'

'I have this weird feeling,' Moremi says now.

It's the kind of intimacy that develops after having sex for the first time.

'You've seen my memories,' he explains. 'From behind my eyes. You do know me. Better than before, at least.'

'It's not just knowing though, it feels like . . .' *Love*. The

223

word darts into both of their heads at the same moment. Moremi bites her lip and winces.

There is a word that some programmers and psychiatrists use for what happens when people share dreams. 'Inversion Syndrome'. Orpheus imagines it feels like this. An awareness of the proximity of her, her light breathing, bathwater dripping down the side of her face, making the baby hairs at her temple curl.

'Can I kiss you?' he asks, and they reach for each other as if they've been lovers for years. The warmth of her lips on his makes his nerves ring like a tuning fork. He delights in everything about her, the sweetness of her tongue, the way that she buries her palm into his hair and pulls him close, breathes deeply through her nose, bites playfully at his lower lip.

It takes everything he has to pull himself away. One time he trapped his fingers in a lamp socket while it was still plugged in. It was the first and only time he'd ever been electrocuted and the feeling was terrifying. The vacuum pull of the electricity at his skin, the fight to free himself and then the way he felt after, as if every nerve in his body was a live wire.

Orpheus gets unsteadily to his feet and staggers back, leaning against the furthest wall, his eyes wild and confused. 'Sorry ...' he says, at the same time as she does. Sitting up, Moremi touches her lower lip in confusion.

Orpheus tries to remind himself that the attraction he feels to her is probably not real. It happens sometimes among people who share dreams. But then, he looks at her now, and she's almost too beautiful to bear.

'It's not real,' he tells her. And she nods in quiet agreement. The sound of the traffic in the street, pedestrians and commuters, wafts up through the half-open bathroom window. A good time for her to leave.

'I should ...' Moremi is already getting to her feet as well, looking around the room for where she left her clothes, folded on the lid of the toilet.

'I don't want you to go.' The words surprise him, but then he feels her relief. If she leaves he'll never see her again. 'You must be pretty tired.'

'Yeah,' she says. 'Funny thing how tired I am even though I've only just woken up.'

'Your constellation was working hard. Stay here,' and adds, 'Please. You can take the bed ... though it's a mess. I can sleep on the floor in the living room.'

She's still standing in her underwear. He can see in the afternoon light her dancer's body, stronger than his. The muscles in her thighs are taut as the string of an archer's bow, a dark film of skin ripples over her broad shoulders, biceps, delicate lovely hands. Through the soaked cotton of her bra he can see her nipples. A smile twitches at the edge of her wide mouth and he has the sense that she can feel his desire. The colour rises in his cheeks. With some effort he lowers his gaze to the floor.

'I'll give you a minute,' he says as he leaves the room.

Orpheus takes a pillow and a blanket into the living room and tries to fall asleep on the rug.

Hard to believe it's still daylight outside. Buses hiss and idle at the traffic lights. How can he sleep when he knows she's only in the next room?

He closes his eyes and tries to make himself. This has never happened to him before, though he knows enough people who hack and dream-share to be familiar with it. Inversion Syndrome. He'd been warned, when he started coding dreams for other people, that it happened to almost all dreamers at one point or another. The symptoms had been clearly defined to him: over-identification with another dreamer, intrusive obsessive thoughts about the dreamer. A certain balance of hope, an uncertainty. A kind of limerence that took a week or two to fade, during which time the sufferer was encouraged to avoid all physical contact with the 'love object', try to wean off Nox, to seek counselling, in less mild cases, or a short course of SSRIs.

When Orpheus closes his eyes, he dreams of her dancing again. God-crazed Agave, and he is Pentheus, being torn limb from limb. He wakes covered in sweat, thinking, *I'm in love with her,* when a sound on the threshold of the door attracts his attention.

Without turning around, he knows that it's her. He mustn't move. He doesn't have the will to tell her to leave but . . . he's distracted by the thought of her bare feet on his worn carpet. Padding towards him. He pretends to sleep.

'Orpheus?' He's already in love with the sound of his name in her mouth.

'It's not real.' He squeezes his eyes shut. 'It just feels real because—'

'We shared a dream.' She's beside him now. Her proximity a wild delight.

'This is a dream. In an hour or two, when we wake

up tomorrow, we'll be strangers to each other again.' But when she lies down, her leg hairs next to his feel like static electricity.

'Has it ever happened to you before?' she asks.

No, he thinks, but he says nothing.

When he opens his eyes, it's to a room flooded with clementine light. Her face is a few centimetres from his, her head on his pillow, the scent on the top of her head like warm bread, and sweet almond oil. It's not real. It's not real.

'When we wake up,' he says again, 'we'll be strangers to each other.'

'Then I'll never sleep again.'

It's midnight when he wakes, around eight hours later. It's dark outside and she is still asleep, illuminated by the thin light shafting in from the corridor. Her body is splayed carelessly across the rug, covers all but kicked off in the heat. She's only half-dressed, in leopard-print leggings. Lying on her side. He loves the mountain crescent where her pelvis meets her hip, a violin's bout.

He wants to lean over to kiss the dark bow of her mouth – her lips are sticky, teeth unbrushed and sour. But instead he tells himself to be responsible. Gets up and walks to the kitchen. Foil stalagmites of takeaway boxes are piled on the grimy counter. Discarded game of solitaire in the centre of the dining table. He'd hung a washing line up by the window and then forgot about it, boxers like chequered flags above his head. Everything tells the story of a life lived alone.

The Panopticon warns that tomorrow will be another

historically hot day with temperatures in some parts of the country expected to reach 45°C. The Met Office have renewed a heat warning for the whole of the United Kingdom, urging people to 'keep hydrated, find shade and take protection against the sun'. Schools are closing early. Some major sporting events have been cancelled. People are being advised against all but essential travel.

Orpheus grabs a tumbler and fills it to the brim with cherry Pepsi from the fridge. A floorboard creaks behind him as he drinks and Orpheus turns to find Moremi standing on the threshold, the flesh of her cheeks criss-crossed with the rumpled lines of the rug. He feels as if he hasn't seen her for years.

'You left me.' Her voice is tremulous.

'When?'

'Just now.'

Orpheus glances around the kitchen as if he's just noticed it. The fridge door is still half-open, panting cool, wet-smelling air into the room. The grimy table, the wrinkled cards scattered across it, the entire room, the scene of his crime.

'This heat . . . I was finding it hard to sleep.'

'I don't like it when I wake up and you're gone.' She says it as if this isn't the first night they've spent together.

'What?' he teases. 'Should I wake you up too?'

'Maybe . . .'

'Afraid of the dark?'

But when she looks up at him he realises that she really is afraid of something. She glances at the hall behind her, as if it's waiting for her there.

'Okay,' he says. The memory of the first night she spent in Halima's bed without her mother flashes into his mind again, and he says what he knows that her sister said. 'I'm always coming back.' He takes her hand. She examines it as if it's a possession she's lost that's been returned to her, subtly different.

16

Moremi

It almost always happens the same way for Moremi. Love comes to her like a vocation. A noble cause. How many times has she lain in bed next to a sleeping man, watched his lips, the wrinkled arrow of his cupid's bow, eyes flickering back and forth in REM, and determined to make him love her?

So it is with Orpheus, that night. Every time their eyes meet it's with a jolt. Every now and then his memories drift into her head like stray bars of music and they smile as if to a shared secret. But, in between, Moremi is struck by a more acute loneliness than before.

To overcome it she asks, 'Tell me three things you're afraid of.' In the kitchen, after the first night they spend together. When their fingers brush accidentally, her heart flutters. She stares down at his slender hand, at the tiny brown hairs under his knuckles. He has a tattoo on his wrist which reads, 'Is it true?' A few plastic bands, moon-shaped bruises at the crooks of his elbow.

'Do you know already?' he asks, getting up to rinse out two mugs in the sink. Although his memories are already evaporating the way almost all dreams eventually do, if she lets her mind clear, it might come to her. She closes her eyes like a psychic, letting the words float into her mouth. 'Fire. Asymmetrical holes. Dying alone,' she says. He looks coolly impressed, as if she's just picked his card from a shuffled deck.

'What am I afraid of?' she asks.

'Underground trains,' he says, searching around for a teaspoon but then settling on a fork. Moremi shifts uncomfortably in her seat just at the mention of it. 'The wave—'

'Stop,' she says, 'don't say it.' But he says it like a lot that's already been drawn.

'Dying alone.' And then a silence settles between them.

She suggests that she should leave and he says that he'll walk her. She is still staying at Halima's flat. And once they leave his place together she imagines the journey, the tube, the night bus, the walk by the unlit path along the river, glancing over her shoulder every time.

Somehow, Orpheus saves her from it. They take a sudden detour and find themselves wandering through the cobbled streets of Covent Garden, where it's a Saturday night and the roads are thronged with revellers. Moremi loves the city at this time of day, when all the dour commuters have returned to their homes or loosened their ties in pubs and turned out into the bars and restaurants in happy droves. This time of the night. As they head up to the kaleidoscopic streets of Seven Dials a car rides past, all the windows rolled down, blasting 90s hip-hop up the road. Summer heatwave air, sticky and unmoving, ripe with the smell of dustbins, the eggy breath of a sewer somewhere near. The thought of saying goodbye to him fills her with disappointment.

He says, 'I think I'll be heartbroken if I never see you dance again,' and they end up in a cocktail club with a tiny dance-floor. He's awkward at first, scared to embarrass himself, too aware of all his limbs. Lacing her arms around his neck, Moremi pulls him close and leads him with her hips. She can feel the sweat creeping down his neck, and he blushes, apologises. She rolls her tongue along the auricle of his ear and he shivers, falls quiet.

He's only a few inches taller than her and when he leans down to kiss her, her heart bursts with relief. He tastes of noodles and cherry Pepsi, sucralose and saliva. She holds him tight, savouring the desperate way he's clutching at her back, then thighs, breathing hard. She can feel his heart pounding as she tips his head back and pushes her tongue into his mouth. Teeth, smooth as piano keys.

The first boy Moremi ever loved had been a skinny kid called Holden Fraser, who lived in one of the fancy new-build apartments across the street. He was the son of two American Studies lecturers. Falling in love with him had felt like finding something that she'd misplaced in the flood. She'd lost her virginity to him under the Spider-Man duvet cover in his boyhood bedroom, his head haloed by glow-in-the-dark stars. She had thought that the act was all she'd ever wanted, to forget herself in someone else. He left her a week later, via a voice message on Vine. Moremi had collapsed right where she had been standing on the kitchen floor, cried so long with her face pressed against the sticky linoleum that her sisters took to stepping right over her prone body just to get to the fridge.

Zeeba had read her a passage from Plato's symposium about love. It had said that at the beginning of time lovers were a single creature, four-handed and two-headed. That vengeful gods had severed them apart, sentenced them to scour earth with their split selves sick with longing for their other half.

A fanciful notion, that Moremi has begun to suspect she actually believes, because whenever she decides to sleep with a new person she asks, 'Could it be you?' and they always say, as Orpheus says, 'Of course.'

They dance for an hour or two and then stumble out onto the street, laughing, their fingers locked together, both jittery and desperate, casting furtive glances at alleyways, behind shuttered stalls.

Finally they run up the Mall, where the Palace is dimly lit. They climb over the gates into St James's Park, which is almost frighteningly dark and utterly deserted. Rolling down the sun-warmed grass and into the shadow of an overhanging willow. Quiet ripple of water, as ducks pass like distant ships on the algae-choked pond. The air smells fertile and overripe, of pollen and water vapour, of grass turning to mulch in the heat, flower petals dissolving into puddles, the whole world tipping towards rot.

There are so many things that Moremi enjoys about sex. She likes the moment when she knows it's about to happen, the look in his eyes that says, 'Are you sure about this?' and her reply: pushing him onto his back and unzipping his jeans. She'll never say this out loud, but she likes the way that boxers smell, a faint scent redolent of her own body. The way that undressing someone else can feel like Christmas morning, unwrapping a gift that is no surprise at all.

It's one of those things that is totally nice, like stretching before an early morning dance class. As soon as he's inside her she thinks that every hour of her life she spends not doing this is a waste.

Moremi loves to believe that she is seeing the side of a person that few others see. That desperate gasp of his that no one else hears, that wrinkle between his brows, his nails in her thighs.

He tells her that he needs to look at her, leans up on his arms, so she's sitting in his lap, pulling his hips into her.

She'd once had a crush on a boy in the sixth form who'd left her for the blonde leader of the netball team. When she'd asked why, he'd told Moremi that 'her eyes are like the sky', as if to ask, 'How could anyone say "no" to the sky?' She'd said, '*My* eyes are like the sky.' Jet and star-strewn. Right now, Orpheus is staring as if he can find entire worlds in them.

'I'm ... ' he says breathlessly. Her favourite part. She could stop the Earth from turning just to hold on to the sight of his face. The sound he makes. The white icecaps of his teeth.

They come at the same time, staring into each other's eyes, and as soon as they do, Moremi doesn't want to be touched. Even the blades of grass under her thighs feel like nails.

'I want to stay inside you,' Orpheus says, plaintively. He wants to cling to her bones as he might to a wind-tossed raft, but she rolls onto the turf and sighs heavily, inadvertently breathing in the smell of their bodies, chlorine and fish, must and salt.

'Tell me everything about you, from the beginning,' she requests, even though she's already seen it from behind his eyes. 'I want to hear you tell it to me.'

And Orpheus begins with the day he was born on a beach. He tells her that he was raised on an island in the south of England, with no Pulse, no internet, barely any electricity. That when he came to London he was like an alien, still feels like one. Lonely and fatherless, a refugee. The only way he can get back home is in his dreams, where he spends most of his time. Dreamscaper, to Moremi, is a job that seems as magical as ballet dancer once did, astronaut, diver. He's made up his own constellations. As they lie on their backs he shows them to her until she's bent double laughing: the emperor of bees, the countess of marbles, the boy and the bullet shells. He explains that he will have to quit Nox for a while, and Moremi wonders if that is why he talks about Dreamtime with such lovesick longing. She wants to share some of his dreams, the ones of the island he grew up on, the ones where he painted his own sky. Moremi is awe-struck and enchanted, hearing about a place on the other side, where this man is a king.

'I'm an exile at the moment, though,' he says.

By the time the sun rises, she already knows that she is in love with him. They roll over in the grass, bone-tired and slightly delirious, dew sticking to the back of her calves. It's 5am and sunrise is pouring molten gold across the horizon. In an hour the park ranger will drive around in his buggy, and fine them for trespassing. So they vault the gate once more and stride up Pall Mall.

Moremi blinks. There are more cars on the road, more birds singing. This whole night with Orpheus a delicious dream from which she is horrified to wake.

'I should probably go,' he says, shaking grass off the back of his black T-shirt.

London looks the way it always does in the early hours of Sunday morning. As if a circus has blown in and out of town, and left everything behind. Bits of paper debris with the Golden McDonalds 'M' gusting along gutters, gummy starbursts of vomit next to bus shelters. As they round the corner at Piccadilly Circus, driverless taxis lurch past staggering women. A group of girls with neon glitter dripping down their cheeks hold their middle finger up at one of the cars.

'Look where you're going! Bloody car almost killed us.' It's hyperbolic, of course, there have been no car accidents in the capital for years. There are a pair of stilettos on top of a recycler near Piccadilly Circus, and the oversized television screens above them rain down pixellated light.

By the time they get to Soho, Moremi can tell that Orpheus is tired and is looking for a polite way to suggest it's time to part. They stop outside a club, still disgorging throngs of teenagers. Girls in leather miniskirts negotiating for an Uber. A hen-party, the bride-to-be singing, her tissue-paper veil flapping behind her head as she sways.

Moremi is so sleep-deprived that she feels drunk,

and the surrounding atmosphere of uninhibited revelry encourages her to ask, 'Stay with me?' What she means is 'Come home with me?' For some reason she says, 'Marry me?'

Orpheus is checking the bus timetable, but turns to her with a smile. 'Are you serious?' he asks.

'I don't want to be alone,' she tells him. Already it feels like a bad idea. She will never see him again. Well done, Moremi, you creep.

'Does anybody?' he asks her.

Rose-gold skin, lips purple as boysenberries. 'Marry me?' she asks him again.

'Okay,' he laughs, as if this is the funniest thing he's heard for ages. And she, flushed and surprised by his answer, can only stare.

The spell is broken; a few stragglers leaning against the window of a boarded-up sex-shop break into happy applause. A six-foot man in drag blows them a glittery kiss and shouts, 'Give us a snog, then!'

The onlookers think that the whole thing was staged, the couple in the middle of the road, waiting for a night-bus, the proposal. They are just happy to be part of it, even the bouncer outside the closing club, compulsively checking his watch. Even the couple sharing a kebab on the doorstep of an off-licence.

'Okay,' Orpheus says again, as if encouraged by all the witnesses. 'Okay, let's get married.'

And as he leans down to kiss her she wonders, *Will it happen? Should it be this easy?* As soon as they part, the laughter fades. His mouth is cold. She'd read somewhere that mothers can taste it, in the salty sweat on their baby's brows, that they will die young. She thinks that she can too, on Orpheus. Immediately, she wonders at the premonition. Perhaps she is just uncomfortable because he was won too quickly. She does not know yet that this is the story she will be asked to tell again and again. Their origin story. She will leave out the failed audition and the fall, the hospital stay, her healing bones. But never the dream he gave her. Never staying out all night, her flash-of-madness proposal.

By the time they board the bus, her life before him is already an event horizon. This is the day that her life begins. It begins with Orpheus.

17

ORPHEUS

On the way to the registry office two days later, Orpheus lists, in his head, everything he hates about himself. That he's never kept a promise in his life. If he had to choose between his own suffering and another's he would always choose another's. He never keeps appointments, he can never wake up on time. Two of his back teeth are threatening to fall out. He's a twitcher, a loner, a flake.

He can taste bile in the back of his throat. It's the middle of the day and all but the most foolhardy are indoors sheltering from the sun. A warning flashes in the corner of his Pulse, telling him that it's 43 degrees. Seek shade, it tells him. Lower core temperature. But they have two more stops until they reach the town hall and Orpheus cannot tell if the nausea he feels is entirely because of the heat or because he hasn't used Nox now for quite a few hours.

This is the longest he's been without for over a year and

his head feels as if it's gripped in a tightening vice. One of his hands is shaking, he squeezes it into a fist and plunges it into his tracksuit pocket, wills himself not to vomit.

They get off the tube at King's Cross station. And emerge onto the bright street to a hectic road that feels hotter than usual, the tart smell of petrol on the air. The town hall is across the road from St Pancras station and the gorgeous gothic revival hotel that makes him think of Harry Potter.

'This is the place where my parents got married,' she says as they enter through the revolving door into a shadowed hall facing a grand marble staircase. 'I can imagine my sisters standing up there, or maybe over there, throwing confetti or something. Do people still do that?'

It's like a joke that's not funny anymore, he thinks, this entire plan. But she takes his hand and smiles at him. Moremi looks as if she's stepped right out of the pages of a picture book, dressed for the heatwave in a sports bra and a pair of his trousers, using the only tie that he owns as a belt. There is a dewy sheen of sweat on her forehead, yesterday's make-up, sticky grit around her eyes. It would be crazy to actually marry her. She's nineteen, a child-bride, and she looks even younger than that, with her lithe dancer's body, ripple of abs under the lining of her bra-strap. It would be crazy to marry her, but the thought fills them with a foreign giggly hopefulness. It occurs to Orpheus that it would be easy to grab the reins of his life and steer it suddenly, recklessly, in an utterly different direction. This easy.

'Let's do it,' he says.

It turns out that Britain is not like the movies – they are told they will have to 'give notice' and then wait twenty-eight days to get married. Their names will be displayed in a public place during that time, and after the interview with the registrar, they watch as their names appear on the console in the waiting room under 'notices of marriage'. Moremi notes that, 'It's pretty old-fashioned that they ask for only your father's name and profession.' Neither of them have fathers.

They have to take part in an interview, together at first, giving their addresses and dates of birth, but then apart, between themselves and the registrar. Moremi goes first. During that time Orpheus passes through the corridor of the town hall, the sound of water coolers and air-conditioning. The news playing very low on a television somewhere. A couple waiting as if in a doctor's office, both of them in suits, to go into one of the suites to get married. The whole time he reminds himself, *This is the right thing.* It's not a head decision. It's intuitive.

And then Moremi emerges and it's his turn. His hands are shaking. The sun is streaming in through a crack in the blinds and he wonders if the registrar can see right through him. 'You do weddings every day, don't you?'

'We sort of rotate around,' says the woman. Whatever that means. She is West Indian, middle-aged with hair in tiny dreadlocks. 'Keeps things interesting.'

'Can you tell who will be happy?' he asks.

She looks up from her console and shakes her head. 'Every love story is a tragedy.'

*

By the three-lane highway outside, Moremi bursts out laughing. Laughing like someone who's just hung up after a prank phone call. 'We really did it,' she shouts, and she has to hold her stomach, she's shrieking so much. When she gets her breath she tells him about the time all the children in her year group had to line up for the HPV injection. Describes the clutch of nerves in her gut as one by one they all emerged from the nurse's office in tears. And then her turn came and, when the needle finally broke the surface of her skin, the laughter that erupted sounded like marbles she'd accidentally spilled. 'We're really going to do it.'

Orpheus tries to smile, but he's seeing double. All of a sudden his diaphragm pings like an elastic band, and he has half a second to rush to the open mouth of the recycling bin before he retches all over it.

'Orpheus?' Her voice is coming from far away, stars spotting his vision. A hand on his back. More sickness. His whole body shaking.

'Is he alright?'

'Look at his hair, he's a fucking twitcher.'

The ground lists under him.

'Orpheus!'

Hot concrete meets the side of his face.

When he opens his eyes, the first thing he sees is the mosaic pattern on his bathroom tiles. He comes to in an empty tub, smelling of sick. And she is asleep on a towel on the floor. Her eyes flutter open when he stirs and it's dark outside.

'I put you in the tub so you wouldn't be sick any-where else.'

Orpheus could cry with shame. His fingers are sticky, his hair matted. How could anyone ever love him?

'You don't have to stay,' he says.

'I know.' She rolls over on the towel like a sunbather on a beach.

'It's something I hate about myself,' he admits, looking away. 'I can't stay in meat-space.'

'I'd stay in Dreamtime too if I could,' Moremi says. She lifts up her arms to rest her hands behind her head, revealing a soft fuzz of armpit hair. Her dark eyes trace patterns along the ceiling and she says, 'I think I used to really think that things in life would work out for me.'

Orpheus tries to get up but simply putting his weight on his elbows makes his head feel like a fishbowl. Something like the worst hangover he's ever had. He relaxes back against the cool porcelain, letting his eyes lose focus.

Everything is different with her in it. This entire house, he thinks. That empty jam-jar on the tiles that she's been using as a coffee mug. The springy short hairs in the pile of the bathroom rug, the way that she hums the opening bars of 'Thriller' to herself when he walks up the hall. If she leaves now, he'll be undone.

'Something I hate about myself . . .' Moremi offers, then holds a hand out in front of her. He'd have to be blind not to notice the dark ridge of scars running up her forearms, a hundred tree rings, a dozen orchid vines. Moremi tells him that she wears a long-sleeved leotard or applies heavy make-up to them before a performance or an audition.

He's seen that she's carved the word 'LOVE' into her thigh. When her first boyfriend left her, she scratched the name Holden Fraser on the soft skin on the inside of her forearm. It's mostly faded now, so it looks more like the words 'HOLD FAST' are etched into the half-healed palimpsest of cut skin.

'There was a time I'd do it every day. I'd get into sort of a loop. It's not as if I'd decide to do it when the day began but then something bad would happen and I would ... There are lots of things people don't understand about it. It's not the same as wanting to kill yourself. It's just ... it's doing what everyone else does, you know. Coping the best we can.'

'How did you stop?' he asks.

She smiles ruefully and says, 'I think I'm coming to realise that the journey is not like ...' She traces a finger up, up. 'It's more like ...' Wild loops, turning back on themselves, dead-ends, false starts, a maze.

Is it naive to think that love could fix either of them?

As dawn begins to flush the sky, Moremi tells him about her plan for 'radical togetherness'.

'You know that's the school where Kimiko works?' Orpheus says.

'Yes, I like the phrase. It sounds like "perfect love", a good plan. A way to make our marriage last.' She explains that their marriage can be the third thing, they can build it together. 'My great-aunt lived until one hundred and two and she was married for eighty years. She and her husband went everywhere together, their desks faced each other. They were never sarcastic. They never lied. They took care to be kind, never called each other names, even in an argument. My mum says that if they were eating with the family and her husband made a point she would rest her chin on her palms and stare at him, fascinated. Even if she'd heard the story a hundred times before. And she'd heard every single one of his stories. All his memories were her memories. They would say to each other every morning, until they died, "I'm happy I married you."'

Orpheus is enchanted by the idea. He wants to turn his life around and maybe he can't hope to do it alone. Her vision becomes his vision. He pictures them at thirty, making snow angels, at fifty, carving their names into love locks. It's a happy, new dream. One he can make come true.

'I'm never going to look back,' he promises. 'Moremi.' Her name is earthy: coffee grounds, a secret river, clay pots fired in solitude. He tells her that he's in love with her and when she says it back he realises that he will never grow tired of hearing it. The way it's impossible to tire of hearing any true thing.

Someone in the world loves him. He should give up everything and just be with her. What if that's all the universe ever asked of him? Not to live a thousand lives in Dreamtime, but to find this one love, to live this one life and die content?

18

MOREMI

Watching him withdraw from Nox is frightening enough to make her never want to use it again. The first two weeks are the worst. She'll leave in the morning for work and return, scared of what state she'll find him in. Bone-pale in bed? Or curled up on the bathroom floor? Or, worse, comatosed in the tub, surrendered to Dreamtime?

A couple of days after they meet, Halima calls, panicked she hasn't seen her sister in a couple of days.

'I've met someone,' Moremi tells her.

'Oh,' she says, with all the tension of a nervous person bracing for a transatlantic flight.

'It's different this time,' Moremi promises, but Halima doesn't sound convinced. 'I'm going to marry him.'

'Isn't that what you said about Lionel?'

Moremi feels so separate from her old heartbroken self that she says, 'Who?'

Everything is a distraction: work, her sisters, the

246

referendum – she would much prefer to spend every hour in his flat, eating ice, ordering takeout and having sex. She is thrilled by every new thing she learns about him: that he likes to sing to himself in a dulcet falsetto when he thinks no one can hear, that he's fluent in seven languages, even though, thanks to the Pulse, almost no one learns new languages anymore. He likes to play chess, but if it looks for a moment as if he might lose, he'll be stonily silent for the rest of the day.

Sometimes she catches him standing in the bathroom, staring at the maps of labyrinths he drew on the mirror, and she knows he's homesick for Dreamtime. 'You told me not to let you use Nox,' she'll say, taking him by the arm. The bruises inside his elbows are fading already from violet to green.

She suggests they make their own dream by telling each other stories about the life they'll live together. In one, they have eight adopted children and live in Prague. Moremi teaches them all to dance. In another they work as horticulturists, have no children at all, trek through rainforests and devote themselves to coaxing rare plants from the edge of extinction. He tells her a story where they are assassins from opposing factions; halfway through, she reminds him it is the plot of a major blockbuster he insists he's never heard of.

She falls asleep and when she wakes he's staring at her with the kind of love in his eyes that she's never seen before. 'I hope you don't think this thing is, like, serious,' she teases.

Orpheus kisses her lips, chin, sternum, and she leans

back, trying not to giggle at the tip of his tongue on her navel. Her nerves leap under his lips. 'I'll never leave you,' he promises. 'I love you.' How many times has she prayed to hear those words?

Orpheus pushes apart her thighs and tastes her body happily, playfully. Moremi leans back, her heart in her throat, eyes staring blindly at the ceiling. She tries not to squirm against the rough hot surface of his tongue. She tries to keep her mind centred in her own body, fights to stop it from drifting. A week ago, in a second-hand bookstore, she came across a book subtitled *How to Eat Your Husband*, a novel about a woman who murdered her spouse and slowly devoured his body over the course of a year. Right hand, left foot, teriyaki fillets of his thighs, bone-marrow soup, a stir-fry of his white matter. Each chapter began with a recipe.

Moremi had been terrified. And yet she finished the book in one white-knuckled night, and lay next to Orpheus, listening to the sound of his steady breathing. Now, she catches herself looking at the gooseflesh on his thighs and wondering.

Husband. The word sounds foreign even in her mind, like a country she's never considered visiting.

The next morning, Moremi thinks she'll get out early and surprise him with a coffee. Perhaps breakfast.

But it's a Sunday, and a lot of the high-street stores are closed.

Moremi buys two lattes in the station. They're so hot they burn her hands, and then she drinks them both before she returns to their front door. On her way back, she passes a vintage clothes store with a yellowing wedding dress on a mannequin. She hadn't planned on wearing anything special to their wedding – hadn't seen the point – but now she regrets not choosing something nice to wear.

It's not too late.

Inside, the store smells of dust and mildew. Disney theme tunes and 1980s music are playing obnoxiously loud over the speakers. Moremi slides her hands over the rail of flannel men's shirts. Neon Hawaiian tees, sun-faded and second-hand. Then she comes to the dresses. Fake flapper dresses with plastic sequins, linen prairie dresses and Jacquard swing dresses. There are a few wedding gowns. A lace frock yellowing like net curtains at the train. A polyester 1950s-style dress with a flared skirt. One that buttons right up to the neck with a chaotic spray of tissuey flowers down one side.

Moremi picks the most extravagant one, an ivory satin gown, with a stain on the back that she manages to rub off with a thumb wet with saliva. She's changing into it behind the tie-dyed curtain when a call notification appears. Halima.

Moremi's first thought is emergency. She's having her baby. Zeeba is hurt again. But instead the two of them call to tell her not to marry Orpheus.

'We thought you were joking at first,' Zeeba says.

'I thought you meant eventually, not tomorrow.'

Moremi assumes they must be using the holo function on Zeeba's console because they both appear as holograms in the corner of the changing room.

249

'You look like Princess Diana,' says Halima at the sight of her.

'Is that a good thing?' Moremi asks.

'None of this is a good thing.' Zeeba's voice comes over the phone. 'Don't do it! He's literally a total stranger.'

'What she's trying to say' – Halima catches her sister's eye and gives her a warning look – 'is we're scared for you.'

'I thought they ... fixed you,' Zeeba says.

'What do you think "fixed" means?' Moremi asks. She has to remember to keep her voice low, so that the customers milling outside don't hear.

'That you'd stop doing crazy things. Things like this. Marrying someone you've only known for a week.'

'Twenty-eight days,' Moremi corrects.

'We haven't even met this person yet,' Halima says.

'You'll meet him tomorrow,' Moremi tells them.

'Did he do something to you?' Zeeba asks, staring at Moremi intently.

'No, what are you talking about?'

'I'm talking about the Panopticon. He makes dreams, Moremi. Hallucinations. Don't you think that's kind of sick? Kind of creepy. Also, I have a friend in school who says that he's a twitcher.'

'Not ... ' Moremi says, with a wince at Halima's horrified expression, 'anymore.'

'You're too young to get married,' Halima says, her fingers pinched on the bridge of her nose as if she's trying to stave off a migraine. 'Too young for this to be anything but a mistake.' That word.

Moremi feels cornered now, furious. These women don't understand her, she thinks, never have.

Then, Halima lists Moremi's other boyfriends and lovers like empires she's watched expand and collapse. That red-haired drama student? The tennis coach a decade her senior? The guy with cornrows and the possessive twin sister? Holden? Lover after lover and then Lionel, only a few months ago. How is this boy different from those boys?

They won't believe her if she tells them that she has found a way to be alive and it's Orpheus. How can she be level-headed about this? Rational and pragmatic? In this uncertain world, one good true thing. She makes herself sick some nights thinking about all the ways she could lose him, as she certainly will one day. Last week she frightened him at a zebra crossing by clutching his arm and blurting out, 'I hope that we die at the same time.' She'd wanted him to say, 'Me too,' but in response to the flash of fear in his eyes she'd played it off like a joke. Smiled, apologised for saying it. For saying it out loud.

'How can you even know?' Halima asks.

And Moremi replies, 'It's not about knowing. You can't make a choice like this based on knowing. It's a brave thing to get married to someone. It's an act of optimism, of hope. I'm not like you, I can't go through my life never needing anyone, not wanting anything. It's not about knowing with me, it's about belief. I believe in him.'

Her mother had married her father after only knowing him a few weeks. They'd been young too, in their final year of university. Halima still owned a Polaroid of

251

them; the way they had looked that day. There had been an outbreak of meningitis in their halls of residence, and a student had died. They both pulled through the world swimming, their future bright, and realised that they didn't have all the time in the world. They registered at the nearest town hall as the fever broke, and were surprised to find themselves, weeks later, following through with it. In the only picture taken that day they are grinning like Jack-o'-lanterns on the stone steps of Camden Town Hall. Growing up, whenever Moremi looked at it she envied them. Her father was wearing those oversized wire-rimmed glasses that were fashionable and then dreadfully unfashionable and now hipster-cool. Her mother looked happy and delicate as a daisy, wearing an indigo dress, holding a fistful of wildflowers. Dozens of shiny plastic Mardi Gras beads hung around the sheer cliffs of their collarbones. An embarrassment of riches. Both of them were so glamorous and charismatic that Moremi wanted to be friends with them. At the same height of five-eleven, they looked like fraternal twins with the same manic gleam in their eye. Moremi imagined that they were one of those couples you couldn't look away from. Their whole relationship had been like a speeding car.

Maybe it had been a mistake. They'd had three daughters together and then, one day, he'd got up and left all of them. Left their mother to struggle and then die alone.

Her mother had this mystical idea that the children who want to be born haunt their parents like ghosts; incite them into acts of madness, passion and irrationality, any way they can, because their desire is to be born. Looking at the Polaroid, her mother used to shake her head at their foolishness and then smile at her daughters and say, 'You just wanted to be born.'

Once, Moremi had asked her mother if she regretted the marriage. Would she go back and undo it? Unsay those vows if she could? Unsign those papers? Her mother had said what Moremi says now: 'It could be a mistake. But you can't tiptoe through life never making mistakes. I'm going to take this love, take all the love where I can find it and pray that it lasts.'

When she emerges in her big dress, half the people in the shop are looking at her. The shop manager, a tall man in a neon boilersuit, claps his hands and tells Moremi that she can take the dress for free.

When she walks out wearing it, in the blazing sun, the world seems like a miraculous place.

He's still asleep when she returns. Lying on his stomach in zebra-print boxer shorts. Curtains drawn. In the lights of his monitor screens, Orpheus' thick locks are the almost-blue of a raven's plumage. His face is half buried in pillows. The curve of his back satined with sweat. Beneath the blanket, his thighs will be sticky, his body cloyingly hot, and yet Moremi is overjoyed to get in next to him.

When they'd visited the town hall, the lady at the registry office who had told her that 'every love story is a tragedy' had asked Moremi if she knew what had happened to Orpheus in the Greek myth. When Moremi shook her head, the woman had told her, 'When they tore his head off, he was still singing,' and Moremi couldn't help but picture her future husband. His Pharaoh's nose and jet hair like barbed wire. Lips bruise-purple, with a sticky sheen of saliva across them. Voice raised in falsetto exultation as a furious crowd pulls his head from his shoulders and sets it singing on the Thames.

'Orpheus?' He sleeps like the dead. Undisturbed by the roar of the fan, the stifling heat and the din of traffic outside. Although he rolls over to face her, his eyes are still closed. When they tore his head off it was still singing. A sudden sickening thought: her eyes fall on the tiny bulge of a vein pulsing in his neck, and she imagines it snapping like a wishbone. Twist of nausea. Intrusive premonition.

'It's okay,' she assures herself out loud. When she was a child her mother took her to the National Gallery to see Salome holding John the Baptist's head on a plate. *Don't think about this,* she urges herself, *think about good things.* 'This time tomorrow we'll be married,' she whispers, brushing his face.

When he turns to her he's waking up, his pretty eyes flutter open. 'Hey, you came back.'

'Of course I came back.'

He smiles lazily. Tomorrow, this stranger, this skinny kid, will be her husband. Maybe they'll be entirely happy. Maybe they'll never argue. Maybe they'll grow old together and die at the same time.

Am I making a mistake? Moremi can't help but think. It'll be over tomorrow and she won't be able to undo it.

'Hey.' His dark eyes flutter open. His sweet breath like steam on the bridge of her nose. But then his eyelids slip shut again. She wants to go where he's going. Into untroubled dreams.

Before she knows it, Moremi's eyes fill with delirious tired tears.

'What is it?' he asks.

When they tore his head off it was still singing. 'I miss you,' she says.

'I'm not going anywhere,' he promises.

'Yes, but I miss you,' she says, 'when you sleep.'

19

ORPHEUS

On the morning they get married, Orpheus buys a blue bow-tie and Moremi shows him how to tie it. She places a plastic rose in his front pocket and plants a lipstick kiss on his cheek. She buys a bouquet of camomile and white chrysanthemums from Marks & Spencer, tears all the plastic wrapping off and leaves it on top of a bin. On the tube commuters make way for her and her taffeta train, too polite to say anything. Three stops to King's Cross station and it's too crowded for a seat. Orpheus holds the railing above his head and Moremi holds Orpheus. He strokes the back of his hand against her cheek. Filled with a giddy tenderness for her. In the dark glass of her eyes the world is still and Orpheus sees that they don't need many things. Sees that they will make their makeshift marriage like their makeshift wedding, nothing too serious, nothing but fun.

By the time they reach the station, he is sure they are

going to be late. They dash through the turnstiles and across the road just as the lights turn amber. On the marble steps two people have just been married. A Black woman with frizzy hair and a white suit, a balding older white man, and Orpheus sees that the two of them aren't so special after all. This is the most important day of their lives but they are also only extras in someone else's love story.

The receptionist asks them what they're here for and they say 'to get married'. He looks for their names on a console, as if this is a dentist appointment or a booking to talk with a mortgage adviser. 'The Tavistock Suite,' he says, and points them in the right direction.

When they arrive, the door is closed because another couple are still inside. It's as if they're on a wedding conveyer belt.

'You came!' Moremi says, relief in her voice at the sight of her sisters.

Halima rolls her eyes. 'Of course, we weren't going to let you go through with this alone.'

'What are you wearing?' Zeeba asks Moremi. Zeeba is dressed as if she's about to go to a disco, neon face-paint and blue-feathered false lashes. She pretends not to see Orpheus, reaches over to hug Moremi and says, 'It's not a bad look,' tugging at her puffed sleeves. 'They're coming back around.'

When it's time for the ceremony – in the low-ceilinged room with lush bouquets of flowers on console tables – it all passes in a blur. A city skyline from the rear window of an express train. Almost too quickly to believe.

The registrar pronounces Moremi's surname wrong on several occasions.

They say: '*I call upon these persons here present, to witness that I— do take you— to be my lawful wedded—*'

They say: '*Do not urge me to leave you or to turn back from you. Where you go I will go. Where you die I will die, and there I will be buried.*'

They say: '*May the LORD deal with me, be it ever so severely, if even death separates you and me.*'

The registrar declares them husband and wife and at the end of the ceremony someone plays an icy synthesiser version of Beyonce's 'Crazy in Love' on the speakers as the papers are signed. Halima and Moremi have a snappy argument about her signature. Orpheus' gaze lingers on the part of the form that specifies, 'Father's profession'; the registrar had rolled her eyes when Orpheus had said, 'Philosopher king.'

More people gather on the steps outside. One or two of Halima's work colleagues, an old neighbour. Zen is there briefly. One of Moremi's old classmates from dance school. Whoever could be rustled up at this short notice.

The motto most commonly associated with Anne Boleyn is the one she adopted for her coronation: *La Plus Heureuse* – the most happy. A phrase which comes into Orpheus' mind as he stands beaming on the steps, sweat creeping down his back, his hand in hers.

It's done. They're married and he imagines himself emerging triumphantly into the rest of his life. He's determined and dizzy with love. Thousands of couples enter through the town hall's revolving door and emerge married. But, Orpheus thinks, their love is like no other love. Theirs is an epic, rare thing.

A passing cloud momentarily dims the light of the sun. Zeeba tosses another handful of confetti at them and they run into the waiting taxi. 'We'll do it,' Orpheus tells her as they roll into the seats.

For a while it will be true.

'We'll be the most happy.'

20

MOREMI

When she wakes up, he's not there. Moremi runs her hand along the bleached hotel sheets, the crease in the cool cotton where his head had been. Her husband, she thinks with a thrill.

'Where are you going?' She finds him in the ensuite, dressed in his white linen wedding suit.

'Probation meeting with Sai,' he says to the mirror.

'Already?' Moremi says. Although, she's not sure why. It feels like almost a year has passed since he was put on sick leave. Everything's different, now.

Orpheus leans in to examine the whites of his eyes, then lifts his hand and they both notice the way his fingers still tremble.

'Maybe it takes a while to go away,' Moremi says. Orpheus looks at her in the mirror and clenches his fist. All she knows about Nox addiction is what she's read in magazines.

'This is the longest I've been in meat-space,' Orpheus says quietly, in awe at himself, 'since I learned how to leave.' Moremi smiles and he looks back at her.

'I never wanted to, until now . . .' He looks down, seemingly embarrassed by the feeling in his voice.

Moremi is still naked. The night before, when she'd tried to put on her bra, Orpheus had tossed it playfully behind the bed and said, 'No more of that.'

'When are you coming back?' she asks.

'I have the meeting and then . . .' He shrugs. 'It's the symposium's opening gala tonight. You still up for coming as my plus-one? Or . . . I guess you're already Halima's.'

'She told me already that she's not feeling up to going.'

'It goes on quite late,' Orpheus agrees. 'But I'll see you there?' He kisses her.

In between . . . he says in her head.

. . . *only longing*, she replies.

He leaves after breakfast and she checks out for both of them. Carrying both their rucksacks and her wedding dress – stuffed in a Sainsbury's bag for life – back to the flat.

Everything looks the way they left it the previous morning, and she raids his cupboards for something to wear. Moremi has only ever read about the Quantum Hill Ball on the Vines of *Harper's Bazaar* or *Tatler*. From what she's read it seems something like the Met Gala and something like a TED conference. So she settles on a shirt of his, paired with her own sequinned leggings and a string of pink freshwater pearls she bought once from a farmers' market. She's booked in for an afternoon shift with the pollinating company so she puts all her things in the rucksack, ready for the gala.

She's back at the Quantum Hill campus that evening and it takes her over an hour to get through security because she'd entered via the wrong gate, behind an army of journalists and photographers eager to capture the first pictures of the night's most esteemed attendees: teenage heiresses, top executives, as well as Hollywood royalty, influencers and two duchesses. By the time Moremi arrives, there are almost a thousand people in the main atrium and surging out onto the lawn. An orchestra have set sail on a flotilla of boats. Moremi can't help but marvel at the sight of them, oboes, and trombones, saxophones and violins, the bells of trumpets like disco-balls in the strobing light.

It's like one of Gatsby's parties, she thinks, awestruck, as she approaches the palatial campus and catches sight of a group of women dancing across a levitating glass platform, their laughter rising like smoke. The banks of canals are lined with buffet tables that heave with food: goose-liver foie gras and fresh truffles, beluga caviar, vol-au-vents with wild mushrooms, chocolate delice, pistachio crème brûlée. Moremi's stomach twists with desire at the sight of them. Next to the bars are crystal towers of champagne flutes, waiters in spotless white tailcoats flying around on Zephyrs, balancing trays of glasses miraculously in their hands.

Moremi scans the crowd for Orpheus now. Dotted among the masses are people she has only ever seen in films or on television. By the fountain a British-Somali model with a waist-length weave is taking a selfie with a famously left-wing actor. A boisterous group of men are singing a cappella, their lips painted deep purple. A pastor from a local mega-church arrives like a king in a driverless Rolls-Royce, striding through the crowd in a flowing *agbada* embroidered with silver lace. A TV presenter with gold Ray-Bans is interviewing a tattooed grime artist in a leopard-print vest who sits on one of the outdoor sofas with three other men who could be friends or could be bodyguards. By a stone pavilion is the former shadow minister for transport, fanning herself with a handful of crumpled Vote Yes leaflets.

Everything is fairy-tale lovely. With the long shadows and the sun about to set, casting its final majestic rays of golden light across the lawn, there is a sense of febrile excitement about the party. It's a celebration of the future. It will be born here, Moremi thinks, caught up in it herself. Everything feels possible suddenly, inevitable.

A waiter hands Moremi a champagne glass and she nods at him sympathetically. Her muscles ache at the sight of his Zephyr, two metres of polished balsa-wood, reminding her of her own afternoons spent hovering over trees, baking in a yellow and black polyester jumpsuit.

Where are you? Moremi asks Orpheus over the Panopticon.

By the stairs. Can't you see me?

Moremi scans the crowd, unsure which stairs he's talking about. Then she thinks she sees Halima in the shade of a plane tree, waiting near the canal with a strange tension in her body. But in the next moment the light from the stage flashes across the woman's silhouette and Moremi realises that she can't be Halima. She's clearly not pregnant. Except . . . she knows that face . . . Moremi's own wide nose, and Halima's hooded eyes, the sharpened edges of Zeeba's wolfish teeth. Could it be? Her mother? Older, with a big scar across the side of her face. The ground rocks under Moremi. How is it possible?

'No . . .' she's saying as the blue wheel of the ReCog function keeps turning, indicating that the Panopticon is having trouble recognising the face, but Moremi has no trouble at all.

'Mum?' She is barely conscious of dropping her champagne glass as she dashes towards the trees, trying her best to dart and slalom through the crowd. 'No,' Moremi mutters to herself. It can't be.

Without seeing her, the woman turns and begins to walk away, towards the canal. By the time Moremi reaches the edge of the woods she is panting. She almost trips over an abandoned drinks tray, but keeps running. The undergrowth snatches at her heels and when Moremi closes the distance between them, she shouts her mother's name.

The woman turns suddenly at the sound of it, and calls, 'Remi?'

They regard each other for what feels like a long while, looking as if they've both seen a ghost. Moremi is thinking, *How can this be possible?* Telling herself that maybe it's not true, anything she's ever been taught about life or death. Her intuition had been right, all those years ago. There is a way around it, ways to survive it.

The sound of a speedboat coming up the canal breaks her mother out of her spell. In the shadow of the leaves, Moremi hears the urgent whisper of a couple of people. Her mother looks torn, as if she wants more than anything to run back up and take Moremi's hand, but the voices behind her grow more panicked.

Finally she looks at her daughter and says, 'Get out of here. Get as far away as you can.' A couple of the hooded figures in the boat are hurrying her away now and when she turns to find Moremi fixed to the spot she shouts, before vanishing, 'It's not safe here. Run!'

21

ORPHEUS

Sai Kaur congratulates him that morning on his return to work. His blood is clear of Nox and he passes their psyche evaluation.

Orpheus feels like a different person now. 'You look different, too,' Sai says.

'I got married,' Orpheus tells him.

'Oh, wow.' A certain surprised hollowness rings in the man's voice.

'Yesterday,' Orpheus says, almost to remind himself, as Quantum Hill and all his colleagues seem a million miles from that sunlit afternoon.

'Newly wedded newlyweds.'

'Almost the newest,' Moremi had said that morning at breakfast when they'd bumped into a boisterous Canadian couple. 'We were married yesterday,' she had told them, and the man had shouted, 'Yesterday? Yesterday! We have to get you a drink. It would be a different thing if it was a week ago. Or even two days ago. But yesterday.' They are the newest thing in the world. Barely twenty-four hours. Their marriage like a creature just born.

'How old are you, fourteen?' Sai laughs, though Orpheus' profile clearly says twenty. 'You're racing through life.'

The rest of the day is mainly spent catching up on messages he missed and downloading quartz recordings of meetings. It's over before the gala starts and then he wanders out of the School of Sleep and takes a walk around the campus which is a flurry of activity. Automated mowers are flying up and down the lawn, leaving the smell of fresh-cut grass in their wake. Orpheus breathes deeply as he walks up the promenade, a smile on his face. It's summer and the air is heavy with pollen. All around him, rhododendrons are lolling their violet tongues. Sai had said he was happy to have him back, and Orpheus is surprised to realise that he's glad to be back. He's returned with a renewed passion for the work he does, and an unfamiliar hopefulness about his life.

Once most of the guests arrive, his Friend Finder notifies him that Moremi is nearby.

Where are you? Moremi asks Orpheus over the Panopticon.

By the stairs. Can't you see me? But he's interrupted a moment later by a hand on his shoulder.

'I didn't get a chance to congratulate you yesterday.' Orpheus turns to find Zen and her partner Kimiko. They both look beautiful. Zen wears a jacquard black waistcoat with gold brocade blossoms, and Kimiko is in a gold dress. They've always seemed like a slightly odd couple to Orpheus. Mainly because Kimiko is almost fifteen years older than Zen. A widow, according to her profile, a head of development at the School of Radical Togetherness. Orpheus has known Zen as long as they've been together though. They have a habit of pairing their Pulses, so whenever the other is nearby one of them will prickle all over and look around like a meerkat. They finish each other's sentences, or talk silently with each other unless prompted to do otherwise.

'Right,' Orpheus says to her comment, although he hadn't seen Kimiko yesterday because – like most people – she hadn't been able to take the time off at such short notice for their weekday wedding.

'You look better,' Zen says, then reaches out for one of the locks of his black and silver hair that have fallen loose of his ponytail. 'You just need to dye them—'

He shakes her away. 'It's a look. It's fashionable.'

'Well, I'm just glad you're back,' Kimiko says. Since the two of them don't know each other so well, Orpheus is surprised by the warmth coming from her.

'And maybe,' she continues, 'I can take credit for this whole union. Since I'm the one who introduced you to—'

Orpheus interrupts her: '*Zen* introduced me to . . .' But at their conspiratorial smile he suspects a trick is being played on him. 'Are you . . . ?' Orpheus doesn't know if it's rude to ask. 'Pairing your Pulses right now?'

'We've – I've – permanently paired, now,' they say in such perfect unison that Orpheus' hairs stand on end.

'I thought that was impossible,' he says. Though the

idea of permanent Pulse-pairing has been widely discussed, Orpheus had thought the technology was a little while away. 'Since when?' Orpheus asks.

'A couple of weeks,' they say.

'You didn't ...' He's speechless, doesn't know if he should be happy for them or confused. 'I didn't guess.' Although he should have, he realises now. From the way that they were moving, from their strange symmetry, the way that they blinked at the same time, or the way that one's gaze seems to draw the other's. 'Kimiko – actually, sorry, should I call you that at all?'

'Mercury,' they say. 'My new name.'

'Mercury,' Orpheus says.

'In one of my childhoods ...' and Orpheus' head reels at this notion. In his cohort in the children's division there had been a pair of identical twins, Ivy and Holly, with the same green eyes and vivid red hair. In a biology lesson, Orpheus had asked about identical twins. Stared at the cluster of cells on the worksheet display on his console. A zygote. A whole planet. They had been one once. One thing that was both and neither of them. Orpheus considers this now as he watches Mercury. The new and strange thing they have become. Both and neither.

'How does it feel?' he asks.

'Someone else's mind? I've been to so many places, Orpheus. I've seen Buddha's light on the Huangshan Mountains. Leaped from a plane. Seen an orbital sunrise, but nothing compared to ...'

'... waking in her head.'

'The taste of her teeth under the roof of her mouth.'

'Her own particular sadness.'

'Another mind.'

'A different universe.'

'Never again.' And the look of serene love that passes between them makes Orpheus want to look away.

'You know what it means to be in love,' they say. 'It's a sudden othering. Your entire world becomes alien and new. A totalling desire to know everything, learn everything about her inner life. Which is our ambition.

'Radical togetherness,' they say. 'Complete love. Its most perfect realisation. It turns out that if two people pair for long enough they begin to dream each other's dreams. My minds reverberated together like a tuning fork and I discovered that it's true. Consciousness is like a bowl of mercury. The same stuff in her that was in me.'

Mercury explains that it is useful to view the brain like a hologram. 'The entirety of the information of a hologram is contained within a part. So if some parts are lost or damaged all of the information remains. Quartz memory storage seems to exhibit similar properties if two constellations are paired for long enough.'

'Then both of you become all of the whole,' Orpheus finishes, his mind reeling at the implications of this. 'So if Kimiko's old body jumped in front of a bus . . . ?'

'Her mind would survive in the body that belonged to Zen.'

Orpheus takes an involuntary step back, his stomach rolling at the thought. 'And if you paired again with another person?'

Mercury says, 'There may be a way to—'

'. . . live forever.' Orpheus' hands are cold. Suddenly he's sickened by the sight of them. He wants to throw them down the marble staircase, burn them at a stake. 'I don't understand,' he says honestly, confused by the sudden grief he feels for his friend Zen. 'I don't understand why you would choose this. To lose—'

'Oh no,' they say, 'there is no loss at all. Only gain.'

On the edge of Orpheus' awareness he begins to notice the sounds of the music growing louder. Distant peals of laughter. Moremi is probably still looking for him. Mercury explains, with the hope of setting his concerns at ease, that the merging of their minds feels more like a 'revelation'. 'Do you ever have dreams,' they ask, 'where you open a door in your flat and discover a room that has always been there?'

'Doesn't everyone in London have that dream?' Orpheus asks.

'I woke up and remembered an entire childhood. New people I'd always known. A different but intimately familiar inner voice. Old desires resurfacing. No "hers" or "hers".'

Kimiko's hand reaches for Orpheus'. 'A lot of people are frightened. Worried that they will lose themselves. There is no loss, only gain. The "self" does not have to be defined by boundaries. I will tell you again that I'm more myself now. More fully aware of both of my selves.'

Orpheus pulls away, keen to leave them and find Moremi. 'Maybe I'll never understand,' he says.

'Oh,' Mercury replies with a smile, 'soon, you will.'

271

22

MOREMI

It takes Moremi a second to recover from her shock at seeing her mother, for her limbs to unglue and to chase after her. Which she does, tearing through the trees until she reaches the canal, shouting her name all the way. But she's already gone, speeding down the canal in an electric boat. It's only once the skin on the water settles and Moremi wipes the tears from her eyes that she remembers what her mother had said. *Run.*

She looks around now in confusion and dread.

Where are you? Orpheus' voice on her Pulse.

By the canal.

Stay there, I think I'm close by.

He finds her on her knees in the dirt, scoops her up in his arms, asks what's wrong. But before she can tell him, she sees Zen and her partner – although a new name is flickering on their Panopticon profile. 'Something's about to happen,' Zen says as a hushed silence begins to descend. The band come to the end of their symphony and a high squeal of feedback tears through the speakers, making everyone wince. An excited hush descends upon the crowd, like theatre-goers waiting for the curtain to ascend. They've timed it perfectly, captured everyone's attention at the exact moment of sunset, when the final blaze of red light vanishes under the trees.

Everyone is looking around the garden wondering what will happen next, when Professor Itō appears, like Neptune, in a bright empire dress, on the balcony of the watchtower – the tallest building in the centre of the campus. At the sight of her the crowd erupts into such riotous applause that Itō has to wait a whole minute for them to settle down.

'Orpheus . . .' Moremi wants to tell him what she just saw but he's not listening.

'I wonder what it's like up there,' he gasps, staring up at the watchtower. Camera flashes flicker and reflect off the whites of his eyes. The entire symposium is being live-streamed across the Panopticon right now. Moremi can see from the feed that almost a billion people are watching. People in Beijing, where it's already tomorrow, are up at 4am to watch. People in Sacramento, on their lunch breaks, people crowded around consoles in Soweto, Lima, Ouagadougou.

Professor Itō smiles like an aged priestess. 'Here we all are. Twenty-five years since the day we first switched on the Panopticon.' Professor Itō promises the watchful crowd that 'History will be made, right here, again.'

Moremi casts a quick glance around at the crowd. She,

Orpheus and Zen and Kimiko are quite far away from the watchtower, although they can zoom in on their retinal interface for a better view of the professor. Although everyone around her is mesmerised, like a congregation gathered before a televangelist hoping that they too can be healed, she is still distracted by what she's just seen. Unsettled by her mother's warning.

'Some people believe that one day we will create a super-intelligence that surpasses human capability. That this invention will be our last. That it will usher in an age of unbridled technological growth. They call this the Singularity. We believe that machines will not transcend human intelligence, but that we will all transcend together.'

A notification appears in her vision; it asks if she wants to take part in the demonstration. 'Say yes,' Zen and Kimiko urge. So she does with a flick of her eyes.

The demonstration begins and when Moremi looks around she sees, from the flickering lights on everyone's constellations, that all of their hearts have begun to beat at the same time. The same steady rhythm. Blue calm. It happens all at once. Moremi closes her eyes and then opens them in another body. A body with two thousand faces and many names. Every mind is a facet; cool and mathematical, spiteful and introverted, needy, self-confident, proud, streaked with narcissism, tempered by other minds; the soulful, the reserved and introspective. A revelation, all of these minds. Hundreds of thousands of memories, desires, dreams. What haven't I seen?

I have lived thousands of years: this thought

reverberates in all of their heads. Each of its bodies turn to each other with a collective sigh of exaltation. All their eyes fill with tears. It feels sublime. It feels like perfect love. The happiest of reunions, all of their minds. A true and total end to loneliness, to strife, misunderstanding. Time expands to meet this new reality. Five seconds, like a held breath.

And then, the pairing is over. The creature rent into splinters. Two thousand bodies, once again. Only one of them, Moremi. That old pain of being alone feels almost unbearable now.

The body called Moremi falls to its knees, wiping tears from its eyes, as everyone else is doing. How will we live now, they are all thinking, when we've glimpsed eternity?

'Now you see,' Mercury says, 'what it's like to transcend ego.'

'Different from . . .' Orpheus looks dazed, shaken. 'I imagined it would be different.'

Hayden appears then on the glass balcony of the watchtower. The rushing fountain a few storeys below him sounds like a long endless applause. Though he helped develop the Panopticon two decades ago, his face is still flushed with an uncanny boyhood. Impossible to tell how old he is. He wears a calico shirt with a monk's collar and matching trousers. Through the transparent balustrade it's possible to see his bare feet and the black marbles of his toes.

'It's okay.' His voice is a comfort to them all. 'The loneliness is just for now. Just for this lesser time before we achieve Total Adoption.' The word itself has taken on a completely new meaning now. It sounds like a promise. The end of their suffering. It's possible, Moremi thinks.

Hayden says, 'It is possible. It's probable. It will happen soon.' The three founders are all standing together on the balcony. Hayden Adeyemi in the centre, Jitsuko Itō, Bertram Fairmont and a few of the other dream scientists.

Unlike Hayden, Bertram is growing old and it's clear to see. He wears his beard long and his platinum-blond hair has turned seamlessly grey, thick locks that fall into his eyes. He explains, 'For those watching the live-stream, what you just witnessed was a demonstration of the world's largest Pulse-pairing. Two thousand two hundred and thirty-one constellations and quartzes synced together for five seconds. It's a function that is due to become universally available to everyone in the world, with a Pulse, by September. Our team who developed this new system update must be feeling great right now.' The camera pans in to the group of bald-headed women and men crowded near the fountain. Almost all of them are laughing, their eyes wet and happy, the light of their Pulses flickering wildly to the beat of their hearts. Engineers, coders, computational neuroscientists.

'Emerson said, "Man is a God in ruins",' Hayden says. 'It wasn't meant to be this way. We were not supposed to grow sick, insignificant, to age, to die. Every day, we tremble at the unfairness of it.' The crowd have fallen silent again.

'We do,' Professor Itō tells them. 'This body only has months left.' Gasps of horror in the crowd. An eruption of chatter on the gossip spools that's so frenzied, Moremi has to mute it. 'But that's only corporeally.' *What does she mean?* they all wonder.

Hayden says, 'What a singular thing a mind is. A pattern of neuronal connections that will never be replicated in the cosmos again. What a tragedy. What a vile injustice that when you die, as you surely will, all your memories will be lost. Along with your particular aptitudes and strange associations. The way that the air smells to you on weekday mornings during your walk to the train station. The first time you ever heard Chopin remixed on a synthesiser on your brother's old laptop. The way the light looked to you at age six, coming through the frayed net curtains. The dappled pattern of it on your mother's cubic zirconium earrings. The way she looked like a goddess to you before you grew up. All you knew.

'The day you die,' he goes on, 'the delicate pattern of information that encodes all of that is lost to the universe forever. And we're all poorer for it. The problem is that our consciousness is an island. An analogue system with no redundancy. No external back-up. That's the reason it takes only a generation to lose everything that we gained. Only a generation to forget the structure of DNA, that bacteria causes disease, that the arrow of time bends towards increased entropy and that everyone should be free.

'We've built a machine that allows humans access to the phenomenal life of every other. After Total Adoption and the roll-out of this upgrade, everyone will be able to opt in to the Singularity. Perhaps this really will be the last invention, the one that ushers in a new epoch of complete togetherness.' He explains that, once connected, every individual's memories will diffuse through the minds of others, fragments of it saved, and stored on everyone else's Pulse, in a way that means a consciousness is retrievable even after death. It's hard for Moremi to imagine, to even comprehend, although – as she's discovered from touching their mind – Mercury has already done it.

'The end of death,' Hayden promises, 'revealed here, today. People will no longer ask, "How will we know when the Singularity has arrived?" It has already begun. It's happening here.'

Moremi's breath fails, her eyes still brimming. She wants more than anything for it to be true. To be part of it.

But as Bertram steps forward again to say something else there is a shout at the back of the atrium, near the entrance of the hall: 'The Panopticon is for prisoners!'

A sound like a whip cracking. Phosphorus head of a match igniting.

'Bomb!' someone screams.

With a hiss and crackle, a bolt of lightning flies at the watchtower and explodes before the lectern. A gunshot? A flaming arrow? Bertram is struck in the chest. His face fills with dread and then his mouth opens and blood spills out. People are screaming before he falls. Moremi is already sure that she will watch this moment, like the flood, again and again, as he tumbles fifteen storeys from the balcony of the watchtower and into the fountain below. She will see from a thousand vantages how his skull cracks like a pumpkin on the side of the marble basin. She will see that when he slides into the water, he is just a body after all. Just blood and bone, an effervescent pattern of information.

The audience freezes for a moment, in total silence. Surely this is part of the demonstration? But then Itō screams, clutches her chest and crumples.

'No!' Hayden shouts, and a thousand people erupt into chaos, turning heel to run.

'Terrorists?' Mercury asks. Moremi's blood turns to ice at the thought. Ever since the flood, she's found it impossible to ignore any story she reads about bombings, stabbings, militants driving cars into pedestrians. She already understands how suddenly a life can be torn apart.

'Get down,' Orpheus screams as a ball of flames heads right for them and bursts. Moremi hits the ground just in time, although her shins slam the stone floor so hard she winces. A shower of sparks rain over her head and she holds up an arm to cover her hair. Moremi looks up as a round shell of electric-blue lights sputter and spiral up the isle and says, 'What's happening?'

'Fireworks,' someone shouts as a rocket launches on a shrill jet of fire and party-goers thunder downhill towards the canals, screaming. Someone knocks over a tower of champagne flutes, an avalanche of glass explodes into razors and the terrified crowd scatters. Someone stumbles, a heel snapped, grabbing at a banner to slow her fall. Half of the hanging decorations come crashing down, taking five other people with them. In front of Moremi, another person loses his footing, slides to the floor in a puddle of champagne and before he has time to stand his fingers crunch like ice under someone's shoe.

'Freedom from our body makes us slaves to technology.' Three waiters in animal masks are standing on a flotilla where the orchestra had been. 'Dreams should be private,' they chant. 'Dreams should be free.'

'The Revelators,' Mercury says as they take cover under the white linen cloth of a buffet table. It makes sense, this high-profile event would be at the top of their list to target.

'I know a way out,' Mercury says to Moremi.

'No!' Although she is on her hands and knees, she cranes her head to look around. 'Where is Orpheus?' She can't see him in the fray. Did he duck for cover? Was he hurt?

'If we go now, we can make it.' There is terror in Mercury's eyes as they point to the forest. 'That way, to the north bank. I can call my car to come and we can take the bridge off campus.'

'I can't go without him,' Moremi says, looking around frantically.

A golden Catherine wheel cracks like a whip at eye-level. In the dry weather, everything is going up like a tinderbox, the grass begins to hiss and fry along with the wooden tables and chairs. The two-storey hanging banners fly up in a crisp, a swift *woof!* as they go. Party-goers and Panopticon employees are barrelling, pell-mell, away from the watchtower. Some are trying to take cover in the trees, others dash towards the river, gathering up their skirts, hoping to swim around the building. Most scatter across the garden, clambering over casualties to hide under the roofs of the stone pavilions or inside the glass refectory to their far left.

'Orpheus!' Moremi thinks she sees him. A black head of curls, someone crumpled in pain on the edge of the forest. *He's been hurt,* she thinks. What if he's crushed? She imagines, with a twist of nausea, a boot flying at his head.

'I'll find you,' Moremi says to Mercury, and without even looking back she runs towards him, though it takes all of her energy to push against the solid wall of people surging in the opposite direction.

'You won't make it,' Mercury shouts. About their heads, ash is falling like snow.

The crowd is pushing so hard that, once or twice, Moremi is shoved back.

'Get down!' someone shouts just as another firework explodes. Something hot catches the skin on Moremi's forearms as she throws them up to shield her face. Her nose fills with the smell of her own roasting flesh. She grits her teeth, her eyes stinging from the pain and the rising smoke.

The crowd scatters further, and in the glittering trail of a comet, Moremi sees that Kimiko's body was struck down. They are curled in the grass, writhing in pain. Moremi runs across to them.

'Where are you hurt?' Moremi asks.

'I was hit,' Mercury says, their teeth gritted in pain.

'Okay,' Moremi says, her first-aid training coming to mind. 'You need to put pressure on the wound.' Only when Mercury moves their hand, she sees no blood, no mark at all.

'My other body,' they shout, their face scrunched in agony, 'it's dying.'

Moremi's head spins in confusion. The shouts and the caterwauling sirens, the flames, and the sound of her own pulse throbbing in her ears, are an assault to her senses.

'You're okay, though?' she asks. 'Not injured?'

'Moremi!' Orpheus vaults an upturned table and runs towards her. When she sees him her heart leaps. 'This way,' he says, 'through the trees, I think I know a way.'

'We can't leave them,' Moremi says, pointing at Mercury. Orpheus deliberates for just a moment, looking back the way they came – the watchtower is no longer visible behind a rising wall of smoke – then he leans over and together they help to lift Kimiko's slight body up. Moremi notices how much her own body aches. The skin on her arm feels as if it's still on fire and so do her bruised shins.

The three of them stagger through the woods, which are so dark and smoky that Moremi has to blindly reach out a hand in front of her to feel for where she is going. 'This way,' Orpheus shouts once, when she almost trips on a tangle of roots. Another time she starts as her foot catches the soft edge of a limb. A body on the ground.

And then they make it to the other side; the clearing in the forest where a fleet of boats are tethered. All around, smoke-blackened and injured guests are leaping onto boats or into the water. Moremi takes a moment to catch her breath. Glasses are shattered like eggshells in the mud. On the other side of the bank is the car park where sirens wail and paramedics are already tending to people.

Moremi lets herself believe, for just a moment, that they have made it to safety when a knife-bright shaft of pain lances across her vision. The world bursts into static, like an old television set, and she cries out. A noise as loud as a plane taking off howls inside her head.

Orpheus cries out at the same time, but the pain inside her ears is so bad that it strikes all thought clean from her mind. Through tears she shouts, 'My Pulse. There's something wrong with it.' As she motions frantically to mute all noise on the audio feed she realises that her Pulse is not responding. This has never happened before.

Through her pain, she can hear that everybody around her is screaming too, holding their ears, dropping to their knees.

'Make it stop!' Mercury yells.

'Ah!' Orpheus falls too. 'They've done something to our constellations.'

Moremi has heard of attacks like this before. 'Noxious transmissions' is the word the authorities use. Pirate Panopticon channels that hijack all the Pulses nearby. They have been utilised in the past in neo-Luddite protests or like water-cannons by police officers trying to break up prison riots.

'It's not real,' Orpheus spits through tightly gritted teeth. 'It's causing your constellation to fire at your cochlear nerve. It's a hallucination. Moremi, breathe. Fight it.'

But each breath is terrifying. 'I can't,' she cries. The pain is so bad she thinks her skull will fracture. Moremi imagines her eardrums like rent animal skins flapping.

Along the riverbank, Mercury is yelling, pulling at their hair. A woman opposite is banging her head against a tree trunk. A collective wail of agony rises up from the cinders and smoke.

'Make it stop,' shouts a man in a dinner jacket. Picking up a shard of shattered glass, he drives it into his ear with a howl. Sweet relief, Moremi thinks at the sight of him.

'No!' It's only when Orpheus shouts that she realises she's grabbed the neck of a broken champagne bottle, intent on gouging her own Pulse out as one might saw off a gangrenous limb.

Orpheus disarms her with trembling hands. She can barely see him through tears, his face strobed with the red and blue lights of the sirens. 'Breathe,' he tells her, placing his palms on her cheeks. Both of them are on their knees in the dirt. Blood dribbles from his nose, down his lips. 'It's not real. Breathe,' he says again through gritted teeth.

She tells herself that it's true. The pain is not happening to her, it's happening to another body.

And the shouts all around.

'It's not real.'

In a few minutes the police will come. The ambulance.

'Breathe.' She just needs to hold on.

On the other side of the bank the firemen have arrived. They are already tearing down a banner, strung between two trees. The letters hand-painted, red and slanting, read: WHO WINS THE WAR FOR YOUR MIND?

PART TWO

23

MOREMI

Someone is screaming. Moremi realises, only when a nurse rushes in, that it's her.

Almost every part of her aches, and she has no sense of what time it is because – she discovers this when her fingers touch the bloody skin on the side of her temple – her Pulse is not working.

'*Calmati*,' says the nurse, '*il dottore ti parlerà presto.*' Moremi's hands finds that a patch of hair has been shaved off around her ear. Is her Pulse still there? She tries to rip off the dressing to find out; all the while her hands are shaking.

She's had nightmares like this, ones where she wakes up without a Pulse. Each time she wakes from them she thinks, *I'd rather pluck an eye out.*

She feels dizzy without it, totally bereft.

'*Starai bene,*' the nurse says, '*presto.*' And something in her tone conveys her sympathy. The door swings open and

Halima appears, looking harrowed, her face tear-stained, hair wild.

'You're awake,' she says. 'Oh, thank God.' She runs over to kiss her sister.

'What's happened to me?' Moremi asks. 'Where is my Pulse?' She can only remember the previous night in flashes. A riot of sound in her head, and pain, pain, pain. The fireworks, the fire, the attack. 'Orpheus? My husband.' And then a strange surprise at the sound of the word. She hasn't said it out loud before.

'It's okay,' Halima says. 'Everything—' but then the doors fly open again and the doctor dismisses the nurse saying – the blue translation light on his own constellation flashing – 'Don't worry, Valentina. This patient can't understand you. She's Pulseless.'

Moremi hears the word like a blow to the chest.

'I'm Dr Wells, the consultant neurologist here at London Bridge Hospital.' He does some quick checks of her neural function, flashes a light in her eyes, asks her to follow his finger with her gaze, to touch her nose and then touch his stylus, which he holds about a metre from her face.

'Okay,' he says finally. 'You, and everyone else who was present during the symposium last night, were exposed to a virus.'

'A virus?' Moremi asks.

'Not a biological virus,' the doctor says. 'One that infects computers. Malicious software written to alter the way that your Pulse operates. This one is well known to the authorities, it has been used every now and then in certain attacks. The virus targets the arrays on your auditory nerve, makes you feel as if you're hearing an unbearably loud sound.' The thought of a virus, like a tapeworm inside her brain, is nauseating.

'They wiped it off your CPU,' Halima says.

'But you will need to keep your constellation off for at least thirty days. Then you can come back and we can assess if there is any remaining damage.'

'Thirty days?' Moremi says.

'I just thank God you're going to be okay,' says Halima. 'You're lucky it's just that.' Halima's eyes are welling up again. 'It could have been so much worse. It was for so many people. I feel sick just watching the videos. Hundreds of people died last night. Even more of them are in intensive care. In comas. People died from trying to cut their own Pulse out. Permanent brain damage. Some people will probably never be off ventilators again.'

'It would have been me,' Moremi says, sitting up again and looking around frantically. 'Where's Orpheus? Orpheus saved me.'

Halima casts a warning look at the doctor and then says, 'He's on his way.'

'From where?' Moremi asks. If only she had her Friend Finder open, she could see his location. 'Is he okay, is he safe?'

'He's fine. Don't worry about him for now. Just worry about yourself. About getting better.'

But Moremi can't shake the sense of violation she feels, waking up without access to her constellation. 'Does it really have to be thirty days? I feel so—'

'Lost without it,' the doctor says. 'I do this every day.

In the neurology department, we deactivate and try to fix faulty constellations. And do you know that's the first thing that my patients always tell me. I tell them, don't forget that your constellation is not actually a part of you.'

'But,' she says, knowing how irrational it sounds.

'But it feels that way,' he says. 'It does for everyone. But you'll just have to survive a short while without it. You need some time to heal. It will be inconvenient, it will hurt. But there is no other way.' He takes out an envelope from his pocket with a letter in it, the details of her situation. 'Here is a doctor's note. Most workplaces, now, they don't even let you pass security without a Pulse. You're not planning on flying, are you? Good, the Pulseless have a lot of hassle at the airport.' He signs it with an ink pen and then hands it to her. Moremi feels as if he's sending her out into the wilderness with nothing she'll need. What will she even do with this . . . paper? She looks at it as if it's a scrap of papyrus covered in hieroglyphs.

'I have to warn you, as I warn everyone,' he tells her seriously, 'about the health complications of losing your Pulse. You might find for the next few weeks that you feel lonely. I have to tell you that the pain of loneliness is completely normal, an evolutionary tool. A pain that prompts us to renew the connections we need to survive. Humans are social creatures.

'Some reports suggest that loneliness is as bad for your health as smoking fifteen cigarettes a day.'

'It's okay,' Halima says, grabbing Moremi's hand, 'she has me.'

'And Orpheus,' Moremi reminds her sister. 'He saved me.'

The painkillers they've given her make her sleepy, and when she wakes again she sees her mother's face. But then it resolves into Halima's.

'I saw her,' Moremi mumbles, half into her pillow.

'You're just sleepy,' Halima says, brushing her cool hand against her sister's brow.

'No,' Moremi says. It floats back to her now, amid the haze of memories from that night. 'I saw our mother yesterday. She spoke to me.'

Halima shakes her head sadly. 'Remi, you know that's impossible.' Of course it's impossible, they'd both seen her body. 'A lot happened that night. And your Pulse got infected. You're just confused.'

'Of course,' Moremi says, though it feels unmistakable. 'It's impossible.'

Her other injuries are minor in comparison to most of the people admitted. Other than the damage to her constellation, her forearms are bandaged, first- and second-degree burns. She's scratched and bruised. There are bloody half-moons where she dug her nails into her palms.

While Moremi waits in the hospital for the neurologist to discharge her, Halima runs out to a local hardware store and buys a cheap console. 'It's almost retro,' she says, laughing at the sight of its touchscreen.

'I can't believe they still make these.' Moremi wants to scoff at it, turn up her nose at the old thing. A toy for the

Pulseless and the elderly. But she feels as if she is already in withdrawal from the Panopticon. Feels the tightening clutch of the kind of boredom and loneliness that haunted her childhood. She needs to know about yesterday's attack. Needs to find out if Orpheus is okay. Moremi lays the console flat on the charging dock and waits the fifteen minutes it takes to boot up.

When it finally does, the Panopticon is like a cool draught of water. Her Vine is flooded with information about what is already being called the Quantum Hill attack. Hysterical ticker-tape headlines: *Terror strikes London ... at least hundreds killed, many more in critical condition in biggest civilian loss of life since the Thames Barrier strike ... City under lockdown as citizens flee ... Late breaking news: Bertram Fairmont and Professor Itō murdered by neo-Luddite radicals. Hayden Adeyemi injured.*

Her console comes with a Jelly, a device that feels like a wad of Blu-Tack which she can push into her ear. As soon as she does the ambient chatter of all of her groups starts up on the edge of her consciousness. Everyone she has ever known has left her a volley of messages that erupt all at the same time: 'OK? ... are you okay? ... R U OK? ... I heard you were ... Heard about the attack? ... Heard you were there ...' On the events app, she marks herself as present but injured, and then scrolls through the list of names of other people involved. There are stomach-curdling videos of young Panopticon employees smashing their skulls into walls and trying to gouge out their constellations. Many of them are dead now, or in medically induced comas.

'Where is Orpheus?' Moremi asks Halima. 'You said he was on his way.' But even as Moremi says it she realises that Halima was lying.

'I just didn't want you to worry.'

'What does that mean? Where is he?'

'I don't know.' She furrows her brow. 'Lots of people are missing, you know. It's not easy to locate them with their constellations offline. He'll turn up though. He'll be here or in one of the other hospitals probably. Just give it a couple of hours.'

Moremi wants to roam the streets as she did when her mother died, and shout his name.

He is not marked on the event app, and when she searches for him on Friend Finder nothing comes up. It seems impossible to find a person without a Pulse. When she searches the hospital's directory he is not there either. Moremi considers sending a message to some of his friends who might know his whereabouts but – and it occurs to her only now – he doesn't seem to have any friends. She settles for Zen, whose Pulse is also offline, and for posting the question in some of the groups he's part of. As she waits for any response, she bats away the dreadful thoughts that come. Orpheus dead like so many others, Rorschach blots of his blood in the mud, his head floating down the river. No, she promises herself, it's too horrible to be true.

There is something so claustrophobic about using the console. Like staring through a dim window into the Panopticon when she used to live in it. Moremi opens another tab and the image of Bertram Fairmont falling from the watchtower like a comet is all over the internet. It breaks her heart to see it, Bertram's head and all its holy contents spilled on the granite lip of the fountain.

Is this the day the Singularity died? asks a *New York Times* op-ed. *What now for the Magi?* asks another.

No one is surprised by the global outpouring of grief for the two founders of the Panopticon. Obituaries are hastily published by all of the major news outlets. In east London, crowds have gathered on the North Bank outside the police cordon overlooking Quantum Hill, clutching each other and crying. Makeshift shrines have sprung up all around the world. Memorials covered in flowers, candles, the Panopticon logo graffitied across walls, drawn in the sand, built out of LED lights, displayed on every screen in Tokyo's Shibuya Crossing, Piccadilly Circus, Times Square. It feels as if the world has stopped turning for them. Sidewalks are carpeted in lilies, which unfurl everywhere like ivory tongues. Handwritten love letters with bleeding ink. Jitsuko Itō's face is projected, three storeys high, on the glass facade of a tech store in Shanghai. People are holding a vigil in the Panopticon's Sydney campus. Students in Hayden's Catholic primary school are reported to be praying ferociously for his speedy recovery.

Opinion pieces have begun to hastily materialise. They changed the world, people agree. They stood at the intersection between technology and religion. The speech that Bertram made at the Symposium has taken on a new prophetic meaning. It wasn't meant to be this way, he had said. So let him be a martyr, some people argue, the last of us to die before Total Adoption. Stella Stratton agrees. In a statement released by Downing Street in response to his death, she says, 'This act of terrorism only serves to illustrate how necessary Total Adoption is for Total Security.'

Moremi agrees. She not only believes what the founders had promised, but for five ecstatic seconds during last night's demonstration she lived it. The better life that awaits them all if they only vote 'Yes'.

Perhaps the worst thing is that no one seems surprised by the attack. 'Violence, riots and revolutions are way more likely to take place in the summertime,' Halima says. 'That's like, a known thing. July the fourth. The storming of the Bastille. Both in July.'

'What about the October Revolution?' Moremi says. 'Or the Arab Spring, which – I literally just discovered – didn't happen in spring?'

'I said *more* likely.'

Moremi won't deny that the air had been feeling electric, seemed to prickle with fury. There is a referendum coming up in a couple of weeks and the 55 per cent of the population who are for Total Adoption have been radicalised against the 45 per cent of Brits who are not. Moremi herself has moved from being fairly sympathetic to those who plan on voting 'No' to being repelled by them. She sees now that the stakes are so much higher than she thought.

Police arrest 12 in hunt for associates of Quantum Hill attackers: Armed police launched a series of raids in east London on Saturday as officers hunted members of the neo-Luddite groups who carried out the attack. The Metropolitan Police said 12 people – five women and seven men – were arrested from at least three addresses in and around Tottenham.

One Anti-TA op-ed says that the Quantum Hill attack, tragic as it was, underscores a particular weakness in certain security systems known as Pulse-blindness. It turns out that the Pulseless assailants were hired by private contractors to cater for the night. While the security systems in place at the Panopticon are designed to scan the constellations of everyone who enters and leaves, those without a Pulse, hired by the external company, were not as rigorously examined. And, after the attack, although a handful of them have been arrested, the majority of them are still at large. The thought of this makes Moremi sick.

Later in the day the neo-Luddite organisation who call themselves the Revelators, who have publicly taken responsibility for the attack, release a statement that says: 'In these radical times we must take radical action.' Revelators, Moremi thinks with a shudder. The word has taken on a new menacing resonance. She can't help but consider her young sister, Zeeba, who had called her up the morning of the symposium and begged Moremi not to go. What had she known? 'Pulseless is dangerous' is the mantra being whispered among Moremi's cohort. So what does that make her sister?

'She's away this weekend,' Halima says, the same concern in her own voice.

'Yeah?' Moremi is uncertain.

'At some . . . I don't remember.' Halima bites her lip.

'You don't think . . .' Moremi ventures. She doesn't want to say it out loud. She's thinking of the last time they were in hospital together and the blood from her asterisk scar matted in dark crystals at the nape of her neck.

'No,' Halima says. 'She would never—'

'Of course,' Moremi hastily agrees. 'I feel bad for even thinking it.'

By the time she is discharged, Moremi is frantic. No one can tell her where Orpheus is. He'd given her his oversized white jacket to keep her warm, the night of the symposium, and she wears it now, even though it's blood-spattered and muddy.

It's dark outside, already ten-thirty, and the halls of the hospital are chaos. Still packed with gurneys and weeping relatives, the victims of the previous night's attack still in their singed and blood-spattered finery. Someone's fur bolero kicked under the leg of a waiting room chair. A string of pearls burst by the reception. Doctors fielding volleys of questions. Moremi is just another in the fray, asking people if they know where he is.

She begs one of the dozens of officers in the lobby to search for his name on the Protect database and finally he does. 'It says that you're his next of kin. That some of our colleagues were trying to get hold of you but . . .' He eyes the side of her head.

'My Pulse was—' Moremi begins to explain.

'Right. Like most of the others.'

'And Orpheus?' she asks. Her chest is so tight that she can only take shallow breaths. Dead, she is thinking, and the sight of those bodies piled high in the wake of the flood flashes before her mind with Pavlovian quickness.

'No,' he says, 'detained in custody last night.' He shares some files with the flick of his hand to her console. But she's not sure she understands what these words mean.

'Arrested?'

'That's right, ma'am.'

In her confusion she can only recognise two words on the notice. 'Conspiracy' and 'Terrorism'.

24

ORPHEUS

He and Moremi had barely made it out of the symposium before the protection officers grab him, and push his head into the asphalt. There follows a harrowing journey in the police van where they answer none of his questions.

After they process him, one of the doctors wipes the virus off his constellation and deactivates his Pulse. When they throw him into his cell, the silence is unnerving. Orpheus falls into a fitful sleep, one plagued by nightmares. Professor Itō in a bellied pool of her own blood. It could have been him, his constant thought. It could still be.

In the dream, like a few he's had over the past month, he is running from a crowd. When they catch him they grab him by the hair and grind his temple into the pavement. They want his head. They want freedom from the machine. They wrench his skull from his spine.

Orpheus awakes on a single foam mattress, pressed up

against a cement wall. On one side of the room is a lidless toilet that smells of bleach and bile. The sound of a passing train rattles the bars in the solitary window.

They come for him early the next morning. Two officers, who escort Orpheus from his cell and along a long hall. They take a turn around a mezzanine deck that gives Orpheus a wide view of the facility. The ground floor is a hive of activity. It looks something like an open-plan newsroom or the trading floor of the New York Stock Exchange. Orpheus can't help but slow his pace a little to take in the sight of it. The ground floor of a protection office is such a stock location in movies and TV shows that Orpheus imagines he might already know his way around it. The screens and monitors, consoles and schematics. On the furthest wall is a giant projection, a map of London, flickering with points of light at roads and intersections, residences and public parks, bubbles of red and orange inflating and vanishing. The silver lance of the Thames splitting the whole thing in two. A clock running in the top corner of the display is dated 24 hours in the future.

'Is that,' Orpheus can't help but ask in fanboy wonder, 'Tiresias?'

He used to enjoy watching re-runs of a show called *Twelve*, a glamourised US show about a blind cop who worked for the NYPD and used a Panopticon software called Tiresias to solve crimes. At the start of each episode he'd have twelve hours to find a killer, or prevent an attack, a traffic accident or a suicide.

Protect is the branch of the Panopticon that won the

government contract to police Greater London, because they claimed that their particular software – Tiresias – produced the most accurate predictions. Orpheus supposes it must be true, because the Panopticon have access to an unprecedented amount of user data. They are able to look into the minds of three quarters of the people on the planet. To see what they see and hear what they hear. A constellation can record whether or not the wearer is sleep-deprived, or is over the alcohol limit. Its sensors can record the wearer's level of cortisol or dopamine. And this wealth of data is aggregated and analysed by computers all over the world, used by the Panopticon to predict outcomes with varying degrees of certainty. This is one of the many ways that the Panopticon is able to make its money. Although most of their apps and services are free, governments and private entities pay the Panopticon huge amounts of money for the future. How much to predict the likely outcome of an election? The likelihood of certain security breaches, or civil unrest, the probability the country may be struck down by an epidemic in the next year, or nuclear war.

Although Orpheus understands that Tiresias' forecasts are not quite as accurate as those depicted in *Twelve*, they grow more accurate every day, with each new person who implants a Pulse.

'Move along.' The officer gives him a hard shove between the shoulder blades. Orpheus catches sight of his reflection in the polished elevator door. He is still wearing a stained shirt from the night before. There is a crust of blood on his lower lip and one of his eyes has swollen shut.

The interview room looks like a dentist's surgery with a reclining chair in the centre. Two armrests with handcuffs snap out. There is a large projector in the back of the room. A two-way mirror, behind which sit white-suited technicians and police officers, he's sure.

'No.' Orpheus steps back at the sight of it. The last time he was in a room like this was after his father died. When a Pulse was forcibly implanted in his skull, when they mined his memories for evidence. Sometimes in his nightmares he awakes in that chair.

'No!' Three officers have to drag him, kicking and shouting, into the chair. A noisy altercation, where Orpheus bites down hard on the wrist of one of the officers, leaving a bloody crescent in the scattered shape of his teeth. Finally, one of them hits him hard with the butt of a rifle, leaving Orpheus dazed and weak, stars igniting across his vision, and by the time he comes to again, he is handcuffed to the chair at his wrists and ankles, uselessly thrashing.

A technician straps a helmet over his head and locks it under his jaw. Orpheus can see nothing but the projector screen in front of him, awash with static.

'I know my rights,' he says to the crunch of boots on the linoleum behind him. 'I know that police aren't allowed access to my memories without my consent.'

'You missed your calling,' says the voice of a woman behind him. *One of the technicians?* Orpheus wonders. *One of the officers?* 'Should have been a lawyer.'

'I know I'm owed a lawyer,' Orpheus says. 'That I don't have to speak until I have one. And you're supposed to tell me what I'm being detained for.'

Two officers step into his field of vision: a large man who introduces himself as Detective Inspector Branson-Lewis, and a woman in her mid-fifties, Assistant Commissioner Melissa Palmer, who introduces herself as the head of the Pre-emptive Protection Division of the counter-terrorism command.

That word, 'terrorism', makes him shiver with dread. 'There must be some mistake,' he says.

DI Lewis explains to Orpheus that he is being arrested for 'conspiracy to commit acts of terrorism' under a section of the law that applies to future crime. For that reason, they explain, protection officers are entitled to view the last week of his quartz recordings and may apply for a warrant to view more. Orpheus has been through this before and knows that there is no point in struggling. He grits his teeth as his brain appears on the screen. A request for access floats into his field of vision, which the technician quickly overrides.

It's a sickening experience, to watch one's own memories anywhere but behind one's own eyes. On the projector screen, his recorded visual and audio feeds appear like a mumblecore movie. The lighting and focus all wrong, the image shaky as a handheld camera. Audio punctuated by the click and snap sound of his own teeth in his head.

Orpheus' heart flutters at the sight of Moremi on the screen. The police have started the recording twenty-four hours ago, when Orpheus and his new wife were in bed in a hotel room. She's naked, stretched luxuriously out on top of the duvet cover, too hot to sleep much longer. Sounds of traffic outside, sunlight through the gap in the heavy satin curtains, room service calling on the ancient hotel landline to warn them that breakfast will be over in thirty minutes. His heart aches for it, for her. Orpheus squeezes his eyes shut but the feed flashes in his head all the same.

'Forward one hour, please,' states the commissioner. 'None of us are interested in his love life.'

The police make him relive the whole of that night, though without the smell of smoke in the air or the iron bite of blood in his mouth. Bertram's twisted body in the fountain. A woman screaming, her hair on fire. The panic after the Pulse attack, people leaping into the canal, slamming their heads against trees, gouging their constellations with penknives or broken glass. 'Make it stop,' Orpheus shouts, straining against the gurney, banging his fists.

The technicians behind the glass look pale too. 'Speed it up,' DI Lewis says. They play the rest of the recording on 1.5 speed until they reach the part where Orpheus was arrested. He'd been grabbed by some protection officers who had tackled him to the ground and twisted his arms behind his back.

'You see,' Orpheus says, once they pause the recording. 'I didn't have anything to do with this. If anything, I'm a victim. Shouldn't you have been arresting all those people in masks? The ones actually committing acts of terrorism? Isn't that your job? What good is any of this' – he gestures to the projector – 'if you couldn't stop any of that from happening?'

The officers exchange a glance.

'That is what we're working to do,' says Palmer. 'We

have intelligence that there is going to be another attack on the capital, something more devastating. Something like the flood. Worse than, if you can imagine it. Something that will have far-reaching global consequences.'

'On the Quantum Hill campus?' Orpheus asks.

'We don't know,' the commissioner says.

'When?' Orpheus asks.

'September 7th.' Three months from now.

'What's going to happen?'

'We were hoping that you would be able to tell us.'

Orpheus' head is spinning. *How could they have it so wrong?* he thinks. 'Why?' he asks, straining against the helmet to stare at them.

'Let me show you something.' The commissioner makes a hand motion and a file appears on the projector screen. It's the kind of display that Orpheus has seen every day on the news or projected up the glass walls of the sky-scrapers in Canary Wharf. The FTSE 100 index. The old graphic that's always been indecipherable to him. Green mountains and red valleys. A timeline at the bottom runs into the future. August 10th, just over two weeks after the referendum, where the line makes a nose-dive that even Orpheus, with his limited knowledge of finance, can tell looks disastrous.

'A few months ago,' says DI Lewis, 'a contact of ours who works in the forecasting department of Goldman Sachs told me that their models are predicting the biggest point-drop in history.'

'I don't know anything about economics or money,' Orpheus says. 'This has nothing to do with me.'

'I'm not a banker either. But no one in her department had ever seen a prediction like this before.' A few more graphs appear on the screen: the FTSE, the Dow Jones, the Nikkei 225. 'Markets everywhere from New York to Hong Kong. Graphs only look like this in the wake of devastating global events. Wars, tsunamis, pandemics. So now, what we're trying to uncover is what happens that turns the world upside down.'

'Something you think I have any idea about?' Orpheus laughs now. 'This is a joke.'

Melissa Palmer says, 'Do you want to know why I do this work, Orpheus? I lost two boys in the flood. Oscar and Charlie. Five and seven. Obsessed with trains, scared of the dark. Loved Nutella. Died with a hundred other children in their primary school that day.'

She is quiet for a moment, although her eyes are steel. 'There isn't a word for it. When you're not a mother any-more.' Orpheus twists in his seat. 'There were whispers, even then, that the Panopticon could have known. Clues. Canaries in the coalmine. When Stella Stratton promised nothing like that would ever happen again – no mothers had to lose their children that way again – I wanted to believe her. I wanted to be part of the team. That's how Protect was born.' She glances at the screen, its static-y light flickering off the pale cliff of her forehead.

'It's like a weather forecast. It uses all the data available, anonymised, of course, collected through the Panopticon. It runs calculations, looks for patterns. Where has crime occurred before? Who? How? And we use the predic-tions to make the world a safer place. The incidence of almost every kind of crime has decreased by up to 90 per cent.'

'I've heard the Vote Yes adverts,' Orpheus says.

'In the 1960s,' she says, 'a mathematician and pioneer of chaos theory, Edward Lorenz, suggested that no one can predict the weather beyond a certain time horizon.'

Orpheus has heard of this too, mainly because the police officers on *Twelve* are always referring to it. 'The predictability horizon.'

'That's right. It turns out that crime and global events are similar, too. Most software can't predict much beyond sixty days; even with near-perfect models and a broad understanding of initial conditions, there is a limit. So, last night, when we ran the prediction again, Tiresias produced some more information. A name. Yours.'

'So,' Orpheus summarises, 'all you know is that there is going to be a devastating attack. You know it will happen in just over a month's time and I have something to do with it.'

'There was another name too,' DI Lewis says. 'Warsame.'

Orpheus' body stiffens. His father?

'Yes. We've been aware for many years that was one of the aliases your father used. Mustafa Matan.'

'But you know my father is—'

'Dead.'

'Killed,' Orpheus spits.

Palmer nods. 'Any loss of life is a tragedy, but I can assure you that your father's death saved many more lives.'

'Is that what your computer algorithms were telling you?'

'He was a dangerous man.'

'And apparently I am, too!' Orpheus shouts, angry now.

'No,' she says, trying to diffuse some of the tension. 'No, Orpheus, you're a good man. You want to help us to save lives. Save your wife. Her sister. Your friends. And it's increasingly clear to us that you really did have no idea who your father was.'

When she turns, the screen resolves into another image. Some of the familiar video footage of Professor Itō connecting her mind to the first computer. The birth of the Panopticon. Commissioner Palmer manipulates the picture with her hands. Zooms into the corner, reconstructs a face. On the threshold of the door is a man who looks like Orpheus. Darker-skinned, but with the same long face and dark locks, same thickly lashed eyes.

'That's my . . .' He's clean-shaven as Orpheus has never seen him before. 'It's not possible,' Orpheus whispers. Although the timelines match up. His father was likely in his early twenties when the Pulse was first created.

'Your father was one of the men on the large team who helped to create the Panopticon's original operating system.'

'He was a primary coder?'

'That's right.'

Orpheus wants to insist that it cannot be true. Do these people understand the way that his father lived? But then, Orpheus considers, this information does make a backwards kind of sense. Orpheus thinks about how fiercely clever his father was. How he seemed to know everything Orpheus cared to ask about computers or engineering or physics. What technical skills it must have taken to construct the life that he had for the two of them.

Orpheus closes his eyes, the ground falling away from under his spine. Finally he says, 'I can't help you.'

Palmer smiles ruefully as if she had anticipated this response.

'You can't lock me up for a crime I know nothing about and haven't yet committed.' Orpheus is wrestling vainly against the restraints now.

'Save your energy,' she says. 'This is about keeping the country safe. Preventing as many attacks as we can. And, as a matter of fact, a recent amendment to the Predictive Policing Bill gives us the power to hold you in custody, for a suspected future crime, indefinitely.'

25

MOREMI

The East London Protection Office is like a fortified castle. An old brutalist building, with tall wire fences guarded by men in riot gear and a fleet of buzzing drones. After she had been discharged from the hospital, Moremi had insisted on travelling there.

'What are you going to do?' Halima asks again, as she had when they'd hailed the car. 'You think if you ask them nicely they'll let him out?'

Moremi doesn't know, but as she steps onto the pavement she sees the vanity of any efforts. There are a couple of protestors gathered by the gates, some shaking the bars and shouting, 'No crime, no justice.' There is a couple camped out in front of a spray-painted tent, holding a picture of a young man. Their son, Moremi assumes from the blue in all of their eyes. They have a flip chart which reads, '764 days and counting'.

'God,' Moremi whispers. A punch in her gut at the sight

of them. How long since Orpheus was taken? Less than a day. But, her mind catapults forwards, the next week, the next year ...

'He's gone,' Halima says, not unkindly. 'They say that they're holding him and he's not coming back. Terrorism ... they don't arrest people for petty future crimes, Moremi. They won't let him go.'

'But ...' Moremi is crying now. 'He didn't do anything.'

'But' – Halima hugs her, rubs her hair – 'he certainly would have.'

She wants to shake the bars and shout his name, to enter the office and tell the analysts that this can't be true. Do you know what a gentle man he is? How quiet and kind? Can she camp outside too until they bring him out? Can she offer them something in return? Can someone appeal? The Panopticon doesn't seem to have a clear answer on this point.

'They're not even in there,' says another protestor in a Vote No T-shirt. 'After they book them, they take them away to some bunker, on the outskirts of London, in the middle of nowhere.'

'It just ...' Moremi is almost too frightened to voice her doubts. 'It doesn't seem fair.'

'Oh!' the man says in mock surprise. 'You thought this would be "fair"?'

'I didn't even get to say goodbye,' she says, fresh sobs coming to her throat.

'He's as good as dead,' another protestor says to her, 'where they've taken him.'

*

311

Halima wants to take her back to her flat but Moremi doesn't want to go. She wants to return to the place she shared with Orpheus for a month. It's the same as the morning they left it. A few hours before they were married. Mason jar of cherry Pepsi on the windowsill, a scum of dust gathered on its black skin. The bonsai tree Halima gave them as a wedding gift. Poplin shirts piled in the hall, his slender footprints on the kitchen tiles.

She lies in his bed and cries herself to sleep that first night. Halima is next to her in the morning, but she has to leave to go to work. 'It'll pass,' she says before she goes. And Moremi knows she's talking about the heartbreak. 'It always does.'

'No,' Moremi says, still in bed, her eyes sticky with tears. 'He was different from all of them.'

Halima only shakes her head and closes the front door. 'Is!' Moremi shouts at it. *'Is!'*

When she tries to scrub the stains out of his linen jacket, she finds his father's pocket-watch in the breast pocket. She'd seen him hold it before, its weight like a yo-yo in his palms, but had never examined it herself. It's been years since she's seen a watch and this one is lovely, with its delicate dials and brushed gold case.

Moremi wanders like a ghost through the house, counting backwards. The day they filled the bath with pillows and ate instant noodles. The day they went out to the museum and lost each other. She'd found him a little while later, staring at a display case with a hand-written label that read 'Spectacular Shells' – the abandoned homes of molluscs, sea snails and cephalopods. Some of them as small as hat pins, others ridged like fans and large as pots. He had been struck by the sight of a nautilus shell shaped like a French horn, its pearlescent inner layer reflecting the museum's thin light. At the sight of his face in the glass she had said, 'You're beautiful,' and he had turned and said, 'I'm only beautiful to you because you love me.'

'You're beautiful and I love you.'

Is it true what they're saying? That it's over now, forever? Will he never come back? The thought is too horrible for her to bear. But she has no idea what to do to try to conjure him back.

She discovers a couple of expired sleeping pills in the bathroom cabinet, takes them and lets the hours skitter away. Each time she wakes, it's to a knife-twist of pain under her lungs and a sound in her ears, like seashell resonance. An undulating whoosh that mimics a lapping tide.

She used to be frightened of it.

When she wakes again, her face is wet, and the poly-cotton pillowcase has stuck to her cheek. Halima is helping her up into a bath. Her sister swears under her breath as she almost trips over the consoles and monitors scattered about the bathroom. Rogue wires and processors.

'Did he ever actually use the bath for bathing?'

The next thing Moremi knows, luke-warm water is sliding down her back, and she feels her muscles unknot. Her sister's hands in her hair. Suds on her arms.

'Do you know what day it is?'

With her quartz deactivated she feels senile, unable to remember the most basic things. Names, places, dates, even words slip from her grasp. Zeeba liked to claim that people used to memorise the epic poems before reading and writing. That their grandmothers knew phone numbers off by heart. Moremi's memory is a muscle she's allowed to waste.

Halima asks another question she doesn't know the answer to: 'Have you heard of "Inversion Syndrome"?'

Halima examines her sister's face for a while before she says, 'I've only just heard of it and I've been doing some research. It's kind of like love-sickness. If love was a sickness. Obsession is one of the symptoms. Impulsive behaviour. Some people I trust have suggested that you fit the profile. Did you and he' – she's not saying his name any more for fear it will tip Moremi over into tears – 'ever dream-share?' She says it the way that doctors say, 'You're not in trouble, but we need to know what you've taken.' When Moremi doesn't reply, Halima says, 'It's okay, we can get help.'

She sounds so much like their mother sometimes, Moremi thinks. If she closes her eyes she could convince herself of it. And at this thought, a memory floats up from the sedative haze. 'Halima,' she gasps. 'All my memories from that night are foggy because of what happened to my Pulse and the confusion and everything. But, on the night of the Quantum Hill attack, I saw Mum.'

Halima only looks crestfallen. Not curious and excited as Moremi had hoped. 'Do you think there's a way—'

'No,' Halima says firmly, dropping the sponge into the bath.

'No. It was. She was real. She called my name. She—'

'I don't want to hear it.' Halima gets as quickly to her

314

feet as she can with her bump. Stands clutching it, looking as if she's about to cry. Before Moremi can say anything else, she says, 'How long do I have to keep doing this?'

'Doing what?'

'Looking after you. You and Zeeba and all your terrible choices. Running after you.' The words are a gut-punch. On Halima's face, there is an expression Moremi has never seen before. She wonders if her sister is counting up the cost. Of dropping out of Oxford to help her sisters. All those years. The meals she skipped just to ensure the two of them wouldn't go hungry.

'You keep coming up with schemes to try to "fix" me,' Moremi says. 'You know I'm not some mess you can try to clean up. You can't return me to the shop for a less defective sister.'

'You know what?' Halima says, and moves quickly for the door. 'Sometimes I wish I could.'

Almost as much as anything, she misses the Panopticon. Its static embrace. Her love for the Panopticon has the intimacy of almost any other. Isn't love made up of a million moments? The profound and prosaic; the thousand videos that make her attention skate off into tangents – ASMR baking, kinetic sand, a Thai craftsman meticulously constructing a bench, cats, puppies, celebrities disclosing what is in their bag. Thanks to the Vine, for all of fifteen minutes, she'd been famous. An audition video she'd submitted to a company went viral and she'll never forget the endorphin rush of a hundred thousand hands clapping her.

Is it normal to feel ...?

Am I the only one who ...?

She misses those nights when her mind, untethered from her body, had soared like a satellite through cyberspace.

She'd sunk the majority of her teenage years into caring for PanoptoPets who eventually starved. Into meticulously constructing a Vine profile and examining the profiles of others, into reliving the memories of minor celebrities as they applied make-up. Into building VR cities in order to watch them burn. Hadn't most of it been fun, though?

It's a shaman, it's a magic 8 ball. It knows her better than any lover, any friend or sister. Only the Panopticon knows what kind of fantastical hentai she likes. Or which medical conditions she's convinced herself she contracted. Only the Panopticon has cast about for answers to her private anxieties.

Will I be alone?

Will I be happy?

Will everything turn out alright? For me?

The nights after Halima leaves, Moremi stays up, searching on her console for memories of the symposium. She wants to know if anyone else saw her mother.

But the virus that attacked everyone's Pulse has rendered most of their memories of the event unwatchable. When she thinks back to that night, she'd been in too much shock to chase after her. Moremi curses herself for it now, though.

*

She wakes one night to find Zeeba sitting on the edge of her bed like Queen Mab.

'I came to see if you're looking after that bonsai tree,' she says. It's on the windowsill gathering dust. It lost all its leaves overnight, and they flutter like confetti around the radiator. 'They need loads of water,' Zeeba says, taking its terracotta tray and putting it into the kitchen sink.

'Where were you?' Moremi asks. 'The night it happened?'

'First the art studio. Then, my friend Raffi's house,' Zeeba says breezily when she re-enters the room. She sits back on the edge of the bed. It's dark outside. Ten, Moremi thinks, or eleven, based on the sounds she can hear on the street. As it's the summer, the roadsides and apartment blocks seem to reverberate constantly with the sound of heavy bass blasting from someone's balcony or the rolled-down window of someone's car.

'Shall I tell you something disgusting?' Zeeba asks. She rummages in her rucksack and brings out a paper copy of the *National Geographic*.

'Where do you even get those?' Moremi asks. 'Museums?'

'Libraries.' Zeeba rolls her eyes, licks a finger and turns a page. 'So I've been reading about anglerfish mating.'

'Of course you have,' Moremi says. Zeeba has a slightly suspect fascination with the mating rituals of different species.

Zeeba rolls over onto her stomach and reads from the magazine.

'So,' she summarises, 'there is this sub-order of the anglerfish family with a name that begins with a C that, honestly, I can't pronounce. In the 1800s biologists could only seem to find the female of the species and never the males. Where were they? In the 1920s the mystery was solved. One biologist found a female anglerfish with two weird appendages attached to her body. What the hell were they? Children? No. When the fish was dissected it was discovered that these lumps on her body were the male fish.'

'That sounds gross,' Moremi says.

'It's worse than that,' Zeeba says, excited now. 'So this suborder of fish swim around for a long time deep in the sea. When at some point a male comes across a female he bites a hole into her belly and hangs on. After a while, their tissues fuse, their blood supply becomes one. Many of his body parts begin to atrophy: eyes – what does he need them for? – fins, and some internal organs. Soon he's nothing but a lump of flesh fused into hers. A parasite, basically. Supping nutrients from her body, providing sperm whenever she's ready to spawn.'

'Okay,' Moremi says, blinking up at the ceiling. 'So nature is terrifying.'

Zeeba holds the pages up to the thin light coming from the window in order to read. 'Naturalist William Beebe said, "But to be driven by impelling odour headlong upon a mate so gigantic, in such immense and forbidding darkness, and wilfully eat a hole in her soft side, to feel the gradually increasing transfusion of her blood through one's veins, to lose everything that marked one as other than a worm, to become a brainless, senseless thing that was a fish – this is sheer fiction, beyond all belief unless we have seen the proof of it."'

Moremi feels cornered now, irritated. 'Did Halima tell you to do this?'

'Do what?'

'Read me some weird story about inversion.'

'In-what?'

'She thinks my love is a sickness. That she can cure me of Orpheus.' Moremi's voice falters at the end of this and her vision blurs a little.

'I think your love for the Panopticon is a sickness,' Zeeba says.

Moremi replays every day they spent together in her memory and wonders, was it love or inversion? Does it matter?

Moremi wants to believe it was inversion. Wants to believe it's something that science can fix for her. She feels she's out of options. Either science cures her pain or she'll die this way, in this flat, of missing him.

When she tries to convince herself, by searching online, she uncovers a hologram of the brain in love, and then an inverted brain, drenched in neon colours to indicate wild trains of action potentials in all the same places, the 'ventral tegmental area' and the 'A10 cells'. Some chemical madness, some people say. In that way, others ask, how different is it from love?

Psychologists have reached no consensus on the best cure. Some doctors believe it fades on its own. Others recommend a course of therapy, antidepressants, avoidance of the love object. The thought of another long journey, another slow climb to wellness, exhausts her.

She wants to be free from this pain, and she wants it to be easy.

A couple of weeks after the attack, Mercury visits and tells her that it's true, that there is a cure for heartbreak. Mercury's Pulse is back online. They arrive with Cher Siu Boa buns they bought from the street-food stall near the tube station. It's the first thing that Moremi's eaten in a while and as she sits on the edge of her bed to greet her friend she is self-consciously aware of the state of herself. The ripe smell of her unwashed body. Sticky crust of tears dried on the side of her face.

It's been weeks now, and Moremi hasn't had the strength to do anything. To get up, to change her clothes, to practise dancing or go to work. Notifications flood her console and she dismisses them all. The air in the house is putrid, the sun through the windows rotting everything. Fruit flies fling their bodies against the glass.

It's still strange to talk to Kimiko's body, knowing that, although Moremi had seen Zen's corpse covered in the hospital and wheeled into a morgue, her friend is alive and here. Kimiko's body is the picture of wellness. In a yellow linen tunic, and matching culottes, they smell of jasmine and gardenia, look as if they've just rolled in from doing yoga in the park.

'Don't you miss her?' Moremi asks.

'It is strange,' they say, 'only this one body.' They spread their fingers as if they've never seen them before. 'And it was strange,' they say, 'to die.'

Moremi shudders at the thought. Some morbid part of her is longing to ask what it had been like but another is too frightened.

'Is there a way to know,' Moremi asks, 'if it was love or inversion?' Mercury shakes their head. 'Some part of me wishes we could be like you,' Moremi says. 'I'd rather be with him forever than never see him again.'

Mercury reaches over and squeezes Moremi's knee in quiet comfort. Moremi is jealous of them. Jealous, not just because her whole body aches from missing Orpheus, but also because Mercury radiates the kind of otherworldly calm that makes Moremi think she's crossed the Rubicon. Crested the hill to technological enlightenment. Zen and Kimiko could live forever and never suffer. *What is it like to be them?* Moremi wonders. Not a doubtful thought, not a prick of anxiety, just a full head of eternal light.

'There is a cure, you know,' they say to her, 'for whatever you're feeling.' Mercury explains that they can perform it in the Panopticon's School of Sleep.

'A cure,' Moremi says, the word itself another promise.

'Only if you want it.'

Moremi isn't sure. The cure, she thinks, is getting him back. 'I want it, though,' they say. 'Want it for you. I feel as if it's my fault.'

'What?'

'All of this.'

'It's not your fault that Orpheus was arrested.'

'No, but I encouraged you to do the treatment. I thought it would help. I didn't know it would lead to all of this.' They look around the room, the miserable state of their friend.

'Don't apologise,' Moremi says. 'I'm glad it happened. I'm glad I met him, that I knew him even for a little bit.'

'But it doesn't have to ruin the rest of your life,' they say, then reach over and take her hand, imploringly. 'Don't you want to get better?'

'Of course,' Moremi says, as she'd said before. Mercury thinks that if Moremi can rid herself from the pain of missing him she might have a chance to move on with her life. To get back into her job, to get back to dance class and auditions. To being a good sister. Mercury makes it sound as if there is a way out of heartbreak, and the Panopticon can make it easy. Moremi wants it to be easy.

So when they say, 'Will you let me help you?' Moremi says, 'Yes.'

Only a few weeks ago it had been beautiful to her, the Panopticon's vast campus. But it seems haunted now. The site of the attack, the last time she'd seen Orpheus. Over there, under the shade of those cedars, he'd held her. If she'd known it would be the final time, she wouldn't have let him go.

There is a mournful air among the employees who have returned. Many of them wear black, tracksuit bottoms and trainers. The constellations of those wearing Pulses flicker with a slow pink ebb as if they're all in pain – the same pain.

Moremi could have imagined Quantum Hill was the safest place on Earth. And now, how can she ever look at the watchtower and not see Bertram falling like a comet from it, smashing his head on the fountain below.

'They're not allowed to say "dead".' Mercury is looking in the same direction, their eyes shadowed with grief.

'What do they say?'

'There's a process. Bertram and Itō would have been placed on a tilting surgical table. All the fluids in their body will have been drained, replaced with cryo-protective agents. They will be suspended somewhere in a tank called a dewar. In some low-ceilinged room in the bowels of Quantum Hill.' Cryo-preservation, just as they'd promised.

'I saw it, though.' Moremi must fight hard not to conjure the stomach-turning image again. Bertram's blood and shards of bone. 'Itō, maybe, but do you really think that any science can bring him back?'

'He might not come back the same,' Mercury says. 'He'll be changed. They both will. A universe of code. Wonderful data. Sun-bright shards of their consciousness in a machine maybe, or in the mind of another. Someone who has elected to pair with them. New face, old memories. The technology exists. They could be here now. Or maybe their bodies are being born half a world away, waiting.'

Something has changed in Moremi. Only a few weeks ago those words would have filled her with hope, but today she thinks she senses some profound emptiness in their promises. But as they walk towards the School of Sleep and Dreams, she tries to shake the doubt away.

Mercury explains that they can do the procedure them-selves, in one of the vacant therapy rooms. Before they paired, Kimiko had performed this procedure on hun-dreds of people with inversion syndrome or heartbreak. She will have to reactivate Moremi's constellation. And then, the machine will scan her quartz for memories of Orpheus. It will delete them with the precision of a dentist. They explain that, in spite of the past few Pulseless weeks, Moremi's brain has rewired itself so that her long-term memory relies heavily on her quartz. After the procedure, she will have trouble remembering him. When she does, the pain of his absence will feel as if it happened a long time ago, the edges of it dulled or forgotten.

The intervention sounds extreme, but Moremi trusts Mercury. And trusts the thousands of reviews she's read online. People across the country say it's worked for them. A couple of members of the groups she's part of – families torn apart by the Predictive Policing Bill – say that the procedure is the only thing that has helped them to find any measure of peace.

Moremi follows Mercury through the school's grand atrium like a sleepwalker. On the way, they bump in to Sai Kaur, Orpheus' manager, who reaches out his hand and says to her, 'I'm sorry for your loss,' as if she's a widow. Moremi wants to pull away and say that it's the Panopticon who stole him from her. You people. But she doesn't.

Looking down, Moremi notices a pattern of scars etched into the back of Sai's hand. Hypnotic swirls similar to the ones on Orpheus' wall. 'The labyrinth?' she asks, gazing at them now.

He pulls his sleeve down to cover them, and says with some shame in his voice, 'So I wouldn't get lost on the other side. But that was back when ...' He shakes his head at the memory, and admits, 'I don't dream anymore.'

Then before he walks away he says, 'I really am sorry. I never met a man who could do what he could do. Maybe I never will again.'

It was more than three months ago, the recollection procedure. The last time Moremi had visited the sleek treatment wing of the School of Sleep. The reception is something like a cross between a dentist's office and a spa. There is a changing room that Mercury directs her to, where she can take a shower and swap her unwashed clothes for bleached white pyjamas.

As she changes, voices from the other cubicles float to her. Back when she had a Pulse, the background chatter on her apps meant she never overheard a stranger's conversation. There is a woman crying. 'It's funny,' she says, through sobs, 'the way it feels. Like something really is broken in my chest. Ribs, sternum ...'

'It's okay,' a soft voice replies. 'Everything you're feeling is normal. It shouldn't have happened. Inversion is just a trick the mind plays.'

'Right. Hazel keeps saying that I need to stop looking back.'

'She's right. We'll help make it so it never happened.'

Moremi must have made a noise in her neighbouring cubicle because they fall quickly silent.

'Are you ready?' Mercury asks when Moremi emerges in pyjamas. She gets a sudden flash of herself at thirteen, standing in the nurse's office, scared of how the Panopticon would change her.

Mercury indicates the sleep-pod. The first time, the water inside had been so cold that she'd cried out. She can either ease herself in slowly or dive in and let the pain swallow her. She chooses the latter, does it with a held breath, eyes screwed shut, but then lets out a cry as the water comes up to her neck.

Moremi watches as the servers across the room begin to hum. She's thinking about the way that her name sounded in his mouth. As Mercury prepares the IV bag of Nox, she remembers the way he had looked, thrilled and nervous, on their wedding day. As they wipe the gummy vein on the inside of her elbow with an alcohol swab, him frying eggs in his chequered boxer shorts. The sandy sachets of three-in-one coffee he drank from a soup bowl when he was too lazy to wash a mug.

'Don't look back,' everyone is saying: her sisters, Mercury, the people on the forums. But it's all Moremi wants to do. She imagines the exquisite pain of missing him replaced by some vapid contentment.

'When you wake, you'll feel a lot better,' Mercury says. When has she heard this promise before?

'Maybe I don't want to feel better,' she says quietly.

'Then what do you want?' Mercury asks.

'I want him back,' she says. 'I want . . .' And then it occurs to Moremi, as if it's always been clear, that the Panopticon can give her nothing she wants.

When she climbs out of the tub, the cold air clutches her immediately. Water pools at her bare feet.

'What are you doing?' Mercury asks.

'I don't want any more dreams,' Moremi says. 'I want it to be true.'

Before she knows it, she's running. Back through the waiting room where onlookers in white pyjamas turn to her in surprise. Through the bright atrium of the school, barefoot down its paved walkways.

By the time she reaches the main road, it feels as if the stones have cut her feet to ribbons, her breath coming in ragged gasps as she tries to hail a taxi.

It's a terrible thing, losing faith. It seems to happen to Moremi all at once. Her faith in the Panopticon, her faith that their technology can save her from any heartache, from loneliness or mortality. *Shake even the dust off your feet,* she tells herself. The automated voice of the taxi asks her where she wants to go. *Where to, now?* she wonders, leaning back in the leather seat, pressing her thumbs against her eye sockets and catching her breath.

Home. Her sisters had been begging. For a while, 'home' was wherever he was. And now?

Moremi considers the journey back to Halima's flat. The two-bedroom apartment in East London. Moremi and Zeeba had shared bunkbeds until she turned eighteen and moved in with her boyfriend. After that, Moremi had only ever returned at the end of a relationship. After Lionel had broken up with her, hauling her belongings back in the trash-bags he had packed them in had felt humiliating. The older she gets, the more that sleeping in that shadowed bunk, under a pile of her sister's clothes, feels like a failure. The failure to launch her own career, to move out, to make any kind of love last.

But then, Moremi is not sure she will recover in Orpheus' flat. In those rooms scattered with the maps he'd scrawled on sugar-paper. The flecks of his skin that probably float in the dust.

She thinks about the way that Halima smells. Like whole milk. The wide ivory spades of her nailbeds. The hands she's used to plait her sister's hair in the static light of the television a hundred times. She thinks of Zeeba, drawing while listening to the radio or labouring quietly over a puzzle. Her inventive cooking, her high, clever forehead.

How could she have believed that any other love could save her?

Come home, they had begged. And Moremi finally does.

26

ORPHEUS

Venice in the summertime is brutal. The air humid and still, mosquitos everywhere. But all Orpheus wants to do is marvel at the sight of the place. Sleepy city on the lagoon.

They arrive early in the morning when mist is still peeling off the water, in a vaporetto that takes them right up the Grand Canal. A place so lovely it could break his heart. Even the water is frighteningly blue. Moremi clutches the gunwales of the boat and stares in unblinking awe at the floating cathedrals, the once-grand palazzos. Ornate gates that open right onto water. The city appears to defy physics. It's some eccentric fairy-tale of a place – dead-eyed palace fronts, shuttered windows of shops brimming with gold-leafed masks, lintels hung with the black capes of plague doctors. Moremi says, 'It's like a museum on water,' as another boat disgorges shoals of tourists. 'Who even lives here?'

'Yes,' Orpheus agrees. Orpheus remembers reading that

the population has rapidly declined since the millennium, that there are 95 tourists for every one Venetian. It looks that way. Orpheus turns his nose up at the guided groups with their expensive cameras. Glassy-eyed schoolchildren listen dumbly to AI audio-tours over their constellations. 'You know, we're tourists too,' Moremi reminds him. But he shakes his head. 'We're not tourists. We're ... honey-mooners.' A different breed altogether, emerged from the water like mayflies, slender short-lived beings that feast only on delight.

They plan to stay for a week. The days are torpid and interminable, and yet by Friday, Orpheus can remember almost nothing they did. They visited no museums, except by accident, slipping through open doors to seek respite from the heat. They woke up late and got up later, squint-ing at the afternoon sun as it pushed through the heavy curtains of their hotel room. From the window, they could see the Rialto Bridge being trampled by people in Crocs.

There was not a cloud in the sky the entire time. They watched as cruise ships the size of apartment blocks slugged along the Giudecca Canal. Orpheus returned home one evening to discover that mosquito bites had left a mottled chickenpox-like rash along his shoulders and arms. Moremi bought gelato every day, sometimes two or three, luxurious flavours like fior di latte, stracciatella, bacio and crema del Doge, a silky mixture of chocolate, cream and oranges. They ate pasta or pizza for every meal, were totally swindled in every tourist trap.

There is a legend that gondoliers are born with webbed feet. Orpheus and Moremi can't afford to ride in one of their lacquered boats, so they watch them take off and return from the *traghetto* in their ribboned hats and striped vests, polished leather shoes with designer labels, too small for webbed feet.

On Friday, they take the vaporetto to San Michele, a quiet island of the dead. A walled cemetery with cloistered churches and long ranks of tombs. They stop in front of Igor Stravinsky's grave where someone has arranged white stones in the shape of a treble clef. Sergei Diaghilev's is strewn with piles of sun-bleached ballet shoes. They take photographs on a disposable camera, although their thumbs eclipse their faces in every one, and then they fall asleep in each other's laps, in the shade of cypress trees.

When Orpheus opens his eyes that day, suddenly he forgets how he came to be here. Looks around at the graveyard, which is bright and overexposed. 'Moremi.' He shakes her awake and she rouses with a grimace. 'How did we get here?'

'We took the boat,' she says, rubbing her eyes and gazing at him in confusion. Shading her face from the fierce glare of the sun.

'And before that?'

'Orpheus?'

'Before that?' he asks with a sudden urgency. 'How did we get here? To Venice?' Suddenly he doesn't remember. A plane journey? A coach? Dread turns inside him, and he fumbles for his father's watch.

'Orpheus.' Moremi takes his hand, stares deeply into his eyes and says, 'Be here now.' Just as quickly, a calm comes over him, a flush of love. His wife, wherever she is, is home, he tells himself. It happens again the next day though. She wants to see glass blown on Murano, but they arrive too late and all the factories are closed. Even the shops with their extravagant window displays are shut. Moremi collapses on the pavement in sudden despair, the stones so hot they burn the skin on the back of her thighs. She will never get up, she says. 'It's okay,' he replies, a smile still in the corners of his mouth. Not sure if she is joking.

'We can come again tomorrow,' he promises.

'But ... every day will be like this.' She sinks down, lies flat on her back in the middle of the street. 'Every day will be like this,' she says again, with what he can see is a sudden sickness at her situation.

'Don't worry,' Orpheus reminds her. 'We're going back to London the day after.'

Only there is a certain hollowness in her gaze, a confusion, as if she's never heard of the place.

They have sex to make it up. Her body, another lovely thing. When he's inside her, he tries to pair their Pulses. Orpheus reaches out for her mind but finds nothing. It's a strange sensation, like the shock of not finding a stair when you expect it. But she takes his hand and rests it on her hips, the way she did the first time they ever danced together. 'Yours,' he tells her. She gazes so deeply into his eyes that time splits open, and when he rolls over onto his back the notion comes to him, that this is the dream.

This time he waits for her to fall asleep before looking for his father's watch, which – though he searches in the drawers, again and again, in the bottom of the suitcases, under the bed, and in his washbag – he cannot find. Orpheus tries to rationalise away the panic. Does a few more reality checks; he knows he has a tattoo on his left wrist which reads 'Is it true?' but when he lifts up his hand he sees nothing but clear skin. Looks again and it's there. Blinks, looks again, and the letters have turned to numbers.

Time is normally different in a dream, too. When he opens the curtains, the sky is blood orange, the sun setting, but all the shadows are falling in the wrong direction.

'It's not real . . .' He says it out loud. Moremi stirs then, and looks up at him with a strange calm. 'How did we get here?' he asks.

'I don't . . .' She rubs her eyes. 'I don't remember.' She's part of it too, he thinks, the dream. And suddenly she seems alien to him, empty as a porcelain doll. Orpheus dashes for the door and heads out into the hall and begins to run.

Down the steps, out into the lobby. Worn wood that feels surprisingly solid against his soles. There are not too many inconsistencies in this dream. If he pinches his forearm he can feel pain, which suggests to him that he's in Dreamtime, rather than a dream of his own mind's making. If only he could remember how he got here. Could remember anything from the past couple of weeks in meat-space. The last thing he saw before he fell asleep.

It's midnight and the streets of Venice are frighteningly quiet. Orpheus runs down an avenue so narrow he can't hold his arms out on either side.

How can it not be real when the details are so vivid?

Orpheus bursts into the staid lamplit bustle of Campo San Bartolomeo at the base of the Rialto Bridge, where stylish women are dining al fresco. Middle-aged couples with cicchetti and Bellini cocktails. Orpheus examines their eyes for the dead-eyed hollowness he's used to seeing in the eyes of dream avatars.

Across a bridge and down more streets, wandering like a sleepwalker, from San Marco to Dorsoduro, and as he slows he finds himself next to a shuttered fish market. Venice is shaped like a fish, and Dorsoduro is its jaw. The city at night is nothing like London or Paris or New York. Only a few hours ago there were heaving shoals of tourists, photographers, school groups and guided tours; now, after the setting of the sun, they have vanished like a legion of ghosts after an exorcism.

Breathless, lost, Orpheus almost trips into the lagoon as he gets to the waterfront on the Zattere, the long quay-side that opens out onto the Giudecca Canal. The water is inviting, dark blue with wet waves of steam peeling off it. The marble facade of Il Redentore with its white crown seems to float in the near distance.

Orpheus kicks the rusted chain off one of the many boats lined up by the quay, grabs the oars, gets in shakily and begins to row. As he does, he remembers that the last time he was in a boat was that cold morning with his father. The last time he saw his home from a distance.

As he rows he tells himself the story of his life. Of being born on a beach, of how he came to live in London. Of how he found her, his only love. Moremi.

And as he rows the city disappears and the details of the

stars emerge. Further out from the nexus of the dream and everything begins to fade. Orpheus has often wondered if there is an edge he could drop right off.

Sweat trickles down his back, and the wooden seat rubs at his thighs.

Whose dream is it? How did he get here?

In his waking life he'd travelled only once to Venice, to meet a client during the Biennale. He'd been working at the Junkyard, then, when an oligarch had paid him handsomely to design dreams for guests he had been entertaining on his yacht. Orpheus had stayed awake all night and slept all day. Saw almost nothing. He'd wanted to travel out through the lagoon into some of the lesser-known islands. Sant'Erasmo, which was once a Roman pleasure ground, or Sant'Ariano where the bones of dead Venetians were taken.

Orpheus rows for what feels like hours, feels delirious with exhaustion when his eyes alight on a shore. A city skyline, the domed roofs of churches. He musters what strength he has left to row there, and the closer he gets, he begins to hear voices. Shouting, people calling his name.

The sun is rising behind them, shedding light on faces as Orpheus approaches.

'It's him!' someone shouts.

'Orpheus!'

'Orpheus!'

'E *vivo!*'

He sees with a sinking heart that somehow he's ended up back where he began. That the nexus of the dream has pulled him back.

And there is Moremi. The glassy-eyed avatar who is not his wife. There are the hollow faces of the shouting people with no inner lives. Nothing but holograms, all of them, and Orpheus despises everything.

As he reaches the shore, the memory comes to him all at once. The thing his mind had been grasping for all night. Suddenly he remembers the detective inspector, the interrogation room with his dreams projected on the wall. 'The power to hold you in custody, for a suspected future crime, indefinitely.' He'd shouted, thrashed his arms, but they'd dragged him out of the interrogation room and into the medical centre and strapped him to a gurney. He'd never been so terrified. He'd heard of jails where all the inmates were asleep, and ones where people woke as shells of themselves because they'd forgotten which life was the dream.

'I must remember,' he had told himself in his head, as the technician attached him to an IV and cold fluid burst into his veins. He had tried to fight the sleep that came. 'This is the prison,' he'd said as he does now, with Moremi's hand in his. 'This is the prison.'

27

MOREMI

When you have to go home, they have to let you in. Halima is in her nightgown when Moremi arrives. 'Never change, then,' she says, reaching out to hold her, and finally, 'Please don't?'

'I don't think I could if I wanted to.' Moremi laughs though her eyes are wet.

Halima sets up a bed for her sister in the room that is going to be the nursery, on a plastic-wrapped mattress on the floor – the daybed Halima has ordered hasn't arrived yet. The room smells of wallpaper paste and plastic. There is a nightlight throwing little goldfish across the windows. Origami cranes hanging from the ceiling. Zeeba's painted hot-air balloons on the back of the door.

In the middle of the night, the silence in her ears becomes the crash and shudder of the wave. Moremi opens her eyes and, in the darkness, she thinks she sees it, rising up on the other side of the open window. 'It's back,' she cries, leaping to her feet, her heart pounding wildly. She'd thought she'd never see it again, she'd relied on the Panopticon to save her from it, but now it rears up as if to swallow her. This time, Moremi stands still, shivering in its path, and doesn't run.

She and Halima used to play a game on the beach; they'd rush out along the shingle, chasing the tide as it receded from the shore and then, just as the surf rose up to return, they'd plant their legs in the stones and scream. Icy water would wash right up to their knees, sometimes as far as their waists, with the force of a steam train. Sometimes it would throw them onto their backs, gasping and smashing in the foam. Other times the force was too weak to overpower them. Every time, no matter how fierce the current was, it would wash back out again, leaving them wet and shivering and laughing.

She has to face the despair like that, it occurs to her only now. Let it do its difficult work while she plants her feet in the shingle and waits.

It's a slow journey back to herself. It seems to happen like the seasons turning. She notices that her appetite is starting to return when Halima brings her a box of gold pralines she bought on her way back from work. They're in a pretty tin box with champagne and amoretto truffles, candied orange slices coated in dark chocolate. Sweet and tart.

Zeeba sings a Vote No campaign song that she's composed on her tiny keyboard. A nonsense ditty that juxtaposes the two meanings of the word 'party': 'let's have a party, it's a party'. Moremi laughs and then catches herself as if she's almost slid on some black ice.

'What is it?' Zeeba asks.

Moremi is too nervous to say it out loud. For half a second, she almost forgot. It's the first time she begins to believe that it's true what they say. That one day, whole hours will pass and she won't think of him.

Another evening, Halima cooks them a vegan curry and Zeeba braids long extensions into Moremi's hair. 'It's the witching hour,' Halima says, pointing to her tiger-striped belly. 'Can you see her foot?' Something that could be a heel rolls under Halima's ribs.

'Her?' Moremi says.

'She just hopes they're a her,' Zeeba says.

'Obviously . . . healthy baby' – Halima waves her hand in that 'blah blah' motion – 'and all the things a pregnant person has to say before I say that I can only think of one name. Mum's.'

'Call them Mum's name either way,' Zeeba says. Halima shrugs. Moremi reaches out to touch her warm skin.

'I worked hard for her,' Halima says, almost to herself.

'Yeah?' Moremi asks. 'I thought Zeus came to you in the form of a swan.'

Zeeba snorts, then yanks on the braid that she is weaving. 'Keep your head still.'

'Okay, okay! I'll tell you.' Halima sits on the sofa with her bowl. 'I knew that I wanted to be a mother, but I've never really wanted a partner. With both of you getting older and Zeeba going to uni next year—'

'Possibly!' Zeeba reminds her.

'. . . I just thought, if not now, then when?'

'Next year,' Zeeba says. 'Or the year after. I hate that phrase.' But Halima ignores her.

'So,' Moremi says, feeling the blood rise up her neck just imagining it. 'Was this like, a donor kind of situation or . . . ?'

'Sort of,' Halima says. 'IVF. One of my best friends went through six rounds. All I'd heard were the tragedies, crying in the car park, months of injections, a sonograph quiet as space. That can be part of it. But do you know what else is part of it? The way an egg looks like a moon. Apparently there is a flash of light at the moment of conception. A firework display. I hear it has something to do with zinc, but it's hard not to think that it has something to do with magic.'

'Just because it's science doesn't mean that it's not magic,' Moremi says, and Halima smiles.

'I want to be a mother. I'm bone-deep certain. I wanted a baby the way I used to want sisters before you two were born.' As if they'd been misplaced by time, not yet Earthside. 'It took a while. I tried the normal – cheaper! – ways at first, but there are some problems, it turns out. AMH, eggs, that word: infertility,' Halima admits. 'It's the loneliest thing. Not a month went by where I didn't cry a little. In the Bible, Rachel says to Jacob, "Give me children, or else I die!" You'd be surprised how soon it starts to feel that way. Everyone says the wrong thing. Everything hurts. Everyone has their story about what finally worked and I came round to believing them all. Acupuncture, ubiquinol, prayers to St Gerard. I used the last of that holy water that Auntie Bola brought back from Lourdes, rubbing it on my belly, I felt like a villager doing a rain-dance. This Vine meditation that tells you to imagine your follicles growing healthy and strong. "Imagine your baby", it said. I did it so often I missed her ...' Halima breaks off as tears roll down her cheeks and Zeeba lets go of Moremi's locks.

For a moment they are stunned. 'I feel so bad,' Moremi admits finally, 'that you felt as if you had to go through this alone.'

Halima smiles and wipes her eyes. 'It's okay,' she says, shaking her head. 'It's okay, because I never was alone.'

A week later, Moremi makes a list of the things that used to make her happy. Before Orpheus, before her mother died, before she fell in love with the Panopticon.

Moremi goes to the cinema alone, in the middle of the day. She buys a ticket to a matinee at the Phoenix Picturehouse, watches a film about an astronaut stranded on an international Martian station. She finds herself alone in the cinema except for an old man in the second row who keeps falling asleep and then biting awake.

Right after the credits roll she walks outside, where the sky is a pacific blue and the day-lurking moon waxes big as a dinner-plate, and she remembers, with a start, how she got here. How she came to find herself alone. Strolling back, she gets lost the way that she used to before she had a Pulse. Takes a few wrong turns and finds herself in a cemetery. A quiet green, lined with trees. Moremi gazes at the lichen-pocked stone and feels distantly sorry for the people beneath them, sorry that they can't behold this bright day.

It's the most alone she's been since the attack. She can barely hear cars on the neighbouring road, and it's totally silent, the distant chatter of voices in her cochlear nerve. Dandelion clocks frustrating gravity, flying up. The smell of honeysuckle. The distant echo of vespers being sung under the crumbling vault of the chapel across the road.

She used to think that she would die without him. And now, as she wanders through the streets, she makes a list in her head of all the things it's possible to do alone. She splashes out on a sandwich from PAUL, half a shopping basket of reduced fruit from Sainsbury's, three pashminas from a dusty-smelling Trinity Hospice charity store, a sequinned cape, and takes herself on an impromptu date. A picnic in Victoria Park. She sits and watches the sunset on the pond, slowly pulling the sticky heads off strawberries and watching mallards and geese bob on the water.

She tells herself that it was a small thing. A childish happy dream, the month she spent with him, and she almost believes it.

It gets dark so slowly she doesn't notice it's happened. She lies flat on her back under the shade of a willow tree. The grass is damp with condensation as the temperature falls. She's never looked carefully before, but the soil is writhing with life. Centipedes and ladybirds, spiders the size of pinheads are living a billion lives. She lies back and pushes her right hand under the waistband of her pants; her middle finger finds its usual electric spot between her lips. When she was a teenager she used to share a bedroom with Halima and Zeeba, but sometimes she'd run home after school, to their room, and lock the door like a girl in the throes of a love affair. It had been. She had relished the silence then, as she does now, pushing her other hand under her shirt, staring sightlessly up at the underside of the willow leaves and fantasising only of herself.

28

ORPHEUS

While he worked at the Panopticon, sometimes Orpheus would shun the light-filled communal dining hall and eat lunch on the observation deck of the dream labs. He used to watch people fall asleep. Watch their consciousness represented in an oscillating trace on the OEG monitor. Waking perception and cognition caused a busy high-frequency thrashing, but, as the volunteers relaxed, the needle of the trace began to dampen. Their eyes closed and it was like sitting near the orchestra in the moments before an opera, the cellists and oboists tuning up their instruments. Strings of melody interspersed with the snicker of a drum, the misplaced snort of a horn.

Orpheus would watch as, almost all at once, sleep began. The nocturnal symphony. Oneirologists saw it a dozen times a day. Spindle waves and k-complexes. Lower frequency bursts of excitation as the neurons in their brains began to fire in harmony. The sensors attached to their skin which measure their body temperature, pulse and skin conductivity showed everything slowing down. Orpheus could always hear it, their breathing coming in more evenly like waves lapping a shore at low tide.

For some reason, when he watched these measurements on the different monitors, his stomach always clenched a little. It had been like watching these strangers drift alone out to sea. He could do nothing but stand at the shore and bear witness, and he had to remind himself to think like a scientist. That there was nothing frightening about sleep. After all, humans spend about a third of their lives asleep. It is dreams that are the real mystery.

'What even are they?' he sometimes muttered to himself, turning up the resolution on the oneiroscope feed. A random string of action potentials? The mind sorting through memories to delete? Or a voyage into death and back?

The Mesopotamians believed that the soul, departed from the body of the sleeper, was carried sometimes by the god of dreams. He knows that the ancient Greeks used to believe that dreams were something outside of the dreamer's mind. That the sleeper portalled into the world of the dreams, close to Hades to encounter the dead, and the immortal.

The neuroscientists of the early twenty-first century, coming of age post-Freud, believed that the sleeping brain is the true and lone dream-maker. That dreamers bore witness to the vivid line-up of midnight shows projected across their cerebral cortex.

And now there is a notion, floating among the physicists,

that for string theory to work it requires more than the one temporal and three spatial dimensions that we all currently inhabit. They believe that there are possibly twenty-one dimensions and many of them are beginning to suggest that one of them could be where dreams come from. That the sleepers' consciousness bears witness to a dimension above time and space, beyond current laws of physics logic and determinism. On Quantum Hill they had been building radios to try and broadcast to it. Perhaps the dreamer really does leave her body when she sleeps. Drifts into hyperspace, dream space, the hinterland of pure consciousness where time is flat, where other realities are possible. Orpheus always looked at the sleeping volunteers and wondered, *What if they never return?*

Orpheus imagines he's somewhere similar. In a sleep lab filled with prisoners, connected to a program that is running this simulation. If he could somehow wake up from it ...

Moremi comes to seem to him like a watchful prison guard, intent on encouraging him to forget – as he does several times a day – that this is the dream.

The sight of her begins to make his skin crawl. She is no flesh and blood person. She's a hollow construct built from his memories, but her eyes might as well be panes of dark glass. There is nothing behind them, he must keep reminding himself, no spark of life, nothing that makes the woman he loves, not her vivid particular mind. Now, when she touches him, he rolls away. To kiss her would be to betray his own Moremi. To give in to the dream.

It's hard work, every day, making himself remember.

Orpheus discovers that if he ever eats food from the dreamworld, his mind fogs and he forgets again. So, although he fasts, he loses no weight at all. But his mind stays as razor-sharp as he can make it.

Instead of sleeping in the grand carved bed, he falls asleep on the rigid recliner and tells himself again the story of how he got here. Of how he was stolen from the island where he was born. Taken from one prison to another.

'Come back to me,' Moremi will say, her eyes full with disappointed tears. And at those times, his loneliness cuts like a knife. He's the only thinking head in this universe.

How much time has passed in the real world? he wonders. Days, months? If they ever wake him, what kind of man will he be?

29

MOREMI

When Moremi returns to work she hears that a woman has died. Margret, Maggie. From heatstroke, people are speculating, although they'll probably never know for sure. What little Moremi does know about the woman comes back to her that afternoon as she works; that she was in her mid-forties, a mother of five. She'd been train-ing to be a doctor before she came to the UK and, though Moremi had never asked how Maggie had ended up in this low-skilled gig work, one time she had spotted Moremi crying behind the Portaloos. She hadn't asked what was wrong but she said, 'My dear, no situation is permanent,' reached into the pocket of her jumpsuit and offered Moremi a Pink Lady apple. Its bruised skin, the colour of a ballet slipper. What kindness. Moremi had smiled then the way that she always smiles when she is offered something that isn't close to what she wants.

The heat today could kill a woman. It's in the

mid-forties and many of the shops are closed. The only people walking about the centre of town are tourists and campaigners, holding up umbrellas to shield themselves. The air is like an open grill. Smells of melting rubber and rubbish baking in green wheelie bins. Glittering clouds of bluebottles.

It's nearing the end of July and the pollination work is drying up. Every week fewer and fewer coaches are leaving from the station, which means that if Moremi wants to get a job that day she needs to arrive early. Some people camp out all night just to make sure they can get on the buses that arrive just before dawn to drive labourers to the meadows and fields, on the outskirts of London where their work is required. Moremi had to wake up at 3am in order to make it to the queue, behind temporary barriers, around the street, into an alley behind a restaurant. Stench of food waste and water-stained crates. Crumpled wrappers. Broken glass and five people asleep on trodden cardboard boxes. The weeks she spent out of work have depleted her few savings and now Moremi has decided to sign up for as many shifts as possible, to make up for it before the work dries up and she will have to look for something else.

She's worked for five hours by lunchtime and her body is already a litany of little injuries: bug-bites and chafing, nettle-stings and blisters. She is slightly dehydrated, it's making her nauseous, and her mind baulks – as it always does – with dread at the notion of doing this kind of work for another season. In some vision of hell she is pollinating acres of orchard all alone. A drone overseeing her progress, persistently as a gadfly, setting a timer when she goes to the bathroom and docking her pay if she is absent from her quadrant for more than four and a half minutes.

'Thought you'd made it out,' says Renata, one of the regulars. A young woman about Moremi's age whose skin isn't suited for the sun. They'd joined around the same time. Moremi knows that Renata dreams of being an actress, tries not to sign up for too many shifts during casting season, and, like Moremi, dreams of the day she can toss her polyester jumpsuit in the bin and never return.

'Not yet,' she replies, though it hurts her to say. The two of them are sitting in the shade of the van on upturned crates, eating sandwiches. Renata has developed a rash and has unzipped her jumpsuit as far as modesty will allow. Feels so strange to be back here, after the break she took. Almost a month. It's like returning to school after a holiday. 'I haven't danced for a little while either.'

'Oh no,' Renata says, 'you have to keep that up. Even if you're not performing.'

'I know,' Moremi says, peeling the tomatoes from her sandwich and letting them fall with a splat on the parched ground. 'I was sick.'

'You look fine to me,' another colleague, a tall man named Kendall, says. 'Better, almost.'

Moremi nods. She is feeling better too, as if she's emerging from the womb-like world of her grief and back into the world of the living.

The drones caw like ravens at the end of their lunch-break and, with a sigh, everyone heads back to their quadrants. 'At least we're doing something different this time,' Renata says, glancing into the distance, dismissing some notifications from her Pulse.

'Yeah,' Moremi says. 'Playing with fire.'

'I keep wondering if that's why they've introduced this new security screening at the gate.' It had been strange, once the van had dropped them off at the field this time. They'd been forced to go through airport-style security at the gate. Protection officers had been gathered at the entrance, scanning employees with Pulses, patting down and questioning everyone who didn't. Moremi still doesn't.

'It's because we're near the Wasteland,' Kendall says.

'The what?'

He shrugs, 'I don't know what they actually call it, but there's a prison over there.' He nods out at seemingly endless fields.

Moremi squints into the heat haze. 'I can't see it.'

'It's underground. Storeys and storeys underground, from what I've heard. Like a rabbit warren.'

'How do you know?' Renata says it with an accusatory spikiness.

'Maggie told me,' he says. And then another drone swoops by and they must return to their work.

Riding a Zephyr is nothing like riding a bike. It's more like dancing. Every day you're not doing it, you're forgetting how to do it. Whenever Moremi boards – especially since she hasn't for a while – she is certain she will fall. She taught herself how to ride, after her mother died, on a board a boyfriend lent her that she refused to give back.

She taught Zeeba how to ride it as well. She had said, 'As soon as you remember you're flying, you're falling.'

Riding a Zephyr is all about belief – suspending belief in the laws of physics. As dreaming had been, as falling in love with him had been. Halima had never been good at it because she was too afraid of falling. She said that her favourite part of learning to ride a Zephyr had been the feeling of solid ground under her heels after. Or watching her sisters making impossible shapes in the sky.

Moremi had been offered her job as a pollinator because she was such a skilled flyer. Dancing had given her the balance and strength required to stay in the sky for hours at a time.

This job is different from anything they have been doing for most of the summer. It involves spraying some noxious chemical on a mutant strain of willow-wort, a knobbly, diseased-looking plant that is swallowing up wildlife on the edges of London's greenbelt. For the rest of the month, they're riding Zephyrs around Ragbrough Farm. Moremi watches as her shadow falls across the knotted weed. Exhausting, mind-numbing. Sometimes she'll come across a cluster so dense she will be authorised to summon the python – the device like a tractor that rolls through the vegetation and snorts out a great geyser of flames. Her favourite part, watching the plants burn. Watching them shrivel and change. She promises herself she will do this with her whole life. She can start again. She'll emerge next spring a new thing. She'll do it without the Panopticon. She'll make herself okay.

30

ORPHEUS

From the roof of the hotel, Orpheus can almost see all of the dream. He can see the way the roads curve in on themselves as his maps of the labyrinth had. He thinks of the way his friend Sherif had looked, that horrifying night, the night he'd climbed up the fire escape, his face sheened with sweat, holding his arms wide like wings, and told Orpheus that he knew a way to cross to the other side.

'Orpheus!' When he turns, he finds Moremi scrabbling up the ladder the same way that he had, squinting her eyes against the fierce wind. 'Please don't.' He has to remind himself that she isn't real, none of this is. That this is possibly the only way to get back.

Orpheus runs forward and leaps as one might off the edge of a diving board. For a distended moment, he is weightless. It's an act of reckless desperation and even in the dream it's terrible. Blood pounds behind his eyes and as he falls a dreadful thought occurs to him. What if he was wrong about the other side? What if the other side was this dream and this is all there really is?

What if he doesn't wake up? What if he actually dies here on the street?

He hits the cobbles with such violence it's as if the world has crashed onto him, the entire brutal force of it.

He's going to die.

Sheer panic as his stomach slaps the ground, turning his chest into a vacuum before he jolts awake.

Awake! Blinded, gasping for air, thrashing in a shallow tub. Where is he? The sound of an alarm filters into his consciousness. He's attached all around to wires. Pulse oximeter, OEG and EEG. In something like a coffin. Or the medicalised sleep-pods he was used to seeing in the Panopticon.

This is the prison.

He might have less than a minute before technicians rush in, in response to the alarm, and once they come they are bound to put him back to sleep. Thwarting any chance he might have to escape.

It takes supreme effort to pull himself out of the tub. He's been asleep so long that his legs aren't working and so he pulls himself up on his arms and rolls over the lip of the tub onto the vinyl floor.

It takes him a moment to get his bearings. He's naked in a room that's as chilly as a morgue. It looks like a hospital ward, with long ranks of sleep-pods surrounded by consoles and a polyphony of beeping monitors.

The sight of the other sleepers strikes terror in his chest.

This is his future, he thinks. They look dead. Naked men and women with sunken faces and white hair. Aged far beyond their years, devoured by Nox.

At the sound of feet coming up the hall, what little hope he had is extinguished.

A group of masked technicians troop in. 'Breach!' one of them shouts.

'Check the Nox valve.'

'It was inventoried yesterday.'

'Then how did we get a breach?'

They descend upon him. Hands on his back and arms. They pin him to the ground once more.

'Please!' Orpheus shouts. 'Please don't send me back.'

'Code Seven,' someone else is saying. 'Have you got the—?'

'Here.'

A sharp scratch in his thigh.

'Don't send me back,' Orpheus pleads as the world slips into blackness.

When he opens his eyes again, his head is buried in a soft cotton pillow. The sun is rising. From the window he can see the Rialto Bridge. A beautiful woman, his wife, already awake, who rolls over and kisses him.

'I miss you,' she tells him, brushing the hair delicately from his eyes, 'when you sleep.'

31

MOREMI

There is going to be a riot. That's what the police and protection officers are saying on the Vines. Neo-Luddite protestors are already organising in Trafalgar Square. They have hung three plinths with hand-painted banners that read 'Live free, vote No', and Londoners have been advised to steer clear. Although the mayor has given them a 5pm curfew, most people expect violence to break out.

There is static in the air, an anticipatory buzz like the kind before a lightning storm, clouds gathering over drought-starved brush. Moremi is neutral about riots. The first and only one she's ever been a part of happened near Vauxhall, when she was fourteen. The year of the flood. Those harrowed weeks when the streets still smelled of rotting flesh and the sewage that overspilled its banks. People were living in overcrowded temporary apartments or tents. Morgues were glutted with corpses and everyone was talking about blame. Moremi's neighbours gathered in the courtyard and commented that the majority of the bodies pulled out from under the water looked like them.

Moremi had been on her way back from school on the day of the riot. Grinding her teeth after being held for an hour for a detention. The sun was setting when the bus rounded the corner near Pimlico and stopped suddenly. The driver commanded that all the passengers get off. Groans of protest and confusion.

Moremi got on her way to another bus station and it was only when she reached Page Street and saw the tenement flats with their chessboard facades that she realised the last time she had been here was three months ago when her mother had died.

That evening, there had been an unnatural quiet all around. Flickering streetlamps overhead. Nothing to see except a few commuters and after-school shoppers. Groups of people in hoodies who would hurry past every now and then with a kind of high-stepping energy. Young people from what she could see, shadowed faces, Pulses flashing. Excited volley of chatter between two girls in puffer jackets, in a hurry to get to the same place, their breath smoke in the brisk air.

Moremi used her Pulse to try to get her bearings and it was only then that she noticed the pub doors shut and shuttered as if there was a curfew. Cafes and restaurants prematurely closed. An update flared across her eyes telling her that all buses coming in this direction had been cancelled. Moremi looked around in confusion, wondering how else she could make it home.

Her app told her that the best option was the train

station, a seven-minute walk away. So, zipping up her jacket and scrunching her fists into her pockets, Moremi followed its instructions.

When she rounded a street corner, Moremi was thrust towards the edge of the fray. The sound of burglar alarms shook the air with a multi-tonal hysteria. On the pavements, it was like a festival. People were running in all directions, shouting. A group of young men were smashing the windows of a parked car with cricket bats. Another in a skeleton mask stood atop the bonnet of a car with a smoke bomb. Violet clouds of smoke gusted up the road, and faces emerged from it, people with crowbars and sticks. Four shops down, two women hurled a fire extinguisher into the window of a clothing store and everyone cheered. The burglar alarm exploded and people stormed in with whoops of delight. The JD Sports and the computing store were all in various stages of being gutted by leaping crowds. With night falling, the siren lights made their retinas flash rabbit-amber. Two men were kicking in the Perspex screen of a bus shelter, shouting, 'What haven't we lost?'

'What are you doing here?' asks a man with a bandana wrapped around his nose and mouth. 'Kid, run . . .' And Moremi started backwards. 'Run!' he barked. She recoiled in alarm and bolted like a whippet after the firing gun. Up a side road where a group were spray-painting a police car and then another street where so many shop windows were being smashed that glass crunched and glittered underfoot. She slowed her step, mesmerised, unable to shake the sense that she was glimpsing something strange and totally human.

Where had all these people come from with their wild-fire rage? Was it something contagious or was it the same thing that was already inside her? 'Take what they took,' they were telling each other.

Moremi will never forget the sound of a Molotov cock-tail going off. A group of men turned out from the local pub. The bottle was hurled through the open window of a clothing boutique. People stopped what they were doing and gathered around to watch the fire. Something irresistible about the sight of the ruby blizzard against the iron-black of the sky. A couple of people pitched a few more bottles of spirits into the blaze and the shop went up like a tinderbox. Moremi watched fire grip the polyester edge of a mannequin's dress. Trainers on a stand melted.

The shop was an inferno. The sight of it lulled everyone on the street and for a while they stood in reverent silence, like celebrants at a pagan festival, their eyes sparkling. When Moremi opened her mouth hysterical laughter spilled out. She knew what it felt like to burn.

The conflagration roared like an unpenned beast, tear-ing down arches, toppling scaffolds. What was left of the flooring crumbled in on itself and crashed to the ground in dark waves of rubble. The brilliance of it struck Moremi like a fever. It ignited a primal joy in her. This is what to do with the fire inside. She'd spent so long swallowing it that she didn't understand fire is pure energy. Fresh illumination, clamour and fervour. It gorges entire for-ests, whole cities. It swallowed London, once. Swallowed Rome, and here, now, they had invoked its delicious destruction again.

Then the sound of sirens scissored through the air. The police and fire brigade. Like everyone, Moremi bolted, dashed down the nearest and darkest side road, where a group of people were kicking a man on the ground. Then another street where cars were parked and people were coming out of their houses, tugging at their dressing gowns and asking questions. Another street, and then another until she could barely see the grey tower of smoke flung up at the sky. Leaning against a bus shelter, shivering and gasping and laughing.

The riot had felt like a fever dream, it had come and gone and taken her rage with it. She'd headed back there on her way to school, the next day. Early in the morning, just after the police cordon had been removed. She'd felt the glass under the rubber soles of her school shoes as she walked down the street. Cracked spider-webbing of glass in the shop windows. A hole like a meteor strike in a TV screen. An empty fire extinguisher abandoned by the traffic lights. Naked shop dummies with melted faces. Moremi wondered where the rioters were now. On their way to work? On the top decks of a bus? Still out on the streets somewhere vaulting traffic cones? That had been one of the last riots.

A couple of weeks later the Legacy government took over and armed protection officers were on every street corner. The fire-gutted shops were rebuilt. The businesses were compensated. The soot was wiped off the walls.

Moremi is making her way to a ballet class when she notices that same tetchy static in the air, an unnatural quiet in the surrounding streets. She tries to ignore it as she walks, taking the long way to the studio, gathering her nerves. This will be the first ballet class she's attended since Orpheus was arrested. Something about the grief of losing him, and her failure, earlier in the year in front of Raphael Gabor, made her lose her way for a while.

Her mother used to scold her any morning she didn't wake early to practise. She'd say that any day she wasn't dancing, she was getting worse. If Moremi ever skipped a practice, or left rehearsal until the end of the day, she would imagine talent seeping out through her pores. Some nights she dreams she's forgotten how to dance, and wakes with her heart pounding, her calves twisted with cramps. This afternoon, she is almost afraid to go. Afraid she might discover that her mother had been right.

Moremi has been invited by an old classmate to a company's open class. In spite of the circuitous route she takes there, Moremi is embarrassed to discover that she is one of the first to arrive. The studio is on the top floor of a church. Rusted barre and, along the far wall, an antique-shop assortment of mirrors, most of them so old it is difficult to make out her own reflection in the tarnished silver. Moremi gazes ahead at a mirror in which she can see clouds scudding past.

She changes slowly by the bench, and soon the other dancers begin to pour in, thin cotton summer dresses over leotards, skin bronzed and tanned by the inner-city sun. They enter in droves, filling the hall with chatter, tossing bags into the corners of the room, kicking off flats and tying up their hair. The studio is suddenly a third of the size as dozens of girls enter.

'Remi!' Her name is Anna; the two of them hadn't known each other very well in school. Although, they had been paired a couple of times for certain performances, and are in enough of the same Vine groups to have a vague grasp of the other's life so far. Anna had turned down a place at a prestigious dance company when she accidentally fell pregnant in her final year of school and was forced to drop out. For months, her name was whispered as a cautionary tale.

She's put on weight, Moremi notices, with some competitive glee, the roundness in her arms, some loss of definition in her knees and calves. She smiles brightly and they hug as if they know each other better than they do.

'I heard on the Vine that you're not part of a company,' Anna says, 'and I thought, we could keep each other company.' Moremi smiles.

They chat about the heatwave, and the travel disruptions on the way to the studio because of the road closures. They speak about the rumours of a riot with the same disbelief. Anna explains that she is trying to get in shape so she can audition for a part in a revival of an old ballet that is opening at the end of the year. One that tells the story of Ariadne, the Minotaur's half-sister, who fell hopelessly in love with Theseus. Moremi knows that her mother had once auditioned for the same part, in the original run, but never made it. Her mother had explained that the word 'clue' was the variant of a word that meant 'a ball of thread', like the kind Ariadne had given Theseus to help him navigate the labyrinth. Moremi resolves to get in shape so that she can audition too. She'll do it for her mother.

Her optimism wavers a little, though, before the warm-up starts and they all line up in position. Moremi grows irrationally frightened, as she sometimes does, that she won't remember how to do it. That she's forgotten the name of every position, that her body won't bend the way that she trained it to for all of those years.

'I'm nervous as well,' Anna whispers conspiratorially. 'It's been so long for me and everything's changed.' At the teacher's instruction they both rise up onto their toes. 'But it's been calling me back.'

'Yeah,' Moremi says, and she lets herself surrender to it, lets her limbs unfurl to the music, lets her fingers and tendons and arms remember; this is a love story as well, her body and dance. 'It's been calling me back too.'

Halima is worried that Zeeba's in trouble. She calls Moremi on her way back from the ballet class. At first, Moremi is only half listening. She's too giddy thinking about how well the class went, about her new desire to audition for the upcoming ballet. But Halima thinks that Zeeba could be in central London, taking part in the pro-tests that, according to the Vine reports, are beginning to turn very violent.

'I know you'll laugh at me if I told you it's a "feeling",' she sighs, her voice buzzy through Moremi's Jelly. 'I wish you both had Pulses.'

'Where did she tell you she was?'

'She's supposed to meet me here, at her art show.'

'Damn it,' Moremi hisses, hitting her head, 'I forgot!'

'Well, apparently, she has too. I even took the afternoon off work. That's what I get for making plans with teenagers.'

'You know I still count as a teenager for two more months.'

'Well, where are you, anyway?'

'Near Holborn,' Moremi says.

'Today's the last day of the show, so if you don't have plans for the rest of the day, can you meet me?'

The art school is twenty minutes' walk away, just off Aldwych, near high-rise office buildings, university campuses and Lincoln's Inn. The summer exhibition takes place in a high-ceilinged atrium and Moremi follows the floor plan, through abstract sculpture, holograms and interpretive dance videos, hoping she will find Halima.

Zeeba's work takes up a significant portion of the far wall. A show called, 'Things we found in the flood'. Everything that Zeeba has ever said about it comes back to Moremi. Objects that Halima uncovered years ago while clearing buildings, and things that Zeeba collected in the weeks after the flood, from those street-corner shrines that sprang up all across the city that year. A baby's rattle that's cracked like a duck egg, a fuseless radio, emulsion photos of old women Moremi has never seen, ink running. Water-bloated books and dated maps. Fountain pens and sugar bowls. Shattered disks and lost keys. A dozen shoes. All piled together as if after a landslide and drowned in a salt solution. Zeeba had waited for months for crystals to form, and a bumpy crust of them glitter now, on everything. Fat glassy spears, lancing from a music box, indigo dusting on the inside of a wedding ring.

At the sight of it, Moremi's breath catches, in awe of her sister. Her ability to make something sublime from heartache. Even the banner that hangs above, as if on a washing line, 'Things we found in the flood', all of the letters fading, except for the word 'FOUND' which is efflorescent. Delicately illustrated dandelions, nettle-leaves and ferns explode from it.

'Zeeba? I thought you were going ahead?'

When Moremi turns she sees the face of a man she thinks she's seen before. Perhaps only a year or two older than herself. For some reason he is carrying Zeeba's faux-leather rucksack. Moremi recognises the frayed handles and the collected assortment of badges.

'Oh!' He gasps at the sight of her. He has dreadlocks, no Pulse, sharp teeth and earnest eyes. Tattoos ring his biceps. 'You're her sister. Moremi.'

'Right . . . and you . . . ?'

'Raffi.' He holds out a hand for her to shake. Where has Moremi heard that name before? There is a tenderness in his expression.

'It feels strange, asking someone's name,' she laughs.

'Old-fashioned?' he teases with a smile. 'You know, you look just . . . I mean, she . . .' He shrugs. Moremi glances down at her bag, which he's still clutching in his hand. Along with a mirrored motorcycle helmet. 'I'm just collecting her stuff for her.'

'So she's not here?'

He shakes his head. 'She's gone ahead to the demonstration.'

'You mean, the riot?' Moremi's eyes flash with alarm.

'Don't believe everything you hear on the news.'

His eyes dart to Moremi's unlit constellation. She feels quite self-conscious about it, even now. At the strange way her skin has reacted around it, grown inflamed and stippled with rash. A GP reassured her that this type of reaction is natural after a Pulse deactivation, but she can't help her finger fluttering reflexively up to it whenever anyone notices. The explanation she always volunteers too early: 'I had it removed because . . .'

Raffi smiles and says, 'Welcome back to meat-space.' He holds up his free hand to high-five her, but Moremi realises too late. 'They don't tell you this part in the Vote Yes campaigns, do they? You still have the traumatised look of someone who's just been turned off. They don't tell you that the quartz will burn holes in your memories. Or about the children who will never learn to write because they've never had to.' Maybe he catches sight of the nauseated look on Moremi's face. 'Might be too late to save a whole generation of people, but the next . . .'

'There you are.' Halima appears looking sweaty and flushed, fanning herself with the exhibition pamphlets. She looks between the two of them and smiles. 'Rafeaq?'

'You know him?' Moremi asks.

'Yes, he's Zeeba's friend. From that church thing, right?'

'New Day,' he confirms.

'I'm sure that's when all this started,' Halima says, and Moremi knows that she's too frightened to say the word

Revelator in public now. Halima rolls her eyes and blows a raspberry. 'It's a sauna outside. They keep saying the weather is going to break soon but ...'

Moremi regards the man again, the wooden cross on his chest, more perturbed than before. She wants to grab her sister's rucksack from his hands.

'Hey!' A man in uniform runs up the hall, his heels squeaking on the linoleum. 'You guys are going to have to leave.'

'But we came to see the show,' Halima protests.

'I know ...' His eyes flit away to some holographic notification. Halima sees it too. 'They think the violence might spread down here. Probably being overly cautious but they're telling us we need to close the premises early today. I'm sorry about the show.'

'What about Zeeba?' Moremi asks. She has no Pulse and neither of them can get through to her console.

'She told me she's going to meet up with her—'

Raffi stops himself and says, 'A friend of ours. At the demonstration.'

'How will we find her?' Moremi asks.

'The old-fashioned way' – Raffi grins, and then puts his motorcycle helmet on his head – 'with our eyes.'

London is burning, Moremi thinks. The nursery rhyme rings a hysterical cannon in her head as she flies. For the first time in her life she's grateful for the ubiquitous Zip Zephyrs docked all around the city.

The entire city is like a struck match, shimmering in a rainbow bubble of heat haze and embers. The cries of protesters and counter-protestors rise like smoke. When Moremi motions her Zephyr up two storeys, she can almost see the crowds gathered on the Strand. She has no idea how she will find her sister.

Armies of protection officers are hurtling through the sky, coming up behind her like locusts. 'You are entering a no-fly zone,' a drone announces. Moremi looks around in confusion. She has no chance of finding her sister if she lands so she keeps flying, searching the ground like a raptor for any trace of her. When she glances at the road behind her, she realises that she's somehow lost sight of Halima and Raffi. Have they fallen behind, or raced ahead?

Moremi leans forward on her board and accelerates to maximum speed. She is not wearing her board-appropriate shoes, which makes balancing a lot trickier, though she is wearing a safety pack that should break her fall if she slips off. Spreading her arms like a surfer, Moremi struggles not to topple off as the wind whips her eyes into slits.

She speeds further up the Strand and towards Trafalgar Square, where the streets are heaving. It's like a parade, the heads of people with their home-made placards, and Moremi slows as she approaches, scanning the crowds for any sight of Zeeba or Halima or Raffi. 'Total Adoption = total control', some of the signs read, or, 'Not in my head'.

'We don't want your world,' they shout. There are thousands of them, Moremi is shocked to see. It's like an occupation, with people settled by home-made barricades on one side of the road. Moremi only wants to find her

sister and she scans the crowd, searching the sea of faces
for any that look like her. Her braids, her dark limbs.
Moremi's head fills with nightmares: Zeeba injured;
Zeeba burned by a Molotov cocktail; Zeeba carried off
by the police and locked in a preventative centre where
Moremi can never hope to see her. Too horrible, she
tells herself.

As she rides, the rising smoke sears her eyes. 'Zeeba!'
she shouts. Closer to Trafalgar Square and the ground is
like a threshing floor. Masked protestors and counter-
protestors in bloody altercations. Others smashing shop
windows. The police are trying to move out the protestors.
A drone comes up behind her and announces, 'This is
now a no-fly zone. Any airborne vehicles will be grounded
by force.'

She's shot in the back too late to dismount. It's a
rubber bullet, though the force and surprise of it makes
her topple. The fall is terrifying, for as long as it lasts.
Moremi takes a second to activate her parachute pack and
it inflates too slowly. She tumbles, all the world a dizzying
blur and, when she hits the ground, the air is knocked
from her chest. Her vision whirls with stars. The sound of
sirens are all around, tear-gas canisters being released and
boots hitting the tarmac. Shouts and the crackle of fire.

Moremi groans in pain, too frightened for a moment
to try to get up. Taking account of all her joints. Nothing
broken. She leans up on her elbows, blinking away stars.

'Hey, come on!' Raffi hurtles past, his heavy boots
crunching on the concrete just shy of her face. 'Her group
ran this way.'

'What about Halima?' Moremi asks.

A fleet of riot vans are speeding up the road behind them, the sirens razoring into her consciousness.

'Hurry!' Raffi shouts, and Moremi bolts upright, her joints protesting at her suddenness. Raffi takes her hand to help her up. She fights the rush of blood from her head, the stippling of darkness at her peripheral vision.

They run together, down a side street behind a clothing store, Raffi in the lead. 'Tear gas!' someone shouts, and then everyone is stampeding in the same direction. Moremi loses Raffi then, and finds herself gridlocked, crouching among the other protestors, waiting for the chaos to pass.

She's in a narrow alley, pushed up against a brick wall by the crowd. All around her, people are shouting, she can hear sirens and protection drones, the squeal of tyres on parallel roads. A metre away, someone is screaming, and a couple of the other protestors crowd around him, pouring water bottles over his face to wash away the tear gas. Moremi thinks that she can smell the vinegar scent of it in the air.

In the confusion, someone else elbows her in the back and she topples over, the rocky ground needling the skin on her knees. Something falls out of the pocket of her shorts and when Moremi reaches for it, she realises it's Orpheus' father's watch. She'd gotten into the habit of taking it with her, reaching for its cool weight occasionally. A flutter of relief that she hasn't lost it.

'It's not working,' the young man who was tear-gassed says with gritted teeth. There are about a dozen of them crammed in the foul-smelling alley. He says, 'We need to do something else, something bigger. Use their tools against them.'

'How?' asks a girl about Zeeba's age. Her face is painted with wild shapes that are supposed to fool the ReCog software, though it's smudged around her temples and under her nose.

The sirens of a fleet of drones squeal overhead and everyone pushes themselves up against the wall to avoid being spotted from its vantage. Moremi is waiting for a chance to leap out and keep looking for her sisters.

'Milk Wood,' says the young man, and Moremi senses a ripple of dread go through the crowd.

'I thought that was just an urban legend,' someone says.

'What is it?' another voice asks.

'I heard it will destroy the Panopticon for good. It's sort of like an "off" switch.'

Moremi doesn't know whether to be alarmed or amused by their discussion. She had been taught that the Panopticon, like the internet, relies on redundancy. 'Switching off' the Panopticon would be like stopping all the rivers in the world all at the same time.

'They've been talking about Milk Wood for years.' Moremi recognises Raffi's voice among the crowd. 'A virus that attacks constellations. A bit like the one that was released during the symposium.' Moremi's fingers twitch to her ear, to her own scarred constellation.

'Wow ...' The girl with the paint on her face rubs her forehead, inadvertently wiping some more off. 'On a larger scale? Are we talking, like, all of London? All of the UK?' The thrill that goes through the group at the mention of the attack makes her dizzy.

'Maybe,' Raffi says with a smile, 'at least, that's what people are saying.'

Moremi is thinking about Zen bleeding out at the symposium and she can't help herself. 'People died,' she says. 'Show some respect.'

The group regard her with suspicion, all of their eyes falling on her unlit constellation. By now, Moremi is used to this search; they're establishing if she is for or against them. 'Destroying the Panopticon would be a total disaster. A devastation greater than the Thames Barrier attacks. Not only would it be a global act of terrorism – putting everyone's life in danger – it could start a war.'

'You know what they say,' a woman in a fox mask shouts, 'one man's terrorist is another man's . . .' Her last word is drowned out by cheers of agreement.

'No!' Moremi says, surprised now by her own fury. 'I was there. I was there at the symposium when the virus was released.' They all fall silent now. 'I almost died, I know lots of people who did. People who didn't deserve to.'

'Look,' Raffi says, his tone more conciliatory, 'I'm sorry about what happened to you, but forcing us to wear a Pulse is fascism. Not only is the government telling us what to do with our bodies, they're telling us what to do with our *minds*. What types of dreams we're allowed to have.'

'This is what people want,' Moremi says, 'what they're going to vote for.'

'Fifty-five per cent of people.'

'But that's how democracy works!' Moremi shouts. 'The plan you're proposing won't free anyone, it will just be imposing your beliefs on them. The way that you want to live.'

'What are you even doing here?' asks the woman in the fox mask, stepping over to shove Moremi in her shoulder so she almost trips backwards, and her head hits the wall hard enough to bruise.

That voice. Moremi recognises it, the undulations of a Nigerian accent, the abrupt edges. Behind the glass eyes of the fox mask, Moremi thinks she sees a spark of recognition too. She's about to say her mother's name, but then an alarm splits the sky above them, a drone descending.

'Run!' they shout, and it's a mad dash to scramble out of the alley in order to avoid being crushed. Everyone scatters, the street is chaos, people shouting or screaming and pouring water on themselves, protection officers in riot gear dragging protestors into the backs of vans. A plastic mask snaps under her foot as Moremi runs out. It seems as if there is no chance she will find Zeeba or Halima in this fray. Moremi hopes they've made it out already. That they're on their way home.

She finds herself chasing after the woman in the fox mask, who is sprinting down a different side street in the opposite direction from the crowd. Moremi dashes quickly after her, up a tree-lined residential street, across the road, slamming the bonnet of a car that almost runs her over.

For a fraction of a minute she thinks she's lost her, but then she finds her again, scrambling over a wall and into a garden. Almost without thinking, Moremi follows her, cutting her hands on brambles and landing on a pile of toppled bins. Moremi is determined. She won't let her go this time.

Her feet sink into the mud just in time for her to see the orange ears of the fox vanish around the corner of a house. Half-blinded by determination, Moremi leaps over the hedgerows and between the shadowed alleys. How can this woman move so fast? She takes a sharp turn under a railway bridge and then vanishes.

'Damn it!' Moremi gasps, her chest on fire. There are the metal struts of the bridge on one side, trash cans on another, an abandoned shopping trolley filled with rubbish. Everything is speckled with solid mounds of bird poo.

There is a rumble overhead, the tracks groaning and straining as a train approaches. The noise makes Moremi's hair stand on end. The wave. Flushed with adrenaline, she looks for a place to run, but she freezes at the crunch of heels on the cracked pavement behind her.

The next thing she knows, her head whacks the floor, her teeth snapping down on her tongue, mouth and skull full of pain. White flurry of stars. Solid weight on her chest.

'Who are you?' The cool of a blade at her neck. Her jugular throbs against it.

'Please, no,' Moremi says in terror. She's thinking of all the cautionary tales she ever heard. Since she is Pulseless, they might not find her body here liquefying among the bin bags, heavy with flies.

'Why are you following me?' the woman says.

Not my mother, Moremi thinks, and then realises, of course not. She had been blinded by hope, that first time at the symposium. The strange hope she still harbours, that there is a cheat code for death. A way back.

Hadn't she seen her mother's body in the funeral home? In the bright wax-print dress that Halima chose for her?

There is a jagged scar on this woman's wrist. Those long fingers, elegant hands that Moremi had seen floating grey in their bathtub.

'Auntie?'

As soon as she says it, the woman's hands fall slack. Moremi reaches up and pulls the mask off her face. As she does, the train tornados past, with the whine and howl of machinery and metal. Flashes of light slash across that face. Dark eyes and wide nose. That face which had been a fixture of her childhood until she'd vanished.

She has dreadlocks and the asterisk scar carved into the skin behind her ear. She looks so much like their mother, it makes Moremi feel nauseous. 'Bola? You're alive?'

32

MOREMI

She's been living on the run for years now, Bola. On a narrowboat called *Double-Down* that she bought battered and wind-tossed several years ago and tried to make beautiful.

When Moremi steps tentatively in, it smells faintly of incense and cigarette smoke. The plants in the saloon have roasted in the sun blasting through the portholes.

'Want something to drink?' Bola asks as she enters.

'What have you got?' Moremi asks, watching as her aunt bends over to examine the mini-fridge. 'Milk . . .' She removes the lid and makes a retching sound. 'Okay, well, flat tonic water and ginger beer?'

'Maybe just normal water?'

Bola vanishes behind a beaded curtain in search of a cup. While she does, Moremi takes her console out of her pocket. It's been buzzing for a little while and the first thing she sees is a message from Halima that says, 'Found Zeeba, heading home, where are you?'

'Safe. See you soon,' Moremi replies simply. Her aunt still feels like a bird she could frighten away. She doesn't want to say anything that could make that happen. Putting the device back quickly, she looks around. The boat is like a fortune-teller's shop, Moremi thinks, crystals and dream catchers. A soy wax candle in the shape of an armless woman. Carved masks, a deer skull, bowls and plates piled high with cigarette ash.

There are Polaroids pegged to a washing line, and Moremi's heart flutters when she catches an unexpected glimpse of her mother. There she is, a teenager at some music festival, her eyelids spangled with glitter. There again, on the sofa playing with their family's cat. Her mouth is half-open in this one as if she's in the middle of a funny story. Her father is there too.

'You look like him.' Moremi starts at the soundless way her aunt can move, recovers quickly and takes the chipped mug. She'd said it like an accusation.

'I want to look like her,' Moremi says, glancing back at the Polaroids. Strange how different they are from quartz recordings. With their fuzzy edges and low resolution, they look more like memories. A darkened window into a vanished moment.

'Don't we all?' Auntie Bola says. Her features are harder, she has a square, almost masculine chin and wide nose. She's startlingly tall, just under six foot, and moves as quietly as a panther. 'You're like her where it matters.'

Then she reaches out and touches Moremi's unlit constellation. 'I thought you were dead,' Moremi says, brushing the woman's fingers away. She'd seemed to disappear from their lives after her last suicide attempt. And, like their father, after the flood she had been impossible to track down.

'I feel as if I was, for a long time,' she says. 'And for years I wanted to be.' She sits on the futon. 'I'm pretty ashamed of how you found me, that last time.' Moremi tries not to flinch at the memory. Back when she had her Pulse it had been papered over by the recollection procedure, but without access to her quartz that old pain of it is still there.

'In the hospital they took me to there was some sort of religious group that met every Wednesday. I didn't believe in anything but I wanted to so badly. That's how they found me.'

'The Revelators?' Moremi asks. She thinks she's starting to understand how they recruit. Raffi and Zeeba seemed to have joined after Zeeba started attending a religious youth group. Sherif claimed he'd been 'saved' by some Revelators in his hospital. And now Bola.

'They think that nothing the world offers will satisfy us, in the end. Money, fame, their meagre consolations against the fact that everything is passing away. The Pulse, stuffing our eyes and minds with dreams. They told me that it would take courage to turn my back on all of it.'

'Okay, they convinced you and you joined them, but what about after that? What about after the flood? We would have grown up in a children's division if it wasn't for Halima. Why did you never come back for us?'

Bola winces. 'I wanted to. I swear to you, I did, but . . . I'd done too many things by that point. If they ever find

me, I'll be dead or asleep in some Protect prison.' Moremi
flinches; even the word makes her think of Orpheus.
'I've been keeping an eye on you, though. Trying to keep
you safe.'

'Was that you?' Moremi asks, shaking at the memory
again. 'Was that you at the symposium? Was that you
trying to keep me safe?'

Bola lowers her gaze. 'I know, I should've tried harder.'

'Yes, you coward, I could have died!' Moremi is shaking
with fury now. 'You should have tried harder the whole
time! You should've come back for us!'

'You don't know, Remi, what a mess I was then. I
wasn't in a space to look after children. I'm still not. I
must have cycled through a dozen different diagnoses
before I was twenty. If I didn't feel numb, I was underwater. Everything a huge effort. Getting out of the house,
even brushing my teeth. Except for the perfect things that
would sometimes lance the darkness. A piece of music,
a mild day, a new lover.' Moremi feels uneasy at how
much of this description she recognises. Bola notices it
and says, 'It's alright. I have a theory about it. I used to
love this man who suffered from anxiety. For years it was
about health. And it occurred to me that we all live with
some element of uncertainty. We all get headaches and we
think, "Is it cancer?" and then we think, "Well, probably
not, right?" We feel the ground tremble and think, "Is it
an earthquake?" A car back-firing is probably not a gunshot. We're mostly okay with "probably". With eighty to
ninety-five per cent. But I sometimes wondered if this man
just couldn't look away from the five per cent.

379

'Maybe it's the same for people like you and me. After all, everything we care about will vanish. Everyone we love will certainly die. All our endeavours will return to ash. Humans only manage to live, shop, watch movies, love, because they spend most of their time turning away from that fact. And yet, you and I make our way through the world in the shadow of it, forced to stare it down though it threatens to floor us and almost never does.'

Moremi swallows. Surprised by the tightness in her throat, she says, 'So are you "better" now? Did they save you?' There is some mocking in her voice because Moremi has heard enough of this kind of story to understand the arc of it. The suffering person travels or learns to meditate or is blessed by a cardinal, or goes to therapy or has their quartz wiped for memories with bad effect and wakes changed. She's heard enough of this story to feel like a failure that she isn't completely better already. Moremi is coming to think that the journey could span her entire life. That she might always have to keep working at feeling better.

Bola shakes her head. 'Shall I tell you what worked for me, finally?'

When Moremi nods, Auntie Bola puts down her cup, walks past and leads her niece outside as if she's about to show her something on the bow of the boat. It's a quiet night, already dark.

'Something changed in me after my sister died. Your mother. For a long while I couldn't get away from it, the void. The thing inside myself that I had been trying not to look too hard at. The pain I needed to anaesthetise.

I used to be frightened of it. But do you know what is better than fear? Better than grief or despair?' She looks at Moremi, who turns to her in curiosity, then says, 'Rage.'

Moremi might have moved quickly enough to stop her if she'd been expecting it. Bola leaps forward and pushes Moremi into the river. The water slaps the side of her body, and before she knows it the water shuts like a vault over her head.

This is her nightmare. Moremi has been terrified of drowning since the day her mother died. Peers at every body of water in fear, will never ever go swimming, even in a pool and especially not in the sea.

But this is shallow water and it's not long before her foot catches the sharp rocks on the riverbed and she's able to push herself to the surface. As soon as she does, though, a hand comes down on top of her head and shoves her violently back under.

Moremi clenches her jaw shut for as long as she can manage, but soon the pain of oxygen deprivation grips her so tightly that her mouth flies open.

She is going to die.

Wild panic as bitter water surges into her mouth and nose, over her vocal cords and into her lungs. This is the moment she'd feared, exactly and suddenly real-ised. Drowning.

Her kicks and thrashes only serve to hasten the end, drag her down further. Moremi's bare foot brushes some-thing rough. She bends her knees and bounds upwards, breaking the surface of the water once more with a gasp.

A hand reaches again to grab her, but Moremi seizes it, unsettling Bola and pulling her into the water with a shout of surprise.

This gives Moremi enough time to scramble onto the sun-warmed pavement at the edge of the canal. Enough time to heave up the silty water and fill her lungs with night air.

'Do you feel it, too?' Bola's voice.

Moremi's eyes are still blinded by tears and water, she scrambles away, her leg grazing the chain where *Double-Down* is moored and setting the boat rocking.

'Get away from me!' she shouts, her heart pounding wildly.

'Rage,' Bola says. She's already pulling herself out of the water with a wild grin on her face. 'That' – she points at the foam-laced water – 'is what the Panopticon did to my sister. This is what Hayden and the Legacy government did to your mother.'

'What are you talking about?'

'And all the thousands named and unnamed. They knew it would happen, Remi. They knew it would happen and they did nothing to stop it.'

Moremi has heard this conspiracy theory before. Has dismissed it too, like everyone she knows. 'Yes, and the Mars landing was a hoax,' she gasps, her words irritating her throat, tapering off into a fit of coughing.

'They create the sickness,' Bola says. 'They sell the cure.'

'You're the sick one,' Moremi says, getting shakily to her feet. Bola comes towards her. 'Don't touch me.'

'I was trying to make you see.'

'I've seen enough.' She starts to run away then but Bola shouts.

'There's a plan to save him, you know.' And when she shouts, 'Orpheus,' Moremi stops in her tracks, all the hairs on her body standing on end. 'You can be part of it, but you must be ready.'

'What does that mean?' Moremi asks. 'What do they want with him?'

'Did he ever tell you about his father, Mustafa? Or he might have been known as "Warsame".'

One of Orpheus' memories flashes before her eyes, his father standing on the threshold of their house.

'Warsame,' she confirms.

'He was the first Revelator. He and Hayden built the Panopticon together. It was a joint vision. Mustafa— "Warsame"— started out as a true believer.'

'But Orpheus told me that his father hated the Panopticon,' Moremi says, shaking her head in disbelief. The cold is starting to settle into her damp clothes now.

'He was on the team of software engineers who helped to invent Tiresias.'

'That can't be true,' Moremi says. 'He lived analogue.'

'What would cause a man like that to make such a radical change?'

'I don't know.'

'Think,' Bola urges.

'I don't know, I guess he could have seen something. Using Tiresias. Something he didn't like.'

'He saw the flood,' Bola says. 'During the attack, terrorists hacked into unmanned British drones in order to drop bombs on the Thames Barrier. The software the drones used was created by the Panopticon. And the attackers took advantage of a Zero Day vulnerability in order to hack into them.'

'What's a Zero Day?'

'A Zero Day is a security flaw that the Panopticon can't predict. The company have 'zero days' to fix the flaw with a patch or a software update before another party has a chance to exploit it. The story we've heard is that Orpheus' father discovered that Hayden had intentionally left this vulnerability in the drones.

'After the attacks, Legacy won by a landslide and then everyone was rushing to get a Pulse.'

'I don't believe any of this, and I don't understand what this has to do with Orpheus.'

'Warsame had begun designing a computer virus which would take advantage of certain other Zero Day vulnerabilities in the Panopticon. Our system is deliberately opaque, but I've just had word that at the right time, when all conditions are in place, Orpheus will help us to use the virus to destroy everything.'

Moremi's head is spinning again. There are disaster movies where the Panopticon stops working. Patients in hospitals die, highways flood, miners are trapped, people run out into the streets screaming. She feels sick even thinking about it, wants no part at all in it.

'Don't come near me,' she says again. She wants to believe there is a way to bring Orpheus back but she doesn't believe anything that Bola has to say. Moremi really is running now, back the way she came, before she knew who this woman was. Some part of her wants to go back there, back to having no aunt at all.

'Everything is in place,' Bola shouts, the whites of her eyes flashing. 'The hour, the individuals. We know it will happen because *they* know it will happen.' She grins widely. 'We're going to do it, Remi. You can be part of it too.'

33

MOREMI

Moremi is not the same after she hears it. Everything that her Auntie Bola says. She jumps on the first bus home, where Zeeba and Halima are watching the fallout of the riot on television. Stella Stratton is saying that in spite of the protest, polls show that the public are overwhelmingly in favour of Total Adoption. 'And I aim to serve the public.'

It turned out that Zeeba hadn't been hurt at all – she'd been trapped in a police kettle for two hours somewhere further from most of the action – though she seems annoyed she missed it. Moremi is relieved that both of her sisters are unharmed.

When she tells them she's just met Auntie Bola, Halima insists that Moremi must have been mistaken, but Zeeba admits, 'I've been thinking she must be one of us.'

'Why?' Moremi asks, feeling a little betrayed that Zeeba never mentioned this earlier.

'It's weird with the Revelators,' Zeeba replies. 'Everything is so secretive. Some big whisper network, I can never figure out how anyone knows anything. As I told you guys before, I didn't have anything to do with the symposium attack. Unless you're directly involved in an operation they don't tell you anything that's going to happen. But I was hearing some rumours about a person involved, Reynard the Fox, she's involved in a lot of the covert operations in London. So, she's like a ghost. Raffi saw her only once without her mask on and he said that she looked . . .'

'. . . like us,' Moremi says, dizzy now. She needs to sit.

'I haven't met her myself,' Zeeba says, 'but I want to.'

'She told me that there is a plot to rescue Orpheus,' Moremi says.

'From prison?' Zeeba looks dubious.

'Yes, I didn't believe it either, but—'

'I haven't heard anything about it. But, I'm a newbie, and young. No one actually tells me much.'

'Apparently there's a virus that Orpheus' father—'

Suddenly Halima drops heavily to the sofa, her eyes glazed with shock, one hand on her belly.

'Are you okay?' Moremi asks her.

'No!' Halima says. 'I'm just trying my best to keep you all safe and it's like you don't care.'

'I do,' Zeeba says, kneeling on the rug in front of them. 'I'm sorry, Halima, I'm grateful. You didn't have to risk your safety to come and save me.'

'But Auntie Bola,' Moremi says.

'I don't care about our criminal aunt who disappeared. But if you care about me, Moremi, Zeeba, you'll promise to stay out of any more of this.'

387

The two of them fall silent for a while. Moremi keeps thinking about what Bola had said, that there is a plan under way to save Orpheus. She wants so badly for it to be true.

Stella Stratton is still speaking in front of Downing Street, promising to crack down on violent protests and lawbreakers in the coming weeks.

'At least until after the referendum . . .' Halima says, her eyes on the screen.

'What happens after that?' Zeeba asks.

'Then, everything is decided,' Halima says. 'And everything can go back to normal.'

'It never felt normal,' Zeeba says, 'to me.'

For the rest of the week Moremi is looking for signs. Signs that none of what Bola told her is true. But the world has changed, as if in a trick mirror. She sees Legacy not as the restorers of peace but the instigators of disorder.

They create the illness, they sell the cure.

A week after meeting Bola, Moremi returns from a ballet class to Orpheus' flat where she finds the backup of his quartz he stores in his bedroom. Moremi had sworn that she would never do it – use the disk to access his memories – it's an almost unforgivable violation of his privacy, but it's the only way, she starts to think, that she might find the answers to her questions.

The quartz can read the hippocampus like a disk. Memories saved from before the constellation was implanted have the grainy poor quality of old movies. Moremi connects his quartz to the OEG machine and watches as his memories play out on the monitor. The last thing she sees is her own silhouette in the bathroom, leaning over the sink, brushing her teeth. The night before their wedding. Must have been the last time he backed it up. She swipes away from it, to earlier ones. There is his friend Sherif and the flat they'd shared. Their mould-spotted bedroom in the children's division. Then a forest, the ocean, and finally, his father, Warsame.

He died the same year that her mother did, though he looks a lot older than her. His dark skin and matted afro remind her a little of her own father, that baritone roll of his voice. There he is on the threshold of their house, the day that he beat Orpheus for trying to run away. In the next memory, his father sits, softly illuminated by a kerosene lantern.

'You don't know what it's like for children out there these days,' he says. 'They're probably tagging them at birth with that Thing now.' He points to his temple and shudders. 'It's only going to get worse after the flood.'

'The flood?' Orpheus asks in the memory, and Moremi's vision goes black for a moment as all the blood rushes to her head.

This is the moment it happens. It feels like cresting a mountaintop and glimpsing the whole prospect of the world. The tectonic plates of her belief shifting. It's all true.

Moremi collapses on the bed clenched with despair. Suddenly she's counting everything that she lost, her mother, her husband. The wave has a face, she thinks; it belongs to *them*.

34

MOREMI

The day of the referendum is flying ant day. Thanks to Zeeba, Moremi knows that it's called 'nuptial flight'. The winged virgin queens seek out males to mate with in midair. She knows that the males die soon after, while the queens chew off their wings and bury themselves underground to found a colony.

Moremi is stepping over the sticky bodies of them when she returns from work that evening, tiny puddles on the pavement that she only half notices. She'd been burned, accidentally, by the python. As she walks, now, from the coach station, the dressing on the back of her calf itches. It had been a long shift, and the sun had felt like a battering ram. Moremi is about to turn the corner for the bus station when someone on a Zephyr almost knocks her over.

'You know you're not supposed to fly those over pavements,' Moremi says.

'Who are you, the traffic police?'

It's Zeeba, who lands nearby, wearing a Vote No shirt that's covered in sweat stains. 'I brought you a Zephyr so you can come with me.'

'Come with you where?'

Zeeba rolls her eyes, incredulous and affronted. 'Tell me you haven't forgotten.'

'Forgotten what?' Then Moremi slaps her forehead, 'Oh, I'm sorry!'

'How could you?'

'I honestly, honestly forgot! I got up early and this lady from my work died last week and ... it's because I don't have a Pulse. Any other day a bunch of reminders would be flashing up telling me to vote. And everyone I know on the Vine would be posting smug pictures saying "I voted" or "Stand up and be counted".'

Zeeba's brow is still knitted in irritation. 'You know, people used to vote even before they had computers in their heads.'

'Our great-grandparents still wrote PhD theses without the internet. They met up in the centre of town without mobile phones. Who the hell knows how any of those things happened?'

'Well,' Zeeba says, touching her thumb to the scanner and unlocking a newly charged Zephyr from the docking station along with a winged helmet. 'Just be glad that you have a sister like me.'

Zeeba's still too young to vote, a fact that sickens her with frustration. This will be the first time that Moremi ever has.

'You are registered, right?'

'Of course I am,' Moremi says. 'You keep asking me. Everyone with a Pulse is automatically registered anyway.'

'That's why Vote Yes can rely on such a high turn-out,' Zeeba mumbles.

'I think I'm still registered at the flat I lived in with ...' Does it mean she's not totally healed, that she can't even say his name? Every now and then she'll let her imagination float back to the possibility Bola offered. That there might be a way to free Orpheus. But then she shakes it away. As far as she knows, no one has ever left a Protect prison alive.

'So then, I think your polling place is in the primary school around the corner from Marylebone Station. We can go together.'

'You don't need to escort me to make sure I do it.'

'I know. I'm just going near that way anyway. Still campaigning.'

'What do you still have to do on the day of the referendum?'

'Knock on doors to make sure the people who said they would vote actually do vote. I've been up since the polls opened. Then I did a few hours of this' – she nods a head at the docking station – 'and then I thought, oh, right, my *sister.*'

It doesn't take them long to get from Victoria coach station to the primary school in the centre of town, although Moremi's calves ache from her day at work. The air is threatening rain and she can almost feel the static. It's as if the entire country is holding its breath. As they ride,

Zeeba tells Moremi that the polls indicate the vote is close. At 49 per cent voting No and 51 per cent Yes, it could go either way. The only people on the streets are wearing the black VOTE NO T-shirts, or else they're handing out white flyers that read 'YES' at the entrances of train stations and the arcades of shopping centres.

If 'No' wins, Zeeba explains, it will make history. 'How many times have men in jeans stood on podiums and told us how they want the world to look?' She laughs. 'So maybe we don't want their world. Maybe we don't want drones and to merge brains. Maybe we don't want your cars and your oil spills.'

They lean on their boards, turn into a tree-lined avenue flanked by houses. Moremi notices Zeeba glaring into the bay windows to see how many white and how many black posters she can count. On one street corner, Vote No campaigners are gathered around a clipboard, crossing off doors that have not been knocked. As they fly past, a couple of them shout Zeeba's name and she waves.

Moremi can't believe how many of them there are. 'Everyone turns up the closer we get to the referendum,' Zeeba says, and paints a picture for Moremi of what it was like in the beginning. She explains how, after the referendum was called, she met with four people in the rain outside a pub to discuss tactics. It's clear that Zeeba regards those people – the foul-weather canvass-ers, the Friday-night phone-bankers, the protestors and petition-signers – as the true believers and she is glad to be numbered among them.

Seeing her sister in this milieu, knowledgeable and comfortable, makes Moremi feel proud of her.

Moremi is surprised by how uneventful the act of voting is. She gets worried about forgetting to bring her polling card, but she approaches the desk and the smiley volunteers tick her name off a list and wave her on. Ballot sheet, stubby pencil. 'Should the UK government pursue a policy of Total Adoption?' and two boxes.

It's laughably low-tech. Pencil and paper, and canvas sacks. Moremi votes then folds her paper up quickly. Posts it through the box and rushes back out into the afternoon light, seeing a vote, for the first time, for what it is: a birthday wish, a stab in the dark. An act of hope.

When she's outside again she feels an odd excitement rise up in her. She made it within less than an hour of the polls closing. At the gates of the primary school are rosette-wearing tellers dressed in black or white, ticking names off a tablet. And other people heading in to vote before it's too late.

'Did you see the last poll?' shouts a man pulling a tall green bin like a wheelbarrow up the hill, glancing at the 'No means NO' stickers Zeeba has patched haphazardly all over her canvas holdall. The lights of his constellation glimmer quickly in the gloom. He laughs and says, 'Doesn't look good for your people.'

They ride their Zephyrs quickly down the river. Zeeba is silent, clench-jawed and trembling the entire way. Vote No's campaign headquarters is located in the vaults under

Waterloo, the maze of abandoned railway tunnels beneath one of London's busiest stations.

Hundreds of campaigners, reporters and politicians have gathered to watch the results come in. The figures for the exit poll are projected onto the curved stone facade of the BBC's Broadcasting House in central London. It says: *46% for No and 54% for Yes.*

People are already crying.

'I don't believe it,' Zeeba says, shaking her head. And breathlessly, she tells Moremi something about margins of error and under-represented groups that everyone seems to be repeating.

Almost an hour later, the atmosphere is buoyant again. The polls have been wrong before. And there is a notion among them that NO will win.

Netted up in the ceiling are black and gold balloons ready to rain down at the moment of victory. *What will happen if they lose?* Moremi wonders. Will canvassers and cleaners take them down and sorrowfully deflate them? Go at them with kitchen knives, cursing the course of history?

Projected on one of the walls is a map of the UK sliced like a Battenberg. Constituencies will turn black or white as soon as they declare. Looking at the map now, Moremi feels a strange sense of inevitability. It's as if anything could happen but the votes have already been cast, a winner among them. Now the country has to wait for the rest of the night to find out.

At eleven o'clock, the first result comes in, Sunderland as expected. Vote NO wins that seat and everyone cheers at the numbers. Same with Newcastle. Several high-tech displays on the wall break down the results along several metrics, examining swing and turnout.

It's almost midnight by then and Moremi realises that she's been up for twenty-one hours. As Zeeba moves through the crowd, Moremi retreats to the corner of the room, where she finds a sofa, and lets the chaos swirl around her.

She falls asleep and wakes three hours later when the crowd has thinned out a little and the mood is more sombre. She can't find Zeeba, though the map at the far end of the room is covered now with a zebra-print pattern of black and white squares. Hard to tell, from the sight of it, behind her sleep-dazed eyes, who is winning.

'I heard you met her.' The man standing before her is Raffi. 'Reynard the Fox.' She examines Raffi now, and wonders what he knows. 'Look,' he says, glancing over his shoulder as if he's afraid that someone might be listening. 'She can be a bit intense sometimes.'

'She tried to drown me!' Moremi says.

'She wouldn't have let you get hurt,' he insists. 'She was only trying to . . . wake you up. Maybe she didn't go about it the right way.'

'"Maybe".' Moremi rolls her eyes.

'Have you . . .' He searches her face. '. . . reconsidered?'

'What?'

'Did she tell you that we need you?' Moremi shakes her head.

'I only just heard today, but there is a change of plan.' He leans in further to whisper, 'They wanted to break him out two weeks ago. We had an inside woman at Ragbrough Farm but she was killed.'

Moremi can't help her sharp intake of breath. 'Maggie,' she says.

'I don't know her real name,' Raffi says. 'They're about to launch another attempt but they need someone who's already been cleared to work there.'

'So it's true,' Moremi says, 'there's a prison nearby? That's why the security is so tight in those fields?' Raffi nods. 'And ... Orpheus?' He nods again. Bewildering to think that he's been asleep in some rabbit warren under her feet. That she's been setting fire to the ground above him for weeks. If it's true what Raffi's saying, that there is a chance to save him, then she is desperate for it, but then Moremi is quiet for a while. Looking through the crowd she sees Zeeba, who is holding court with a couple of people her age wearing Vote No T-shirts.

'I promised Halima I wouldn't put myself in any more danger.' Though Moremi loves Orpheus as much as her sister, the last person who tried to save him died in the attempt.

'We're all in danger,' Raffi says, and Moremi isn't sure what he means by this. 'Has Zeeba told you about my sister Hana?' Moremi shakes her head. 'My parents died when I was young and Hana raised me.' He reaches into his trouser pocket and pulls out a photograph.

Moremi stares at the laminated picture of a pretty woman who looks a little older than Halima, holding a baby and smiling.

'That's her daughter, Leilani, but we all called her Lala.

Hana was pretty committed to raising us all analogue and when the school began to stop accepting children without a Pulse, she joined the protests against it. I don't really understand the series of events that led to it, but she was one of the first people to be arrested in the Preventative Policing Programme. One day she was there and the next . . .' He pauses, then sighs. 'Me and Lala weren't put in a division, thank God, but we were bounced around from relative to relative. Five years of living without her and then my grandma gets news that they're letting a handful of people go.'

What?' Moremi asks. 'I've never heard of something like that happening. Someone being released from Protective custody?'

'Yeah. I mean, I don't think it does happen. And we were never given a good reason why. Something about "risk levels" and "caution".' He shrugs. 'I don't know. She was arrested pretty early on in the programme and my hunch is that someone messed something up.'

'But it's good news, though,' Moremi says, 'right? You got her back.' Raffi's face darkens then.

'She wasn't "her" anymore,' he says, 'still isn't. She'd been under for three years, and that kind of thing takes a toll on the body. Hana had to learn to walk again, how to sit up even. And she never did learn how to talk. She lives with my grandma still, she needs pretty much round-the-clock care, which the government so kindly provided.'

'She can't talk?' Moremi's stomach twists.

'The carers who come have nicknamed her "Lala".'

'Her daughter's name?'

'Yeah, my niece. It's the only word she still knows how to say. I'll say, "How are you?" and she'll smile and say, "Lala".' He shrugs. 'Apparently there's a maze on the other side. And the sleepers stay there so long they lose every part of themselves. We have this theory that the only way she managed to survive it was by holding on to the one thing that mattered to her. Her light and purpose.'

'Lala.' Moremi imagines the pretty woman in the picture, aged the way Nox addicts are. Hair brittle and white, eyes sunken and empty. She imagines Hana; maybe she'd lived for centuries on the other side, and awoke, time-displaced, an ancient creature in a weakened body. Stay in Dreamtime long enough and people say that eventually everything flays away: time, language, any notion of reality. To stand a chance of surviving it, the dreamer has to hold on to a hope that is like a talisman. Hana had repeated it to herself again and again.

Suddenly Moremi is too hot. Needs to get up, to go outside to breathe.

'It could be you,' Raffi shouts after her as she runs. 'It could be Zeeba or Halima. It will be him.'

As Moremi pushes her way through the crowd to find the exit, she notices that the mood in the hall has totally soured. It's the hour of the night when the results are coming in thick and fast. Although a lot of Scotland has voted No, more Yes votes than anyone expects are being returned in the Midlands and northern England. People are wringing their hands. Counting all the ways that Vote No could 'still win', what kinds of swings need to happen and where. Moremi notices that on the map almost all of London is covered in white squares. She's not surprised. It's where the idea of Total Adoption first took hold. Families torn apart by the flood. 'Total Adoption will bring safety for more and a future for all,' explains a commentator on the BBC now. 'Who amongst us would reject that?'

Zeeba's outside by the docked Zephyrs, crying. Shaking her head at her own naivety. At her misplaced faith in this country. Zeeba tells Moremi that she has a taste in her mouth like steel. Disappointment.

'I need to go,' Moremi says over the tinnitus ringing of her own blood in her ears.

'Where?'

Moremi looks back at the hall. The crowd has thinned, and the music has stopped. The once-smiling staffers are already discussing in hushed tones 'what went wrong'.

'Can I borrow your board?' Moremi asks. Zeeba has figured out how to hack the navigation system on hers to keep from being caught.

'Okay, but—'

'I'll see you tomorrow,' Moremi promises as her sister unlatches it from her backpack. As it settles under her weight, Moremi says, 'Don't wait for me.'

It's a quick ride. To the west end of the city, past the Regency buildings with their painted stucco, towards the canal. Last time, she'd run it with tear gas stinging the corners of her eyes. This time, she keeps putting her hand in her pocket to feel for Orpheus' watch. She's doing this for him, she thinks, she has to.

By the time she reaches *Double-Down*, Bola is standing

outside, squinting up at the sky as if waiting for an eclipse. 'You came,' she says.

Fireworks are exploding above rooftops and bridges. Vote Yes has won. Somewhere in the city, Moremi imagines, Hayden Adeyemi is looking out with glee.

'Yes,' she says. 'I'm ready.'

35

MOREMI

Apparently the plan is already in motion. On the night of the referendum, when Moremi returns to *Double-Down*, Bola seems to be waiting for her, in the moonlight on the embankment. Before she can step inside, a skinny white boy with braces leaps out and holds up a device like a Geiger counter, first to her ear and then down her body.

'It's okay,' Bola says, stepping onto the paved embankment, 'we can trust her,' but he keeps going. When the scanner reaches her chest it makes a high-pitched squeal and, with a catlike quickness, his hand slides into her jacket pocket. He pulls out her folded console and tosses it into the canal. Moremi feels that old rush of panic and rage. All that money, all her data.

She swears at him and shouts, 'You better pay for that!'

'Sure.' He rolls his eyes. Then, wiping the scanner up and down her Zephyr, he asks, 'Who hacked it for you?'

'It's mine,' calls a voice. Raffi and Zeeba come running up behind her in the darkness.

'Were you following me?' Moremi asks. Zeeba's still wearing Raffi's motorcycle helmet.

'I wanted to see her too,' Zeeba says, turning to Bola as if she's a ghost.

The boy with braces sighs. 'This family reunion is very touching but we're trying to keep the number of people involved in this mission limited.'

'Well, you can't keep me out,' Zeeba says, pulling her helmet off and shaking her hair out. 'If this works, if Remi and your inside man manage to break Orpheus out, then we're all on the run.'

'She's right,' Raffi says.

'Wait.' Moremi looks between them all. 'Why?'

Bola scoffs, 'You think you can break a man out of prison and then go back to your little life? To dance class and spiced lattes and walks in the park? Were you two going to live in the suburbs and raise 1.6 kids?' Moremi's mouth opens then closes. The truth is she hasn't thought of any of this. She didn't really believe that she would ever see Orpheus again until a couple of hours ago. 'After this, we're all on the run.'

'All?' Moremi asks. 'Halima too?'

'She'll have to come,' Zeeba says.

'She can't travel anywhere,' Moremi says. 'Her due date is next month. And she told us ...'

'I know what she told us, but Silo Six will probably be one of the safest places to be after ...'

'Milk Wood,' Bola says. 'She's not going to want to be in a hospital or anywhere near a big city once it starts.'

403

Moremi steps back, feeling a weakness in her knees. She wants to rescue Orpheus before he suffers the same fate as Raffi's sister, but to live on the run as Bola does? It doesn't seem like a life that she can handle. 'Where would we go?' Moremi asks, though she's already thinking about everything she doesn't want to leave behind. London, the dance classes she's been going to. She's been entertaining herself with daydreams that she might get to dance in the ballet about Ariadne.

'Silo Six,' Bola says. 'All of us. We hide out for however long it takes. After Orpheus is free. Tonight.' Moremi notices that they're all looking at her. There is an unspoken understanding that this next part of the plan relies on her. The five of them pile inside the boat, and Bola mixes them all grainy instant coffee, which burns the back of Moremi's throat with every drag. Her hands are shaking so much she spills a little.

'You okay?' Zeeba asks, not for the first time. Moremi shakes her head. The enormity of this decision is weighing on her.

The teenaged boy with braces is a hacker nicknamed Peak. He explains that their inside man has been working for months as a night security guard in the facility where Orpheus is being held. Peak's remotely activated program should create a doorway in Dreamtime, which Orpheus can use to wake up. The inside man will switch off his Nox valve and help him out of his sleep-pod. He will take him up to an automated delivery truck, which has been hacked to bring them both to Silo Six.

'So,' Moremi asks, starting to let herself hope that this

can happen – that they really can save him. 'Where do I come into this?'

Peak pulls out a paper map, covered in his shaky handwriting. 'The delivery trucks come from here.' He points a nail-bitten finger to something he's highlighted in green. A patch of land next to Ragbrough Farm, where Moremi has been working. 'This whole area is almost impossible for us to reach because of security.'

'But I could,' Moremi says. 'I've been working around there for a month. I've probably seen that truck depot.'

'That's right. If you can get into it before your shift ends and load this . . .' He hands her a glass key. The kind that looks a bit like a quartz, with little spots of data etched into it. 'I'll show you the diagrams of the van so you know exactly where it needs to go. This will give me remote access to the van and I'll be able to shut down its GPS tracking, making it invisible once it leaves the prison. When Orpheus is inside I will redirect it to Silo Six.'

Moremi takes the key, feeling the cool weight of it in her hand.

'Six months ago,' Bola says with a smile, 'the Revelators flew a drone that sprayed thousands of seeds of wild willow-wort all over that area.'

'Wow,' Moremi says, shocked at how far back their planning goes. If it hadn't been for the outbreak, she wouldn't have been allowed anywhere near the restricted area.

'Once you get out,' Peak explains, 'you'll need to wait for us at the rendezvous point.' It's a couple of miles away, at the end of a cul-de-sac by a river.

'I guess I'm never going back to work there again,' Moremi says, quietly.

'Well' – Zeeba shrugs – 'you always said you hated your job.'

Moremi stares down at the key. If she agrees to take it, she'll be part of all this. 'Maggie,' she says. 'Was she part of this too? A Revelator who died trying to do this?'

'We've had a couple of false starts,' Bola concedes. Then, at Moremi's expression, she adds, 'I never promised you "easy".'

'You never promised me anything at all,' Moremi says.

Peak explains that the first part of the plan is already in motion. He's already hacked into Orpheus' dream and opened a door. Moremi lets her eyes drift out the porthole window to the cloud-blackened sky, fireworks spilling across it. She tries to imagine it happening right now. Orpheus, in some deathlike slumber somewhere, waking up.

36

ORPHEUS

'You don't remember me, do you?'

The young man who approaches him has slender features, copper skin with jewel-like eyes that flicker, now, with disappointment.

'I don't . . . ?' Orpheus searches his memory.

'They told me you could be completely gone by now, forgotten everything, though I had hoped . . .'

'Sorry, what did you say your name was?' Orpheus asks, hoping it might prompt some recollection. He hates situations like this.

The two of them are in one of the long courtyard-facing galleries in London's Victoria and Albert Museum. They are in a hall of statues, busts on pedestals, marble, stone and alabaster. Over there, Theseus sits triumphant on a Minotaur, and there, Samson slays a Philistine with a jawbone.

'Sherif,' the man says, examining Orpheus' face. But the name means almost nothing to him.

'I've come to bring you back,' he says.

'Back where?'

'To the other side.'

Some unhinged mystic? Orpheus wonders. A New Age con artist? When Orpheus looks over his shoulder, he sees that Moremi is a couple of metres away, by the gift shop, waiting for him.

'Orpheus.' The man looks concerned now. 'Tell me that some of you is still in there?'

'I don't know what you're talking about,' Orpheus says, stepping back quickly. Maybe this person is violent, he thinks. Sherif grabs his wrist and says, 'I've known you for years. Brother?' He looks like a shipwrecked sailor, scouring the horizon for a sign of shore. 'We went to school together. Shared a bedroom. I had my appendix out and when I opened my eyes you'd been there the whole time.' Orpheus pulls his arm from the man, sorry to disappoint him.

'You've got the wrong person,' he says, turning away.

But then Sherif shouts, 'Is it true?' Words that make Orpheus start, ring distantly in the halls of his memory. He feels suddenly sick, disorientated. The man's question has startled him into some lucidity, brought him back up from whatever swamp of forgetting he had been mired in.

The question that comes to his lips is almost a surprise then. 'How long have I been here?'

'How long do you think?'

'Four years.' He rubs his head. 'It's our anniversary tomorrow. Fruit or flowers or linen or silk. Electrical appliances.'

'Except that they don't properly work on this side,' Sherif says.

'How long on the other side?'

'Six weeks.'

For a long while, after he and Moremi returned from Venice, Orpheus would do reality checks every morning. Avoided food, reminded himself none of it was real. But after a while he fell out of the habit. The loneliness of being the only thinking head in this world of shades became too much for him. Now he's ashamed about his loss of faith.

'How did you get in here?' Orpheus asks. Did Sherif break into the prison facility and hack into the servers?

'They call it a "protective holding", not quite as secure as jail.' Then he looks around the grand room. 'Which is how we got in.'

'What do you mean by "we"?'

'The Revelators,' Sherif says, and glances over his shoulder. There is a sound of commotion coming up the hall. 'I can't tell you everything now but there is a plan under way to break you out. You don't know how far this goes, how many people are involved. And you probably never will. We've opened a seam in Dreamtime. You'll have to jump to get through it.'

'Hey!' a uniformed man at the far end of the hall shouts.

Sherif looks panicked then. 'Fucking dream security,' he hisses. Boots on the mosaic floor.

'Intruder!' someone shouts.

Sherif says the rest quickly. 'I'm waiting on the other side for you. Get up to the roof and jump.' By then a dozen security guards have materialised from the crowd.

'Orpheus?' Moremi is behind him, reaching out for his hand. 'Who is—?'

'The dream will do everything it can to try and stop you,' Sherif shouts as he makes a beeline for the courtyard. 'Don't let them win.'

'Is this man bothering you?' asks the security guard as Sherif vanishes. Orpheus knows that if he speaks to any of them he'll soon start to forget.

'Let's go,' Moremi urges, trying once again to take his hand. He turns and with the familiar revulsion remembers that she is no more real than a hologram. As soon as he does, he notices her pore-less hands and hollow eyes.

'It's not true,' he says, shaking her off. And Orpheus races away, back through the gift shop, knocking stunned people aside. How to get to the roof? Orpheus turns left into the bright domed entrance hall through a busy gallery and into the cast courts. In Dreamtime, it occurs to him, the casts are fakes of fakes. Orpheus dodges a group posing for pictures by Trajan's Column. The helical frieze crowded with soldiers, statesmen and priests, cut in half like a magician's assistant to fit beneath the ceiling. Sunlight is pouring in bright squares through the tall mullioned window. Orpheus dashes up one echoey flight of stairs and finds himself in the gallery of sacred silver, where procession crosses, relics and alms dishes reflect his face in a thousand splendid shards. Everything is deep-sea blue, refracted through the ancient stained glass.

According to the map in his head, he's almost halfway there, and the crowd has thinned out. *The dream will try to stop you,* he thinks, just as he rounds the corner and sees the smoke.

White plumes of it spume out from the painting gallery. Orpheus rubs his eyes. When he peers through the smoke he can see the paintings burn. It's a heartbreaking sight, the work of all those old masters set alight. Botticelli, Rembrandt, Tintoretto.

When Orpheus feels it against his skin, a solid wall of heat, his first instinct is to turn back, but Sherif is waiting for him in meat-space, and by the time he returns to the main atrium it's likely he will have forgotten everything that his friend has told him. But to keep running, headlong into the flames? The past few years have taught him that even if he might not die in this simulation, this body feels pain the same way it does in the waking world.

If his dream created this problem, though, Orpheus thinks, perhaps it also provided a solution. Looking around, between one of the glass display cases in the hall, Orpheus finds it, a fire extinguisher. He'd received some fire safety training when he took up his position at the Panopticon, and as he unlatches the heavy tank from the wall it comes dimly back to him.

In the training, they had donned VR masks, and aimed the nozzle. Although the displays had been realistic, Orpheus thinks now, no one had trained him for this. Their charismatic instructor, an ex-firefighter, had not told him how the blistering heat would tear at the skin on his face and forearms, or that the bitter smell of it would fill him with terror.

Flames roll down the hall in boiling waves. Sparks fly,

installation wires near the door begin to melt. Orpheus struggles to loosen the extinguisher because his fingers are already slippery with sweat. Not much terrifies him more than fire.

The inferno is spreading so wildly that by the time Orpheus squeezes the trigger on the extinguisher, the smoke has already turned black. The first gush of foam from the nozzle evaporates with a defiant hiss. Orpheus' heart hammers in panic as he comes to a dark understanding of the danger he is in. This could be his last chance to escape; if he doesn't make it he could be trapped in the dream indefinitely.

Gritting his teeth, Orpheus empties the entire contents of the extinguisher out onto the fire in front of him. Enough to clear a path for him to run through the painting gallery.

He has to do it with his eyes in slits, ducked low to save his lungs from the smoke. It feels like one of the longest distances of his life. The air is a thunderstorm of embers. By the time Orpheus reaches the tapestries, the edges of his vision are flickering with stars.

Orpheus finds himself on the emergency stairwell, eyes streaming, lungs on fire. When the heavy door slams behind him, he is plunged into darkness. Nothing but the distant glow of the exit sign. Orpheus takes a moment to slow down, his head spinning, gut clenched with nausea. Sets the fire extinguisher on the ground and waits for his eyes to grow accustomed to the darkness.

Orpheus holds tight to the banister and then runs up the steps, taking them two at a time. From his memory of the place, he needs to scale two more floors to make it up to the roof.

He's halfway on the first landing when he hears the sound of a match lighting above him. When he looks up, there is a hooded figure outlined in the darkness. 'Who's there?' he calls. The figure lights another match, and in the brief illumination, Orpheus sees her dark eyes. 'Moremi?' he asks, warily. There is an alien glitter in her face.

'Where are you going?' she asks.

Orpheus takes a careful step towards her, but when his hand touches the banister again he realises that it's wet. Oil, he thinks, but the sharp smell of it tells him it's something different. Something flammable, white spirit or turpentine. Orpheus realises that she is planning to set this place alight to stop him from leaving. 'Moremi,' he says again, with the gentleness of a hostage negotiator. 'None of this is real.'

'Stop saying that,' she shouts at him. 'What am I?'

I don't know. His heart is pounding now. A string of code? A figment of Dreamtime? Of his own mind? The flame crackles at the end of the match and then sputters out, plunging them once more into blackness.

What happens next seems to take place in seconds. First, the sound of her feet on the steps, then the blade of a knife flashing green in the exit light, its hilt coming down first on the side of his face – his vision goes white with pain – and then its blade plunging for his throat. When Orpheus ducks to avoid it, he loses his balance, his ankle gives way on the oil-slicked floor, and he crashes hard on the landing. She misses his jugular by a few

413

centimetres, and the blade slices deep into the connective tissue just under his shoulder. Muscles, tendons and flesh. 'Please,' Orpheus gasps, his chest tight with agony. Hurts to breathe, hurts to flinch. 'Let me go.'

'What happens to me,' she asks, 'when you leave?' Her bloody hands clenching the knife. Those hands were almost as familiar to him as his own. Lips he's kissed, face he's woken up next to for four years. There is almost nothing she could do that would stop him from loving her.

'I don't know,' he says. He can feel the blood seeping in a pool under his neck. 'None of it is true, what is between us.' She is the sword-hand of the dream, lancing back to thwart his escape. The words seem to hit her like a shove in the solar plexus. Orpheus presses his advantage then by lunging for the knife. Rush of adrenaline as they wrestle. Orpheus manages to get out from under her and up the next couple of steps. As he does, he hears another match ignite and realises that she is planning to set them both on fire. At this point, his clothes are covered in turpentine, and he thinks of the way that the tapestries went up in flames. With a sudden panic, Orpheus grabs the fire extinguisher, then realises, from the lightness of the tank, that it's empty.

'Don't do it,' he shouts at her, but all he can see is her grin flashing like ivory keys in the match-light. With his one good arm, Orpheus pitches the fire extinguisher down the stairs. It's an awful sound, a crash that echoes up the concrete walls. His wife topples backwards. Shout of surprise, metal crunching bone with the force of a baseball bat. It sounds as if she hits every step on her way down. The match strikes the white spirit and the ground explodes with a blowtorch-like flame that knocks the hair from Orpheus' face. He feels his ear drums burst inwards and, in the blue light, sees his lover's skull shattered on the step.

There is only one escape. Orpheus scrabbles up the next flight of stairs, half-blinded by the smoke. *It's not real,* he tells himself at the smell of his own burning skin, at the pain.

At just the last moment, though, he is struck by doubt. Had he imagined the encounter? His old friend appearing and then disappearing into nowhere? What if he's wrong and this is meat-space? He stands now, sickened by the height. If he's wrong, if this isn't a dream, then, if he jumps, he will certainly die. But then he thinks of her. Moremi, the way she'd looked lying on the rug that first night he met her. *I'll never let myself sleep,* she'd said, and he told himself, *I love her.*

Before their wedding she had said that love is an act of faith. It will take an act of faith to get back to her.

When Orpheus leaps, he's falling for so long he's sure he'll die – hit the tarmac below and shatter his bones beneath the wheels of a car. But when he lands, Orpheus opens his eyes; the world is bright and an alarm is wailing. He's on the other side. Sherif peers into his smashed sleep-pod and says with a wide, relieved smile, 'Welcome back, brother.'

37

MOREMI

Moremi has nine and a half minutes to do it. The drones monitor her walking speed and distance from the Portaloos and allocate a window of time for a bathroom break. If she's not back at her quadrant after the allotted time, an alarm will sound and the drones will come looking for her. They won't find her, of course, if everything goes to plan; she will be miles away before they realise that she is missing.

All day, Moremi has been reminding herself of the plan. She was in *Double-Down* for a couple of hours discussing the details of it with Peak and Bola, memorising the map, the mechanics of the truck, the route she must take to the rendezvous point before it was time to leave with Raffi. He'd driven her to the coach station at the start of her shift and wished her luck. Difficult to believe that she'd stood in the same spot here twenty-four hours ago, before any of this happened.

London had looked different to her as they drove through it, and not just because of the people who had clearly been out all night celebrating or commiserating the result of the referendum, but because it's her home and she loves it and she doesn't know, now, when she'll see it again.

Moremi has volunteered for an extra-long shift. Though, that morning, as the protection officers patted her down and rolled the scanner over her body, her heart had been in her throat. She'd tied her braids up in an intricate bun at the top of her head and used Peak's glass port key to keep it up. It looked decorative, barely noticeable, but she could still only let out the breath she'd been holding when the officers waved her through the security barricades.

This is the last time she'll wear the polyester jumpsuit she despises, the last time she'll chat over lunch with Renata, who – like everyone else – is busy discussing the result of the referendum. 'For a little while I thought it would change everything, but now I can't think of one thing it will change. Everyone I know has a Pulse already . . .' Moremi's mind keeps drifting back to her sisters. Zeeba, who won't be able to go to university unless she gets a Pulse; Moremi, too, will have to get hers reactivated if she wants any chance to participate in society, to keep any job, to pay for food, to vote in the next election.

The whole day, spraying down willow-wort or watching the vegetation burn, Moremi keeps glancing at the neighbouring field. She can see the truck depot in the distance. A building the size of a supermarket. She keeps trying to guess how long it will take to vault the fence and run towards it. A couple of minutes at full pelt? Can she do it without any drones catching her? Can she do it before a protection officer shoots her for trespassing?

She must do it before the end of her shift. Bola has given her an analogue watch that she keeps compulsively checking, along with Orpheus' watch which she is keeping for luck in her pocket, imagining that some time tonight she might be able to give it to him. Just the thought of seeing him again fills her with a Christmas morning kind of anticipation. Though, they've warned her that he won't be the same as he was before. He might even have forgotten her – but any risk feels worth it for a chance to hold him just one more time.

Thirty minutes to the end of her shift and Moremi presses the button on her security bracelet to let the surveillance drone know that she is taking a bathroom break. She climbs off her Zephyr and gestures for it to follow behind her. At lunch she swapped her own hacked Zephyr with her trackable work one. If everything goes to plan, once she's completed her task she will be riding the hoverboard off the estate and heading to the pick-up spot where Peak and Bola will be waiting with Halima and Zeeba.

Moremi's tracking bracelet flickers with a countdown. Nine minutes and thirty seconds. The Portaloo is further away than normal.

It takes everything she can summon not to race towards it. She doesn't want to draw attention to herself, because with every stride she is watching the seconds count down.

She has eight and a half minutes by the time she's

inside and struggling to pull the security tag off her wrist. The smell in the loos always makes her feel sick. Some chemical tang on top of human waste. Her nerves, now, as she digs her nails under the lip of the tag and wrenches with all her might, are enough to make her want to vomit.

The window on the tag reads seven minutes by the time she's pulled it off – along with a layer of skin on the back of her knuckles – and she already feels as if she's failed everyone. If the alarm sounds before she makes it to the depot and she doesn't manage to deliver the port key, Orpheus and his accomplice will probably be killed. They might make it out of the prison and into the truck, but without Peak shutting down its GPS system and remotely directing it, they will soon be discovered. If not on their way out of the prison, then at the truck's original destination.

Once the security tag clinks to the floor, Moremi kicks it behind the toilet and dashes out. The depot is half a mile away, she can see it on the horizon. She may make it, if she runs. The hard plastic door of the Portaloo slams shut as she scrabbles up the wire fence behind it and into the neighbouring wheatfield.

Peak had reminded her that this part of the mission is all about stealth. She needs to get as far as she can before the surveillance drones spot her. Which is why she chooses to run through the long heady-smelling grass instead of riding her Zephyr across the field as she would like to.

The metal barbs in the worn fence scratch at her as she climbs over and when her feet hit the soil on the other side she feels a tug at her sleeve. The cheap polyester of her jumpsuit is caught on the fence.

'Damn it,' she hisses as she pulls herself free. A scrap of yellow fabric tears, and cracks like a flag in the late afternoon breeze.

Never mind, Moremi tells herself as she races into the long wheatfield. She can barely see it as she dashes through the grass, stems crunching under the heels of her plimsolls. How long now? Six minutes, maybe, six and a half. She runs so fast her thighs burn inside her jumpsuit and her breath comes in hard gasps.

The setting sun throws her shadow in front of her as she races. Then, Moremi thinks that she feels a rumble in the sun-warmed earth. *It's back,* her first thought. She's probably imagining it because she's nervous. Moremi turns to dismiss the fear, focuses her eyes on the corrugated roof of the depot and keeps running.

Half a minute later, though, and she is sure she can feel the ground shuddering all around her, the fluffy heads of wheat are trembling on their stems, shaking grains free. She looks back down at her shadows to see something that looks like a wall, rising up behind her.

Moremi turns to discover that an automatic harvester is flying up the path behind her. She's only ever seen them from a distance, on her Zephyr in the neighbouring field. They had been compelling to watch as the wheat was drawn into the crop dividers and reeled down to the cutters. She'd had no idea how large they were close up. It makes a terrifying sound as the threshing drum beats the crops to break and shake the grains away from their stalks.

It's tall and wide. Its speed is ferocious, it's moving much faster than she can run, and is too wide, she realises now, for her to duck out of the way of it. The wave, she thinks, all over again. She's heard of people who die in automatic harvesters; a shoelace or a sleeve gets sucked into the divider and reeled down into the cutter. She's heard of people who have lost limbs this way, or been hacked to pieces. From this vantage point it looks like a mouth full of teeth, its blades menacing in the sunlight.

Moremi pushes her feet as far as they can go, her lungs and legs on fire. Every time she looks over her shoulder, it's closer. Is this how Maggie died? Was she torn apart by a machine?

Something snags at her heel. Moremi feels the harvester pull violently at her. Her heart leaps into her mouth. 'Nonononono . . .' she gasps, the world flashing before her eyes. There is a blade at her calf. When it sinks into her flesh, the pain is almost blinding. She must bite down on her tongue to stop herself from screaming.

Moremi tugs her leg back, feeling her blood spray against the grain heads, and banks right, towards the fence. She can't outrun the machine fast enough to save herself but, through the tears, she sees it. Her flailing arms find a bough of an oak on the other side of the fence. In two desperate leaps, she manages to grab it and swing her body forward like a gymnast on a bar, grateful as she ever is for her athletic body.

The stunt is enough to save her. She hangs on, pulling her legs up as the harvester rows past, but then, watching the sun gleam on the flat top of its grain tank, another idea occurs to her. Taking another deep breath, Moremi lets go of the branch and lands on its hot metal roof, letting the machine propel her to the end of the field, where the depot comes into view.

She probably has a minute or so before the alarm sounds. Jumping on the harvester saves her a minute or two but as it reaches the edge of the field, she must carefully jump off, making sure to land on her knees and roll through the grass. By the time she stands, the harvester is already hurtling in the opposite direction and she pulls her bruised and lacerated body over the wall.

The depot is on the other side. Sixty seconds, she guesses, running around to find a window. Moremi grits her teeth against the bright knife of pain that carves into her muscle with every step.

There are no easy ways into the building, the door is sealed and the windows too are firmly locked. Standing on her tiptoes, Moremi can see the van that Peak had pointed out – a large automated delivery truck with the number plate she's already branded into her memory.

How to get to it, though? Moremi looks around, frantic, thinking about the seconds the drone must be counting down before it comes to the Portaloo and finds that she isn't there. If the protection officers discover her on this side of the fence she'll likely be jailed for trespassing. Or worse. Moremi is not sure how easy it will be for them to connect her to the Revelators, but if they do she'll be facing a terrorism charge.

Think, she urges herself, but only the most basic and reckless idea comes to her – she picks up one of the rocks lying at the edge of the wheatfield and hurls it through the window of the depot. Just as she expected, alarms tear through the air. She'll have less than a minute now, she thinks, grabbing the window ledge to haul her body up with all her strength. Broken glass pierces the skin on her arms and shins as she pulls herself through the shattered window and stumbles inside the depot. Shards of it snap under her plimsolls. The light outside has rendered her sun-blind. The depot smells of hot rubber and motor oil. At the moment, most of the trucks are hooked up to their charging ports.

Moremi spares no time running towards the right one. She remembers, from Peak's diagrams, that there is a door she can open in the front of the vehicle which will give her access to the Controller Area Network bus. 'The can bus,' as he had told her, then laughed to himself that 'It's called the can bus, not the can't bus, because once I've got access to it, there's nothing I can't do.' Plugging the glass key into a nearby port is what will give him remote access to it. She knows it's worked as soon as she does it because, once she pulls the key out of her hair and pushes it in, it flashes green.

Her chest lets her release some of the breath she's been holding. But the relief lasts only a second. When she turns, trembling and covered in blood, she sees that protection officers are already pounding at the door of the depot.

No, she thinks, they mustn't find her here.

Moremi stumbles back the way that she came and clambers through the window, looking frantically around. Her Zephyr should be waiting for her. Moremi makes the hand motion to summon it. But the board doesn't seem to be in range to sense her. Her heart sinks as she looks up to find that a fleet of security drones are flying towards her like a murder of crows, the setting sun making it look as if the sky behind them is on fire.

Moremi looks around. On her left are the protection officers, and in front are the drones. Her only option is to run and try to hide. If she goes back through the wheat-fields she risks getting torn apart by the harvester.

She will have to try to make it on foot to the rendezvous point, which, by her calculation, will be about an hour's walk by a river. She's not sure her injured leg will let her limp that far, and if by some miracle she makes it there before the protection officers catch her, she could end up leading them straight to Halima, Zeeba, Peak and the others. Moremi's heart sinks at the predicament. Should she just give up now?

She reminds herself that if she keeps running, she might see Orpheus one more time. And this possibility gives her the strength to try and think of another escape.

Moremi tries to lose them by darting around the building, scrabbling over the fence and diving into a neigh-bouring apple orchard. Although Moremi doesn't have the capability to outrun them, she hopes that the long shad-ows of the trees combined with the setting sun might make it difficult for her pursuers to find her. But, she remembers as she runs, this orchard was slated for treatment today. Sprinting past the plants, she can see that they have been covered by the weed. Willow-wort, the spiny shrub that grows around the roots of the trees, choking them of nutrients. The few fruits on the twisted branches look poisonous, their leaves are shrivelled and discoloured, littering the parched ground. Distantly, Moremi thinks she can hear a couple of Zephyrs, her colleagues working at the edges of the field.

Moremi keeps running as sirens howl overhead. Although there is no chance she can outrun them, at least she might find somewhere to hide from them. But, by the time she reaches the edge of the field, she thinks that she is in too much pain to keep running, nothing but adrenaline and terror powering her legs. With some difficulty she climbs over another fence and walks straight into the python. It's on her right, rolling through shrubs as the harvester had, and then she recognises the warning countdown it makes when it's about to set fire to the vegetation.

The spikes on the willow-wort catch at her, pull on the threads of her jumpsuit. It's hard to find her footing on this unstable ground. As Moremi leaps over a tangled mass of shrubs, her ankle twists. She's sent flying forward, her face hitting the dirt with a hard smack. All the breath is knocked from her lungs and stars erupt behind her eyes. As the blood whooshes through her ears she hears the python's countdown, the particular beeping she's grown used to. It sounds like *three, two, one,* as the formidable machine powers up and, with a *whump* sound, snorts a gout of flames at the overgrown weed.

Moremi can do nothing but duck her head and hope not to be hit. When she opens her eyes the world is burning. Every direction she looks the weed is going up like a bonfire, its wild growth during the rainless weeks making the fire gallop through the underbrush.

With a shout of pure terror, Moremi looks down to find that her polyester suit is also on fire. Unzipping it quickly, she manages to pat some of the flames away. The sky is now completely black with smoke. A dizzy storm of embers. Moremi doesn't know which way to turn.

She stays low for a little while, her heart pounding, every breath roasting her lungs and lips. Using the caterwaul of the drones to orientate herself, Moremi tries to picture this field on the map that Peak had showed her. There had been a river. Under the rustle and crackling of flames, Moremi thinks she can hear it. South-west, it had been. At an angle to the way the sun was setting.

On some intuition, she runs for it. It's like walking over hot coals now, the burning weed, the awful smell of it. The ground under her feet is black or veined with light, and every step is agony. Every breath.

She's not sure how she makes it, except that, finally, she reaches the edge of the field and her heels sink into thick mud. The river is bright with the reflection from the fire. Lancing like a bronze sabre away from the depot, and the orchard, and the farm she'll never see again.

Moremi leaps into it, and the cool of the water closes over her head. As she sinks lower, she's reminded of her encounter with Bola on the boat. The way the woman had pushed her head down into the canal; the terror Moremi had felt then is nothing like the relief she's experiencing now.

Moremi lets her feet touch the sludgy bottom of the

river before she pushes herself back up, head breaking the surface a little distance from where she'd dived in. The sounds of the sirens are further away now, the fire must have made it easier for her to lose them. The water is moving fast; if she surrenders to it, it might take her where she needs to go.

38

ORPHEUS

Orpheus is shunted back into the upper world. Into the squealing of sirens. Sherif is dressed in the white linen jumpsuit of a technician and leaning over the shattered pane of the sleep-pod. Though Orpheus has never been so relieved to see his old friend, before he can answer, his diaphragm pings, he jolts upright to dry heave, and then slides back into the tepid water of the pod with a groan. Shards of glass float about his head and clatter like ice cubes against the lip of the pod.

'Probably the worst wake-up you've ever had,' Sherif says sympathetically, removing the breathing tube from under his nose. With dark panic, Orpheus realises that he can't feel his legs. 'It's okay,' Sherif says, 'they told me it would take a while for everything to get back to normal. Just be glad we managed to get in sooner rather than later.'

'Glad ...' Orpheus' voice comes out scratched, and he

has to strain to get the words out. '... you ... came ... at all.' Then, 'Sorry,' as he fights the urge to be sick again.

'Not a thing I haven't seen,' his friend says, pulling electrodes off Orpheus' skin. 'That's a true thing.' How many times, when they were room-mates in the children's division, had Sherif returned to discover Orpheus, half-conscious and hypothermic, vomiting in a bathtub after a hundred hours of Dreamtime?

Sherif jumps at the sound of voices outside the heavy door. 'Okay, we're going to have to hurry.' He says this quickly, unplugging the pod and kicking aside wires. 'There is an automated delivery van in the depot right now. It leaves in seven minutes and we have to be on it.'

'Can't ... walk,' Orpheus rasps.

'It's okay.' Sherif's mouth twitches. 'You've never weighed very much.'

He's naked under the water, and as Sherif helps him upright, Orpheus sees the toll that over a month of Dreamtime has taken on his body. His skin is grey and he can almost see his heart slamming against the jutting cage of his ribs.

'Take this.' Sherif gives Orpheus a papery hospital gown, attaches a muzzle to his constellation, then wraps an arm around his friend and helps lift him out of the pod.

Sherif's hair is long now, tied back in a greasy ponytail. It smells faintly of cigarettes and body spray, as his side of their dormitory had. People used to mistake them for brothers, and for years he was the closest thing Orpheus has ever had to one.

'You ... saved me,' Orpheus says now as Sherif bends his knees to bear the weight of him.

'You saved yourself,' Sherif replies.

It's like a three-legged race, Orpheus' feet dead weights under him. It takes all of Sherif's upper body strength just to hold on to his friend, who is gritting his teeth and breathing hard in the rush to get them both out.

'Breach!' The door behind them flies open as security storm in.

They're a couple of metres away, on the other side of the wall, and Sherif is fumbling with the security pad on the emergency exit. He presses his thumb against it and the pod slides open.

'What?' Orpheus stares at his friend in surprise. 'You're an inside man.'

'One of many.'

Orpheus tries to imagine the shadowy ranks of Revelators, infiltrating facilities. 'Been working here for a month,' he says with a smile, then as the heavy door opens the wailing of alarms tears their eardrums. 'Six minutes until the van leaves – damn it! Might have to throw you down the stairs to make it.'

Boots thunder behind them, up the long ranks of sleep-pods. About a dozen guards in heavy vests with mirrored visors.

'Freeze!' a couple shout, their constellations flashing wildly as they point guns at the two fugitives.

'Nononono,' Sherif hisses under his breath. Dragging Orpheus with him, he takes a sharp left and runs down the hall towards the stairwell. Only another troop of guards are right behind them, running up the other end of the hall. Too quickly for either of them to escape.

Orpheus wants to tell Sherif to go without him, but the confrontation happens almost too quickly for Orpheus to take in. A smattering of gunfire, bullets hitting the windows of doors and glass flying everywhere.

Sherif falls with a howl of pain and Orpheus scrabbles on his hands and knees to push the fire door open and haul his friend through. In a few seconds they are on the other side, leaning against the heavy door, breathing hard on the concrete, tears of panic in both their eyes.

'Five ... minutes,' Sherif hisses through gritted teeth. His words echo up the dank stairwell as the motion-sensitive lights come on with a clink. 'You need to get down there,' he says, nodding his head at the banisters.

'Okay,' Orpheus says. 'Can you walk?'

'Fuck, no!' Sherif's holding his side, and Orpheus sees, with a roll of dread, blood gushing through his fingers. The exit wound of a bullet in his chest, his face a mask of pain, turning greyer by the second.

'I won't leave you,' Orpheus says. Sherif is clearly looking at a holographic display on his Pulse. 'Four ... and a half ... now. You have to go. Go now! Now or they'll kill you.'

'Don't make me,' Orpheus says, his vision blurred with tears. He says what they used to say when the other was in pain. 'I wish it was me.'

'I wish it was you too,' Sherif gasps, gritting his teeth in pain. A collapsing lung, Orpheus thinks from the sound of his breathing. 'I'm twenty, I didn't want to die.' He winces;

the sides of his mouth are black with blood. 'Go now, and make this worth something.'

'I don't deserve it,' Orpheus says, but then he's startled by the sound of boots coming up the stairs and adrenaline jolts through him. Sherif is already slipping away, his lips turning blue, his eyes drifting. 'They say you're going to save us,' he mumbles.

'Up here.' The guard is three flights up. Orpheus will have to outrun him if he wants any hope of making it to the delivery truck on time. With every last bit of his strength he pulls himself up on the banister, using his strong arm to get himself down the stairs.

He trips and collapses on the seventh-floor landing, cursing his lame feet. By then, the guard is almost upon him, two flights away and running.

How long now until the van leaves? Orpheus thinks. Three minutes? Holding on to the banister he stumbles as fast as he can down the stairs. Sixth floor, fifth ... the men above gaining on him with every step.

He almost falls down the final two flights, counting the seconds in his head. The dim basement lot where trucks are lined up like cows, lit with fluorescent bulbs.

One minute.

Gunshots.

'He's on the ground floor.'

A figure appears at the exit and shoots. Thirty seconds. Orpheus leaps into the one open truck, doesn't even notice that he's been shot until he collapses between two aluminium drums, and then touches his gut, with a dreamlike disbelief.

The doors of the van close and he's in darkness, curled up between barrels of rotting food. The ground rumbles under him as the vehicle's freight programme starts up and it begins to move. With his blood pooling like treacle between his fingers, the pain clutches at him. That darkness ushers him back as it had that first time, when the technicians pushed the cannula of Nox into his arm. Sleep used to be delicious, Orpheus used to love the other side, but now his mind flails against it.

Where are we going? he thinks as the van rumbles under him, inclined upwards for a long while, through the tunnel that leads out of the underground prison. Wheels on tarmac, then gravel, then road. Sherif crying. 'Make it worth something.'

The van is a ferry ride into Hades. The highway, the River Styx. That sordid god, Charon, distantly visible in the enveloping gloom. His flashing eyes are sodium lamps and holograms, street signs lighting the way back. To her.

39

MOREMI

It is a harrowing ride, from the outskirts of the city to Silo Six. Zeeba and Peak found Moremi, half-conscious, cut, burned and bruised, in the riverbank by the rendezvous point. They'd helped to drag her to their getaway van, an old manual one with blacked-out windows. Bola drives in the front wearing a rabbit mask. Raffi and Halima were in the back. Everyone shouted with joy when they saw her, in spite of the state she was in.

Halima had helped tear off her clothes and bandaged her burns with an old first-aid kit. They were mainly on her back, blisters coming up in a way that made her feel as if she was still on fire. Cuts on her hands and shins that were cleaned with antiseptic, and the big gash at the back of her calf that made her feel as if her flesh was minced meat. Moremi could have cried, she was so relieved to see her sisters, but Halima looked tense and when Moremi asked what it was she only held her stomach and shook her head. 'Braxton Hicks,' she said.

Peak was riding next to Bola. 'Did it work?' Moremi kept asking as they drove. 'Is he safe?'

'There's literally no way to know that until we get to the van.' Peak was following its progress on a console where the van, a little flashing icon, was coming towards them. 'If the two of them are in there, then they made it.'

Moremi must have fallen asleep again soon after that because when she opened her eyes the white delivery van with the Protect logo had come veering down the half-deserted street. Without thinking, Zeeba had leaped in front of it to stop it. 'No!' Halima shouted. The sensors in the front had flashed and whined, giving Bola and Raffi enough time to jump into the back.

'You didn't have to do that,' Peak shouted at Zeeba. 'I'm controlling it remotely.'

Ignoring the argument, Moremi followed Raffi and Bola around the back. They all saw it, though, the blood everywhere. Moremi had screamed, pushing the aluminium drums aside to find him.

She'd thought he was dead, when she first saw him. Waxy skin, lips turning purple, his arms dead weights. He was still bleeding generously, from a wound that took a moment for Bola to find, tearing off his hospital gown. Moremi had never seen so much blood, and as they climbed into the back of the van, Bola began shouting orders.

'The main thing is to stop the bleeding,' she barked, as Zeeba appeared again with the first-aid kit. 'A person can bleed out in minutes,' she said.

Bola treated him with the efficiency of a field doctor, staunching the flow of blood. They all watched as she checked his vital signs and determined the entry and exit wounds. 'Small central entry wound. Can you see it there?' It had a black halo around it. 'Abrasion collar.'

That thought playing a baleful cannon in her head: *he's dead, he's dead.* She could barely see through the tears.

Bola turned to Moremi then, untucked her shirt from her belt and revealed a star-shaped gash. Knobbled scar tissue, faded now. 'People come back from this,' she said. 'And he's lucky, it doesn't look as if it's damaged any major organs. When we get to Silo Six they will have to debride the wound and give him antibiotics.'

Peak brought out something that looked like a piercing gun and held it under Orpheus' chin. 'What is that?' Moremi asked.

'It's an implant,' he explained, and then fired. 'It will keep his Pulse dark, so no one can find him.'

Halima winces at the sounds of it. In the thin light, Moremi notices that she has a matching wound under her chin.

'Good,' Bola said. 'If we turn up at Silo Six with active constellations, they'll probably shoot us.'

It took three of them to pull Orpheus into the back of their van. By the end of it, they were all covered in his blood. 'It'll be a long night,' Bola said, climbing back into the driver's seat.

She's right. It will be sunrise by the time they arrive.

They don't know what happened to Sherif. They can only assume that he didn't make it. Everyone seems saddened and shaken by the absence of their friend. Although Moremi only knows Sherif from a handful of Orpheus' memories, the loss of their co-conspirator makes her even more aware of the danger they are all in.

It takes a lot to look after the wound for as long as they are driving. They take it in turns, though it is mostly Moremi who holds him.

Through one of the van's small windows, Moremi watches the moonlit squares of fields and farmland flash by. They're taking a circuitous route, away from the main roads, where the most surveillance is.

As they drive, now, Bola promises them that they will be safe in Silo Six. She describes it like a promised land. An analogue community of people who have lived for decades in a mountain range in South Wales, where the Legacy Party have less control over the devolved government. She tells them that children grow up without the Panopticon there and they've learned to be self-sufficient.

The railway tracks and highways winnow into country lanes and rolling hills, dramatic landscapes, the thunderous clouds wrestling across the sky.

Moremi is half-delirious by the time they approach. She's injured and terrified, adrenaline has frayed her nerves. Zeeba points out the settlement through the window, tents and caravans, little wooden houses with green roofs, a lake of solar panels.

All of a sudden, chaos erupts around them. Banging on the sides of the van. Hoarse voices telling them to 'Get out!' and 'Put your hands up.' Moremi pulls back one of the beaded curtains that hang over the window and sees the barrel of someone's gun. When they open the door, Moremi stumbles out and retches on the dirt-road. She's had nothing to eat or drink but the Lucozade she found in the bottom of Zeeba's rucksack and her bile comes up blue.

Protection officers, she thinks as Zeeba, Bola and Raffi stumble out, squinting, half-blinded by the sunlight.

Moremi was too badly burned to want to put more clothes on. She's wearing nothing but her underwear and a frayed T-shirt of Bola's, which is blackened with Orpheus' blood. She puts her hands up, her heart pounding.

The air outside smells of smoke, and her bare feet sink into the mud.

'Are you she?' someone shouts.

'Who?' Moremi asks.

There is a tense silence among them all. No one wants to explain who they are. Raffi says that if the police find Orpheus they are sure to execute him, and Bola has been on the run for years.

'Queen Mab,' Bola says. Someone has her head pressed against the bonnet of her van. 'The fairies' midwife? "She comes in shape no bigger than an agate-stone ..."'

Raffi swears under his breath and squeezes his eyes shut in misery. 'Is this the right fucking time?' he asks. Zeeba looks as if she might wet herself as she stares down the barrel of a rifle. Moremi is trying to control how hard her hands are shaking.

'Sometime she driveth o'er a soldier's neck,' Bola says, clicking her finger and thumb together as if to get herself to remember. 'And then dreams he of cutting foreign

438

throats ...' She squeezes her eyes shut in recollection as a couple more people appear from the trees, riding on Zephyrs, wearing animal masks. 'Something about Spanish blades?'

Moremi gasps, then says with such breathless speed it's almost all one word. 'And in this state she gallops night by night. Through lovers' brains, and then they dream of love.' It's the part of *Romeo and Juliet* that their mother had once challenged them to memorise.

'Welcome!' Voices from the crowd, everyone lowers their guns and steps back. The woman wearing the moulded plastic face of a cheetah, says, 'People with a Pulse can't memorise a thing.' *Oh,* Moremi thinks, *it's a codeword.* And then she wonders why their mother had made them learn it. Did she have some inkling a day like this would come?

It's only then that Moremi notices the scar on the side of all of their heads. The Revelators search everyone with the machine that sounds like a Geiger counter. A woman pulls Moremi's braids back and eyes her constellation.

'Everyone's dark,' Bola assures them. They pat down Zeeba too, and examine everyone's Zephyrs.

'Okay,' says the barrel-chested man in a ram mask, its decorative wooden horns curving behind his ears. In his pocket, a walkie-talkie buzzes. 'Have to be safe, you know.' He pulls it off and she sees that he's around Bola's age, with a scruffy beard and dirty blond hair. 'We've had a lot more people coming this way since the vote.'

'You should have been expecting us,' Bola says, an edge of annoyance in her voice now.

'What's wrong with him?' the woman with the cheetah mask asks as she searches the van.

'He's Orpheus,' Raffi says, and the mood suddenly changes. In a flash, everyone is moving, rushing to get him out, and into the back of the mud-splattered pickup truck that has been riding up the side of the road. They all keep saying his name in whispers to each other, their voices light with awe and disbelief.

'We've been waiting for years,' someone says.

'I thought it might never happen,' says another.

Moremi climbs into the back of the truck with him and the man in the ram mask slams the accelerator to speed them towards Silo Six and the field hospital. 'He's gonna make it,' he shouts at the steering wheel. 'He has to.'

And the other man in the front seat says, 'We haven't come this far to lose Orpheus now.'

Something about the motion, or perhaps everyone saying his name, makes Orpheus' eyes flutter open. Moremi is lying next to him, her face buried in his neck, breathing in the salty smell of him, iron and sweat, his blood turned to jelly on her clothes.

'Remi . . .' He mumbles her name.

'Orpheus!' she says, sitting up and holding his face in her hands, crying again now.

'You came back for me?' A look of sleepy relief in his glassy eyes.

'I'll always come back to you,' she promises, 'wherever you go. On this side or the next. I'll look for you and won't give up.'

PART THREE

40

ORPHEUS

He awakes to the sound of singing and the smell of smoke. Sun, peering through tiny gaps in tarpaulin. Silo Six is more like his childhood home than anywhere he's ever been. A vast and rambling site built around an abandoned grain factory. Some two hundred people. A community of neo-Luddites and runaways nestled among the Brecon Beacons.

Orpheus has been in the city so long that he's forgotten what it is to go to sleep to the sigh of the wind through trees and to wake up to the sight of thunderclouds rolling up from the offing sky.

For over a week he is in and out of an opiated sleep, recovering in their field hospital – an old barn filled with whatever they can steal or salvage. The details are fuzzy. Their improvised surgery, removing the bullet, the members of their community who donated pints of blood. The days it was 'touch and go'. The nights he woke half the campsite screaming and clenching the bedsheets from the pain. The implant under his jaw jams the signals from his Pulse. The silence between his ears is sublime. So is the dark.

He's unconscious for the worst of the Nox withdrawal, though he still wakes sometimes seeing phantoms at the end of his bed. His father, Zen, Sherif. Sometimes he wakes to Moremi's face and each time he asks her, 'Is it true?' and she kisses his eyelids and leans in.

And tells him, 'Yes, yes.'

He's been in the dream so long, living with only the pallid shadow of her, that her flesh and blood self is almost alien to him. The pores on her nose, the way her braids smell of smoke, her sour breath on his cheeks. 'I never want to dream again.'

Moremi tells him that the world changed while he was sleeping. That Total Adoption is coming. She also explains how they broke him out of prison, how she was injured trying to save him. That, after a long labour, Halima gave birth to a girl.

Orpheus wishes he'd imagined Sherif's death. Wishes he could open his eyes, as he had so many times growing up, to his friend's crooked teeth, to hear him say, 'brother' one final time. Orpheus will never completely understand what it took for Sherif to come to rescue him. And it breaks his heart that he will never be able to thank him.

It's some time before he's well enough to take short walks around the campsite. One arm around Moremi and the other on a cane, wary of any sudden movement that might cause pain to lance through his taped-up guts. She shows him the way that the elaborate security system has kept the group hidden for years. She chats excitedly about the things she's learned and the people she's met since they have been in hiding here. But Orpheus doesn't know what to do to bridge the gap between them now. In his head, four years have passed since he last saw her. The real her. Years he spent in Dreamtime with her dead-eyed avatar who had tried to kill him. Every now and then, the sight of her at the bottom of the staircase, blood pooled behind her cracked skull, will flash before his eyes and he will have to remind himself that it never really happened. More than anything he wants to get back to their old easy way with each other. To the private happiness they had before the world rushed in and rent their lives apart.

'You never got to see Angharad,' Orpheus says to Moremi that morning as they look at the community.

'I've seen it in your dreams. It looked a lot like this.'

'My father wanted to bring us here. The night he died – before that actually – growing up we always had a plan that if our location was ever breached we would make our way to Silo Six.'

'You never told me that.' She stops for a moment in surprise. Orpheus winces at the motion and she apologises.

'You know, you're famous here.'

'Famous?'

'They did all of this for you,' she says. 'The attack on the symposium, the breakout.'

'Why?'

'Because they think you're the key to destroying the Panopticon.'

445

As they walk, Orpheus begins to notice that people fall silent when they approach. The group in cotton dungarees working out in one of the fields, the woman pushing a wheelbarrow. The class of small children collecting feathers to make dream catchers.

'Don't they all look as if they hatched out of eggs?' Moremi laughs. In their homespun clothes, tousled long hair, grass-stained harem pants and sun hats. 'They look like children on a magazine cover about childhood. And don't you think they look different because they don't have Pulses? Their eyes maybe ... a kind of faraway look in them?'

A couple about their age, a man with a long ginger beard and a woman in yellow corduroys, come up the dirt road and offer to take Orpheus and Moremi for a short tour on the cart attached to the back of their tractor. Alder and Meeghan, they say their names are. They explain that they also knew Sheriff briefly. That they too were heartbroken at the news of his death, had planted a tree at the edge of the estate in his honour.

When they ride, Orpheus feels each bump in the pit of his stomach, and clenches his teeth against the pain in his wound.

It's a short journey up the side of the valley, and from that vantage he can see that the community sprawls across seven or eight hundred acres, with a river running through it. On one side are the Black Mountains and on the other, the Brecon Beacons. Orpheus' heart soars at the sight of so much green, as far as his eyes can see.

'We're saplings, me and Alder,' Meeghan jokes,

squinting her eyes against the sun as she turns back to look at them.

'That's what they call people who haven't been living here long.' Moremi's voice rings with the keen interest of a tourist.

'You haven't been living here long?' Orpheus says.

'Two years,' Alder says, his eyes on the dirt road ahead of him.

'And a half,' Meeghan adds.

'Where did you live before?' Orpheus asks.

'Manchester.'

'What made you leave?'

'Oh, you know . . .' Meeghan smiles. 'Looking for what everyone is looking for. Meaning. Kinship. "Industry without drudgery".'

'It's not so woolly as you make it sound,' Alder says. 'It's not as if we had a hundred options. We didn't see ourselves pollinating apple trees for some conglomerate until we were eighty. Or teaching robots how to cross roads.'

'It's not so easy here, either,' Meeghan says, gesturing down the valley. And from where they are now, Orpheus can see the whole of it. The abandoned factory they've converted into the main communal living area. Dining hall, theatre and library. All around it, wooden structures, dormitories or personal family homes, all the roofs scattered with solar panels or grass. A dairy farm, stables, people sheltering from the midday sun under brightly painted gazebos. Wire fences around pastures. Farm animals grazing among rusted agricultural equipment. 'Lots of people come for a while, a month or two, can't cut it and leave. It's a lot of work. We grow all our own food, obviously. Sew our own clothes, salvage what herbs we can for the apothecary. It looks idyllic right now, now that the sun is shining, but when you're up to your ankles in pig shit it does actually feel like drudgery.' She laughs. 'But then . . . we begin every morning in the dining hall with a poem. And sometimes we stay out all night just gazing at constellations. Playing guitar by the fire. And I remember that when I lived in the city I was bone-deep lonely. And not just that, so sad it made me sick.'

'They say that people in intentional communities rate consistently higher on the Satisfaction with Life scale.' The way Alder says this makes Orpheus imagine that he's said it often.

'Is that what you call it?' Orpheus asked.

'We're kind of a broad church. I think at one point there was a horticultural school here, and a couple of the elders still run courses for the—'

'The elders?' Orpheus interrupts.

'A lot of things sound weird if you're new here,' explains Meeghan. 'I keep telling my parents, you know, it's not a cult or anything like that. Nothing kooky or religious.'

'Some people are, maybe,' Alder says. 'We can't, like, account for everyone. There are a couple of different groups. A few religious – a couple of post-Tribulationists and neo-Mennonites – but mainly people come here because they're sick of their lives, or because they hate what they're doing to the planet, or because they hate what companies are doing to their brains and the brains of their children. They come here because we've been on

Earth for a long time, and for a long time this is how we lived.' He gestures again to it.

Alder and Meeghan explain that the Welsh government have granted special licences for small communities to live without the Pulse and free of a large amount of intervention from Protect.

'Though, who knows what will happen now?'

'Since Total Adoption,' Moremi says. And they shudder at the word.

According to the couple, there was a large influx of people the first time Legacy were voted into power, and in the wake of the widespread adoption of the Pulse in schools and workplaces. The increased population had led to infighting, a schism, breakaway groups and then finally a 'constitution of sorts', Meeghan says. 'One of our core beliefs is that we and our children will live Pulse-free.'

By now they've made a loop around and are returning back.

'Of course, living this way, sustaining this kind of lifestyle, can't be the ultimate goal. We might be carbon-neutral and sane and happy, but we can't just pat our own backs while Rome burns. And make no mistake about it, the world is burning. Hayden and the people at the Panopticon desire nothing less than to remake the world. To change what it is to be a conscious human. If that doesn't set our hearts on fire to stop him then we're the villains.'

Every word that they say makes Orpheus dizzy with exhaustion. Can't they see what he can? That there is no running. There never has been from this kind of progress.

It is bound to swallow them all whole like grains in a thresher.

'Everything is in place now, to stop them,' Alder says.

'With Milk Wood?' Moremi ventures carefully.

'Yes,' Meeghan says, her eyes bright. 'That's why we risked our lives to save you, Orpheus. Because you're the one who is going to save us.'

Orpheus shivers at these words. Remembering what the protection officers had said, about the scale of the disaster they were trying to avert. Because Orpheus knows that he owes these people a debt for rescuing him, and he's not ready to tell them that he doesn't want any part of this.

When he looks up, Alder is still smiling and, wistful, he says, 'The whole of the Panopticon will come crashing down. Because of you.'

41

MOREMI

The baby is like a little god, eyes like specks of onyx, black as space. She'd been blue when she was born. It took almost five minutes for her to breathe, and that entire time, Moremi was cursing herself. Cursing the forces that had brought her and her sisters and her husband to this candlelit barn. This makeshift hospital filled with stolen and salvaged supplies. In spite of how it turned out – Orpheus is recovering from his injuries and both mother and baby lived – Halima is also resentful.

'It's not the birth I wanted,' she says.

'In a barn surrounded by the people you loved,' Zeeba says. 'If it was good enough for the Virgin Mary, isn't it—'

'That's not funny, so stop saying it,' Halima says. 'Something could have happened.'

'Nothing did! But you wanted latex and glass. You wanted doctors and needles. If I ever had a baby, and I never will—'

'You guys!' Moremi says to interrupt their argument, 'can we just take a moment' - she inhales and exhales – 'to be really happy?'

They sit in silence for a while in the meadow on the edge of the apple orchard, where a dozen members of Silo Six are busy working, filling up wheelbarrows and singing to each other. The day is dreamlike in its loveliness. The sound of birds singing, the fierce glare of the late-afternoon sun, butterflies winging their way through the grasses. The vinegary smell of rotted apples.

Halima and the baby are stretched out on a tie-dyed blanket and Orpheus is asleep on the grass. In the distance she can see their Auntie Bola teaching eleven-year-olds about the water cycle.

'We could stay.' Zeeba voices the thought just as it occurs to Moremi. Halima doesn't reply for a while, shades her eyes against the sun and frowns. 'Couldn't we? Wouldn't we be happy?' She looks at both of her sisters to measure their responses. 'You and Orpheus could be happy here, and the baby. Auntie Bola is happy here. She says that she's tired of living on the run. That she's going to grow old here. We could.'

'Zee ...' Halima rolls over on the blanket, her skirt riding up her thighs. 'I'm happy with my life. And the Panopticon too. I know what you all think about it but ...' She touches the little implant under her chin that has taken her constellation offline. 'I feel kind of sick without it. And I hate how blurry all my memories are.'

'They say that fades,' Zeeba says.

'Or you just get used to it,' Moremi says. 'Brain-memories

aren't like quartz-memories. They're more ... mutable. You remember flashes, sounds or smells; some memories are just ... feelings.'

For Moremi, though, it's easy to imagine being happy here, learning new skills, teaching other people how to dance. But she also can't deny that she had dreamed of more for herself – taking a second bow on stage at the Royal Opera house.

'What about him, though?' Zeeba lowers her voice a little, worried that saying his name will wake him. Orpheus, asleep under the shade of an apple tree. He's not been the same since they rescued him and Moremi has been finding it hard to get close to him again after all they've both been through.

They all know that Orpheus can't get anywhere close to a city, a drone or even an automated truck with a video feed that might recognise his face. Here in Silo Six, they only have a tenuous link to the outside world – a couple of people who deliver some papers from the local village every morning – but Moremi has gleaned enough to know that he's infamous now. Orpheus' face has been splashed across the covers of a couple of publications. The story is that he broke out of prison and killed an orderly, and a couple of pressure groups are campaigning for his execution.

'Maybe it will be different, in ten days?' Zeeba says, when the attack is predicted to take place.

'What's that noise?' Moremi thinks she can feel the ground rumble, and she sits up quickly.

'The freight train,' Zeeba says. 'I think it carries lumber

from some place and down to some South Wales port. It's a maglev, apparently. Haven't you been hearing it in the morning? The noise is like a thundercrack, it's been waking me up.'

At the sound of it, Orpheus rouses, and rubs his eyes. He looks around in surprise as if he'd forgotten where he was, and leans up on his elbow with some difficulty.

'You let me fall asleep,' he says, looking slightly betrayed at Moremi.

'I didn't—'

'Don't do that,' he mutters, his face surprisingly dark.

The baby starts to cry and Halima says, 'She needs a feed, and I'm too embarrassed to get my boobs out in public yet.'

After she's gone, Zeeba turns to Orpheus and asks, 'When you go to sleep, do you go back there?'

Orpheus is silent for a while, his jaw tight. 'I'm still finding it hard to tell which side is which.' Both sisters shiver at the thought.

She finds him a couple of hours later, at the far edge of the estate, in the wooded area near the trees, staring up at the large fence. He starts when he hears her approach, then winces, clutching his side.

'Sorry.'

'No, it's me, just jumpy still.'

Moremi comes over to stand next to him. Like her, he's wearing clothes rummaged from the 'free closet'. Second-hand and frayed cargo trousers and a sun-faded *Sgt. Pepper's Lonely Hearts Club Band* T-shirt.

It's turning to autumn without her noticing, the ground is already littered with fallen leaves and there is a dampness in the air that she'd forgotten. Orpheus is holding his hands out as if he's hoping to catch rain in his palm. 'It's electrified,' he says.

'I guess they're worried about trespassers? They seem pretty secretive.'

'Right . . .' Orpheus sounds unconvinced.

'Planning on running?' She says it light-heartedly but the look in his green eyes then makes her serious. 'Orpheus? You know we're safe here, right?'

'I don't feel safe,' he says, then lowers his voice as if they might overhear him. 'It's not as easy for me to forget that those people building bonfires and having poetry slams are the same people who killed my friends in the Panopticon. Your friend.'

Moremi thinks of Zen, their Pulse gouged out. 'But they also saved you from prison.'

'For a purpose, for *their* purpose. That's the thing that's making me feel the most uneasy. They made this big sacrifice. Sherif gave his life for something I know nothing about. Milk Wood, they all know as much as I do. I have no idea what my dad was planning and I'm sure in a couple of days they'll realise that and . . .'

'And what?'

'I don't want to be part of it, Moremi. More violence.'

'Then what do you want?' Moremi asks.

'All I've ever wanted!' Orpheus says. 'To be free. To be left alone. I'm seeing it all differently now, Moremi, the life my father built for me. The way he raised me like some mouse in a maze. Everything was a lie, even his name. And then the children's division and now this . . . Now I'm central to some plan to destroy the world and I feel as if I've not made one free choice in my entire life.'

Moremi feels a little wounded by his words. She glances down at the leaves under her sandals and says, 'Not one?'

Orpheus seems to regret his words then; he puts his hands on her chin and says, 'I'm glad I chose you.' Just this, the simple joy of his nearness, she thought she'd never experience again. Moremi is surprised to discover, though, how much she misses reaching out for his mind across the Panopticon. Misses talking without moving their lips. With both their Pulses offline the distance between them seems frighteningly vast.

'I want to stay,' she tells him. 'I want it to be true. Everything they're saying about the virus that will destroy the Panopticon. About—'

But Orpheus pulls away from her, something like disgust on his face.

'You're not thinking about this rationally. People will probably die.'

'I am,' Moremi says. 'I believe it now. This is a war for our minds. It feels almost impossible to fight, let alone win. The Panopticon doesn't just feel unstoppable or irresistible, it seems inevitable. But it's not true. We get to decide the way that history turns too. We get to bend it with our will too. We can't go back to the way we were. Not now that we understand that what they're offering isn't freedom. Freedom to think as they direct us to, to dream what they allow us to.'

'No! It's not freedom for me either,' Orpheus says. 'Obey the algorithm. Tiresias. Obey my father. What am I alive for? What is my will for?'

When they stare at each other then, the gap between them seems almost painfully vast. They've never argued before.

In the silence, both of them hear the rumble of tyres on the bridge a few metres ahead of them. Urgent voices.

Moremi strains to see through the trees. Another van has arrived, as they had a couple of days ago. Alder and Meeghan had said with some pride that people have been fleeing for the silos all across the country since the referendum result was announced.

The voices of the newcomers drift towards them, 'O, then I see Queen Mab hath been with you. She is the fairies' midwife, and she comes in shape no bigger than an agate stone—' but then the sound of a scanner whining cuts through the woman's practised recital.

'He's got a Pulse!' a couple of the masked men shout.

'You didn't deactivate it at the gate?' Moremi hears the heavy metal sounds of rifles.

'He can't!' the woman shouts, and now both Moremi and Orpheus are straining to see what is happening. From this vantage, she can just make out the old man's curly head of hair, pressed against the side of the car, a rifle at his back, in the position Zeeba had been. The old terror of that morning returns to Moremi.

'He's almost eighty!' the woman – his daughter? – pleads, crying now. 'He has Alzheimer's, he can't live without it.'

457

'Then you can't come here,' someone else shouts.

'His quartz is probably recording all of this,' another person hisses. 'Our voices, everything. We can't afford to be discovered. Now, more than ever.' Moremi assumes she's referring to the Revelators hiding out here.

'What should we do?' The masked people are sounding more panicked now.

'Damn it.'

'It's too late,' another shouts, 'take it offline.'

'But—

'Now!'

'No!' The sound of two gunshots rattles Moremi's bones. She thinks she can almost smell them, in the silence. Firework display of blood on the side of the car where the old man's head had been.

When she turns, she sees her own terror reflected in Orpheus' eyes.

42

ORPHEUS

They talk about the time after Milk Wood the way that Christians talk about heaven. Even the children, who turn to their parents in the light of the fire and ask, 'Will we be this happy after?'

'Even happier,' they reply.

That night they're roasting a deer to welcome the newcomers. There's a giant bonfire, and everyone gathers to eat on logs or at the long oak table, buffet-style. It's lovely food, more of it than Orpheus thinks he's ever seen in one place, dozens of trays of roasted potatoes, vegetable curries, pork and venison, carrots and sweet potatoes. But it's hard for him to eat, as he watches some of the people he knows to be Revelators tearing into roasting flesh.

Several bands play, guitars and drums, a sweet chorus of a song that everyone joins in for. Moremi accompanies Zeeba, chatting by the fire. Orpheus feels oddly separate from it all. The pain in his body, and his uncertainty about the group draws his attention inwards.

'You're talking about the collapse of society,' he says to Alder as they talk about Milk Wood.

'Of course,' Alder says.

'It needs to happen,' Raffi says, the fire making his retinas flash red. 'We have to burn everything down before we can start again.'

Some people in animal masks are dancing too. At the sight of their revelry, Orpheus' mind flashes with violent images. He tells himself, even as the children weave corn dollies from dried husks and toss them laughingly into the flames, that he can't let himself forget who these people are. The same people who had torn through the crowd during the symposium, the ones who had watched innocent people die. Orpheus thinks about the flood too, the ruined city, the waste of human life. These people are willing to watch it happen again.

Suddenly the food in his mouth tastes like ash. Orpheus spits it out and gets up.

'Hey,' Raffi shouts after him. 'Hey!'

Orpheus is still in too much pain to outrun the man as he would like too. Raffi and Alder catch up with him quickly, further from the fire, where the cool of the night clutches his face and arms.

'Where are you going?' Raffi says.

'I'm not a violent person,' Orpheus says. 'I don't want to be part of this.' Raffi and Alder exchange a wary look.

'Maybe it's time,' Alder says, more to Raffi than him.

'For what?' Orpheus asks.

'For you to meet Queen Mab.'

Queen Mab is one of their elders, a woman in her late fifties who's been living in the community for almost twenty years. Mirribelle Yenter, she is one of the coders who helped to create Dreamtime. She lives now in a small house in the side of the mountains, high enough to see the rest of the community from her front door.

At another time, Orpheus would have been dizzy with awe to meet her. 'I used to love it,' Orpheus says. 'Dreamtime. I used to believe it was the only place where I could be free.'

'Yes,' she says, some regret in her voice, 'that's an easy mistake to make.' Orpheus wonders if she's thinking about the twitchy Nox addicts on every street corner. Or the Protect facilities trapping people in a maze of their own fantasies.

'What's in this?' Orpheus asks Mab now. They sit by a fire in front of her house, the sky above them wild with stars, and she offers him a flask of a bitter tea.

'Willow bark,' she says. 'For your pain.'

'My dad used to make this for me sometimes,' Orpheus says, taking a long draught, thinking of summer nights in their living room, picking at scabs from after a hard day of labour on the farm.

'Some people say it's gentler on your stomach than lab-created aspirin.' She sits next to him and warms her hands by her little fire. 'Funny how the Earth has already given us everything that we need.'

Over the crackle of embers, Orpheus can hear the sound of singing. Further down by the camp, he can see them lit like a fairy ring, dancing and feasting on the deer.

'How is your wound healing up?' When she asks, Orpheus' eyes go reflexively to his side. The thick ridge of bandages under his shirt. The habit he has now of twitching to protect it.

'Hurts sometimes,' he says. 'When I move.' Smiles bitterly. 'When I breathe.'

'At least you are breathing,' Mab says. 'You know, you don't look anything like Callie.'

'How do you know my mother's name?' Orpheus asks.

Mab's rheumy eyes glitter. 'You children all think that the world began turning when your hearts started. I knew her, of course I did. We worked together for years, she was such a clever, kind soul.'

Orpheus shakes his head in confusion. 'She was part of this too?'

'That's how we all met: me, Hayden and Jitsuko Itō – she wasn't "professor", then – and your mother and father. We were all working in the university's neural computing department.'

'My mum,' Orpheus says, lightheaded at this information. Already more than his father ever volunteered. He wants to ask Mab everything he's ever wondered about her. Were her eyes green like his? Was she plagued by the same nightmares? Could she sing? Had she loved him?

'She was a Londoner. Grew up somewhere near Battersea if I recall correctly? Did her DPhil at Oxford and then joined us. She was a mathematician. A brilliant one.'

Mab smiles to herself in recollection. 'She and your father used to have such interminable debates about – oh, are you familiar with Kozlov's theorem? – okay, well, never mind then ... leave it to academics to get so worked up about something with such low stakes. Maybe that's why they could.'

'So, you all helped to build the Panopticon?' Orpheus asks

'That's right.' Mab looks a little sympathetically at him. 'He didn't tell you anything, did he? Your father.'

'Nothing at all,' Orpheus admits, and she nods.

'He must have guessed they'd scan all of your childhood memories. He did it to keep you safe, I'm sure.'

'But I'm not "safe", am I? Anything but!' Orpheus grits his teeth, his gut twisting with a sudden rage at her words. 'I feel like – like a wasp batting against a spider's web that he spun years ago.' Orpheus' vision begins to blur and he fights the emotion he can feel coming.

'He needed to create a way for his plan to outlive him,' says Mab. 'He knew it was a matter of time, that he couldn't hide forever.'

'His plan to destroy the Panopticon. To destroy the thing that apparently he helped to create. And you too.'

'It's a familiar tale,' she says. 'We were all there at the birth of this world and now we recoil with disgust at the sight of it. You've heard of what Hayden is planning to do? Join our minds up like paper dolls.'

'The Singularity.'

'Yes,' she scoffs. 'I heard that was what he was calling it.'

'Did you know? Then?'

463

'How could we!' A flash of emotion crosses her own face, the embers of the fire thrown against her eyes. She's quiet for a moment, gazing at the yellow tendrils of light skittering up the kindling, cracking, turning white with heat.

'It's curious,' she says, still not looking at him, 'how far you can travel away from yourself in your pursuit of your desires. A better world. A solution to the problem of other minds. Hayden said to me, "Almost every order of human unkindness is caused by a fundamental scepticism of other minds." We don't believe that other people are as conscious as ourselves. That their inner lives are as vital as ours. Slavery, genocide, war. Even smaller injustices, pettiness, selfishness, jealousy. If we could create a machine that allowed us to look into the mind of another, wouldn't it change what it meant to be human forever? To feel another consciousness?'

'I believed him,' Orpheus says. As she speaks he can still remember the euphoria he experienced during the demonstration of mass Pulse pairing at the symposium. And the joy of inversion; seeing Moremi's memories had made it impossible not to fall in love with her.

'That's the problem,' Mab says. 'Maybe I don't want to change what it means to be human. Perhaps no one should dare to. I look at this community we've managed to build here and it occurs to me that the objects of our desires are actually quite simple. It's not only kinship and meaning, shelter and food. It's some element of struggle, and hope in the face of it. Desire. Perseverance.'

'You don't need to convince me of anything,' Orpheus

says bitterly. 'I don't feel as if I have a hand in any of this either way.'

'Oh, but you do, Orpheus.' She leans forward and gazes at him solemnly. 'Orpheus twice-born. Son of Mustafa. He and I, your mother and a whole team of people, helped to make the first incarnation of the Panopticon. It was like being in love, those heady early days. Before the usual things happened: infighting, disagreements, disillusionments. Your father, though, he was a true believer. Like Hayden. I left before he did, just after a major advertising company acquired most of Dreamtime in the hope of using the software to sell products to people in their dreams. And I thought, dear God, there's nowhere to hide any more, is there?' She laughs at herself. 'I started to see what we were doing. We were like children in a sandpit, blowing glass figurines, exquisite lovely things to offer up into the blazing maw of the market. Capitalism. Here, look, we can harness the computing power of a thousand minds. And what do we use them for? To sell things to people.

'I cashed in my shares and helped to found this place.' She looks around proudly. 'But your father. He worked and worked. Your mother too. They became fixated on using the information the Panopticon had harvested to develop some program that could help them predict the future. Tiresias, as it came to be.

'To be honest, I don't know much about that time. I didn't have much to do with them for a couple of years until I heard that they'd vanished, she and him, suddenly, and that the police were looking for them. The story we heard was that they'd been discovered trying to code a virus that exploits a secret security flaw in the Panopticon.'

'A Zero Day,' Orpheus says. Mab explains that, since his parents had a foundational role in coding the Panopticon, they were able to create a secret 'back door', and that his father had been trying to engineer the perfect cyberattack which would exploit it in order to destroy the Panopticon. 'So they were working on Tiresias and then they were trying to destroy the Panopticon? It doesn't make any sense? What changed?'

'That's what we all want to know,' Mab says. 'The two people who could tell us are dead now. The thing everyone suspects is that once they succeeded in building Tiresias, they peered into the future and saw something that terrified them.'

'What, though?' Orpheus wants to go back in time and ask his father.

'Some say the flood – as you know, there's a rumour that the Magi let it happen in order to further their plans for Total Adoption. Some say, they could have looked far into the future and seen whatever Pulse-pairing hive-mind that Hayden wants to turn us into. Others think they glimpsed this.' She gestures distantly to the edge of the estate, the bridge that people arrive over. 'The world we live in now. Whatever they saw, it was enough to convince them that the Panopticon must be destroyed.'

'But I heard that Tiresias can't see that far into the future,' Orpheus says.

'Current incarnations. But maybe the one they were

working with . . .' She shrugs. 'Maybe they learned something some other way. From speaking to Hayden and the others. They were all working closely, after all.'

'I've heard people say that you can't change the future.' Orpheus is thinking about that show *Twelve*. The cop who never manages to fix anything.

'Let's hope not,' Mab says. Orpheus looks back out at the people gathered below the hill, by a campfire. 'Once your parents were discovered trying to destroy the Panopticon they had to go on the run. Everyone who knew them was interrogated or killed by people who worked for the Magi. They wanted to find Milk Wood before we did. Find it before anyone could use it.'

'And you all want to find it too,' Orpheus says. He's been frightened to tell any of the Revelators that he doesn't know anything about Milk Wood. He's worried they might conclude that rescuing him from prison was a waste of effort. Every now and then, the sound of that old man being shot on the bridge echoes through his memory. If he's not useful to them, could he be next?

'He will have left you some clues,' Mab says. 'The virus still exists somewhere, a string of code he could have hidden in anything. A port key. A book. Just before your father died, when he knew they would be coming for him, he devised a plan to bring it here – to people he knew would use it at the "right time" – that was one thing he was very clear about in the letter he wrote.'

'The letter?'

'Oh yes!' Mab stands. 'I've basically memorised it after all these years.' She returns to her house and emerges a few minutes later with a piece of paper in her trembling hands and a pair of reading glasses.

It's been years since Orpheus has seen a handwritten letter, or glasses for that matter.

'Can I . . . ?'

She glances at him with a frown but then, reluctantly, hands the sheet over as an archivist might a manuscript. Orpheus leans into the flickering light of the fire and stares for a long time at his father's handwriting. He knows it from his childhood, that graceful penmanship, the tall slanting letters, that name at the bottom, 'Warsame', with the flamboyantly curled W that Orpheus saw signed in the front of all his father's books. The sight of the letter aggravates his old grief.

As Orpheus reads it, she narrates excitedly. 'He told us to be prepared. He said that he'd laid a plan for the destruction of the Panopticon and that it would survive him. He told us, too, that he was coming with his son, but, as you know, he never came.'

In the letter he says what Sherif must have been quoting: 'There's a design. Aspects cannot be chosen or escaped. The day, him, and his particular make-up. Orpheus is part of it, he will be.'

When Orpheus looks up Mab is kneeling, gazing at him imploringly. 'The instructions are hidden somewhere. Your father had a plan. He and your mother sacrificed their lives to create Milk Wood and to get it out into the world. Your father was killed for it. So now, I have to ask you, do you know where it is?'

It's clear to Orpheus, now, what those officers had been

looking for when they scanned his brain all of those years ago. When he was still a child, just arrived in London. They'd been looking for clues too, and they hoped they'd find it in Orpheus' memories, some indication of what his father had done. And Orpheus felt then as he does now, like a fool. A disappointment. A bit player who's forgotten his part.

'If there was anything that he told me, the authorities would have found it.'

'It's true,' Mab says. 'But I suspected ... I don't know. A code? Or an encrypted memory?' Even as she says it she can see from the look on Orpheus' face that it's fruitless. 'It's okay.' She gets to her feet with some difficulty and steps back as if comforting herself. 'It's okay. You'll stay here for a while and you'll remember.' She tries to smile but her hands are shaking. The kind of nervousness that comes from being within touching distance of your heart's desire. 'Of course,' she tells herself more than him, 'you'll stay here for as long as it takes and you *will* remember.'

43

MOREMI

Moremi wakes from a nightmare and he's not there. She whispers his name in the darkness, quietly enough not to rouse Zeeba or Halima who are asleep in camp-beds opposite. With the rapid influx of people, they have been told that it might be a couple of months before a cabin is built for them to live in. Moremi doesn't mind sharing a tent with her sisters and niece, though; it makes her happy to wake up and know that they are safe.

There is no double camp-bed so she and Orpheus have been asleep on a pile of hand-woven rugs and two sleeping bags on the floor. Moremi must shake hay and dirt from her hair every morning when she wakes.

Tonight, she thinks she can hear his footsteps outside the tent. Slipping her feet quickly into some borrowed crocs, she rushes outside to find him.

'What is it?'

Orpheus is holding the analogue watch that Bola had given her, and staring out to the edge of the property.

'Shh . . .' He presses a finger to his lips and they stand in expectant quiet. There is a distant whoosh then a rumble, like a plane taking off far away.

Orpheus looks down at the watch: 5.02. Not a hint of sunrise yet, stars are still distantly visible outside the sodium blur of London's lights.

'What is it?'

'That's the train that's going to take me out of here.'

'Orpheus!' Her voice comes out louder than she intends, he looks at her in alarm, and they both step into the forest at the edge of the property.

'Orpheus,' she says again, more quietly

'I don't want to stay,' he tells her. 'I don't want to be part of any of this.'

'Okay,' Moremi says slowly, 'but go where?'

'Mab thinks that my father might have left me some clues,' Orpheus says, then keeps walking, to the edge of the property, where they can both see the light glimmer off the electric fence. 'I've been racking my brain all night and I remembered something. The night he died, he told me, "You will find me where you lost me." Where did I lose him? In some forest near Angharad. Home. I think through all the options for what to do next and the only option seems to be, go back home. Back to the old house he built, the island.'

'But the location was breached,' Moremi says. 'Aren't you bound to be discovered there by the people who found you and your father the first time?'

'It is a possibility,' Orpheus admits, 'and I haven't thought of a good way around it except stay vigilant.'

'And how would you get there?' She's still hoping that he will see how unworkable this plan is and abandon it.

'That's the other thing I've been puzzling through. Obviously, I can't board a train, which would be the fastest way. I can't drive a manual car or steal a driverless one. Even if I wear a hood or a mask or paint my face, I'm still best off if I avoid most open roads to save being spied by a drone but . . . then I remembered the lumber train. They're all driverless. I could climb into one of its open carriages and it can take me at least some of the way. Maybe if I steal a Zephyr—'

'They're only good for short distances,' Moremi interrupts.

'Maybe if I go half on foot, half on a Zephyr.'

'All the way down to where, Cornwall? We're in Wales right now.'

'It will take a couple of days,' Orpheus says. 'I'll have to steal camping gear from the barter store, which I feel bad about considering everything, but—'

'You've really thought this through, haven't you?'

'I've been planning it since we saw them shoot that old man. And then when I spoke to Mab, I realised that everything I think I know about my father, someone has told me. He gave me the clue. I need to go back and find out the truth for myself.'

'Just you?' Moremi says.

'Of course, you don't have to—'

'Of course I have to.' Moremi cups his face in her hands

472

so that he can feel the warmth of her palms on his cheeks. He closes his eyes. His eyelids are thin as butterfly wings, threaded with dark capillaries. She didn't know just how much she'd missed him until she saw his face again. 'Wherever you go, I go, remember.' He smiles, and leans in to kiss her.

'What about Zeeba and Halima and the baby?

'I don't want to leave them, either, but I already know what it's like to lose you. And I don't want to again.' She looks back at the shadows through the trees where her sisters are probably still sleeping. 'I guess Bola and Raffi will look after them. For as long as we're—

'But that's the thing, I don't know how long it will be. I feel as if I'm in checkmate. No other moves to make. Stay here? Go back to London? Board a train? Steal a car? I have this idea, though, that maybe I can stop the attack from happening if I stay on the island. Stop anyone from getting hurt.'

'What will you do?' Moremi teases. 'Lash yourself to the mast of a boat until the tenth has passed?'

'If I have to,' he says.

'But don't people say that you can't change the future?'

'I guess I'm desperate enough to try.'

As the sun rises, the trees are a riot of birdsong. Moremi listens to the wind overhead catching leaves, tangling and untangling branches. Animals rustle on the forest floor, and scuttle across the ground. 'The thought of being out here, camping for possibly a week.' She shudders dramatically. 'There's a reason I never signed up for D of E.'

'The what?'

'The Duke of Edinburgh award.' Moremi laughs at the blankness in his face. Orpheus shrugs and turns again to the fence. 'And this is the other thing. I mean, we can probably fly over it with our Zephyrs, but I think we're going to have to keep this escape a secret, Moremi.'

'From my sisters?'

'From your sisters, from everyone. Especially any of the Revelators. I think their plan is to keep me here until I tell them where Milk Wood is.'

Just then, they are both startled by an alarm, a distant howling that sounds as if it's coming from the campsite.

'Fire?' Orpheus asks, looking at Moremi, puzzled.

A minute later the canopy of the trees shudders as if in a sudden wind. Orpheus and Moremi look around to see masked faces materialising from behind the trees, about a dozen of them flying on Zephyrs.

'Intruder!' someone shouts, and all the hairs on Moremi's body stand up. She's shunted back to the night of the symposium. To the masked figures who executed Bertram and Jitsuko. *They're here,* she thinks. Flying through the air, as they are now, these people look just as they had then, in their faux fur animal masks, fox snouts and rabbit pelts, eyes like buttons. Some hold hunting rifles and others crossbows. The hems of their skirts and trousers splattered with dirt.

Orpheus stares down the barrel of a hunting rifle with a strange calm on his face.

'Don't shoot!' shouts the man riding in front, wearing a fox mask. He pulls it off his face, and Moremi recognises Raffi. 'It's Orpheus. And Zeeba's sister.'

Moremi still feels too terrified to talk.

'You tripped the motion sensor,' Alder says, nodding at the barrier in front of them.

'Are you—' Moremi says.

'In the Hunting Party,' Raffi confirms, and as he leans further on his Zephyr he floats into the slanting light. Moremi can see that his trousers are splattered with what looks like blood. His fingers and flannel shirt are also stained. Her hands turn cold. Hunting, she thinks, and imagines them riding through the woods like maenads, on their hacked Zephyrs, tearing unsuspecting campers limb from limb.

'We killed a deer,' says a woman, bringing her board to a halt beside him. Meeghan, Moremi thinks, from her voice.

'We'll eat well again tonight.'

44

ORPHEUS

Two days later, he wakes her just before dawn. 4.30am, with a plan. At 5.02am, the day's first freight train will leave from the nearby depot. If they vault the electrified fence using the stolen Zephyrs – which Moremi's left charging out in the sun for some time – they might be able to cross the woodland and climb aboard the train that he hopes will take them as far as they can get, as quickly as possible.

'I was awake,' she lies, her eyes flying open when he creeps across the tent to shake her.

He's not slept at all. Since his meeting with Queen Mab, he's noticed the way the mood has suddenly soured in the camp. People still fall silent when he walks past, children point and stare, he'll turn in the dining hall to hear whispers behind him, only now there is a certain hostility in even Raffi's remarks. He has been the 'promised one', the man they sacrificed so much to save, yet he is unable or – they clearly suspect, now – unwilling to help them.

It's taken him a couple of days to finalise his plan. Inside his stolen rucksack is almost everything they will need for the long hike. In an ideal world, they'd be leaving with tents, sleeping bags and water-purification tablets, but although Orpheus was not able to get his hands on any of those things he was able to steal some other supplies that will be useful to them: a torch, a couple of Ordnance Survey maps of South Wales and other parts of the UK, and a first-aid kit. He's searched around the supply sheds, the free cupboard, the barns and kitchens for other things. Changes of clothes, a lightweight tarpaulin, some lengths of cord – which he knows are useful for building shelters and fishing, even as an emergency tourniquet – some bottles of water, though not enough. And a knife.

Yesterday morning, after breakfast, he'd volunteered to help with the cleaning duty and stole what food he could find. Some bags of caramelised nuts, vegetable crisps and flapjacks. He found a couple of other useful items in the drawers, a lighter, and bin liners. There are a few surprising items that his father taught him can come in handy. Orpheus has learned that a condom, which takes up no space at all, can be a sturdy way to carry up to two litres of water. They're also good for keeping tinder dry. He's also learned that a tampon can be anything from a water filter to a candle, though he's not certain how to find either of these.

'Shh,' he says now. They're sleeping in the tent they share with her sisters and Orpheus doesn't want to wake them. It's a cool night outside and he can hear that it's raining slightly.

Moremi gets silently out of her sleeping bag and rolls it up quietly. Orpheus flinches every time the polyester cover of it rustles. 'Just roll it up outside,' he whispers. She bundles it in her arms, and they creep towards the door. As they do, the baby makes a noise and they both freeze. Their eyes dart to the camp-bed where Halima is sleeping.

They run out into a moonlit clearing behind the tents and work quickly together to bundle the sleeping bags into Moremi's rucksack. 'I left her a letter,' Moremi says, 'telling them I'll see them soon.'

'That sounds good,' Orpheus says distractedly, though he can't shake the thought that he will never see them again. Zeeba or Halima or the baby.

They make a beeline for the forest, where the rain is not coming down quite so heavily. Through the trees he can see the remains of that night's bonfire. Wood scorched white, final embers quenched by the downpour. A pile of bones they'll gather for the compost.

It's not long before they see the moonlight glimmer off the fence. Moremi makes a hand motion for her Zephyr and as Orpheus summons his, she asks, 'Are you definitely sure you can ride?' in a whisper. His core muscles were decimated by the injury and he knows there's no way he can pilot the Zephyr without pain.

'We just need to get over the fence,' he says, 'and then we can run.' They're wearing black hoodies from the free cupboard and macs, light clothes they can fly in, and walking boots with some grip in their soles.

'Okay.' Moremi is about to motion for him to get on to his when they see a shadow in the trees. They both freeze. A wild animal, Orpheus thinks, a trick of the moonlight, but as his eyes grow more accustomed to the dark he sees the outline of a figure.

'Please,' Moremi says, her voice tense. 'We're just . . .'

Orpheus' hand flies to his pocket and he brings out a knife. It flashes silver in the darkness. 'We're leaving and you can't stop us.'

'Where are you going?' the figure says, and at the sound of her voice they both relax. Moremi almost starts laughing.

'Zee! You scared us.' But as she steps out from the shadows in the trees and into the light her expression is serious.

'Where are you going?'

'We can't tell you,' Orpheus says, 'and you can't come.'

'You have to stay,' Moremi says regretfully. 'Look after Halima and—

'They won't let you go,' Zeeba says. Though she makes it sound more like a promise.

'Zeeba—

'No!' She shakes her head. 'This isn't about you and me, Remi. This is about something bigger.'

'Bigger than sisterhood?'

Zeeba raises an arm, and Orpheus sees that she's holding a large rock in her fist. She pitches it at them and they both duck. Turning back, Orpheus realises that she wasn't aiming for either of them but for the fence, which sparks and sputters. Mist curls up in the rain and an alarm begins to howl.

'Let's go,' Moremi shouts. Orpheus grabs his Zephyr and as he leaps onto it, a bright knife of pain cuts into his side, causing it to wobble beneath his heels. Orpheus grits his teeth, bends his knees and tries to remember the riding stance. The last time he flew was probably as a teenager, playing with Sherif under an underpass somewhere or in a half-flooded skatepark. It's not like riding a bike – what little skill he had seems to have vanished, he feels as if he's trying to balance on a wave, and the rain makes it even harder for him to keep purchase.

'This way,' Moremi shouts. She's already a couple of metres ahead of him, surfing through the trees, her voice carried to him on the wind.

Orpheus allows himself a quick glance over his shoulder, and he thinks he can already see them approaching. The Hunting Party.

A fleet of them rise out of the trees. Like Orpheus, many of them have trained for years in the forest, know how to set traps, how to snare and kill animals. Gritting his teeth, he leans forward and his board accelerates so fast the wet air blasts his hood from his head.

Moremi is trying to lose them, flying like a dancer ahead, slaloming through the trees, making the branches knock crystals of rain in a veil behind her. Leaves eddy across the forest floor beneath them.

For the first time since he was rescued, he wishes that their Pulses were activated, that way he could talk to her. As it is, he just has to hope that she remembers the way, above the canopy of trees to the railway tracks.

At the sound of an arrow flying through the air,

Orpheus' vision turns black for a moment. He's back in the woods, running with his father. Suddenly, the people on Zephyrs look like the ones who killed him. He tries to shake the memory away but when he turns to his left, he sees Moremi slip and fall. She must have been hit, he thinks.

'No!' he shouts, diving after her into the canopy of trees, hitting nearly every branch on the way down.

It's almost pitch-black on the forest floor, and when he shouts her name, no response comes. She's been hit, he thinks, panic making his heart skitter. 'Nonono ...' Sherif, he thinks, Zen, his father; he knows he won't survive watching another loved one die.

'Shh!' She's a shadow by the riverbank.

'Moremi?' And when she moves he can tell it's her. 'I thought you—'

'Cut the lights on your Zephyr.' She motions to do it for him. 'I programmed mine to go in the opposite direction. Hopefully we can lose them, if we're down here. For a while anyway. Give us enough time to catch the train.'

'Brilliant,' Orpheus says, and she smiles.

'You lead the way. If we run, we'll make it.'

It hurts, of course, to run. Once or twice, Orpheus has to stop to clutch his side and catch his breath. All the while, Moremi is looking at her watch and counting down. He's almost blinded by the pain, lungs aching with the effort. Soon every stride is a triumph of will, and his focus winnows into a single mission: to keep his legs moving.

He doesn't know how long they are running, by the

time the wood abruptly vanishes and they reach the railway track. The freight trains look like space shuttles in the
dimly lit depot. As Orpheus and Moremi approach, they
can smell the freshly cut lumber.

'Two minutes,' Moremi says, before the train starts
moving. They will need to climb up into the carriage, but
Orpheus can already see that it will be far too high for
them to climb. Moremi motions for the Zephyr, but as she
does, the lights on it flicker. The board falters and then
makes a nose-dive for the ground.

'It's a maglev train,' Orpheus explains. 'The magnetic
field on the tracks probably interferes with the propulsion
system on the boards.'

'So what should we do?' Moremi asks, panic in her eyes
now. Ninety seconds before the train takes off and they're
both startled by a rush of wind coming through the trees
behind them. Four members of the Hunting Party emerge
like buzzards from the darkness, one of them aiming a
bow and arrow. The sight of it gives Orpheus an idea.

He thinks about watching his father fishing with a
knife. The lightning-quick way his fist could crack the
water. 'I have an idea,' he says, and reaches into his pocket
for his knife. 'Do you have the rope?' he asks. Moremi
unzips one of the pockets in her rucksack quickly.

They have about one minute.

Orpheus fashions something a little like a harpoon,
as quickly as he can with trembling hands, and pitches it
hard. It bounces off one of the felled trees, ricochets off
a metal rung on the carriage, its momentum making it
loop around.

'Is that what was supposed to happen?' Moremi asks.

'Sure,' Orpheus says, and tugs hard on it. It's not fastened tightly enough to carry him for the whole of the climb and by the time Orpheus manages to scrabble up onto the carriage, it slips off.

In twenty seconds the train will accelerate like a bullet from the barrel of a gun, and Moremi is still metres below him, by the tracks, her pupils dilated in terror.

'Hold on,' he says, and works as quickly as he can to tie it to the carriage. Moremi grabs the rope from the other end. And, pulling with enough force to make him cry out in pain, he helps her onto the top of the carriage just in time for the train to hiss and sputter and begin to levitate.

In a few seconds they are leaving behind the valley, the forest, the Hunting Party and Silo Six.

45

MOREMI

Leaping off is almost as terrifying as getting on. By the time they have to do it, the sun is rising. The speed of the train is ferocious, melting orderly fields and heather-clad grasslands into a blur.

How to do it without breaking a bone? When they launch off the back of the moving train their momentum sends them flying.

'Remember to roll,' Orpheus had said before they jumped. Moremi also remembers to tuck her head in, and resists the impulse to use her arms to break her fall. The speed, though, turns her stomach to jelly.

She's flung like a bowling ball off the tracks and down a grassy slope, hitting everything as she falls. Her spine slams into a rock, the side of her face knocks the hard ground. When she finally comes to a halt the world is spinning, and the sound of groaning in her ears is coming from her. She lies still for a long while, rain splashing on her face, craters of pain radiating from her bones.

'You still breathing?' Orpheus' shadow flickers across her closed eyelids.

'Barely,' she says.

'We need to get out of the open. Into the woods a bit more so that no one will see us.'

'Right,' she groans. He takes her hand and helps her up.

The two of them limp into the trees and settle down under the grand canopy of a sessile oak, which shelters them from the worst of the downpour. Orpheus rifles through his rucksack and examines the OS map for a while.

'How can you tell where we are from that?' It might as well be hieroglyphs to Moremi who, thanks to her Pulse, has never had to rely on her navigation skills.

'Somewhere in the Wye Valley,' he says, which isn't exactly an answer to her question. 'If we follow the river down' – he points it out with his finger on the paper – 'we should get to the Severn Bridge, which takes us out of South Wales. From there, we have to navigate down to Cornwall.'

'That's far,' Moremi says.

'It's an insane distance to try to cover on foot. Especially considering the amount of supplies we have. But we still have one Zephyr between us and . . .' he sighs, his shoulders slumping, '. . . and what other options do we really have?'

They walk for what feels like hours because of the rain and her sprained and bruised body. Traversing through steep ravine woodlands to grassy meadows.

'You know how they say that nothing is completely waterproof?' Moremi shouts as a wet gust of wind picks up once more and smacks the side of her face. 'I can confirm that is true.'

Orpheus isn't talking much and Moremi can tell it's because he's forcing himself to walk through his own pain. When he almost slips on a muddy hillside, she suggests they stop for 'lunch', which is roasted nuts and crisps, but totally delicious to Moremi after their morning exertions.

Orpheus scoops handfuls into his mouth and winces at the map. There is a sense of urgency to everything he does now.

'How can you tell we're going the right way?' she asks.

'Well, other than, obviously, just following the river, there are lots of ways the Earth tells us the right direction.' At her look of curiosity, he says, 'The trees, for example. It's getting to autumn so the sides of the trees facing north are getting less sun, and – can you see? – that side is starting to turn yellow first.' Moremi is not sure she can see. 'It's quite damp around here so this is not so accurate, but sometimes the moss can tell you something. It grows in the shade, the north side.

'Sometimes you can tell by the sunlight, put a stick in the ground and mark the end of its shadow, do that again in twenty minutes, when its shadow has moved, and the line between the two will be east-west. Obviously, in the southern hemisphere it would be – why are you looking at me that way?'

'Nothing.' Moremi smiles. 'It's just. You seem different here.'

'Different how?'

''I don't know, calmer? A bit like those children in Silo Six.'

'Well,' Orpheus says with a slightly embarrassed shrug. 'You know, I kind of grew up here. Not in the Wye Valley, but ...' Even his eyes are the same green as the ancient woodland. 'When I was in the children's division, I forgot a lot of it. I don't know if I did it on purpose – because it was too painful to remember – or if it had something to do with the fake childhood memories they gave me, but being back here ...' He sinks his fingers into the spiky moss at the base of the oak. 'It's all coming back to me. Memories of trekking through the woods with my father, foraging, or setting traps for animals. Even just playing, climbing a tree. One time' – he tightens his mouth a little in pain at the memory – 'when I was about nine, my dad took me out into the woods and left me.'

'I know,' Moremi says. She'd glimpsed a few of his most poignant memories the first time they paired their Pulses.

'I thought it was a game at first. That he'd come back. I waited for hours, as the temperature dropped. As it started to get dark, I ran through the woods screaming his name, thinking he'd come back for me, thinking something had happened to him.'

'What happened?'

Orpheus braces again at the memory. 'I got thoroughly lost. I think I wet myself, I was so terrified. And then the night fell and it was pitch-black and I kept thinking that I'd seen things moving in the forest. Which I probably did, woodland animals or something, but my mind was making monsters.'

'Did you get back? Did he come to find you?'

Orpheus is quiet for a moment. 'I found my own way back. The next night.'

'You were out there for two days?' She gasps with horror and her husband nods.

'Yes. And when I got back, my father was in a chair, calm as anything, reading Dylan Thomas – I still remember. "Now you never have to fear getting lost," he'd said, except I think it only made me more terrified, whenever we went out again, that, without warning, he'd abandon me.'

'That sounds like child abuse.'

'Yeah ...' He trails off a little. 'I mean, it probably wasn't much like the children at Silo Six. We weren't learning folk songs and weaving dream catchers. It was hardly ever fun, though I didn't know much else.' He pulls back the sleeve of his hoodie; just under the tattoo on his wrist is a burn like the Nike logo that Moremi had noticed before. 'This was his way of telling me never to touch the kiln.' Moremi tries to hold back her gasp. 'But you don't understand, Remi, or' – he shrugs – 'maybe you do, that he was like my pole star.'

Moremi says, 'It's disorientating when you consider your parents for what they are – were. It makes my head spin to think that I'm almost the age my mother was when she had Halima. I look at myself, all my flaws and shortcomings, and then I look at my childhood and think, "Oh!" She was only human. After all.'

'They've been calling him a terrorist since I was a child. The word itself used to make me sick. Now I think, what else do you call a person who planned to do what he did?

And then I look at my childhood and notice his single-minded focus. The way he shaped me like a tool. That's what I was, what I am to him.'

'Don't say that.' She puts her hand on his and realises it's freezing. The rain has soaked right into his clothes, and his lips are turning purple. 'Hey, how long has it been since you last slept?' When he shrugs, she says, 'You didn't manage to pack a tent, did you?'

'Not one that no one would notice was missing. I feel like an idiot now, I thought it would be warm. I didn't count on the weather turning so quickly.'

'Well, maybe the rain will let up soon. Which will give our board a bit more time to charge.'

'I brought some rope and tarpaulin, though, as well as our sleeping bags.'

'Okay.' Moremi gets to her feet and begins to rummage through the rucksack. 'Then that's all we need.'

She uses their supplies to build a quick lean-to. A long, horizontal branch lashed between two narrow tree-trunks. And, sheltering from the rain, she helps Orpheus – whose mac has a few holes in – to change his clothes.

Pulling his top off, she sees that his bandages are soaked through, still streaked with spots of blood. Her breathing stops for a moment at the sight of the wound, her mind shunting her back to the sight of him, half-dead, on the floor of the van. The glassy look in his eyes, the hours she was sure she would lose him.

'Hey.' He touches her face as she swallows back tears. 'Hey, it's okay.'

'I'm sorry.' She closes her eyes.

489

'It's okay,' he says again, trying to smile.

'I thought I'd lost you. I thought—'

He wipes a tear from under her eye and says, 'I'm here. It's okay. I made it up.'

'Okay.' She leans forward and kisses him. 'Live forever?'

'Okay,' he laughs, 'I promise,' and kisses her back. His lips are cool against hers. She can feel his stubble on her chin as he opens her mouth with his. She pulls away to peel her damp cardigan off, and he stares at her breasts, cupped in a faded wireless bra.

'Was there a me on the other side?' she asks, and his jaw tightens.

'It wasn't you, though. She wasn't.' He really does seem traumatised by it, his time there. Once or twice, during his most fevered nights in Silo Six, he jolted awake in the dark with terrified unseeing eyes and swore that he'd never dream again, that he'd never let himself.

Now, she bites his neck playfully. He kisses her collarbone and tries to run his fingers through her braids, but she swats his hands away and unzips his trousers to find that he's ready. Her whole body has missed him and when she wraps her legs around his waist he groans with relief.

It's their first time since their wedding night, and they are more tentative now. It's awkward and brief and sweet. Orpheus clutches her suddenly, time freezes, and then he rolls back onto his sleeping bag, flushed and laughing. 'I'm sorry!' he says. 'I was in jail for a month!'

They fall asleep to the sound of rain on tarp and, when Moremi opens her eyes, it's stopped and she's shivering. She tries to pull her clothes on as quietly as possible so as not to disturb Orpheus, and then creeps out into the forest looking for a place to pee.

It's grand and lovely, the ancient woodland, still spangled with raindrops. Old trees that soar like cathedral vaults. Autumn leaves the colour of cinder and sandstone. So different from the austere beauty of the city.

'Shall I tell you something cool?'

She almost screams at the sound of his voice, buttons her trousers hastily. 'What did you do, teleport?'

Orpheus grins. He's dressed again, in his black hoodie with his mac. 'Hunting skills,' he says. It must be true, he does seem to move through the underbrush with the fleet-footedness of a roe deer.

'I thought we swore, when we got married, that we'd never watch each other pee. To preserve the mystery.'

'I thought you'd got lost.'

Moremi sighs and asks, 'What's the cool thing?'

'It's something my dad told me about the falling tree.'

'The tree that falls in the forest and no one hearing? That thing? I don't think it ever made sense to me.'

'Not to me either, for a little while. It's a bit like Schrödinger's cat, it's kind of asking whether or not something is real if we never observe it.'

'There's a cat in a box with a radioactive source. Is it dead or alive? Who knows, until you open the box? Except that what I do know is that biology suggests cats do die if you leave them in boxes indefinitely.'

Orpheus rolls his eyes. 'It's a quantum physics problem. Before you open the box there is no way to know if it is dead or alive. Just like the tree, it needs to be observed.

The observation determines the existence and state of the cat.'

Moremi rubs her head and stares at him. 'How is this "cool"?'

'According to my dad, Einstein wasn't totally convinced. He said, "Does the moon exist just because a mouse looks at it?" and the crazy thing is that a quantum physicist might say "Yes". The cool thing is that trees fall and the sun rises and there is a theory that seeing it makes it so. What is consciousness for? Well, what if nothing exists without conscious heads to observe it?' His face is bright with excitement now, dappled shadows flitting across his forehead. 'I used to go for walks alone, and imagine that was true. By the beach or among the trees, with this kind of responsibility. I'd imagine that my mind was conjured up by the universe simply to look at itself in gladness and awe.'

They cover a lot more ground before nightfall. It's a steep learning curve, figuring out how to ride the board together. At first it feels like trying to stand upright on a seesaw, its surface bobbing and weaving under them, knocking one or both of them off. But then they discover that it works if they hold each other tightly. It's something like a dance; Moremi leads and Orpheus follows, matching a shift in her weight or stance with a corresponding change in his.

They fly low, to avoid notice, following the river, only taking detours when their route passes some of the historic towns and villages. Once the rain stops and the sun comes out, it's a lovely ride, filled with stunning views, dramatic limestone gorges, ruined castles and abbeys.

The sun is setting by the time they reach the Severn Bridge, the sound of traffic, cars and drones an assault on both of their senses. The lights of Bristol are like molten lava against the sky. They keep their hoods up, faces covered, and try their best to stay out of sight.

At Orpheus' urging they take a convoluted detour in order to avoid any main roads and find themselves bone tired by midnight, in Rowberrow Warren, an area of woodland south of Bath and Bristol.

By then, something of Moremi's excitement at their adventure has curdled. They're running out of water sooner than they'd planned, and the forest, in the darkness, is fresh from her nightmares. Even after Orpheus builds a fire and puts up the shelter, she starts at every sound, and shudders at the sight of bats against the navy sky.

He wakes her the next morning with a fish that he'd caught with a night line. To her, it might as well be a magic trick. Even after they cook and eat it, she's still hungry.

Moremi finds herself, every time they stop, gazing longingly at the map, at the names of cities she's visited – Bath, Bristol, Exeter – and feeling a pang of homesickness for something she recognises. For half the morning she complains about her caffeine withdrawal, and when she comes close to suggesting they stop at a nearby town or village, they get into such a heated argument that they ride in a stony silence for the rest of the day.

But by nightfall, they miss each other. They make love under the star-strewn sky and before they fall asleep

Moremi's mind changes. 'Why don't we just live this way? Just the two of us?' In some fantasy world they're living in the house that Orpheus grew up in, the two of them like Adam and Eve, foraging and hunting and fishing. They have a child, maybe two, and Moremi teaches them how to dance. Except that even as she says it the dream evaporates, and they go to sleep clutched with anxiety about the coming week. Six days now until the attack and no matter how far they travel from the city, with every passing hour, Moremi can feel its grip tightening on them both.

By the third day, they've traversed a large portion of southwest England on their hoverboard. Moremi has blood blisters on the soles of her feet, all her joints ache and they have run out of water. They wake near the Tamar Valley, on the border between Cornwall and Devon. Moremi feels run-down and grimy, the way it's only possible to feel after living in a tent for a couple of days, with no access to plumbing.

Orpheus tries to explain the best ways to collect water from a river – make sure it's moving fast over rocks, hold your bottle so that the opening is facing downstream and debris does not flow into it – and then he uses an unworn sock to filter it. Moremi refuses to drink it at first, mistrustful of his technique. They ride for half a day, her mouth dry as sand, head light with dehydration, and when she observes that he doesn't appear to have cholera, she gives the water a try herself. While she does, Orpheus explains some of the different ways it's possible to collect water and make it safe in the wilderness: 'Gypsy wells and solar stills. Collecting dew with an absorbent fabric. Even moss can act like a sponge. Also' – and she's sure he's saying this to provoke a reaction from her – 'urine is almost sterile when fresh.' Moremi promises herself it will never come to that.

46

ORPHEUS

By the fifth day, Orpheus is forced to admit that they are lost. They'd found themselves wandering through a succession of hamlets and villages in south Cornwall, most of which had been abandoned a couple of decades ago due to flooding and demographic shift. Literal ghost towns, Moremi had muttered, although she'd found a well outside one of the churches and filled up their flasks.

Then, they'd ventured into a forest that was not marked on their map and something in Orpheus told him that this was the place.

That had been the fourth day, and now they've been turning back on themselves, veering onto country roads and out into windswept coves. Every now and then they'll see a beach, a shoreline, and Orpheus' breath will catch. *This one?* he'll think, but never see the tidal island, Hunter's Tryst, his house.

'What do you even mean by Hunter's Tryst?' Moremi

asks, crouched under their shelter, examining the map. 'There is nothing with that name on the map.'

'I don't think any of these places were called what my father called them. I've never managed to find an island called Angharad.'

She exhales heavily then and he can see the tension in her face. 'Are you sure he ever wanted you to find the place?' She closes her eyes and lies back on her mud-streaked sleeping bag. It's a chilly morning, one that feels more like autumn, she's been wearing the same hoodie for days and now it's grass-stained and pocked with twigs the size of hedgehog quills.

Their time living outside is starting to wear on him too. His joints ache, his arms and calves are covered in insect bites, the skin on his ankles has been slashed and stung by thorns and nettles.

'It sounds as if he went to some extreme lengths to hide this place from the world. I mean, a tidal island? I can't even find a place like the one you've described on this map.'

'That map is probably out of date, I just got it from one of the storage cupboards in the silo.' Orpheus is standing by the front of their makeshift tent, trying to encourage Moremi to help pack up their things in order to keep going. But she's run out of the will to continue hiking now that it's clear they are going in circles. 'Coastal erosion and flooding means the shoreline doesn't look like that. Angharad probably wasn't a tidal island to begin with, but rising water levels—'

'Well, how do you know that it's not all underwater

now?' But at the sight of his face, she apologises quickly for the suggestion. 'Let's try to get into your father's mind then,' she says. 'After my mum died whenever we asked, "Where is the hot-water bottle?" or "the booklet of instructions that came with the boiler?" we'd think, "Where would Mum put it?" We don't know everything about your father's plan or motivations but we know a few things.'

'We know that he knew my thoughts would likely be scanned by the police if they ever captured me.'

'So he was careful not to tell you anything too explicit. Anything that would give you or his plan away at an early stage. But you think he eventually wanted you to come back.'

'I've said it and said it.'

'So, he must have given you something that would help you to—'

Her eyes widen and she gasps, leaps to her feet.

'What?'

'You said that once, when you were young, he left you in the forest.'

'Yeah.'

'This forest?'

'I don't know.'

'But he left you to find your way home on your own.'

'Yes, and it took days.'

'How did you do it eventually?'

Orpheus looks away, down at the forest floor. He can see that look in her eye, the one that he'd seen in Mab's face that night. An expectation, and he can't bear to disappoint her.

'I wandered around in circles. A bit like we're doing now. It's hard with this coastline that goes on forever and bends back on itself. I've heard that in Cornwall you're never more than twenty miles from the coast, so I didn't exactly have the sea alone to go by.'

'So what did you do?'

Orpheus pauses at the memory. In the woods they are all returning to him in vivid flashes. 'I wandered around for hours, until the sunset. Fell asleep under a tree and then in the middle of the night a sound woke me.' A tawny owl; Orpheus still remembers its *ke-wick* piercing his consciousness. A couple of weeks before he'd abandoned him in the woods, Orpheus' father had pointed out its dark silhouette against the inky sky and said, 'You can tell, the females make that sound. And the men reply . . .' He'd replied then with a silly *hoo-hoo-hoo* noise that had made Orpheus laugh.

'It felt a bit like when your eyes become accustomed to the darkness,' Orpheus tells Moremi now. 'The sound of that owl, and then remembering the tree we'd passed on the way back, with the roots that bulged, and I'd tried to be careful not to trip.'

It turned out that, in the dark, it had been easier to find his way. Didn't he recognise the feel of that tree? Or the way that the ground buckled under his home-made shoes? The distant sound of the river, the spongy moss underfoot, and how, as he got closer to the beach, it turned chalky. He remembered the old grooves and ridges his feet were used to finding during morning tracking with his father. The direction of the wind, the crannies in the edges of the trees where pillowy mush-rooms bloomed.

He knew this place by touch alone, his memories only bright enough to light the darkness immediately before him. He'd followed his recollections into a clearing in the forest where he found his father's large footprint still visible in the mud. Orpheus had leaned down and touched it, illuminated by the moonlight.

'That led you all the way home?' Moremi sounds dubious.

'Well, every now and then I veered off track but ...' He smiles sheepishly then, with a touch of pride. 'It took a couple of hours.'

Moremi smiles, turns around and begins to unpack one of the rucksacks. Orpheus watches her as she unzips their first-aid kit and unrolls their last bandage. 'Your father wanted you to know the way with your eyes closed, information they couldn't take from you. That's why he left you out here at sunset. So, let's close your eyes and see if you remember.'

In the dark, it takes a while for Orpheus to find his bearings. He's still for a while, letting his mind slip into the kind of embracing silence he could never find with his Pulse active. Eventually, his ears pick up the sound of the forest. Wind in the leaves, Moremi's breathing, her boots on the soil. Wood mice gathering hazelnuts. Distantly, a roe deer. And below that – he almost has to hold his breath to hear it – the sigh of the ocean. The smell of it. Orpheus lets his feet lead him, a certain intuition, long-faded memory.

As he gets closer to the edge of the forest there is a

change of texture in the soil, it begins to get more chalky.
The air turns less humid. His feet lead him as perhaps hers
sometimes do, in a dance she was sure she'd forgotten.

He is walking for a while, touching the trees with his
hands, before Moremi makes a noise, his eyes fly open,
and he pulls the bandage off.

'Is that it?' she asks, pointing a few metres away in the
trees. Orpheus sees first the sunken tyres, ferns growing
through the wheels. Their abandoned getaway truck.
Graffiti scrawled all over its old body.

The shattered window. The backseat has been stolen
but Orpheus knows how it had felt against his spine that
day, when he'd watched his father die. It's a haunting
sight after all these years, like a relic from a dream. Half-
devoured by trees and vines. Teenagers must have used it
as a hangout or hook-up spot and now birds drink from
its dented roof.

He knows the way from here, would know it in his
sleep, and runs through the woods and to the ocean. He
can smell it and hear it before his eyes see it. The cliffs,
the rocky beach, wrinkled dunes and screaming gulls. The
moiling waves chromed with light.

47

MOREMI

She's been in his dreams long enough to feel a shimmer of dread at the homecoming. The tide is out, and as they stride across the causeway, he says, 'I wanted it to look exactly the way it did when I left.'

'Of course you did,' Moremi says, rubbing his arm sympathetically.

The house has been devoured by time. Large parts of the island have been swallowed by the rising water. Now, most of what remains is the crumbled building. Livestock, long-dead, bleached bones like stones in the sandy grass. Algae brushed into the chicken-wire.

'Are you sure about this?' Moremi doesn't know why she reaches out a hand to stop him when he pushes open the front door. It's locked, but it's easy to knock it off its rusted hinges with a few hard shoves. Keeping their eyes and ears alert for any signs of drones or sensors, the two of them walk carefully inside.

There is a haunted quality to the place. It looks like Pompeii or some town that's been evacuated suddenly in the wake of a nuclear incident. Dishes still rot in the sink. Everything says that the inhabitants may still return. On the low coffee table is an unfinished game of chess strung with cobwebs.

'Were you black?' Moremi asks, her shadow falling across it.

'I don't remember,' he says.

Whole empires of spiders have risen and fallen, built kingdoms in every crevice and corner. Dust twinkles on the air. It's a modest open-plan room. Living room on one side, on the other a kitchen with a long wooden dining table that clearly doubled as a workbench. It's strewn with half-finished woodwork projects, goggles and sandpaper, rubber bands, a mason jar filled with nails. Some workbooks, covered in Orpheus' delicate handwriting. Latin. Thermodynamics. Fractal doodles in the corner.

Moremi feels like an archaeologist, unearthing evidence of the way that he lived. The windowsill is a graveyard of bluebottles and mushrooms bloom across the Persian rug. The spidery limbs of climbing vines curl like witches' fingers through cracks in the panes beside the fireplace. On the mantelpiece are letters that the two of them wrote to each other.

'Dear Dad, I don't really hate you, please forgive me. Orpheus.' And another dated two months later. 'Son, Don't worry, we'll try again tomorrow and do it better next time. Warsame.' Orpheus has to close his eyes for a

503

while when he reads them and Moremi's heart bursts with tenderness for him.

'This was your whole life,' she says, and she feels terribly sorry that it was so small.

The tide is coming in outside and they risk being stranded here. 'It'll only be a couple of hours,' Orpheus reassures her as the crash and fizz of waves outside grows louder. Moremi nods, though the thought of spending a couple of hours in this place makes her skin crawl.

It's clear to her that Orpheus is looking for something. Some clue his father may have left, a message, a letter. He searches through the stacks of books and pushes back the sofa. Two mice skitter past and Moremi has to hold herself back from screaming.

'I'll go look ... over there,' she says, just to get away, and heads into the darkened pantry.

It's filled with a couple of years' worth of food. Branded tin cans covered in dust, and many more that Orpheus and his father clearly made themselves. Fruit and oil with hand-written labels that are illegible now. Sacks of grain. A bag of rice drilled through by beetles.

Where would her mother leave a message?

A curtain divides the living area from the sleeping area. Orpheus' bed, a mat on the floor, piles of felt and lambswool. But then, a rumpled Captain America duvet cover. Moremi wonders where it came from. There are no photos. No television or radio. It's a house, Orpheus had explained, built to block any incoming or outgoing EM signals. So what did they do in the evenings? Moremi wonders. Tell each other ghost stories? Read chapters of Dickens novels? Play Go?

His father's 'bedroom' is like a monk's cell. There is a wooden box of his clothes, which she rifles through. A mud-spattered pair of trousers made of burlap-like linen, a thickly woven wool cap. He must have been tall, she thinks, and wonders, for the first time, how much he looked like Orpheus. In Orpheus' dreams, Warsame's face changes; sometimes they are a mirror image of each other, sometimes his father looks menacing, or his features are twisted like silly putty. Sometimes he's Hayden or Bertram or a teacher in the children's division.

When her eyes fall upon the stopped clock on the wall a thought occurs to her and she finds Orpheus crouched before the bookcase, squinting at his father's books.

'Hey,' she says. She slips her hand in the pocket of his borrowed jacket, and brings out the watch she's been carrying with her. 'I think I broke something of yours.' His eyebrows lift in surprise at the sight of it.

'Oh yeah.' He puts the book down on the rug, and turns it over in his hands. 'In my dream, I was looking for it.'

'It fell out of my pocket when I was on a Zephyr.'

'It was broken before, if that's what you mean. When I found it.'

'Where did you find it?'

'It was in my trouser pocket when I woke up after my father died. It used to be his.' At the sight of her expression he shakes his head. 'Don't get too excited. That's already occurred to me. That this was some kind of message he left to me. If it is, I can't decipher it. And I've been staring at this thing for years.'

Her shoulders slump in disappointment.

Orpheus gestures around the house. 'He must have left me something, though.' The sun is beginning to set outside and it flashes like a camera in their eyes. But Moremi is losing hope. How many nights has she dreamed that she would open her inbox and find emails from her mother, postmarked from the grave?

'Is this the only place it could be?' Moremi asks. 'Is there a barn or, it looks like your dad did some woodworking, did he have a studio around the back somewhere or—'

'He did most of his woodwork . . .' Orpheus catches his breath. 'He did have a study.'

'Oh yeah? Where?'

But instead of replying Orpheus rushes back into his father's bedroom. Moremi follows after to find him on his knees by the bed, pushing away a pile of boxes. There is a door she hadn't seen before. 'But it's locked,' Orpheus says, pointing to the keypad on the wall, with a thumb-sized LCD screen above it. 'I was never allowed in.' This piques Moremi's curiosity and she sits on the bed with a frown.

'I'm an idiot,' Orpheus says. 'I guess this should have occurred to me first.'

'Was it locked when you were young?'

'I don't remember a lock. But then . . .' He shrugs. Chews on his bottom lip in thought. 'It's a keypad so it's probably not a number. I'll eliminate the obvious first.'

'Password123?' Moremi says.

'You'd be surprised.' The corner of his mouth twitches in a smile. He tries, first, his own name, and then his father's name. And then the name that the police told him was his father's, his mother's, his grandfather's, 'Angharad', and every time the machine makes a discordant groan and flashes red. Moremi blows a raspberry and brushes mouse droppings off the mandala-print comforter. The sky blazes scarlet, darkness approaching. She leans back and closes her eyes, her stomach turning at the musty smell of the place. The groan of the machine marks every minute.

It's almost dark outside when she's woken, with a nerve-jangling start, by the sound of Orpheus kicking the door. 'Fuck!' he shouts, slamming his body so hard against it that the bed shudders and a cloud of foul-smelling dust and dirt falls.

'Hey!' She grabs his arm, but he shakes her loose.

'He didn't give me anything! He didn't help me in any way. They're right about him. They must be, he left me, and he left me with nothing.'

'Don't say that,' she says, though it's a feeble protest because Moremi hates his father too. Hates the man for leaving his son in this predicament. She reaches for the watch he left on the bed. 'Not nothing,' she says, though she means it in jest. Orpheus is too upset. Red-faced and on the edge of tears, he grabs the thing from her hands and dashes it against the wall.

'Don't!' Moremi leaps to her feet too late to stop him. It cracks like an egg on the rotted floorboards. They both blink at it in the dim light. It doesn't look the way they expect. On the inside, they don't see the cogs and wheels of an ordinary timepiece. There is a piece of glass, the size of a medallion, with a holographic picture of a skeleton watch stuck to one side.

'A quartz,' Orpheus says with surprise, picking it up delicately to examine it in the last embers of daylight.

'His?'

'I didn't know he had one. But I guess it makes sense. He did work for the Panopticon, after all.'

'Did you ever see . . . ?' She raises her hand to her own constellation.

'He wore his hair long.' Then Orpheus shrugs. 'Maybe I did and I don't remember. Back then I wouldn't have been sure what it was.'

'Hey, what's that?' Moremi lifts the brass back of the watch-face, curved like a magnifying glass. She has to strain to see it in the dark but the words engraved into it read, *Only your eyes are unclosed*.

Orpheus tries the phrase on the door keypad and, with a whirr of mechanics, it opens.

48

ORPHEUS

His father's basement study is windowless and dank. When the door closes behind them, the sound of the sea vanishes. Orpheus fumbles for a light, pulls a string and he hears the familiar rumble of their backup generator sputter to life. A couple of lights clink on. As he descends the worn wooden steps, he's not sure why his arms come up in goosebumps. It's like a graveyard of computers. Monitors and motherboards. A room that reminds him of some in God's Own Junkyard.

Cement floor, smell of mildew, of water dripping somewhere. An ozone-like tang from corroded gearboxes and defunct switchboards. Orpheus can feel his father's presence all around. And in his clammy hand, the most precious thing, a piece of his father's mind.

It takes only a few minutes for him to find what he expects. A quartz-reader, attached to an old computer.

Orpheus wipes away years of dirt from the screen with a sleeve over a clenched fist.

'I need to connect my constellation up with the machines,' he says, but then Orpheus realises that his Pulse is not activated.

'I saw them deactivate it,' Moremi says. She reaches out to touch the bump of skin under his jaw, where they implanted a device that switches it off. It's only a little bigger than a grain of rice. Barely visible, and Orpheus can only feel it if he reaches for it.

'Cut it out,' he says, rummaging in his pocket for a knife.

'Wait!' Moremi's eyes flash white in the gloom, and she grabs it from him. 'If you activate it, they might be able to find us.'

'I don't think so,' Orpheus says. 'This house is a Faraday cage. EM signals don't get in or out. And we're in a basement. Maybe he designed it this way, designed it so I can talk to him.'

'Okay,' Moremi says.

'Please?' He glances at the knife. It's hard to imagine cutting himself with it. Orpheus tries to picture the angle.

'I can do it,' Moremi says. And he nods gratefully as she leans forward to examine it as a surgeon might. He has a sudden frightening memory of her on the staircase in his dream, the way that she had come at him with a knife. The way he had said, 'It's not true,' and it had only enraged her. That woman was almost a caricature, though, compared to this Moremi that he loves and trusts.

'Ready?' she asks, putting her hand firmly on his shoulder. 'Three, two—' An act of mercy, she cuts him on 'two' and it's only a short flash of pain, only a little blood. When he opens his eyes the room is filled with holograms and rainbow loading wheels. 'I'll get some antiseptic,' she says as she pulls the little black implant away.

'That can wait,' he says. He's restless to start now, to talk to his father. Orpheus falls almost into autopilot as he sets up the OEG machine, untangles the wires. He's done this hundreds of times. Maybe his father had, too. This one is an older model than devices he's used to working with and it takes some imagination to figure out how his Pulse is supposed to connect to it.

Finally, he sits back in the chair by the desk, and attaches sticky pads to his temple and forehead. 'Can you . . . ?' he asks, but Moremi is already doing it, pushing the quartz like a cassette into the machine's old drive.

Before she switches it on, she says, 'Come back to me, okay?' He smiles and closes his eyes.

He opens his eyes in the same room. Only Moremi is no longer next to him and the door leading back into his father's bedroom is open and pouring bright clear light into the workshop.

Orpheus gets up, unencumbered by wires, and climbs slowly up the stairs. Where he can hear the heaving sea. A low hum of a voice he recognises.

His father, who hasn't aged a day from Orpheus' memories. Haloed by the morning light, sitting on the sofa, leaning into the coffee table where their old game of chess is.

'Apparently, in your dreams, you always return home. To your own front door, to yourself.'

Orpheus has to bite back emotion at the sound of the man's voice. Has to fight the urge to hug him. 'You're an avatar,' he says in order to remind himself. A hologram of his father built from a selection of the man's memories. Confronting an avatar can feel like talking to an advanced AI. And it's not completely different. He's a simulation, running on Orpheus' brain. Running a code made from memories.

'That's right.'

'So you can answer my questions?'

'Depends on the question.'

Orpheus sits on the other side of the chessboard and looks down at the pieces. His father had carved them himself, so all of the pawns' frowning faces look a little different. Of all the pieces on the board – foot soldiers, royalty, knights and battlements – the bishop has always struck Orpheus as the most mysterious. Difficult to imagine, a bishop on the battlefield, wetting his cassock with blood. It moves diagonally, driven, perhaps, by divine knowledge across the board. In French the same piece is called the *fou*, fool, or madman. So, depending on the game, Orpheus pictures a Rasputin-type character, whispering in the queen's ear, leading her family to destruction.

'If you're here, then I'm – I must have –' His father's expression falters, he can't bring himself to say the word. Orpheus simply nods, a knot in his throat. 'Hard to conceive,' he says, his eyes growing distant. 'I'm – I was – alive when I recorded this. When I laid this plan.'

'But you knew they would come to kill you,' Orpheus says.

'Callie and I always knew.'

'Why didn't you tell me any of this?'

'To protect you,' his father says.

'Why did you run away from the Panopticon and create Milk Wood?'

'I can't answer all your questions,' Warsame's program says.

'That's the only question I care about!'

Orpheus looks down at the chessboard. At the opening, it is like a sunlit field, the enemy gathered only distantly on the horizon. A sense of wondrous possibility. There are more possible chess games than atoms in the known universe, his father had liked to remind him. Anything can happen. After four turns there are over 3 billion possible moves a player can make.

'And you're safe?' his father asks.

'No,' Orpheus says. He's on the run, there is nowhere he can hide. At any moment protection officers could batter down the door and arrest them both.

'Are you happy?' Orpheus opens his mouth to answer but then considers. He's confused and totally lost. By a process of slow and then sudden attrition, he's stopped believing in everything that he used to. But then, the past months that he's spent falling in love with Moremi have been the happiest of his entire life. If they can stay safe, and make a life together, he'll die content.

'Sometimes.'

'Well.' His father leans back. Orpheus isn't sure what responses are programmed in for this answer. 'I suppose that's the best any of us can hope for.' Then he looks down at the board. The game they left unfinished. 'Do you want to see how it ends?'

Orpheus knows that he should probe his father for more answers to questions that may help him. But, in the end, Orpheus just wants to enjoy being in his father's mind. He just wants to be fourteen again, to go back.

'If I remember correctly, you were playing white.'

Orpheus sits on the chair opposite and examines the game. Staring down at the board, some of it comes back to him. They had been about two hours in before they decided to adjourn. A game they'd played by candlelight a couple of nights before his father was killed.

Orpheus very rarely beat his father, a fact which always irked him. Warsame used to tell him that the art of chess lay in never letting your opponent show what he can do. Deflect and undermine him, dominate, sabotage, draw blood. That was the way that he played.

Gazing at the board now, Orpheus can already see that he'd been drawn into a few of his father's traps, put in the defensive position and forced to flee squares, narrowly missing check. Years have passed, though, Orpheus reminds himself. 'This is my last chance to beat you.'

'And mine.' His father smiles.

Impossible to tell, sometimes, when the endgame begins. They are drawn into it quickly and after a dozen moves there are only a few pieces left on the board. Orpheus' own king and queen, as well as two stalwart rooks with which he intends to storm Warsame's patchily guarded battlements and murder his king. His father has held on to a queen and two knights, plus a single pawn creeping down the board.

This is the part of the game that his father loves. After most of the lesser pieces have been captured, he says it is possible to witness some of the game's intrinsic beauty. It's normally clear to Orpheus, at this point, if he will win or lose. Like his father, he used to own dozens of well-thumbed copies of books on endgame theory, and as he stares down at the sun-dappled board, a formation comes to him in a lightning bolt of inspiration.

Alekhine's gun, named after the former world chess champion, which consists of placing the two rooks stacked one behind another and the queen at the rear. Orpheus sketched a picture of it once, in the back of a chess notebook, but has never had a chance to use it. Until this afternoon. Yes, he thinks with elation as his mind puzzles through the quick succession of moves he can use to capture his father's queen and then push him into checkmate.

His heart begins to race as he makes his next move, forcing Warsame to take his king out of danger, but opening the way for Orpheus' queen to slide across the board and capture his. His father sees it coming, but there is nothing he can do. As Orpheus grabs his queen, he is filled with a visceral delight at the cool weight of it in his palm, sleek dark wood. A joy to possess her.

In three moves the game will be over.

Sometimes, when he plays, Orpheus imagines a commentator saying, 'It seems, now, that black must lose.' It will be almost impossible now for his father to pin Orpheus in check with only two knights, and that distant pawn. He's at such a material disadvantage that Orpheus wonders why he doesn't resign now.

No matter. Orpheus pushes his rook in front of his queen. Even as he does he's imagining the joy of victory. And the relief.

Warsame pauses before his turn. And, for the first time in the silent minutes that pass between them, he looks up at Orpheus. His lips are wet, eyes glittering the same glassy black as his captured queen.

He doesn't, as Orpheus guessed he would, try to move his knight between Orpheus' rook in order to block his king. Instead, he pushes his lone pawn from the seventh to the eight square. Orpheus realises with horror that he's been so distracted by creating his formation on this corner of the board that he was half-blind. He did not see that his father's pawn was one move away from becoming a queen. Orpheus reassesses the game with horror.

His king is in danger now. But as his mind runs through a dozen moves he realises that they are all impossible. His king is helpless. He makes the one feeble move that he can, out of check. But Warsame's new-born queen trundles across the board.

Orpheus' chequered kingdom traversed, measured across, and destroyed.

The word 'checkmate' comes from the Persian phrase *Shah Mat*, which means 'the King is dead'. A good player never needs to be told.

Orpheus stands up and fights the urge to push over the chessboard – the scene of his defeat – and stamp the pieces into the ground. The crash of the waves outside are like a round of applause. His father shakes his head in disappointment. It's heartbreaking to see. Orpheus knows that he will say, 'How did you miss the pawn?' so when he opens his mouth, Orpheus says, 'Don't!' but his father still says, 'Are you blind!?'

His cheeks hot with fury, Orpheus' own fury. And shame. He didn't see because he was so excited about his own plan to force his father into checkmate. It was a game he could have won.

'I'm tired of your games!' Orpheus shouts, his vision blurring. 'I'm tired of trying to figure out your plan. Just tell me!'

'Okay.' His father is sombre. 'Okay, I'll spell it out for you, since that's what's required.' He narrows his eyes and looks out the window. He says, 'We created Milk Wood as part of a plan that would outlive us.'

'But how would it outlive you?' Orpheus asks. 'Where did you store it? How can we find it?' *How can we destroy it?* he thinks privately, but does not say.

His father stands up. He's still taller than Orpheus by a few inches. Since Orpheus has aged and he has not, the distance between the two of them, now, is smaller. 'It's here,' he says, motioning to the room around him with a smile. Then he leans over the board to hold Orpheus' face like a crystal ball between his hands. 'And now it's in here.'

When Orpheus wakes, Moremi is on the other end of the room leaning against the door, her pupils dilated with terror. 'Orpheus,' she shouts. 'They're here.'

'Who?' He fights back the roll of nausea as he comes to, pulling the electrodes off his chest as if they're infected. But before she can speak, before he has a chance to run to the door, it bursts open and she tumbles down the stairs.

Protection officers pour in, more than Orpheus has ever seen, in masks and hazmat suits, holding rifles.

Assistant Commissioner Melissa Palmer is in front – he recognises her stern face through her visor. She strides across the room and pushes aside the trolley with the quartz reader on. 'Make sure you get all of this,' she tells them. 'It's all evidence.'

'Leave him alone,' Moremi shouts. Three men are holding her back, though she is kicking and struggling with all her might.

'We knew it was only a matter of time before you returned,' she says. At the sight of her face an alien calm descends upon Orpheus. The endgame he'd expected. He's not at all surprised to see her again.

'We've been watching this house for years.'

No one can describe to the uninitiated, his father used to say, the agony of chess. Orpheus feels as if he's been outmanoeuvred one final time. 'Let her go,' he tells them. 'It's me you want.'

49

ORPHEUS

'Hello?' The walls of his cell are padded and Orpheus can tell – from the blinking lights of the transmitters in the corners of the room – that they are watching him.

He has no notion of what time it is. Although, he estimates that a day or so may have passed since he and Moremi were thrown in the back of a van and driven from Angharad to London. He's at Quantum Hill, he knows. Not only from the glimpse of it he caught as he was escorted in. But because he used to work on the other side. They call them 'air-locks', special cells that the security analysts use to observe people who are hosting certain kinds of malware on their constellations.

'I know you're watching me.' Orpheus imagines them in another room somewhere, watching a holographic reconstruction of him pound like a mime at invisible walls. 'Sai?' There is no way his old manager is not there, leading a team of analysts. 'Sai Kaur? Just tell me what's wrong with me. Tell me what you're going to do.'

A long time passes before the lights on the transmitters flash green and a voice comes through a speaker high up on the ceiling.

'I think you know what's wrong with you, Orpheus.' Sai's voice resonates across the room before the transmitter beams flash and a hologram of his body appears like a smoke signal.

'Milk Wood, the malware that my parents authored; it's on my constellation right now.'

Sai nods sombrely, and Orpheus feels a sickness at the invasion. Sai might as well have told him he's harbouring tapeworms.

When he worked for the Panopticon, Orpheus had seen the other side of rooms like these, seen the lightless office with a dozen malware experts and threat analysts, reverse-engineering viruses, studying the dimensions of their attacks on air-gapped computers, as a scientist might examine a viper.

'It's actually a worm,' Sai says, 'one that can take advantage of a security vulnerability in the Panopticon's core operating system.' Orpheus' former manager's eyes glimmer. 'I've probably only seen a handful of these in the wild before and none like this.' Orpheus wonders if uncovering Milk Wood had felt to Sai the way that playing chess had felt to Orpheus. A glimpse of a malign intelligence.

Sai explains that as soon as Orpheus connected with his father's quartz, the worm began its work. When Orpheus left that basement, it had infected every contact on his

Pulse, everyone that he'd ever called or sent a message to, and then spidered out, unfolding with the organic chaos of polyps or mycelium, through friends of friends, networks of networks, at the speed of light through fibre-optic cables.

'It looks as if it can gain full control of the host's constellation. From there it travels across the Panopticon to infect other hosts,' Sai says. 'It's still spreading, though as soon as we were made aware of the attack the prime minister ordered a COBRA meeting and the department of defence have organised a kind of virtual quarantine for the next twenty-four hours, cutting the UK off from the rest of the world while we deal with this threat.

'From what we can see,' Sai continues, 'the worm needs to be triggered before it begins to execute its code. It looks like your Pulse is acting like a command-and-control server. Imagine that your Pulse has sent out troops to enemy territory and they're all just waiting for your go-ahead to detonate their payloads.' The metaphor makes them both uncomfortable. Sai glances at Orpheus with the wariness of a bomb-squad member before an unexploded landmine. What could the trigger be? Orpheus wonders. An EM pulse, a keyword, a specific date or time? And what does it do? Sai himself doesn't seem to be sure. 'It propagates on constellations, but we don't know what it will do inside the host's head yet. We know that it attacks physical infrastructure as well, civilian control systems. So maybe it could cause blackouts, car accidents. It could take out ventilation systems, affect hospitals and navigation. The damage, if this thing is triggered, could be catastrophic.'

Orpheus sits back down on the bed, his gut rolling with nausea at Sai's words. 'It's one of the most sophisticated cyber attacks I've ever seen.' Orpheus would expect nothing less of his father.

'I'm guessing you've tried the normal things,' he says, remembering all he'd learned at God's Own Junkyard. 'Bypassing the malware and disabling it?' Sai doesn't even nod, just looks at Orpheus sorrowfully. 'Releasing a patch?'

Sai shakes his head. He's a doctor giving a miserable prognosis. Orpheus has come across a few bad cases before, in God's Own junkyard and during his work in the School of Sleep. People who had to have their entire constellation wiped, losing all the saved memories and information. It was a heartbreaking prospect for most people but one that – at this desperate moment – Orpheus is more than happy to contemplate.

'Not in the time we have. Obviously, this has already wreaked billions of pounds of havoc, but the home secretary is convinced that our best and first course of action needs to be neutralising the threat that the payload will be triggered.'

'Which means . . .' this is such a delicate way of saying it that Orpheus almost has to laugh, '. . . "neutralising" me.'

Sai flinches and looks down. 'I'm sorry,' he begins. 'We've read your memories. We know that you didn't choose this, but . . .' He sighs and Orpheus can see that perhaps he hasn't slept, stress etching lines in the side of his eyes. 'I can count on one hand the amount of Zero Days I've worked on. I feel as if I've worked my entire career to see this one.' Malevolent, perfect code. 'The only way to disable this attack is to execute you.'

There's a man silhouetted on the threshold of his cell. It takes a moment for Orpheus' eyes to focus in order to recognise him.

'Hayden?' For a while, Orpheus thinks he could be dreaming. Hayden Adeyemi in the flesh. Orpheus discovers in an instant that it's true what they say about him. That he's barely aged. Can it all be fasting and clean living? If his father had survived they would be around the same age.

Hayden enters the cell soundlessly. An alien presence. Another hologram. He's taller than he looks on the Vine. Barefoot, in a white linen sleepsuit. Eyes that seem to suck all of the light out of the room.

Orpheus knows that he should get up off his bed, stand, be respectful, but all he can think is *I hate this man*. He hates everything with the impotent fury of the totally wronged. Despises every free person because he knows, now, that he will live his life from one cell to another and then they will put him to sleep and he will dream of a century of cells. He'll be trapped until he loses his mind. A fate which makes him feel physically ill and totally terrified. And now here is Hayden, not here to save him.

Hayden says, 'It's a cruel thing. His plan.' And Orpheus has a flash of memory. The thing that Sherif had said to him, what feels like so long ago, 'Aspects cannot be chosen or escaped.' Orpheus quotes this and Hayden nods. 'We've been watching it unfold for years. We knew that his son

would be part of it. This day, you, here, and your particular make-up.'

'How long have you known?' Orpheus asks.

'From its inception,' Hayden says. 'We understand
intimately the mind that devised it because it was ours
once, too.'

'My father,' Orpheus guesses. 'You paired your Pulse
with him?'

Hayden touches the bald edge of his temple. Apparently,
after his brother died all of his hair fell out. He stopped
talking, stopped eating, never grew another inch. 'We
still feel him in here, sometimes . . .' Orpheus wonders if
Warsame did as well. If he woke at night now and then,
sweating because of Hayden's nightmares. If his heart ever
broke with grief for the brother he never had.

'We loved your father. Hayden and Warsame devised
the Panopticon together. We experimented on ourselves,
mapped the other's dreamscapes. It wasn't only thoughts
we shared, it was our fears and our desires, everything.'
Orpheus knows all too well the intimacy of prolonged
dream-sharing. But the thought of his father doing this
with Hayden still makes his head spin.

'If that's true then what made him change his mind?'
Orpheus asks what he hadn't managed to ask his
father's hologram.

'Reversion,' Hayden says. A word Orpheus has only
distantly heard of. It describes an inverted mind suddenly
returning to its pre-inverted state.

'It took us a while to discover that he and Callie had
been sabotaging all our R&D efforts from the inside. It

took us years to root out and patch all the vulnerabilities that he wove into our system. A warrant was put out for his arrest but he vanished. Evaded almost all our efforts to find him. Until ...'

Orpheus knows that they are both imagining his father, his teeth slick with blood, his eyes wide open, pupils black panes of reflected stars.

'It was you,' Orpheus says. Details from that night floating back to him. The way his father had said, 'You came yourself,' with some surprise. 'That night. You killed him.'

'It had to be done,' Hayden says. 'But you must believe us when we tell you it wasn't easy. It was, it felt like ...' Hayden grits his teeth and winces as if he can feel the path of the bullet through his own flesh. 'Suicide.'

In Orpheus' misery and rage he feels as if he hates them all. He feels used. He had thought he was fighting with his father against the Panopticon but it turns out that he was a pawn in his father's hand in a decades-long game Warsame had been playing against Hayden.

'You're the final vulnerability,' Hayden says.

'And once you execute me?'

'We can begin.'

'You've got everything now. Now that Total Adoption is on the way, you can roll out the software update and connect everybody's mind,' Orpheus says.

'We might have achieved it years ago, if it hadn't been for your father.'

It's the 'we' that continues to grate on Orpheus. The alien way that Hayden moves. *What kind of man is he?*

Orpheus thinks, and then, an idea occurs to him that makes the ground beneath his heels tremble.

'Who are you?' he asks. Hayden smiles.

'You know who I am.'

'You're ...' Orpheus feels dizzy. 'You're all three of them, aren't you? Bertram Fairmont, Jitsuko Itō and Hayden. All of their consciousnesses inside your head.'

Hayden smiles wider, wolflike white teeth. 'They never died.'

'Wow.' Orpheus almost laughs at his stupidity for not realising it sooner. 'You've been each other for years.'

'On and off,' Hayden concedes, with a fake-modest wave of his hand. Orpheus has to sit down for a moment, the bed hard under his thighs.

'It will be commonplace soon,' Orpheus says. 'In a year or so everyone will be paired, right? That's the dream.'

'Yes, Orpheus. This world was rotten, before we remade it. It's our deepest regret that you or your father will never live to see it.'

'Aspects *cannot* be chosen or escaped,' Orpheus says, at first to himself, but then he looks up and asks, 'Did you ever watch that show, *Twelve*?'

'We know of it.'

'A cop who predicts the future and always gets there too late.' Orpheus smiles then, remembering his father's last words. 'You can't beat him. I've tried. And the protection officers showed me that the attack does happen.' It had been frightening to consider before but it provides him with some measure of hope now, that perhaps he might be saved. Perhaps he won't be executed.

'In every generation some rise up and hope to halt the turning of the world. The Luddites failed back then and they will fail now.' Then Hayden says words that had terrified Orpheus for years: 'You can't change the future.'

Orpheus smiles, finding a bitter comfort in them today. He replies, 'Exactly.'

50

MOREMI

Apparently, Sai Kaur pulled some strings to help to get her out of prison early. Moremi spends three days in a dank cell. Back in London, where their on-staff neurologists reactivated her Pulse to allow the authorities to scan her recent memories, they established that she had committed no crime they could prove. It's almost midnight when they let her out; Sai and Mercury are there, tears in their eyes. They tell Moremi that they've only just heard the news about the execution, and when she says, 'Execution?' they fall into a despairing silence.

When her Vine comes alive for the first time in months, Moremi feels as if she's at the eye of a storm. A dizzying stream of news and messages that she missed flies before her eyes all at once as her different feeds update.

Everyone is saying his name: Orpheus. Her friends and distant acquaintances, news correspondents and MPs. His 'trial' is under way at the Old Bailey and just a couple of hours ago Parliament passed a controversial new law that allows the police commissioner to execute people accused of the most heinous future crimes. 'Common sense,' many say, giving the police power to save hundreds or thousands of lives. All the way up Whitehall, protestors are camped out.

'Execution.' The word makes the ground fall out from under her. Surely, it can't be?

'I spoke to him yesterday,' Sai says, 'and he begged me to help you any way I could.'

'Tomorrow?' Moremi says, and they both nod.

'It's political, more than anything,' Sai says the word as if it's dirty. 'Not justice, not even the only course of action. I still think they could wipe his pulse or surgically remove it. But the Home Secretary has vowed to be tougher on future crime.'

'Yeah ...' Mercury's voice is sour. 'What looks better than executing the man who almost destroyed the Panopticon?'

It occurs to Moremi that her final glimpse of him on Angharad as they were both thrown into the back of the police van might have been the last one.

The flat is a time capsule, or a shrine, to the time they spent together. When Moremi slows her pace she's on the street where she danced the role of Agave for him that stifling midsummer night.

Mercury follows her in. 'I don't think you should be alone,' they say. Up the stairs to his bedroom. Before they'd got married she'd written on the fridge with a dry marker everything that they still needed: flowers, dress, etc. It hits her with a gut-punch of grief. The heady hopefulness of the summer. They'd said 'forever' to each other. They'd said, 'nought but death shall part thee and me.'

Moremi leans over the sink and cries.

The bulbs have blown in the old kitchen lights. A long row of flesh-coloured tights are strung up above the sink and in the gloom they look like cuts of meat. Thighs and calves of bloodless legs, dancers hung out to dry.

Fumbling in the cutlery drawer for a box of matches, she lights the few candles he'd jammed into empty bottles of Famous Grouse. There is a map of the maze drawn on some paper he'd hung above the sink. She takes it down now, and examines the labyrinth. When she thinks about the years Orpheus wasted trying to solve the maze she feels a little sorry for him.

Everything she has read about execution suggests that he will be trapped in Dreamtime forever, that wherever he finds himself, a shopping mall, a graveyard, a castle, he will wake to find the walls or hedgerows or never-trodden footpaths curve endlessly in on themselves in a puzzle that could take him more than a lifetime to solve. It's a night-mare. She knows he'd rather die.

Almost all the lights in the corridor are off, and she fumbles her way blindly down the hall, pausing only when she reaches his bedroom, where the door is ajar, and the wan light of monitor screens flicker. Moremi's body tenses as if she thinks she might see a ghost. *Someone is in there,* she thinks, *in his bedroom.*

When she pushes the door open, though, she sees only the jumble of machines he's set up. On one of the screens, she sees his friend Sherif. Orpheus is watching him draw a face, a young woman with delicate, deep-set eyes. It's magic, almost, watching the picture emerge from his lines.

Moremi must have left the machine on, that one time she read Orpheus' quartz. She switches it off now, but the room feels too haunted to sleep in.

Mercury is curled like a cat on the sofa in the living room. At the sound of Moremi's approach, their eyes flutter open, but Moremi says she'll take the rug.

She struggles to sleep. Sometimes she drifts off into that liminal space between sleep and waking and she can almost conjure him. The house smells the way that he does. Of dust and mouldy fruit and something sweet burning.

There are a few of his long black hairs in the pile of the rug.

I could clone him, she thinks, pinching one between her fingers.

She lies with eyes wide open listening to the *shhhh* of tyres striking tarmac. Waves lapping in just one direction. The dust of the streets rises up on hot currents of air. She falls asleep and wakes up and each time that old pain is like a knife-twist in her sternum.

This time tomorrow, he'll be dead.

Or as good as, in that eternal prison-sleep where she could never reach him. His bones and heart wasting until Nox finally stops his breathing.

Moremi used to have this idea that, when she went to

primary school, her parents went into suspended animation. That they powered down like automata, her father motionless at his desktop, her mother frozen by the phone just waiting for her daughter to call.

But now Moremi imagines herself powering down like her fantasy mother, only to spring into animation when this nightmare is over. *I can't live without him,* she thinks, *I refuse to.*

Getting stiffly to her feet, she gazes out the open sash window. Her Pulse tells her that it is 4.30am. Who is awake, right now? All the windows of all the houses are darkened. The road is suddenly quiet. Nothing but automated lorries careening to dawn deliveries.

What if she is the only one awake? Moremi pictures her sisters half a country away, safe. Halima, asleep with her baby. Zeeba dozing with an old paper copy of *National Geographic* slipping out of her grip. Orpheus . . . ?

Your eyes alone are unclosed, she thinks, and suddenly the way ahead seems clear to her. What had it been? *Only your eyes are unclosed?*

51

ORPHEUS

Orpheus remembers an execution he's never been to. A government-issued memory, implanted in his quartz as part of the Good People Project. In the memory, it's a May morning and the sky is an Arctic blue above the Tower of London. It's the Thames Barrier Ten, the group of terrorists convicted for orchestrating the flood. Orpheus remembers the electricity in the air. The crowds pushing to get close to the square.

Apparently, it's very humane. It's a medical procedure simple enough it can be performed under local anaesthetic. A device the size of a pinhead, which they call a Nerf, is implanted near the brainstem. The Nerf is inserted on the morning of the execution, with a timer set to activate its software. Orpheus has studied its neat code, which contains a logic bomb that causes the host to drift into an eternal sleep.

The strangest thing about an execution is that, by

the time the crowd arrive, or tune in over the Vine, it's already happened. The Nerf has already slid between soft tissues, has already networked with a million neurons, and paired with the prisoner's Pulse. The tiny punctured skin at the base of the skull has already begun to scab. Drops of blood sticking baby hairs together. The timer in the prisoner's brain is counting down the final conscious seconds.

During that time, their verdict and crimes are read out again. The home secretary will sign a document permitting the execution. He will say, 'With this act, we hope to make Britain a safer place.' Then the humanist preacher in her white cassock will say, 'For as long as it's with us, every flame of human consciousness is a precious thing. A more ancient society may have asked themselves during a season of famine or drought, "What can we sacrifice, to bring the sun back?" But we must remember that this act will return nothing we've lost. Although the sleeper will live out the rest of his natural life, blind and deaf, in a liminal space, we hope that he will take something with him. Something of our rage, some part of the world's cruelty, some bit of our collective brokenness and broken-heartedness, and discard it forever, on the other side.'

Sometimes, the prisoner is allowed a final word. At this stage of the execution, they are in a glass cell in the tower, too high up to be properly visible, though their face will be projected across retinas and screens all over the country. They will probably shout that they are innocent. In the case of the Thames Barrier Ten, a couple of them simply cried. One shouted a final word of goodbye to his mother, another spat at the camera.

And the last moment is almost anticlimactic. The timer in their brain ticks down to zero. There is one final glimpse of their eyes, a flash of alertness as the Nerf activates. Pain? Orpheus has studied the faces and never sees it. It's like falling asleep under anaesthetic, doctors explain, happens suddenly and all at once. They won't remember it on the other side. They will open their eyes in some maze of their mind's making and they will have forgotten, already, how they came to be there.

'Have you already done it?' Orpheus asks, reaching a hand for the numbed skin at the base of his skull.

'Yep,' the doctor says, adjusting the height of the chair. 'All done.'

'I didn't know it would be so quick.' Orpheus imagines the Nerf like a worm in his hypothalamus. How is it possible he can't feel it at all?

Orpheus has heard that most of the neurologists try not to make too much conversation with the inmates, for obvious reasons, but this man and the nurse next to him are the first people he's seen in a while. They may possibly be the last.

'I thought they'd give me a last meal,' Orpheus says as the nurse begins to wheel the trolley out. The night before, he'd lain awake devising recipes. Last meals. His father's fish teriyaki. The Werther's Originals he found in the moth-eaten pockets of a vintage-store Barbour. Anything he ever ate with Moremi.

'You're not supposed to—'

'I know . . . Eat for thirty hours before the . . .' Orpheus can't say execution.

After the implantation procedure, they take him into the cell where it will happen. A prison built for this purpose alone, amid the flood-ravaged ruins of the Tower of London. Orpheus supposes that Stella Stratton must have felt like a medieval king, restoring this old fortress to one of its original purposes. Voters had loved it.

One of the walls is made of glass and outside he can see the city has not yet woken up. Dappled streetlights dash across the tiled floor. It's 6am. Peach flush of dawn staining the sky. *And all the people of the lulled and dumbfound town are sleeping now.*

He lies on the ground and doesn't let himself cry. He thinks of Moremi, of the morning they were married, of the open-hearted way that she'd loved him, as if she'd never been hurt before. He'd lost faith in meat-space, in whatever joy he might find there, until he met her. Now he wants nothing more than to stay awake, even just one more night with her. When he thinks of the other side, what centuries of dream captivity await him, his mind blackens with terror, and his looping thoughts rail against the injustice. Then he despises everyone, including his father, who had a hand in this pattern of events that brought him here. It's not fair, but he can only comfort himself by trying to let go of the notion that anything ever would be.

*

536

The morning of his execution is bright. It's the last glimpse of sky and so his heart is pierced by its loveliness.

There are crowds gathering at 6am. News vans and tourists who consider the UK's public executions an almost medieval curiosity. His face is projected larger than life on a couple of screens along the walls of the inner-most and outer keeps. There is a timer in the corner of his vision counting down the hours and then the minutes until the Nerf activates. *How many people are watching this?* Orpheus wonders.

There are so many security guards and police drones, it looks as if the city has been occupied by insurgents. Tower Bridge and the roads around the underground station have been blocked by the police in order to heighten security.

News anchors might be saying, now, over the Vine, what they always say. Words like 'totally humane', 'completely painless'. There are protestors in the crowd, holding banners and projecting holograms; Revelators, vainly lobbying the government for a last-minute reprieve. Pro- and anti-sleep campaigners, religious groups and Vote No advocates with their fading slogan T-shirts.

Orpheus watches it all. As the judge re-reads her sentence, and the home secretary tells the world about the 'heinous crime' Orpheus had conspired to commit, the humanist preacher takes the lectern and says, 'This act will return nothing we've lost.' Except for order, the crowd hopes, and some measure of peace.

This is the face that history will see. In school, will they teach children how the country was rescued from the brink of destruction and, when they do, will they say his name? Orpheus, destiny's fool, a pawn in everyone's game.

His mind is already beginning to float from this moment. Five minutes left, the holographic timer tells him, until his consciousness is snuffed out like a candle.

'Have you prepared any words?' asks the preacher over the Vine. Orpheus sees his own dumbfounded face on the screen and curses himself for his lack of preparation.

The whole world is quiet. Watching. Will he make one last fool of himself? Will he stammer and shrug? Will he tell them that he too has been wronged? That all he wanted was to live a quiet life?

When his tongue loosens, the thought unfolds like a jasmine flower in his mind. 'Only *your* eyes are unclosed,' he says.

Everyone is looking at him, silent, rapt.

That old play his father used to read; as he says one word, the next comes to him. 'And all the people of the lulled and dumbfound town are sleeping now.'

Something is happening.

Only Orpheus sees it at first. A drone plummets from the sky. It shatters like a clay pigeon on the worn battlements of a mount. And then a couple more lose purchase in the air and crash into the grassy moat.

Milk Wood. Finally, Orpheus understands. 'Hush, the babies are sleeping, the farmers, the fishers, the tradesmen and pensioners . . .'

'No!' The home secretary's face is a mask of terror. At the edges of his vision, people are beginning to run. 'Someone stop him.'

Orpheus sees now his father's plan. It involved this day, the execution, his own terror about closing his eyes. Orpheus realises that his father has coded the escape into his memory. This virus, he thinks, can save him, is his way out of that eternal sleep.

It's a relief to give in, to seize it. A relief to play his father's final move, and tear the world down with him.

'From where you are, you can hear their dreams.'

Orpheus triggers the virus with the savage glee of Samson toppling the temple of the Philistines and taking himself with it.

Confusion. Then terror as they realise what is happening. Too late to stop it. Milk Wood is unfolding in everybody's minds like a music box, releasing its malicious code through the vast networks on their constellations, through the Panopticon, and everything that connects to it; drones and traffic lights, cars and TV screens, which all begin to turn dark. Flicker off. Fall from the sky.

As he says the words, he feels his awareness expand, pushing out, through the walls of his cell and into the analysts crouched on the other side. The dark popcorn-smelling room, lit by a hundred monitors and blinking servers. The security guards in the hall. There is a distant cacophony of alarms that start up and then fall silent. The world grinds to a halt. Some of the analysts' heads drop to the melamine counters, the legs of the security guards crumple beneath them. Cleaners in the hall tumble down the stairs.

The city falls under a witch's spell. Traffic lights turn dark, the lights of Piccadilly Circus flicker off. People fall on subway platforms, the trains slugging in and out of stations stop moving. Cars crash. Fires start.

Before the Nerf counts down its final seconds, Orpheus thinks that he sees her face in the crowd. Can it be? Moremi wearing the same hood she wore in the forest, her eyes terrified. He wants more than anything to reach out for her, but his vision turns white. And on the way to the other side, he thinks that he can hear his father laughing. Orpheus imagines him standing again in the bay window of their cottage, his arms outstretched in sublime triumph and, as the world falls asleep, he shouts, 'It's already here.'

52

MOREMI

Overnight, Moremi had come up with the plan. The maps Orpheus had drawn of the labyrinth had been the clue. And Sai Kaur, the scars she had seen on his hand once: 'So I wouldn't get lost,' he'd told her, 'on the other side.' The way that Sherif had coaxed Orpheus out of his dream. As the sun was rising she shook Mercury awake and asked, 'Is there a way I can save him?'

Although they had agreed that the plan sounded feasible, they were quick to remind Moremi that nothing would work if the cyberattack fried all of their constellations before they could save Orpheus. So they'd discussed ways to shelter from it. Mercury had explained that everyone wearing Pulse-blocking headsets would probably be safe. They also suggested turning a room of the flat into a Faraday cage, blocking all electromagnetic radiation from entering or exiting. To do this, they ordered industrial amounts of tinfoil by drone, and then taped it up, on the walls, ceiling and floor. Moremi had covered all the electrical outlets, and stuck the seams together using conductive tape. She pulled up some of the loose floorboards from the kitchen to allow a bridge, so she could walk across the foil without damaging it.

Wearing a muzzle, Moremi jumped on a bus, and then – as the traffic has blocked most of the major roads – ran to the Tower to rescue Orpheus.

She had almost arrived too late. Only a minute or so before the entire world, it seemed, was rent apart. Moremi had stood among the crowds in the heavily guarded outer wards and seen Orpheus' face on the screen. It had been almost impossible, at first, to hear what he had said because of the shouts of the protestors all around. But after a few moments, as the drones began to fall from the sky, everyone fell silent.

By the time Orpheus said the last words of the trigger – 'From where you are, you can hear their dreams' – the screen went black. A woman close by had screamed and then crumpled to the ground. Another had stared at her and said, as the drones began to drop like comets, 'We will not all sleep, but we will all be changed.' She'd looked around at the people on the ground, then stared up at Moremi with terror in her eyes. 'In a flash, in the twinkling of an eye,' then turned to run. It had been a sight stranger than a dream, Moremi thought, looking around to find that everyone with a working Pulse had fallen asleep.

With all of the guards in a virus-induced slumber, and all the doors powered by the Panopticon open, it had been possible for Moremi to find her way through the tower, to Orpheus, who was sleeping on the ground in his cell. He'd looked like a sleep-scientist or a monk, with his hair shaved off. Moremi had been filled with the tenderness she normally felt when she watched him sleep. His heartbeat had been slow and even, and his eyes fluttered behind his lids in REM. *Where is he?* Moremi wondered. Racing up and down the halls of a dream labyrinth?

She'd carried his body down to street-level, trying her best not to bash any of his limbs in her hurry. Found an abandoned shopping trolley and pushed him through the city back to the flat.

All across London there had been little wild pockets of activity. Pulseless children emerging from quiet classrooms with tears of confusion in their eyes. People in papery gowns pounding on hospital windows. Pulseless vagrants were looting the streets up Piccadilly, smashing the gilded windows of Burlington Arcade and emerging with brightly coloured trays of Ladurée macaroons, pockets full of vintage watches and jewellery. Moremi hopes that Zeeba, Halima and her niece are all safe in Silo Six.

When Moremi arrives back at the flat, and hauls his sleeping body up the stairs, it is a relief to find Mercury safe in the sparkly, tinfoil bathroom. But when Moremi examines them more closely, she sees tears in their eyes.

'What is it?' she asks.

'Without my Pulse I'm only Kimiko.' She's waxy pale.

'I'm sorry,' Moremi says. Of course, Zen's mind is saved as some cloud on the Panopticon. Kimiko can only access it when she is connected. As Moremi pulls Orpheus into the blow-up paddling pool she wonders if Mercury regrets her decision to help save Orpheus.

'I'm sorry,' she says, again. She knows what a terrible thing it is to face losing the one you love. Mercury only shakes her head. 'He's my friend too.' She doesn't want to lose either of them. 'And if we fix this, we can bring both of them back. If we wake him, maybe we can wake everyone.' Though neither of them understand the mechanics of this completely. In some hellish world, Orpheus dies and so does everyone else.

Moremi can see the twinkling light of the Nerf in the back of his neck, a scab forming around it. To take it out, they both know, will risk death or serious brain damage, and neither of them are skilled surgeons.

'Though this, too.' Kimiko holds up the dripping blade. 'Carving Orpheus' map into your skin, is this necessary?'

'I got the idea from Sai,' Moremi admits. Then she repeats her plan: 'I use the map, I go in and find him, wake him up. Save him, save everyone.'

'Everyone . . .' Kimiko repeats with a low whistle.

It's a Hail Mary plan. It's almost certain to fail. More likely, as Kimiko fearfully reminds her, she will be trapped in the prison with him, wandering empty halls for hundreds of years, unable to find her way back. Or, worse still, she could die suddenly in real life, as people in Nerf-induced slumber have been known to do, her overtaxed constellation causing a vessel in her brain to burst.

'We need to hurry,' Moremi says to her friend. 'In Dreamtime, in the labyrinth, maybe Orpheus has already been there for two years. If I don't hurry he might not remember me when we meet.' Moremi remembers the warnings that Orpheus gave her. He'd told her that walking into the labyrinth would be like diving into a black hole. She could be there for years before she finds him, but Moremi is willing to try.

'This is going to hurt,' Kimiko says. Although she still sounds a little uneasy, she brings the razor down on Moremi's palm. A white-hot flash of pain makes her dizzy for a moment. She closes her eyes as Kimiko drags the blade in a circle. All the while, she clenches her jaw and tries not to scream.

It takes almost an hour, and Moremi tries to split her mind from her body the way that she had that night at the symposium, when her Pulse had been attacked. Kimiko draws as accurately as she can, from the maps that Orpheus made, both of them hoping that the scars will save Moremi from getting lost on the other side.

Once they've finished, they manually attach her constellation to his, with sticky wires. 'You don't have long,' Kimiko says. 'After a couple of hours, if you don't manage to get out, your constellation will probably fry your brain. I'll play a cue out here, but Nerf-induced dreams are different. If you don't get to the portal as soon as you hear the cue then that's it.'

'Good to know,' Moremi says with mock cheerfulness as the cold lacerates her calves.

'Remember the rules: don't eat anything.'

'Or I'll forget everything,' Moremi recites, her teeth chattering.

'There is only one way through the labyrinth.'

'What does that mean?'

'And don't die,' Kimiko says.

'I'll ... try,' she gasps, the pain of the cold some-how growing less bearable. She's worried she'll wake without toes.

Kimiko attaches the IV of Nox to her arm and says, 'The dream will try to stop you both from leaving. But you'll have to remind yourself of how far you've come.'

'It's okay,' Moremi says, as the sleep begins to come upon her. Before she can say, 'I'm ready,' Kimiko clutches her head and pushes it down under the water.

53

MOREMI

She awakes drowning. Not a second to gather her bearings before her lungs are flooding with silty water. Her first thought is that she's still in the bathtub, that it burst its confines somehow, but as she sinks further she discovers there is nothing beneath her.

Wild panic. Will she fail so soon? Moremi's bare foot brushes something rough. Pondweed or a plastic bag, and her head tells her which way is up, though somehow she can find no force in her limbs to heave her body to the surface.

The river – she thinks it's a river – is moving fast, knocking debris in a dizzy whirlpool around her. This is how Moremi manages to grasp her salvation. A battered crate, which knocks the top of her head. Almost before she makes the choice to, her arms cling to it. And then she discovers that she is able to pull herself up towards the light, though she's still half-blinded by dirty water.

Before she knows it she's halfway out, still clutching the planks of wood like a raft. It takes all the strength she has to propel herself towards what she can see of the shore. She's thankful, then, that years of arabesques have strengthened her calves enough for the swim.

On either side of the river are high embankments and, beneath one of the walls, a little muddy shoreline that comes out about half a metre. It's littered with sharp black rocks, broken glass and the city's rubbish. By the time Moremi surfaces, she is covered in it, though she's so relieved at the air in her lungs, she barely notices.

She doesn't know how long she sits with her knees and palms bleeding on the beach, coughing and heaving, but eventually her vision comes back, and her head stops spinning enough for her to look around.

Is this what the underworld looks like? she wonders. She's found herself among the ruins of an ancient city. From where she sits she can see, up behind the weather-worn stone walls, the corroded husks of cars. Streets, eerily quiet, air stagnant as a funeral home. The once-impressive skyline is crowded with hollowed-out high rises.

Moremi looks down at her palm to find the healing scar. The map, curving and strange. Mercury had guessed that she'd find Orpheus near the centre of the maze. Yes, she thinks, and her focus sharpens again. She remembers that she came with a purpose.

It's only when she notices the dome of St Paul's Cathedral, cracked like an egg, that she realises where she is. London. Only it's a silent London, a crumbling city. London in a hundred years? London if every Londoner fled suddenly, leaving their cars and all their belongings behind without ever looking back.

The sight of it fills her with a strange dread. Once, she'd seen a VR simulation of a Roman forum turned to ruins and had suffered a kind of temporal whiplash as she wondered what parts of her life would survive the ravages of that much time.

For what it's worth, Moremi tells herself, the landmarks will prove useful for navigation. According to her map, if she's reading it correctly, Orpheus will be close to the river. Although, she's not sure which side.

Moremi looks around then, trying to remember some of the navigation tips that Orpheus had given her after they'd run away from Silo Six, but then the dark river swipes at her bare feet, and she looks down to notice that the tide must have come in sooner than she expected. Almost all of the land around her has been submerged in the time she was sitting still. When she regards the water once again, she notices that it is marbled with a strange white foam and the current seems to have reversed.

If she hadn't seen this phenomenon before, she might not have known to run. She might have stood for a while longer and stared, waited for the waters to slide out only to gallop back in with a hundred times the force.

Moremi knows enough to run.

Scrabbling to her feet, she takes the pitted steps up the embankment two at a time, trying not to slip on the thick algae. She finds herself on a once-busy road; the traffic, double-decker buses and rusted cars, eternally stalled. There are people in them, she realises with horror. A uniformed bus driver with his head against the glass, his jaw hanging open, flies buzzing between his teeth. There is a woman slumped in the driver's seat of a car, two children in booster seats at the back.

Some kind of radiation incident? A toxic gas leak? The pavement is littered with bodies too. But then, she realises, not dead, only sleeping. Thousands of them, prone on their stomachs with their cheeks on a flattened palm. Or else curled in foetal balls. On a bench, an old couple have fallen asleep with their heads on each other's shoulders. A jogger in reflective shorts slumps by a low wall. The entire city must be asleep, she thinks. Some fantastical dream sleep that preserves their bodies forever, so their skin is still dewy and flushed with life, their breath still fogs the glass and their eyes flicker behind their lids. But the rest of the world seems to have marched on without them. Vines have grown over and under feet. Mushrooms have sprouted under the shade of someone's thigh. Delicate webwork of capillaries, spiders skittering across it.

The roar of the wave reminds her to run. That dreadful sound, of rubble churned up in its jaws, trees totally uprooted, girders and beams snapping and twisting, the whine of metal. Her reaction time is faster than it had been then. Then, she had stood transfixed by the sight of it, the black waterfall rising up and crashing over the embankments, white foam glittering in the air. It had been Zeeba who had shouted her from her trance and urged her to run as fast as she could to higher ground. Zeeba had saved her. Almost a second later and she might have been one of the many who were devoured by it.

Moremi runs now, at first dashing up whichever street will take her in the other direction. But then she notices a few landmarks that point the way to higher ground; the IMAX – though she doesn't have enough time to find the entrance. A church: she sees its open door and pelts towards it.

She's a couple of metres away from its entrance, and by then the streets have already become black rivers full of oozing mud. It thunders behind her, devouring everything in its path, whipping up cars and the sleeping people, shearing the pavement in two.

She's only a few paces away from the darkened entrance of the church when she allows herself one glance back. Despite her years of watching Vine videos and quartz recordings, something in her mind had muted the edges of the memory. She'd forgotten the perfect, terrible force of the thing. The way her lungs had seized in fear of it. Her mind baulks, now. How can it be true? The wave, conjured here, as if from her darkest imaginings. Exactly the way it had been.

And then, she thinks she hears Zeeba's voice in her head telling her to run. Moremi runs into the darkened church, her steps echoing as she dashes up the nave and past people sleeping in the pews. At the sound of her heels on the ground, she hears the distant scratch of mice and small creatures fleeing. Birds loosen plumes of dust and ash in the belfry. She takes a left into the north transept and is relieved to find a row of steps leading to a second mezzanine gallery.

She makes it up and ducks just in time to hear the

wave tear open the church doors. She squeezes her eyes shut, imaginary light flashing behind her eyes to the wild beating of her heart. *It's not real,* she reminds herself, struggling to breathe. The air smells of it. And although she doesn't dare open her eyes, she can imagine all the sleeping people in the pews whipped into the air and dashed against the walls.

By the time the wave retreats, the city will look as if it was hit by an asteroid. Household items floating in gutters, children's toys and teacups, pages of magazines. The water will have spared nothing, severed lampposts and stripped houses to their foundations. *It's not real,* she promises herself.

Time moves differently in this place.

She must have fallen asleep under those rotted pews, because she wakes as the sun is rising outside, with a riot of birdsong in her ear.

It's as if it hadn't happened. Leaning over the mezzanine to peer down at the church, she had braced herself for the sight of scattered limbs, the lectern and choir stalls slick with mud, but it's as if the wave evaporated into steam before it touched anything.

There are about forty people asleep in the pews. A man in a cassock is curled in the pulpit. The choir are breathing heavily, their faces pressed into sheet music.

Outside, it's the same. A lovely sky, high cirrus clouds edged with gold. The city has been spared, she thinks in dazed relief. From this, at least. She steps over a BioBank bike, its familiar acid-green branding scarred with corrosion. A student is curled on the side of the road, the lip of the pavement like the edge of a pillow, open-mouthed, the side of his skull furred with moss.

So this is the dream, she reminds herself. She wonders how long it will be until she finds Orpheus. Moremi wants nothing more than to run to him.

Sitting on the edge of the pavement, she squints at the map that they cut into her palm. It's already healing, the pain of it a distant memory. It looks like one of the labyrinths she's seen on those enamel plates in the London Underground. Arced and whorled like a fingerprint, tight loops in the centre. Where is she?

When she stares at it, she thinks she can make out the River Thames, the bridges that cut through it. Moremi guesses that she needs to get across the river to find him. She knows she could walk along the south bank, or – since she's wary still of getting too close to the fast-moving water – parallel to it, along Stamford Street then Southwark Street. She knows the way well. It shouldn't take her more than half an hour. Leaping to her feet, flushed with optimism, Moremi begins to run it.

Up Stamford Street, past King's College and the London Nautical School. Except that everything is different now. The streets almost unrecognisable. Her ankle catches on a gnarled root jutting from tarmac, and when she falls on her face, she reminds herself that she might have to take this route more slowly so as not to get lost.

Most of the buildings on this street have crumbled now. If it wasn't so strange, it might be beautiful, Moremi thinks. The city is efflorescent – wild crocuses, irises, asters, Queen Anne's lace blooms where once there had been tarmac or concrete. Nature has reclaimed what they took.

Freezing and thawing have caused pavements to split, trees and weeds have burst from the gaps. Or else, water-logged subways and clogged gutters have turned highways into rivers that flow into the Thames.

Moremi runs for a long while, through cratered streets just marvelling at the place. At trees bursting through department stores, and ivy that has set its talons into the billboards in Piccadilly Circus. Crows and falcons nest in high buildings. Without their humans, house cats and dogs have gone feral, feasting on birds and mice.

It's a long while before she realises that she's lost already. She thinks she must have taken a wrong turn somewhere. Down what used to be Blackfriars Road, perhaps? Heading away from the river, and south of the city. To the edge of the dream?

No, she thinks now. She's seen that building before. The ruins of a co-working space. And that hollowed-out van. Saw them yesterday, when she was running from the flood. Moremi stops, that strange feeling of the ground listing under her which comes from realising she must be thoroughly lost.

There is the IMAX. There is the church she sought refuge in yesterday. There is the cyclist asleep on the pavement. Somehow she's walked in a straight line and come back on herself. Back where she'd started.

'No.'

She turns around, rubbing her head. The sound of her

voice startles some pigeons. The first human sound they may have heard in their lifetime.

Sitting on the ground, she looks at the map. Finds her bearings once more. Tower Bridge, she tells herself. The path is so clear she can almost see it. She must have got distracted. Turned around somehow. It won't happen this time.

This time she is faster, past King's College, past the shattered windows of restaurants and coffee stores. Zip stands and electric bikes. Crumbling Georgian terraces. A group of sleeping schoolchildren by the traffic lights. Streetlamps heavy with vines. She knows the way. A straight line. She can almost see it before her. The towers of the city rising from the mist.

She runs for almost an hour this time; by the end, her calves are on fire. Takes a moment to catch her breath, and when she looks up she sees it ahead of her; the IMAX, the roundabout near Waterloo Bridge. The church.

The third time it happens, she cries. Dreamtime logic. Determination can only get her so far. By the fifth time, the sun is setting and she is wild with panic when she shouts out his name, 'Orpheus!' and drops to her knees. Her echo sends birds flying from rooftops, knocking plumes of dust into the fiery sky.

It takes her a long while to realise that this is the labyrinth. She does it by marking the streets she walks along with a rock she uses as chalk. Not the same street, she realises, but many identical streets, with the same landmarks, the same church, the same people frozen in the pews.

When Moremi refers to the map on her hand, though, she realises that a couple of days have passed and she has traversed only a small portion of the world. It will take much longer than she thinks, she calculates, her chest sinking. Years, possibly, although Moremi is not sure what that will relate to in hours outside. She knows that in the labyrinth, unlike the rest of Dreamtime, it's possible to spend decades that are only hours in meat-space. But will years be enough time to find him?

At first, she marks the time in days. One hundred. When the sun rises, she opens her eyes in the pews of the church, walks out and makes her slow way through the city, searching the faces of the sleeping for Orpheus. Sometimes she calls his name, other times she simply walks, as if afraid to wake them, her whole body clenched with anticipation.

By sunset it always looks as if she's trod some wide circle, as if the silent streets and crumbled pavements have bent back on themselves and she must remind herself that with every day she is getting closer to him.

One year.

It gets harder with every sunrise to remember why she is here. To remind herself, Moremi creates a dance. With the rhythm of her feet she tells herself the story of her mission, of who she is and who she loves, she tries to imagine that the walk through the labyrinth is an extension of the dance.

*

Moremi marvels at the number that she marks in the chalk. If she had known that she would be searching for him for two years, would she have started looking?

She tells herself 'yes', at first.

Three years.

Before the labyrinth she'd never spent a week alone. By the fourth year, she must wake every morning and remind herself of the reasons to keep going. She'd heard that the labyrinth could crush her. Devour hope.

At the sunlight through the church's mullioned window, Moremi feels so griefstricken it's hard to breathe.

The week before they were married, the electricity in the flat went out. Moremi had taken a long bath and woken to find Orpheus leaning over the dining table playing canasta alone. Moremi had turned the kitchen counter into a barre, and danced quietly to herself in the candlelight.

The next morning, Orpheus had told her that he had been happy. He'd said, 'If I were dead or in hell, that's the night I'll remember.'

The sweetness of the statement had stayed with her because, to her, that night had been so ordinary. Funny, he hadn't said that about the time they'd won vouchers to an award-winning restaurant. Not the afternoon they'd made love three times. Just another quiet evening, one she never would have picked from a deck of cards.

Now she turns it over in her mind like a talisman. She

promises herself that they will make it out. That they will have a thousand nights like that one.

For five years, she gets up every day and looks for him.

By the sixth year, so many of her memories are fading that he's almost a myth to her. A distant hope. His name a cypher for everything she's ever wanted.

Mercury had told her that there is only one way through the labyrinth, and Moremi comes to discover that the way is temporal, not spatial. The challenge is not finding her way, her challenge is holding on to hope.

Maybe one day they will ask her how she survived the maze. When they ask what sustained her, all of those years, she will say, 'love', and they may think that they know what she means.

It takes her a long while to discover that to survive the maze she must fall in love with it. Walk around every day and look at those wildflowers, the ones flourishing in the lobby of that hotel, tilting their scruffy heads at the sun through the high window. Scrunched red poppies and fist-sized dandelion clocks. Violet starbursts of milk thistle darting up from under the hood of a car. Everything heavy with bees. The city belongs to her and it takes only a small act of surrender to be moved by it.

To love the labyrinth is to wake every morning and praise the pellucid light. The sound the wave makes as it sweeps through the streets and draws itself back like a breath, every day. The labyrinth requires her to dance its dance. To tread all its routes, and celebrate its perfect strangeness. She must see it for what it is, intestinal, claustrophobic, a wild spool of thread, and still consider it with the humbled awe as she might the ocean.

Moremi discovers that falling in love with the maze involves her falling in love with the journey and what it is transforming her into. It's settling her mind into a cool lake, taking its slow time. All the years of her life have prepared her for this. She tells herself that she already has everything she needs to survive this.

There is only one way, in the labyrinth, and so, the morning when it delivers her to the edge of the river, Moremi knows what it requires of her. Complete surrender, as the wave rises up and swallows her. In its maw, she discovers that she is a new creature, bold and unafraid.

She'd often wondered what it would feel like inside the wave. It takes her up along with the detritus of the city, uprooted trees and rubbish bins, the bonnets of cars and cracked windowpanes. A dark maelstrom she braces her body against.

It sets her down on the other side of the river, tossing her like a rag doll on the pavement before it draws itself back. Moremi pulls herself up and looks around. As soon as she sees the entrance to the subway station, Moremi knows where to find him.

Her heart catches at the sight of Orpheus. Moremi is not sure what she expected to find. That he'd be like those bodies, frozen and asleep? That he'd aged beyond recognition, grown gaunt and blind, hollowed out by time. Or that he'd be beyond saving, like Raffi's sister, Lala.

He looks the way he'd looked on the rug that first night, when she came to find him, on his stomach on the living room floor, trying to sleep.

'Orpheus?' She's too scared to touch him.

He turns with a start, and his hand reaches quickly for a rock the size of a fist. She can see the terror in his eyes. He looks tormented. He makes a noise that sounds almost animal.

'Orpheus?' she says again, stepping back and throwing her hands up to show that she means him no harm. He's still tense though, holding the rock up as if to pitch it at her.

She must be a shadow to him, some apparition. He might have imagined her more times than he can count. Or he might have forgotten her name along with everything else from the other side.

'Are you . . . ?' His posture begins to waver. Voice cracking. 'Please tell me you are. Real. Really her. I couldn't bear this if . . .' He lets the rock drop from his hand.

'Yes,' she says. The next time Moremi opens her mouth a sob comes out. She doesn't know if it's from relief or exhaustion. It's only now that she can let her guard down just a little. Only now she can let herself look back at how far she's come, how harrowing the journey. How tortuous the climb.

Orpheus' shoulders drop, he runs towards her and hugs her hard. 'I was too frightened to hope,' he says, crying too.

'Me too,' she sobs. If she'd come much later he might have been beyond saving.

He smells of sweat and smoke. Moremi laughs the way she had laughed on their wedding day, overwhelming gladness at the sight of him. She could stand here for a year, just holding him, but finally Orpheus breaks away and says, 'Do you hate me for what I did?'

'I could never hate you,' she says.

'I'm ... I did it to save myself. Triggering the attack. Stupid, selfish—'

'It's okay,' Moremi says, though even now she doesn't really understand the scope of the destruction. 'It will be. If you hadn't done it, I could never have saved you.'

'For a long time, I thought I was in hell, and those sleeping people outside were here to punish me for what I'd done.'

'Punish you how?'

'Every time I try to leave, they wake up and pull me back.' He looks beyond her shoulder as if he thinks that they might overhear them. 'I'll be running through the maze when I hear a thunder of feet behind me. Getting closer and closer. There's one hall with a ladder, and I see this brilliant light pouring through. The upper world, I think, or some other side. But before I can get through they'll chase me down and grab me. Last time I tried I thought they were going to strangle me. But then I come back here, and they fall asleep.'

The distant chime of a voice begins to play in the background.

Frère Jacques.

'It's Mercury,' Moremi says. 'Or Kimiko, I don't know. She told me that she would sound an alarm when I'd been asleep too long. She said that there's a portal I'll need to go to, to get out.'

'How long have you been here?' Orpheus asks, worried now.

'Years.'

'How many?' His urgency startles her.

Frère Jacques.

'Six years, but it's hard to count—'

'Six years in the labyrinth ... probably eight hours on the other side. You need to get out of here before your constellation overheats.'

'I know,' Moremi says. 'Apparently there's a portal we have to run through.'

Dormez-vous?

'We?' Orpheus says.

'I'm not going without you,' Moremi says. 'And if you wake ... maybe everyone else will wake too.'

'If I die they might wake up as well.'

'Don't say that,' Moremi says.

Dormez-vous?

He finally gives in and agrees that they'll make the journey together. 'The dream will do everything to stop us,' Orpheus warns. 'So, if we do this, you have to run when I tell you.'

'Okay,' she promises.

'And when I tell you, "Don't look back" ... don't look back.'

54

ORPHEUS

For a long time, people asked him what he had seen the night his father died. The night his heart stopped. His entire life? His father's face? Hers? Had he begun to see the light? Had he heard the voice of God?

It had taken all his life to make sense of the vision. There had been a cannibal crowd, who tore him limb from limb. They'd hoisted his head up with a shout. He'd been haunted by it, the sight of his own dismembered head, his nose, his jet hair like barbed wire, green eyes hollow panes of glass, frozen in surprise. Lips bloody, voice raised in falsetto exultation as it had been set singing on the Thames. But before that, and for one perfect instant, he'd seen her.

Frère Jacques.

'Don't look back,' he tells her as they race hand in hand through the gloomy hall. He doesn't want her to see the moment when the sleeping bodies will jolt upright as if shaken from a night terror and begin to run. But, as soon as it happens, he knows she can hear it. Their footsteps behind come like a roll of thunder and Moremi starts.

Frère Jacques.

'Don't look,' Orpheus tells her, and she pelts ahead. 'You have to face your fears to get out of the dream.'

'I have.' In the dark he can see her braids, silver glitter of beads clipped into them.

'You can only fight the fear with hope. So, hope that I'm following you, that we'll be safe. We'll make it out.' His stomach twists even as he says it.

Moremi uses the map that she has carved into her hand to lead the way. Through the windowless subway, its grimy curved tunnels, its dizzying loops. The song plays in a repetitive canon as they race.

Dormez-vous?

In the dark, flickering light, Orpheus' bare foot finds something soft and warm. A commuter asleep on the platform, mushrooms wax under her skull. The air smells of rot and there are black poppies of mildew everywhere. Half-rotted skeletons of mice are littered under benches.

Down a still elevator, and they dash through another platform where people are piled like litters of kittens, cobwebs draped like bedsheets between them.

Dormez-vous?

Round another corner is a long hall. At the other end is a hatch, a ladder, and the clearest light pouring through. The portal. Orpheus knows it will lead them to the upper world, but he also knows that only one of them can make it out.

Orpheus hasn't had the chance to make many choices

in his life, and even fewer good ones. He's chosen to run when he shouldn't have run, not to help when he should have helped. He's been selfish before, passive. He's never been a hero. But this one time, he will save the woman he loves. He tells himself that she will wake up on the other side, she will become a famous dancer. She will have all kinds of love in her life. She'll be calm and creative, a loyal sister, a devoted aunt. She will make enough money to feel safe, she'll wake every morning with a keen sense of gratitude, with the kind of gladness she can only bring back from the other side.

The crowd are wild, blind and furious, calling his name. Someone grabs his shirt and he stumbles. Moremi hears and, too scared to turn, says, 'Orpheus?'

He scrabbles to his feet, knocking the arm away, but more of them descend upon him, they tear at his clothes, his shirt, then his hair. At the end of the subway tunnel he can see the sun rising. If she can make it a few more metres, she will be saved.

She slows her pace, though. 'Are you here?' she asks. They can both hear the cue from the upper world as it comes to its end. If she doesn't leave soon, they will both die.

Sonnez les matines!

Ding, dang, dong.

Two people snatch his arm and clutch it in a vice-like grip. Someone else takes a fistful of his hair. 'Hey, Moremi,' he shouts, as the crowd descend upon him. They grip his shoulders and jaw.

Ding, dang, dong.

It's then that she turns and he sees her face. He wants to say, 'None of it was a mistake.' Because he is glad it all happened if it led him to her, glad even, for this. But instead, when she meets his gaze that final time he tells her – before they wrench his head from his shoulders – 'I'm happy I married you.'

55

MOREMI

For a while, she was a hero. That's what they were calling her, on the Vine.

There is a version of the story where Moremi saved everyone. Everyone with a Pulse fell asleep and she faced down death to wake them up. In another version, she was the willing participant in a failed coup, a plan to destroy the kingdom.

Moremi awoke next to Orpheus' cold body, and the sun rising outside. Her head was still full of the way that he'd looked on the other side as the crowd had chased him down. The last she'd seen of him, his green eyes flying wide open. A final gasp, as the cannibal crowd rent him apart and scattered his limbs.

'He's dead,' Mercury said, and then – tearing the tinfoil off the window and letting the sunlight pour in – 'It's over?'

Somehow, everybody was waking up. On the street outside, people were pulling themselves up off the asphalt and from balconies, rubbing their eyes and looking around in alarm.

'Someone who knows more about this than me will explain how this works but,' Mercury said, rubbing their eyes, 'Orpheus dying turned his Pulse offline? And that deactivated Milk Wood?'

Security cameras were blinking to life, cars booting up. In the recordings, it looked as if the world was a spinning top that God had set turning.

A Mexican wave of people, getting up from pavements and subway platforms and basketball courts. Mothers in playgrounds, their cheeks pockmarked by the Astroturf. Bars and bathtubs overflowing with cold water. People in stairwells, their shopping spilled, glass bottles and tin cans, felled like bowling pins on the landing. Some bruised, bones broken, limbs a rush of pins and needles. Everyone had dreamed of the same thing. They'd dreamed of him.

At Orpheus' funeral, autumn leaves snap underfoot. It's sparsely attended. Mercury, Moremi, Zeeba and Raffi, Halima and the baby. A couple of people who knew him from God's Own Junkyard, some of his colleagues from the School of Sleep at the Panopticon, Sai Kaur.

On his grave are the words that Zeeba chose: 'But someone will ask, "How are the dead raised? With what kind of body will they come?"'

The protection officers had found Mercury and Moremi. She had been on the flooded floor of his bathroom, clutching his torso like a raft and weeping.

Moremi remembers the rest in flashes: the fluorescent

lights of the hospital, the coroner who ticked the box that said 'aneurysm' on his console, then said, 'You look too young to be a widow.' The word, bitter as wormwood, the furthest thing from 'wife'.

She doesn't have many friends and the few she has fall silent. Discomfort at the strangeness of her grief. An old ballet teacher sends a holographic bouquet of lilies which open with a note that says, 'There are all kinds of love in this world.' Moremi turns the words over in her head for a while, wondering if the woman had been gesturing at what everyone is too afraid to explicitly say; that she was only married for a season. A couple of months. They hope that her grief will pass with the same swiftness. They do not know that she's lived for decades in Dreamtime longing for him. Faced down death to return him.

Instead of flowers, Halima had found Moremi's old bonsai tree. The soil in its terracotta tray had been bone-dry, though leaves little as pinheads were curled like springs on its miniature boughs, waiting to flourish. 'You've made it up once before,' her sister had said, 'from this kind of grief.'

Sometimes, at twilight, she'll think she sees him. In his flat. Candlelit at the dining table playing that game of solitaire. A shadow. A shade. Dressed for a heatwave, in his zebra-print boxers, his shoulders a mountain range she's already memorised. Or he'll be silhouetted in front of the panting fridge, looking for a can of Pepsi. And before she switches on the light she'll say, 'Live forever?' and with a smile he'll always reply, 'I promise.'

*

That autumn she auditions for the role of Ariadne. It's in a practice room near Sadler's Wells, and Moremi wears a red leotard in preparation for the part. This time when they call her number she's completely ready.

It's the role her mother never danced, the Minotaur's half-sister, goddess of mazes and paths, passion and forgiveness.

In some tales she is only a woman, fallen hopelessly in love with that slippery hero Theseus. She betrays her family to run away with him. Moremi always wondered why her mother identified with the Cretan princess so much. Perhaps it was because, according to some accounts, Ariadne was abandoned as her mother had been. Theseus left her while she slept on the shore of Naxos.

Moremi dances as she had on the other side. Dances as if her survival depends on it, tells, with every tendon in her body, the tale. Before them, she is the mistress of the labyrinth, goddess of forgotten things and disappointed love. They may leave honey for her by the threshold and hope she might direct them back. What doesn't she know about coming back?

When they ask for her name, she is face to face with him again. Pellucid blue eyes, wolf's teeth. Rafael Gabor. Blood rushes up the back of her neck as the assistant calls her name.

'You.' A glimmer of recognition in his eye. 'Is it you?' Moremi wonders if he remembers how she ran away from her audition in front of him. It seems so long ago to her now, but his assistant whispers something in his ear and his eyes light up. 'Apparently, you saved the world?'

Moremi shakes her head and says, 'I only wanted to save him.'

The world is changed after the attack. All plans for Total Adoption are suspended, pending several enquiries. It's not what Zeeba and the Revelators had hoped – almost no one shuts their constellation off entirely and swears to live analogue – but there is a new wariness about the tech in everybody's heads. There's increased pressure for schools to wait a couple more years before giving children the implant. Zeeba is granted an exemption, along with many of their other Pulseless friends, which means she will have less trouble enrolling in a university, or travelling abroad.

Although the attack weakens Hayden and his company for a while, even knowing the risks most people shrug and say, 'If you're not a slave to technology, you're a slave to biology,' and get a Pulse.

Once a year, though, the attack is commemorated with a 'twilight hour'. Between the hours of eight and nine, all the non-essential lights in the city are shut off. Constellations go dark, channels stop broadcasting, people gather in candlelight and remember how far humanity has come.

Moremi and her sisters enjoy watching it with the crowds in Piccadilly Circus. The blank screens, the impossible quiet on the streets. Moremi's favourite moment is when it's over. She loves the collective exhale of breath, the explosion of sound and neon as everything wakes up. There's a giant bottle of Coca-Cola on top of the memorial fountain, which blows out bubbles that float to the night-black sky and expand like planets. There's the electric laughter of a drone. People rush back into arcades and shops. Everyone is speaking the same language again. Precious content. Lovely data. Cars start, music plays, everything glitters with phosphene stars, everyone takes a picture of where they were when the world woke up. Holograms flaunt across the clouds and the lights of the city scatter the rain-slicked roads with a hundred reflected suns.

It is always a shock to see everything come to life so suddenly and flamboyantly. One moment, the analogue hush, and the next she's laughing hysterically, in spite of herself. Impossible not to laugh at the audacity of the world. At their willingness to forget almost everything and come back the same.

EPILOGUE

At the end of his short funeral service – after the sprinkling of dirt on the grave, the minister and pallbearers already gathered in a taxi to leave – Mercury put something in Moremi's hand. A shard of glass? A diamond coaster?

A quartz.

'His?'

They'd nodded.

'How did you . . . ?' Moremi asked. They'd disassembled his constellation at his autopsy. The police had taken his quartz and examined his final memories.

Mercury only smiled mysteriously and shook their head. 'A gift. You can have everything,' they'd said. 'Everything that you've lost.' Moremi slipped it into the pocket of her black woolen dress. By then, Zeeba and Raffi were already in a car, calling out for her.

When Moremi returned to his flat that night, she pushed his quartz into the machine in his bedroom. I won't make a habit of it, she'd lied to herself. It will just be this one time.

*

573

The dream begins when the wedding is over. They have left the laughter behind, the music and the quick clicking of heels outside the courthouse. The grinning faces of their guests have vanished like smoke. Their few witnesses, who had lined up to say goodbye, along the cracked pavement, tossing dried petals. Orpheus and Moremi ran between them, she clutching her satin train, he flinching from their balled fists.

'It happened so quickly,' she says in the taxi to the hotel as she shakes confetti from her hair.

'It did,' he says.

'And now we're . . .'

'We are.'

Orpheus, a relief to see him. He leans his head out the window, the summer air tosses his thick locks out of his face, and he closes his eyes in happy surrender. *What a good day to be alive,* she thinks. This beautiful boy is now her husband.

They ride for a while, up tree-lined boulevards, stuccoed houses white as sugar cubes, midday traffic. 'Let's do something *we* would do,' Orpheus suggests. 'We could get a pizza. Eat it in our hotel room.' Moremi laughs and dismisses the idea but he motions for the car to pull up on a side road and they climb out.

The evening sky is blush and brilliant; they are near Edgware Road and the streets are sweet with the smell of shisha. Pixellated ads leap like fireworks off the displays in windows. Vape shops and fabric stores, a halal burger place.

The silk lining of Moremi's dress feels luxurious against

her calves as she walks, and every now and then pedestrians stop to stare. They stop at a convenience store to
purchase fruit and cereal. Moremi holds nothing in her
hand but a wilted crown of orange blossoms. At the till
she tells the shop assistant, before she can even ask, 'We
just got married,' and the girl congratulates them wearily
as if she sees a marriage every day.

On the way to the hotel, Orpheus chews on handfuls of
dried cornflakes as if they are crisps.

'We just got married,' Moremi says to the woman at the
hotel reception desk.

'Well done. Should we show you your room?' The
carpet is plush under her feet, and there is a suit of armour
gleaming by the window. The concierge leads them up the
stairs and then closes the door. The silence is unnerving.
Moremi looks around at the pink flower petals strewn on
the duvet, the velvet soft furnishings, the bed.

'Hey,' she says, 'you forgot to carry me over the threshold.' And so they go outside and do it all again. He lifts
her shakily into his arms, charges through the narrow
door and then lets her tumble off onto the bed, in spasms
of laughter.

Orpheus asks her to take off her dress. She turns around
and he fumbles to find the pearl buttons. She can feel sweat
trickle down her back, between her legs, and she is restless
to leap into the shower. When her dress loosens, her hands
fly to cover her breasts. Orpheus tugs, the silk slides right
down her shins and into an ivory puddle on the floor.

'Let me see you,' he says. Her heart is beating wildly
under her palm.

When she peels off her knickers, she lets her hands drop to her sides. His face falls slack as he stares in silence for a long while at the bronze prospect of her breasts, her black nipples, faded stretch marks on her thighs, calloused feet.

His silence unnerves her.

'Do you like me?' she asks with quiet desperation. She'd meant to say 'my body', but stumbled on the last word.

'I . . . love you.' He kneels down to kiss her.

'I need to shower.' She says it like an apology.

'I don't care,' he says, his mouth full of flesh.

'Are you happy you married me?' she asks.

'I could die of happiness,' he says, his Pulse flickering wildly with the beat of his heart.

Just then, there is a knock on the door and they both start. Moremi leaps into the bathroom, as Orpheus calls, 'Who is it?' Another knock.

He tugs on the doorknob and, crouching naked in the bathroom, Moremi sees the receptionist and the concierge standing on the threshold. *'Félicitations!'* says the concierge, and he hands her husband a dark bottle of champagne, tied with a white ribbon. 'Oh, thank you.' Orpheus blushes.

Moremi leans back against the cool door and decides to climb into the shower. The water is a relief for her muscles. She pulls the pins out of her hair and lets the rough flakes of hairspray dissolve out of it. She rubs soap all over, her back, her breasts, and scrubs between her thighs.

Under the sound of the jet spray she can hear people whispering in hives of chatter on the Panopticon; she lifts a hand to mute the conversations, climbs out of the shower and writes 'WIFE' in the condensation on the steaming mirror. Behind the door Orpheus is singing 'America' in his falsetto voice, the Simon and Garfunkel song she'd caught him singing once before, his eyes growing glassy with tears at the bridge, that line about being empty and aching.

Would she do it again, knowing all that she knows now?

She always does.

The entire summer of their love, the good and the painful. Their days in Silo Six, making their way through the forest. That last glimpse of his face at the execution, the flash of wild hope in his eyes when she came for him in the underworld.

She will live it again. She will return to his memories in Dreamtime again. She will try and fail and try again.

Hadn't the woman at the registry office warned her? Hadn't she told them, 'Every love story is a tragedy.' Moremi wants to return to the town hall, just to shake the woman by her shoulders and ask, 'But, what happens after the tragedy?' What will she do with the rest of her life? What will she do with her love for him?

That winter, she dances the role of Ariadne and cries at every encore, when the curtain rises and the lights come up behind the proscenium, because she wants to know what happens next. Ariadne was abandoned by her lover on the shores of Naxos. And after? Did she tear out her hair in grief? Grow thin with longing? Terrify the islanders with songs of lamentation? Did she leap into the sea and pledge her life to bringing him back? Some say she took her red thread and hung herself with it, others that she joined the maenads in their thralls, or that she married Dionysus and her wedding diadem was set among the constellations.

Moremi likes to hope that she shook the sand from her hair and walked away, that she learned to live out the rest of her days and never once looked back at the quiet sea, the scene of her desertion, where her mercurial lover vanished in the offing.

Every time Moremi returns to the dream, she tells herself that she will not look back this time. This time, she will return Orpheus to the upper world, and they will wake as the sun is rising.

Always, the wave, the ruined city, the frenzied crowd. 'Don't look back,' he will always say, his face lovely in the dream-light. She will tell herself she can save them both. That they will wake on the other side laughing at the jealous maw of death. They will make a good way in the world. They will be entirely happy. Their love will resist the ravages of time.

As she runs, Moremi tells herself that she alone can storm the gates of hell and return them both to the other side. She will grit her teeth against her terrors, and try again, but when he calls her name that final time – *I'm happy I married you* – she will always, always look back.

ACKNOWLEDGEMENTS

Sincere thanks go to everyone at Greene and Heaton, to my agent and literary Godmother, Judith Murray. To my editors, Mina Asaam, Bethan Jones, Anne Perry, and Joe Monti. Also to Clare Hey, Jess Barratt, and Simon and Schuster UK.

I am very grateful to Iwan Price-Evans, who is full of brilliant ideas. The prison that Orpheus is trapped in and the plan to break him out was one of them. I am very blessed that you and Lauren are our friends.

My thanks to Christopher King who was a kind and supportive manager while I was working on this novel and working at BPP.

I have been grateful every day for the love and support of my family. For my grandma, Philomena Agunbiade, for her selfless and steadfast devotion. For my mother Dr Sheila Ochugboju, for everything, including her wisdom and generosity. You are the first person I call when I need someone to celebrate with me or commiserate with. Being a mother is terrifying, but you have made me brave. I am thankful for my wonderful siblings; beautiful Ruth and talented Che who bring me so much joy. And my sister Keche. I'll never forget that, over fifteen years ago, during my first halting attempt at a novel, you consoled me with fudge when my computer broke and I lost all the words I wrote. You've been a rock and a shoulder to cry on ever since.

To my incredible friends Nanci Gilliver, Natasha Djukic, Ella Sparks, and Dr Stella Fielder, who I would vote for in a heartbeat.

To Professor Sionaidh Douglas-Scott, Alexander and Venetia Douglas-Scott, and Anne Alfred and Dr Michael Douglas-Scott.

I'm thankful to God, He has answered my prayers, He has been a 'shield to me, my glory, and the lifter of my head'. To Jubilee, for making me a mother. And to Benedict. I have been writing this book for as long as we've been married. It's been like an illegitimate child you have attended to from the kindness of your heart. I'm happy I married you.

DO YOU DREAM OF TERRA-TWO?

Temi Oh

The Long Way to a Small, Angry Planet meets **The 100**
in this unforgettable debut by a brilliant new voice.

A century ago, scientists theorised that a habitable planet
existed in a nearby solar system. Today, ten astronauts will
leave a dying Earth to find it. Four are decorated veterans
of the 20th century's space-race. And six are teenagers,
graduates of the exclusive Dalton Academy, who've been
in training for this mission for most of their lives.

It will take the team twenty-three years to reach Terra-Two.
Twenty-three years spent in close quarters. Twenty-three
years with no one to rely on but each other. Twenty-three
years with no rescue possible, should something go
wrong. And something always goes wrong.

**Don't miss one of NPR's best books of 2019 and winner
of the American Library Association's Alex Award.
Called 'a major new voice' by Stephen Baxter.**

AVAILABLE IN NOW IN PAPERBACK, EBOOK & AUDIO

SIMON &
SCHUSTER